ROYAL DOOM

Good King Trent sat at the table in the library, an open book in front of him.

"Your Majesty!" Chameleon said. "We have to warn you—"

"Something is wrong," Ichabod interrupted. "He is not moving."

They went to the King. He sat staring ahead, taking no notice of the three before him. This was odd indeed, for King Trent was normally the most alert and courteous person.

Imbri projected a dream to the King's mind. But his look did not change, and his mind was blank. "He's gone!" she said to the others. "He has no mind!"

The three stared at each other with growing dismay. Now, when Xanth faced its greatest danger, it had lost its King.

By Piers Anthony
Published by Ballantine Books:

THE MAGIC OF XANTH

THE APPRENTICE ADEPT

INCARNATIONS OF IMMORTALITY

NIGHT MARE

Piers Anthony

A Del Rey Book

BALLANTINE BOOKS • NEW YORK

A Del Rey Book
Published by Ballantine Books

Library of Congress Catalog Card Number: 82-90817

ISBN 0-345-33698-4

Manufactured in the United States of America

First Edition: January 1983
Thirteenth Printing: January 1986

Cover art by Darrell K. Sweet

For our Mare
Sky Blue
and her girl Penny
our Heaven-cent daughter

Contents

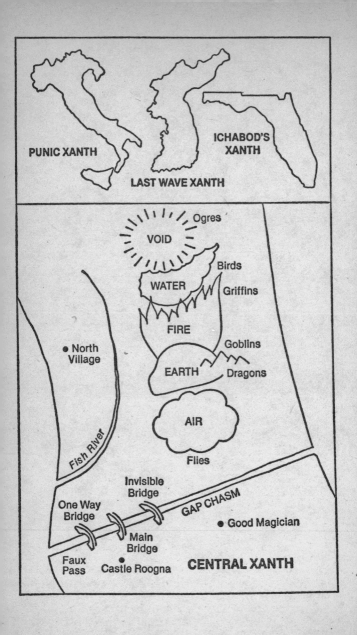

PUNIC XANTH

LAST WAVE XANTH

ICHABOD'S XANTH

Ogres

VOID

Birds

WATER

Griffins

FIRE

Goblins

North Village

EARTH

Dragons

AIR

Fish River

Flies

Invisible Bridge

GAP CHASM

One Way Bridge

Good Magician

Main Bridge

Faux Pass   Castle Roogna   CENTRAL XANTH

Chapter 1. To See the Rainbow

The stork glided to a landing before Stunk's residence and squawked for attention.

"No, it can't be!" the goblin cried in panic. "I'm not even married!"

" 'Snot that," the stork said through his long bill. "In the off-season I deliver mail." He produced an official-looking letter.

"Off-season for what?" the goblin demanded.

"You wouldn't understand. Take the missive. I have other idiots to bug."

"But I can't read!" Stunk protested, his panic shifting to embarrassment. Few goblins could read, but like most illiterates, they didn't like this advertised.

"I will read it to you, bulbnose." The stork opened the envelope and oriented an eye on the document inside. "Greetings."

"Same to you, birdbrain," Stunk said politely. Goblins had excellent manners, though for some reason other creatures seemed unable to appreciate them.

"Don't answer back, dolt," the stork said. "I'm reading the letter, not talking to you. Don't you know what 'Greetings' means?"

Stunk didn't answer.

"Hey, stupid, I asked you a question," the stork said, irritated.

"I thought you were reading the letter, needlebeak, so I didn't answer back. I'm trying to be polite to one not worth the effort. Of course I know what it means. It's an ungoblinish salutation."

"Salutation, ha! You dope, it means you have been drafted!"

"What? I wasn't aware of any draft. It's a very quiet day; no breeze at all."

"Abducted into the army, moron! Caught by the official press gang. Your happy civilian life is over."

"No!" Stunk cried, appalled. "I don't want to fight. Not that way, with weapons and rules and things. Tell me it isn't true!"

"I'll bet you wish you'd had the baby instead, huh, goblin!" the stork gloated, cradling the letter with his wings.

"Why would I be summoned to war? We're at relative peace with the dragons and the griffins!"

"It's the Mundane invasion, oaf. The Nextwave of conquest. The horrible Mundanes are coming to make dragon stew and goblins too."

"No! No!" Stunk screamed, his horror growing by stumbles and lurches and faltering footsteps. "I don't want to be goblin stew! I'm only a young, ignorant lout! I have my whole ornery life ahead of me! I won't go!"

"Then you are a draft evader or a deserter," the stork said, licking his beak with an orange tongue. "Do you know what they do to deserters?"

"I don't want to know!"

"They feed them to dragons." The stork was gloating; waves of gloat radiated out from him like ripples on a greasy puddle. Behind him a dragon loomed, snorting up little warm-up snorts of purple smoke.

"They'll never get me alive!" Stunk cried, working up to a superior degree of cowardice. He charged out of his hole in the wall, fleeing the draft notice. But already the dragon was pursuing him hungrily, pumping up extra-purple smoke, the kind that not only roasted goblins, but smelled pretty bad, too. Salivary smoke.

Stunk fled screaming, feeling the monster's fire hot at his back. He paid no attention to where his feet were going. He was beginning to outdistance the dragon, but knew he was not yet out of its range; that tongue of flame could reach him any time.

Suddenly he was at the brink of a ledge, unable to stop. His horror doubled as he fell off. He saw the hard rock of the bottom of a canyon rushing up at him as his stubby arms windmilled futilely. Better the dragon than this, and better the draft than the dragon—but now it was too late for either.

It was too much. Bawling out his terror, he woke.

Imbri leaped through the wall, phasing into intangibility. She had misjudged the client's reaction to the dream and had almost been caught visible. It was very bad form for any night mare to be seen by a waking person, even one as insignificant as a goblin. She galloped out into the night, leaving only a single hoofprint behind as a signature. That signature was important; Imbri was a perfectionist, and liked to put her personal stamp on every bad dream she delivered.

Dawn was threatening. Fortunately, this was her last call; now she could go home and relax and graze for the day. She galloped across the land, passing through trees and bushes, until she came to a patch of hypnogourds. Without pause she dived into a ripe gourd—a feat that would have surprised anyone who was not conversant with magic, as horses were much larger than gourds—and was instantly in an alternate world.

Soon she was on the dusky plain, with the other mares of the night mare herd converging, all returning from duty. Their hoofprints bore maps of the moon, with its green cheese and holes, and the names of the individual mares highlighted thereon. MARE HUMERUM, MARE NUBIUM, MARE FRIGORIS, MARE NECTARIS, MARE AUSTRALE—all her old immortal friends, all with seas of the moon named after them, in honor of their nocturnal performance over the centuries.

Another mare galloped up to intercept Imbri. It was Crisium, serving as temporary liaison to the Night Stallion. She projected a dreamlet the moment she came within range. It was the scene of an elf, waving his arms in animated speech. "Imbri!" the elf exclaimed. "Report to Trojan right away!" The brief dream faded.

A summons from the Dark Horse himself? That was not to be ignored! Imbri whirled on a hoof and charged across the plain, heading for the stable. Her relaxation would have to wait.

The Night Stallion was awaiting her. He stood huge and

handsome, midnight black of hide and mane and tail and hoof in the same fashion as all the mares, but on him it was more impressive. *Any* male was impressive in the realm of equus, for the real power lay with the few stallions.

Trojan projected a dream set in a lush human edifice chamber, in which Imbri took the form of an elegant human person lady, and he was a gray-haired human creature King.

"You are not doing well, Mare Imbrium!" the Horse King said. "You have lost that special spark that truly terrifies. I am dissatisfied."

"But I just drove a goblin to distraction!" Imbri-Lady protested.

"After hauling in the dragon and the unforeshadowed cliff," Trojan retorted. "You should have had him terrified into oblivion before he ever left the house. Dream dragons must not be brought in promiscuously, or the dreamers will become acclimated to them and desensitized. That ruins it for the other mares. You must avoid overexposure of emergency elements."

Imbri realized it was true. The nucleus of the dream had been the horror of the draft that was supposed to chill the spine of the client and make him shiver. She had lost her competitive edge and made clumsy what should have been precise. "I will try to do better," her lady form said penitently.

"That is not enough," he replied. "The edge is not entirely a matter of trying. It is inherent. Once you lose it, it's gone. I'm going to have to trade you, Mare Imbrium."

"But this is the only work I know!" she protested, stricken. She felt as the goblin had when receiving a dread notice. After more than a century of dream duty, during which time she had earned and held her designated moon sea, she wasn't ready for anything else.

"You can learn new work. There are daydreams—"

"Daydreams!" she repeated with contempt.

"I believe you have the inclination."

"Inclination?" She was stunned. "I never—"

"You were recently caught and ridden by a client," he said firmly. "No night mare can be caught unless she tacitly acquiesces."

"But—"

"Why would you accede to being caught by a client?" The King held up a hand to forestall her protest. "I will tell you why. You saw, in the memory of another client long ago, the image of a rainbow. You were fascinated by this vision; you wanted to see the reality for yourself. But you knew you could never do that as a night mare, for the rainbow shuns the night. It is a phenomenon of day."

"Yes . . . " she agreed, realizing it was true. The vision of the multicolored rainbow had haunted her for years. But no night mare could go abroad by day; the radiation of the sun caused her kind to fade rapidly. So it had always been a futile notion, and she had been quite foolish to let it distract her.

"As it happens, you possess half a soul," the Stallion continued. "You carried an ogre out of the fringe of the Void and accepted in payment half the soul of a centaur, when all you really wanted was the chance to see a rainbow. Logic has never been the strong point of females."

She remembered it well. The ogre had wanted to do her a return favor, but she had not felt free to converse with him in dreamlet fashion and had been unable to convey her interest in the rainbow to him otherwise. He had been a decent sort, for an ogre and for a male. The two concepts overlapped significantly.

"As it happens," the Dream King continued, "that soul has further dulled your edge, interfering with your dream performance. It is difficult to be truly brutal when you have a soul; that is contrary to the nature of souls."

"But it's only a half soul," Imbri protested. "A mere fillet of soul. I thought it wouldn't hurt."

"*Any* portion of a soul hurts in this business," he said. "Are you ready to give it up now?"

"Give up my soul?" she asked, appalled for a reason she could not define.

"As you know, most mares who earn half souls soon turn them in to me for storage, so that their edge will not be dulled, and they receive bonus-credit for extraordinary service to the cause. Souls are extremely valuable commodities, and we grasp and hold any we can. You alone retained your share of soul, passing up the advantage you could have had by cashing it in. Why?"

"I don't know," Imbri admitted, ashamed.

"I *do* know," Trojan said. "You are a nice personality, and you have grown nicer over the decades. You don't really enjoy causing people misery. The soul enhances that liability."

"Yes . . ." she agreed sadly, knowing that she was confessing a guilty secret that could indeed wash her out as a bearer of bad dreams. "I have drifted along an errant path."

"This is not necessarily wrong."

Her ears perked forward—an incongruous thing, since she remained in lady image in the dream. "Not wrong?"

"It relates to your destiny. It will one day enable you to see the rainbow."

"The rainbow!"

"You are a marked mare, Imbrium, and you will set your mark on Xanth. That time is near."

Imbri stared at him. The Night Stallion knew more than any other creature in the World of Night, but seldom told it. If he perceived a pattern in Imbri's incapacities, he was surely correct. But she dared not inquire about it, directly.

"Imbrium, I am transferring you to day mare duty. A more horrendous mare will assume your night duties."

"But I can't go into day!" she protested with fearful hope. She knew how brutal and awful some mares were, with wild eyes and wilder manes; they had absolutely no mercy on sleepers. It bothered her to think of her clients being placed in the power of such a creature.

"One of the distinctions between night mares and day mares is the possession of souls. The creatures of night have no souls; those of day have no bodies. You will actually be a halfway creature, with half a soul and a half-material body. I shall enchant you to be able to withstand the light of the sun."

"I can go abroad in the real world by day?" The hope became less fearful, for when the Stallion neighed, all mares believed.

"You will serve as liaison between the Powers of the Night and the powers of day during the crisis."

"Crisis?" Imbri thought she was confusing the term with her friend Mare Crisium.

"It is essential that the enemy not know your nature, or enormous peril may arise. They must perceive you as a simple horse."

"Enemy?"

"It was in the dream you delivered. You have become careless about such details."

Imbri tried to review the details of the last dream, but before she could make progress, the Dark Horse continued. "Therefore you will report to Chameleon, to be her steed."

"To whom? To be what?"

"She is the mother of Prince Dor, Xanth's next King. She is part of the key to Xanth's salvation. She will need transportation and the kind of guidance and assistance only a night mare can provide. Guard her, Imbrium; she is more important than anyone suspects. You will also bear her this message for King Trent: BEWARE THE HORSEMAN."

"But I don't understand!" Imbri exclaimed, the dream background shaking.

"You aren't meant to."

"I don't even know Chameleon or King Trent! I've never had to take a dream to either of them! How can I deliver a message?"

"Your present image is that of Chameleon," the Stallion said, producing a mirror from air so she could look at herself in the dream. Imbri was not a phenomenal judge of human appearance, but the image appeared quite ugly. Chameleon was an awful crone. "Use your dreamer-locater sense; it will operate by day as well as by night. And if you need to meet King Trent directly—he is my present image." The Stallion's dream form was handsome in an aged sort of way—the very model of a long-reigning King.

"But I understand so little!" Imbri protested. "This is like a bad dream."

"Granted," the Stallion said. "War is very like a bad dream. But it does not pass with the night, and its evil remains long after the combat has abated. War is no warning of ill; it is the ill itself."

"War?"

But the Stallion's kingly eyes flashed, and the dream faded. Imbri found herself standing at the edge of the broad grazing plain, alone. The interview was over.

Imbri traveled the realm of the night, making her farewells to its denizens. She went to the City of Brass, threading her way between the moving buildings, meeting the brass folk. Brassies were just like human folk, only made of metal. The males wore brassards and the females wore brassieres. The brass folk were activated when particular dreams had to be mass-produced; they were very good at mechanized manufacturing. Imbri had been here often before to pick up specialized dreams, and they were always well crafted.

One brassie girl approached Imbri. "You do not know me, mare," she said. "I understand you are going dayside. I was dayside once."

Imbri remembered that a brassie had briefly joined the party of the ogre. "You must be Blyght!" she sent.

"I am Blythe. I changed my name. I envy you, mare; I wish I could visit dayside again. The light doesn't hurt me, and some of the people are very nice."

"Yes, they are. If I ever have occasion to bring a brassie there, it will be you, Blythe," Imbri promised, feeling a kind of camaraderie with the girl. Perhaps Blythe, too, wanted to see the rainbow.

Imbri went on to bid farewell to the paper folk and the ifrits in their bottles and the walking skeletons of the grave-yard shift and the ghosts of the haunted house. All of them contributed their special talents to the manufacture of frightening dreams; it was a community effort.

"Say hello to my friend Jordan," one of the ghosts told her. "He haunts Castle Roogna now."

Imbri promised to relay the message. She went finally to mix with her friends, the other mares, with whom she had worked so closely for so many years. This was the saddest of her partings.

Now it was time to go. Imbri had used up the day and grazed the night, preparing for the awful transition. She did like her work as a bearer of bad dreams, even if she was no longer good at it. It was exciting to contemplate going into day, but awful to think of leaving the night. All her friends were here, not there!

She trotted out toward the rind. No creature could escape the gourd unaided except a night mare. Otherwise all the bad stuff of dreams would escape and ravage Xanth uncontrolled—a natural disaster. So the gourd had to be limited, a separate world of its own, except for those whose business it was to deliver its product. Some few people foolish enough to attempt to glimpse its secrets by peeking into the peephole of a gourd found themselves trapped there for an indefinite period. If one of their friends interfered with their gaze at the peephole, then they were freed—and seldom peeked again. It was always wisest not to peek at what concerned one not, lest one see what pleased one not.

The Stallion was right: Imbri had lost her touch with the dreams. She carried them, she delivered them—but the goblin's draft notice had not been her first clumsy effort. She no longer had the necessary will to terrify, and it showed. It was indeed best that she go into another line of work, difficult as the transition might be.

She focused on the positive side of it. She would at last get to see Xanth by day. She would see the rainbow at last! That would be the fulfillment of her fondest suppressed ambition.

And after that, what? Could the sight of the rainbow be worth the loss of her job and her friends? That seemed a little thin now.

She came to the rind and plunged through it. She didn't need to will herself immaterial; that came automatically. In a moment she was out in the night of Xanth.

The moon was there, exactly like one of her hoofprints, its sea and craters etched on the surface of its cheese. She paused to stare at it, spotting her namesake, Mare Imbrium, the Sea of Rains. Some called it the Sea of Tears; she had always taken the name as a punnish play on concepts. The Land of Xanth was largely fashioned of puns; they seemed to be its fundamental building blocks. Now, with her half soul and her new life ahead, the Sea of Tears seemed to have more significance.

She backed off and looked at one of her hoofprints. It

matched the visible moon, as it always did, even to the phase. The prints of night mares became obscure as the moon waned, unless a mare made a special effort, as for a signature. Imbri had never liked dream duty when the moon was dark; her feet tended to skid, leaving no prints at all. But there was no such problem tonight; the moon was full almost to the bursting point.

She trotted on through the Xanthian night, just as if bearing a fresh load of dreams to sleeping clients. But this time her only burden was her message: beware the Horseman. She didn't know what that meant, but surely the King would. Meanwhile, her equine heart beat more strongly with anticipation as the dread dawn gathered itself. Always before she had fled the rising sun, the scourge of day; this time she would face the carnage it did to the darkness.

The stars began to fade. They wanted no part of this! Day was coming; soon it would be light enough for the sun to climb safely aloft. The sun hated the night, just as the moon despised the day; but Imbri understood the moon had the courage to encroach on the edges of the day, especially when fully inflated and strong. Perhaps the lady moon was interested in the male sun, though he gave her scant encouragement. As long as the moon was present, a night mare could travel safely, though perhaps uncomfortably, even if the edge of day caught her. But why take chances?

Still, Imbri had to brace herself as the light swelled ominously. She knew the spell of the Night Stallion and the presence of her half soul would enable her to survive the day—but somehow it was hard to believe absolutely. What would happen if the spell were faulty? She could be destroyed by the strike of a deadly sunbeam, and her sea on the moon would fade out, unremembered. She trusted the Stallion, of course; he was her sire and he ruled the Powers of the Night. Yet surely the sun was an aspect of the powers of the day, and perhaps did not know she was supposed to be exempt from its mischief. Or if it knew, maybe it refused to recognize the fact. "Oops, sorry, Horse; you mean *that* was the mare I was supposed to spare? Fortunately, you have others . . ."

The brightening continued inexorably. Now was the

time; she would have to stand—or break and run home to
the gourd. Her legs trembled; her nostrils dilated. White
showed around the edges of her eyes. Her body was poised
for flight.

Then she remembered the rainbow. She would never see
it—unless she faced the sun. Or faced away from it; it was
always a creature's shadow that pointed to the rainbow, she
understood; that was one of the special aspects of the
magic of Xanth, that secret signal. But the sunlight had to
fall on that person to make the shadow appear—shadows
were reputed to be very strict about that—so the shadow
could perform.

The mare Imbri stood, letting the dread sun ascend,
watching its terrible beams lance their way cruelly through
the mists of morning. One launched itself right toward Imbri, amazingly swift, and scored before she could react.

She survived. The only effect was a shine on her coat
where the beam touched. The protective spell had held.

She had withstood the awful light of the sun. She was
now a day mare.

After the tension of the moment, Imbri felt an enormous
relief. Never had she suspected the Night Stallion of seeking to eliminate her by tricking her into braving the sunbeam, yet she realized now that some such suspicion had
made an attempt to harbor itself deep in her being. How
glad she was that her trust had been justified!

She took a step, feeling the soundness of her legs, the
solidity of the ground, and the springiness of the air she
breathed. Not only did she seem whole, she seemed twice
as real as before. She was now conscious of the weight of
her body, of the touch of weeds against her skin, and of the
riffle in her mane as a teasing breeze sought it out.

OUCH!

She made a squeal of protest and swished her tail, slap-
ping her own flank smartly. A fly buzzed up. The brute
had bitten her!

She had become a creature of the day, all right! No fly
could bite a true night mare. Few flies abounded at night,
and the mares were solid only when they willed themselves
so. Now it seemed she was solid and bitable—without ef-

fort. She would have to watch that; getting chomped by a bug wasn't fun. Fortunately, she had a good tail; she could keep the little monsters clear.

There was a certain joy in solidity. Now the sunbeams were bathing the whole side of her body, warming it. The heat felt strangely good. She was more alive than ever. There was something about being all-the-way solid that was exhilarating. Who would have believed it!

She walked, then trotted, then pranced. She leaped high in the air and felt the spring of her legs as they absorbed her shock of landing. She leaped again, even higher—

Something cracked her down in mid-prance. She dropped to the ground, bright white stars and planets orbiting her dazed head. Those stellar objects had certainly found her quickly! What had happened?

As her equilibrium returned, accompanied by a bruise on her head, Imbri saw that nothing had struck her. Instead, she had struck something. She had launched into a pome-granate tree, cracking headfirst into its pome-trunk, jarring loose several granate fruits. She was lucky none of those rocks had hit her on the way down!

Now she understood on a more basic level the liabilities of being substantial all the time. She had not watched where she was going, because she usually phased through objects automatically. As a day mare, she could not do that. When solid met solid, there was a brutal thump!

She walked more sedately after that, careful not to bang into any more trees. There was nothing like a good clout on the noggin to instill caution! Though muted, her joy remained; it merely found less physical ways to express itself, deepening and spreading, suffusing her body.

But it was time to go about her business. Imbri oriented—

And discovered she had forgotten what her business was. That knock on the head must have done it. She knew she was a night mare turned day mare, and that she had to go see someone, and deliver a message—but who that person might be, and what the message was, she could not recollect.

She was lost—not in terms of the geography of Xanth, which she knew well, but in terms of herself. She did not know where to go or what to do—though she knew it was important that she go there and do it promptly, and that the enemy not discover whatever it was she had to do.

Imbri concentrated. There was something—ah, yes! That was it! The rainbow! She had come to see the rainbow. That must be her mission—though where the rainbow was at the moment, and what she was supposed to say to it, and why this was important to the welfare of the Land of Xanth—these things remained opaque.

Well, she would just have to look for it. Eventually she would find the rainbow, and perhaps then the meaning in this mission would become apparent.

Chapter 2. The Day Horse

Mare Imbri was hungry. There had always been plenty of grazing in the gourd, but she had been too busy and too immaterial to graze while on dream duty and evidently had not consumed enough during the past night to sustain the elevated material pace of the real world. Now she had to graze—and didn't know where to find a decent pasture, here in dayside Xanth.

She looked about. She was in the deep jungle forest. Dry leaves coated the forest floor; there were few blades of grass, and those that she found were wiregrass, metallic and inedible. No doubt this was where the brassies harvested some of the wire for their constructions. She was roughly familiar with this region, of course, since she had been all over Xanth on dream duty—but by day it looked different, and now that she was fixed solid, it felt different. She had never paid much attention to the potential grazing here. Where would there be a decent pasture?

Well, this was not far west of Castle Roogna, the human-folk capital. She recalled that there was a large clearing north of here, and that should have plenty of excellent grazing. The problem was, there was a minor mountain range between herself and that pasture, and in her present solid state it would be at best tedious and at worst dangerous to climb over that range.

There was good pasturage at the castle, however. But she had seldom gone there, as the bad dreams for the royal human personages were generally carried by night mares with seniority, those who had been in the business for three centuries or more. Imbri would be likely to blunder in that vicinity, especially by day, and she didn't want to do that.

But she remembered that there was a pass through the mountains, little known but adequate. It had a mildly interesting history—

She paused in her thought. There was a nice patch of grass, superverdant! She could graze right here, after all.

She trotted to it and put her nose down. The grass reached up and hooked in her tender nostrils and lip.

Imbri vaulted backward, her nose getting scratched as the awful greenery ripped free. That was carnivorous grass! She couldn't go near that; instead of being eaten by her, it would eat her.

No help for it. She would have to cross the mountains. She set off at a trot, bearing north. She skirted tangle trees and danglevines and the lairs of dragons, griffins, basilisks, nickelpedes, and other ilk, knowing they were now dangerous to her. She had, after all, illustrated such hazards in the dreams she delivered to deserving creatures often enough. Soon she came to the mountains.

Now where was that pass? A little westward, she recalled. She trotted in that direction. She knew the general lay of the land, but exact details of placement were vague, since material things not relating to clients had not had much importance to her before.

Something was coming toward her. Imbri paused, not frightened but careful. She realized that she was now vulnerable to monsters, though she had confidence she could outrun most of them. Few things moved faster than a night mare in a hurry! But there were so many things to remember when one's body was stuck solid.

The reality was a pleasant surprise. It was a magnificent white horse, trotting eastward along the range. He had a fine white mane, a lovely tail, and his appearance was marred only by a thin brass band about his left foreleg, at ankle height. Imbri had never heard of a horse wearing a bracelet—but, of course, the only horses she knew were those of the gourd.

He halted when he spied Imbri. She became conscious of the distinction between them: she was a black mare, he a white stallion. She had understood there were no true horses in Xanth, only part equines like the sea horses, horseflies, and centaurs. Her kind, the night mares, existed separately in the gourd and did not roam freely when not on business. There were also the daydream mares, but they were completely invisible and immaterial, except to others of their kind. What was this creature doing here?

She decided to ask him. She could have neighed, but wasn't sure she could define her question well enough that way. So she stepped forward somewhat diffidently and projected a small dream. It was technically a daydream, since this was day—a conscious kind of imagining, much milder in content and intensity than the night visions she normally carried. It was also less perfectly structured, since she had no original text to work from. Anything could happen in an extemporaneous dream!

In this dream she assumed a talking form, that of a young human woman garbed in black, with lustrous long black hair in lieu of a mane and a skirt instead of a tail. Skirts weren't as useful as tails, since they were no good for swatting flies, but did serve to render mysterious that portion of the anatomy that profited by such treatment. Human people almost always wore clothing over their functional parts, as if they were ashamed of such parts; it was one of a number of oddities about them. "Who are you?" the dream girl inquired with a fetching smile.

The white horse's ears flattened in dismay and suspicion. He wheeled and bolted, galloping away back west.

Imbri sighed through her nose. He had been such a handsome creature! But apparently he was afraid of human people. Had she known, she would have projected something else, such as a talking bird. If she should encounter him again, she would be much more careful.

She proceeded west and in due course located the pass. And there, standing within it, was a man. He was of good stature for his kind, with pale hair and skin, with muscle on his limbs and handsomeness on his face in the humanoid manner. Naturally no human person was as handsome as a horse; that was another of the discomforts the human species seemed to have learned to live with.

"I say, pretty mare," the man called when he saw her. "Have you seen a runaway white stallion? He is my steed, but he bolted. He wears my circlet on his foreleg." And the man held aloft his left wrist, where there was a similar short circlet. There could be little doubt he was associated with the horse.

Imbri projected a dreamlet: herself in woman form, again garbed in black, her female parts carefully covered. She did not want to scare off another creature! "I saw him shortly ago, man, but he bolted from me, too. He ran in this direction."

The man looked startled. "Is that you in my mind, mare, or did I imagine it?"

"It is me, man," she said, continuing the daydream for him. "I am a dream equine. I project dream visions to your kind, but by day they lack the conviction they have at night." She had not realized it before, but obviously there was no qualitative difference between the dreams of night and those of day. It was just that the conscious minds of waking people were much less credulous, so the impact was less. They could readily distinguish fancy from reality. But the dreams remained excellent for communication.

"Ah. And did you project such a dream to my steed, the day horse? No wonder he spooked!"

"I fear my visions can frighten creatures who are not prepared," she projected, her woman image spreading her hands in the human signal of gentle bewilderment. If only she had been able to inspire such fright in her bad dream duty! "I am the night mare Imbrium, called Imbri for brief."

"A night mare!" he exclaimed. "I have often met your kind in my sleep. But I thought you could not go abroad by day."

"I am under special disposition to the day," she said. "But I do not remember my mission, except perhaps to see the rainbow."

"Ah, the rainbow!" he exclaimed. "And a worthwhile goal that is, mare! I have seen it many times and have always marveled anew!"

"Where is it?" she asked eagerly, so excited she almost forgot to project it in dream form; when she did, her dream girl was in partial dishabille, like a nymph. Quickly she patched up the image, for the dream man was beginning to stare. "I know my shadow points to it, but—"

"There must be sun *and* rain to summon the rainbow," the man said.

"But don't clouds blot out the sun during rainfall? There can't be both at once."

"There can be, but it is rare. The rainbow formation is exceedingly choosy about when and where it appears, lest familiarity make it change from magic to mundane. You will not see it today; there is not rain nearby."

"Then I shall go and graze," she said, disappointed.

"That is surely what my steed is doing, though I feed him well," he said. "His appetite is open-ended; sometimes I think he processes hay into clods without bothering to digest them in passing. Left to his own devices, he eats without respite. But he's a good horse. Where could he have gone? He did not pass by me, and I have been walking east until I heard your hoof-falls."

Imbri studied the ground. Horseprints curved into the gap between mountains. "He seems to have gone through the pass," she projected.

The man looked. "I see his tracks now. That must be it. Had I been a little swifter, I should have intercepted him." He paused, looking at Imbri. "Mare, this may be an imposition, but I am not much afoot. Would you give me a lift through the mountains? I assure you I only want to catch up to my errant steed. Once I see him and call to him, he will come to me; he's really an obedient mount and not used to being on his own. He may even be looking for me, but have lost his way; he is not as intelligent as you are."

Imbri hesitated. She had been ridden before, but preferred freedom. Yet she would like to meet the day horse again, and if she was going this man's way anyway—

"Or if you would like to come home with me," the man continued persuasively, "I have plentiful grain and hay, which I keep for my own horse. He is of Mundane stock, you know; what he lacks in wit he makes up for in speed and power. But he is very shy and gentle; not a mean bone in his body. I fear he will come to harm, alone in this magic land."

Mundane stock. That would explain the presence of the horse. Some Mundane animals did wander into Xanth, randomly. Of course, it was not safe for such creatures here. Even Imbri herself, a creature of an aspect of Xanth, could have trouble here by day; there were perils all about. That was probably why the true daydream mares were intangible; it was a survival trait not to be able to materialize by day. "I will take you through the pass," she projected.

"Excellent," the man said. "And in return, I will show you a rainbow, the very first chance I get." He approached, his voice continuing softly, soothingly. She stood still, with a certain nervousness, for ordinarily no waking person could touch a night mare. But she reminded herself firmly that she was now a creature of the day and touchable.

The man sprang on her back. His boots hung down on either side, around her barrel, and his hands gripped her mane. He had ridden a horse before; if she had not known the day horse was his steed, she could have told by his balance and confidence.

She started through the pass, the man riding easily, so that she was hardly aware of his weight. The ground was firm and almost level, and she was able to trot.

"This is a strange configuration," the man said as they passed almost beneath the looming rocky cliffs of the sides of the pass. "So steep above, so level below."

"This is the Faux Pass," Imbri sent in a dreamlet. "Centuries ago the giant Faux was tramping north, and there were clouds about his knees, so he did not see the mountain range. He caught his left foot on it and tripped and almost took a fall. He was a big giant, and such a fall would have wreaked enormous destruction in Xanth. But he caught himself, and his misstep merely kicked out a foot-sized piece of the range, creating a gap that ordinary creatures could use to get through. Thus it came to be named after him, though now people tend to pronounce it rather sloppily and just call it 'Fo Pa.' "

"A most delightful story!" the man said, patting Imbri on the shoulder. She felt good, and felt foolish for the feeling. What did she care for the opinion of a human man? Perhaps her new solidity made her more susceptible to the opinions of solid creatures. "This is a fascinating derivation. Faux Pass—the giant misstep. I suspect that term will in due course enter the language, for many people make missteps of one nature or another."

They emerged to the north. The plain spread out, filled with lush tall grass. Imbri was delighted; here she could graze her fill.

"I think I see a print," the man said. "Over there." He made a gesture.

Imbri hesitated, uncertain which way he meant, as his gesture had been confusing. She did want to find the day horse; he was such a handsome animal—and he was also male. She veered to the left.

"No, wrong way," the man said. "There." He gestured confusingly again.

She veered right. "No, still wrong," he said.

Imbri stopped. "I can't tell where you mean," she projected, irritated, her dream girl frowning prettily through strands of mussed-up hair.

"Not your fault," the man said. "I love your little imaginary pictures; *you* have no trouble communicating. My verbal directions are too nonspecific, and you evidently are not familiar with my human gestures. But I think I can clarify them." He jumped down, removing something from his clothing. It was a little brass stick with cords attached to each end. "Put this in your mouth, behind your front set of teeth." He held the stick up to her face, sidewise, nudging it at her mouth, so that she had either to take it or to back off. She opened her mouth doubtfully, and set it in, between her front and back teeth, where there was the natural equine gap. Human beings did not have such a gap, which was another one of their problems; they could not chew nearly as well as horses could, since everything tended to mush up together in their mouths, unappetizingly.

"Now I will tug on these reins," he explained. "That will show you exactly where to go. Here, I'll demonstrate." He jumped on her back again and got the two cords reaching from the metal bit to his hands. "Turn that way," he said, tugging in the right rein.

The bit pulled back against her hind teeth uncomfortably. To ease the pressure, Imbri turned her head to the right. "You've got it!" the man cried. "You are a very smart horse!"

It had not been intelligence; it had been discomfort. "I don't like this device," Imbri projected.

"You don't? I'm so sorry. Let's turn to the left now." He tugged at the other rein, sending a twinge to that side of her jaw.

But Imbri had had enough. She balked, planting all four feet firmly on the ground and trying to spit out the brass bit. It tasted awful, anyway. But the reins held it in place, annoyingly. She sent a fierce dream at him, of her dream girl self gesturing in righteous ire, tresses flouncing. "Get off my back, man!"

"You must address me by my proper title," the man said. "I am known as the Horseman."

The Horseman! Suddenly Imbri's misplaced memory returned. Her message was "beware the Horseman"—and now she had an inkling of its meaning.

"Beware the Horseman, eh?" the man repeated, and Imbri realized she had spoken her thought in the dream. Angrily she exploded her dream girl image into a roil of smoke, but this did not daunt the man. "So you carry a message of warning about me! What a fortunate coincidence this is, mare. I certainly can not afford to let you go now. I must take you home with me and keep you confined so that you can not betray me."

Imbri did not know what to do, so she continued to do nothing. She had unwittingly put herself in the power of the one person she should have avoided!

"Time to go home," the Horseman said. "I'll come back and catch the day horse later; you are too valuable a captive to let escape. I understand you night mares can pass through solid rock at night, and even turn invisible. That means I must get you safely corralled before darkness comes. Move, move, mare!"

Imbri refused to move. It was true; he could not hold her at night even if he remained awake and alert. If he slept, she would send him a dream so bad he would be paralyzed. Time was on her side. But she had no intention of obliging him one moment longer than necessary. Her feet would remain planted here until she figured out how to dump him.

"I have another little device that may amuse you," the Horseman said. "It makes horses go." And he banged his heels into her flanks.

Pain lanced through her. There were knives on his boots! Imbri was leaping forward before she realized it, jolted by the shock. A horse's natural response to fright or pain was to bolt, as running was normally the most effective defense.

"You appreciate my spurs?" the Horseman inquired. He drew on the left rein, forcing her to curve around that way.

Imbri tried to slow, but the spurs stung her again, making her run faster. She tried to veer right, but the bit in her mouth cut cruelly and she had to go left. The Horseman had subjected her to his awful will!

No wonder the day horse had fled this terrible man! If only she had realized the Horseman's nature! If only she had not foolishly forgotten her warning message!

But these things had come to pass, and she was paying the price of her neglect. If she ever got out of this fix, she would be a wiser mare!

The Horseman rode her back through the Faux Pass and west along the south side of the mountain range. Imbri stopped fighting her captor and found it amazingly easy to yield to his directives. The Horseman did not hurt her unless she resisted.

Imbri cursed herself for her inability to resist. But she was rapidly becoming conditioned to the will of the Horseman. When she tried to resist, he punished her; when she obeyed, he praised her. He seemed so sure of himself, so reasonable, so consistent, while she seemed, even to herself, like a poorly mannered animal. For now, until she figured out an effective course of independence, she had to go along.

But capitulation was not enough. He wanted information, too. "Who gave you that warning to beware of me?" he asked.

Imbri hesitated. The Horseman touched her sore flanks with his awful spurs—they weren't actually knives, they just felt like it—and she decided that there was no harm in answering. She sent a dreamlet, representing herself in woman form, in shackles, her side bleeding from abrasions, and with a brass bar in her mouth. "Ve commands va Fowers of va Night," the woman said around the bit.

"Do not tease me, mare," the Horseman said, touching her again with the spurs. "Your dreams can speak clearly."

She had to give up that ploy. "He commands the Powers of the Night," she repeated clearly. "The Night Stallion. He assigns the dreams to be delivered. He sent the message."

"The Night Stallion," the Horseman repeated. "Naturally you equines revert to the herd in the wild state. But he is confined to the night?"

"To the gourd," she clarified. "It keeps us secure by day." Now she wished she had never left it!

"Explain," he said. "The only gourd I know is the hypnogourd that has a little peephole. Anyone who sets eye to that is instantly hypnotized and can not move or speak until someone else breaks the connection."

"That is the same," Imbri's tattered dream girl said, looking woeful. She hated giving so much information to the enemy, but didn't see how this particular news would help this man. He already knew better than to peek into a gourd, unfortunately. "We night mares are the only creatures who can pass freely in and out of the gourd. All gourds are the same; all open onto the same World of Night. When a person looks into any gourd, his body freezes but his spirit takes form inside and must thread its way through our labyrinth of entertainments. Those who remain too long risk losing their souls; then their bodies will never be functional again."

"So it's a kind of trap, a prison," he said thoughtfully. "I suspected some such; I'm glad you are choosing to tell me the truth, mare. How many spirits can it contain?"

"Any number. The gourd is as large as Xanth in its fashion. It has to be, to contain dreams for every person in Xanth, every night, no two dreams the same. To us in the gourd, the rest of Xanth seems small enough to carry under one of your arms."

"Yes, I see that now. Very interesting. We can carry your world around, and you can carry ours around. It's all relative." After a moment he had a new question. "To whom were you to deliver your message?"

Now Imbri resisted, being sure this would affect the conduct of the war. But the Horseman dug in his spurs again, and the pain became so terrible she had to tell. She had never had to endure pain before, for it didn't exist in immaterial form; she couldn't handle it. "I was to go to Chameleon with the message for the King."

"Who is Chameleon?"

"The mother of Prince Dor, the next King. She is an ugly woman."

"Why not take the message directly to the King?" The spurs were poised.

"I don't know!" The dream girl flinched, putting her hands to her sides.

The spurs touched. Desperately, Imbri amplified. "My mission was to be secret! Maybe it was a ruse, to report to the woman, who would relay the message to the King. No one would suspect I was liaison to the gourd."

"The King is important, then? Nothing can be done without his directive?"

"The King rules the human concerns of Xanth," Imbri agreed. "He is like the Night Stallion. His word is law. Without his word, there would be no law."

"Yes, that makes sense," the Horseman decided, and the spurs did not strike again. "If you reported directly to the King, the enemy might catch on, and know the warning had been given. That could nullify much of its effect. Still, I think it better yet to nullify *all* its effect by preventing the message from being delivered at all. Because, of course, it is an apt warning; your Night Stallion evidently has good intelligence."

"He is the smartest of horses," Imbri agreed in a fragmentary dreamlet. "He knows more than he ever says, as does Good Magician Humfrey."

"Intelligence, as in gathering data about the enemy," the Horseman clarified. "This is the activity I am currently engaged in. But, of course, your Stallion has the night mare network. You mares were peeking into our brains as we slept, weren't you? No secrets from your kind."

"No, we only deliver the dreams," Imbri protested, her pride in her former profession overriding her wish to deceive the Horseman. "We can't tell what's in people's minds. If we could, I would never have let you put this bit in my mouth." That brass tasted awful, and not just physically!

"How, then, did you know about me? I know you knew, because of your message of warning about me."

"*I* don't know. The Night Stallion knows. He has a research department, so he can tell where to target the bad dreams. But he can't usually tell waking people. There's very little connection between the night world and the day world."

"So I now understand. Many secrets are buried in the depths of night! But what of this Good Magician, who you say also knows a great deal? Why hasn't he warned Xanth about me?"

"Magician Humfrey only gives information in return for one year's service by the one who asks," Imbri said. "Nobody asks him anything if he can help it."

"Ah, zealously guarded parameters," the Horseman said, seeming to like this information. "Or the mercenary motive. So for the truth about Xanth's situation, a person must either pay a prohibitive fee or peer into the peephole of a gourd—whereupon he is confined and can not extricate himself by his own effort. It is a most interesting situation. The people are almost entirely dependent on the King for information and leadership. If anything were to happen to

King Trent—" He paused a moment. "His successor, Prince Dor—is he competent?"

"All I know is what I have picked up from people's dreams," Imbri temporized.

"Certainly. And their dreams reflect their deepest concerns. What about Prince Dor?"

"He has hardly had any experience," she sent unwillingly. "When he was a teenager, about eight years ago, King Trent went on vacation and left Dor in charge. He had to get his friends to help, and finally the Zombie Master had to come and take over until King Trent returned. There were a lot of bad dreams then; we mares were overloaded with cases and almost ran our tails off. It was not a very good time for Xanth."

"So Prince Dor is not noted for competence," the Horseman said. "And next in the line of succession is the Zombie Master, whom the people don't feel comfortable with. So there really is no proper successor to King Trent." He lapsed into thoughtful silence, guiding Imbri by nudges of his knees. When he pushed on one side, he wanted her to turn away from that side. He was not wantonly cruel, she understood; all he required was the subordination of her will to his in every little detail.

That was, of course, one thing she couldn't stand. At the moment she could not escape him, but she would find a way sometime. He couldn't keep the bit and spurs on her forever, and the moment he slipped, she would be gone— with a whole lot more news about him than she had had originally. Beware the Horseman, indeed!

They came to the Horseman's camp. There were two men there, Mundane by their look. "Found me a horse!" the Horseman called jovially.

"Where's the other horse?" one asked.

"He bolted. But I'll get him tomorrow. This one's better. She's a converted night mare."

"Sure enough," the Mundane agreed uncertainly, eyeing Imbri. It seemed he thought the reference to night mare was a joke. Mundanes could be very stupid about magic.

"Better off without the white horse," the other Mundane said. "For all the riding you get on him and all the feeding you give him, he's never around when you need him."

"He's got spirit, that's all," the Horseman said with a tolerant gesture. "I like a spirited animal. Now put a hobble on this one; she's a literal spirit, and she's not tame yet."

One of the henchmen came with a rope. Imbri shied away nervously, but the Horseman threatened her again with his awful spurs, and she had to stand still. The henchman tied the rope to her two forefeet, with only a short length between them, so that she could stand or walk carefully but could not run. What a humiliating situation!

They put her in a barren pen where there was a grimy bucket of water. They dumped half-cured hay in for her to chew. The stuff was foul, but she was so hungry now that she had to eat it, though she feared it would give her colic. No wonder the day horse had bolted!

All day she remained confined, while the Mundanes went about their brutish business elsewhere. Imbri drank the bad water, finished off the bad hay, and slept on her feet in the normal manner of her kind, her tail constantly swishing the bothersome flies away. She had plenty of time to consider her folly. But she knew the night would free her, and that buoyed her spirit, her half soul.

Now she meditated on that. Few of her kind possessed any part of any soul, and those who obtained one generally didn't keep it, as the Night Stallion had reminded her. Yet she clung to her soul as if it were most important. Was she being foolish? Imbri had carried the half-human Smash the Ogre out of the gourd and out of the Void, but it was not any part of his soul she had. It was half the soul of a centaur filly. That soul had changed her outlook, making her smarter and more sensitive to the needs of others. That had been bad for her business and had finally cost her her profession. But as she gradually mastered the qualities of the soul, she became more satisfied with it. Now she knew there was more to life than feeding and sleeping and doing her job. She was not certain what more there was, but it was well worth searching for. Perhaps the rainbow would have the answer; one look at the celestial phenomenon might make her soul comprehensible. Yet that search had led her into the privation of the moment.

As evening approached, the Horseman and the two henchmen appeared and started hauling firewood logs from the forest. The wood fairly glowed with eagerness to burn. They threw a flame-vine on the pile, and burn it did. The fire blazed high, turning the incipient shadows to the brightness of day.

Suddenly Imbri realized what they were doing. The Mundanes were keeping the pen too light for her to assume her nocturnal powers! As long as that fire burned, she could not escape!

With despair she watched as they hauled more logs. They had enough wood to carry them through the night. She would not be able to dematerialize.

The sun tired and dropped at last to the horizon, making the distant trees blaze momentarily from its own fire. Imbri wondered whether it descended in the same place each night, or whether it came down in different locations, doing more damage to the forest. She had never thought about this before, since the sun had been no part of her world, or she would have trotted over there and checked the burned region directly.

The fire blazed brighter than ever in the pen, malevolently consuming her precious darkness. It sent sparks up into the sky to rival the stars. Perhaps they were stars; after all, the little specks of light had to originate somewhere, and new ones would be needed periodically to replace the old ones that wore out. The Mundanes took turns watching Imbri and dumping more wood on the fire as it waned.

Waned, she thought. That jogged a nagging notion. She wished it had waned this night, putting out the fire. Waned? *Rained*; that was it. If only a good storm would come and douse everything. But the sky remained distressingly clear.

Slowly the henchman on guard nodded. He was sleeping on the job, and she was not about to wake him—but it didn't matter, because the fire was more than bright enough to keep her hobbled, whether he woke or slept. She might hurl a bad dream at him, but that would only bestir him with fright, making him alert again. She would have to deal with that fire first. But how, when she was hobbled?

Then she realized how to start. She approached the fire and put her front feet forward, trying to ignite the rope that hobbled her. But the blaze was too fierce; she could not get close enough to burn the rope without burning herself.

She turned about and tried to scrape dirt onto the blaze with a hind hoof. But the ground was too solid; she could not get a good gouge. She seemed helpless.

Then a shape appeared. Some large animal was stomping beyond the wall of the pen, out of the firelight. A dragon, come to take advantage of a horse who could only hobble along?

She sent an exploratory dreamlet. "Who are you?"

"Is it safe?" an equine thought came in the dream.

It was the day horse! Imbri quelled her surprise and pleasure at his presence and projected another dreamlet. "Stay clear, stallion! The Horseman is looking for you!"

"I—know," the horse replied slowly. She wasn't certain whether it was dullness or caution that made him seem less than smart. She understood that Mundane animals were not terrifically intelligent, and the Horseman had said as much.

"He wants to catch you and ride you again," she sent, making her dream image resemble a centaur, so as to seem more equine while retaining the ability to speak clearly. Of course horses had their own language, but overt neighing and other sounds might wake up the henchman.

"I—hide," the day horse replied, beginning to catch on to this mode of dialogue. He stepped up to the fence and looked over, his head bright in the firelight.

"Well, go hide now, because if that henchman wakes—"

"You—greet me," he said in the dream, awkwardly. "I run. You—caught by man. My fault. I came—free you."

Imbri was moved. She had pictured him in the dream as a white centaur, and he seemed to like the form. She had made sure it was a very muscular and handsome centaur, knowing that males tended to be vain about their appearance. Males of any species were foolish in a number of respects. But what would Xanth be like without them?

"I can't get away as long as that fire burns," her dream filly image said. "I had hoped there would be a rainstorm, but—"

"Rainstorm?"

"Water, to douse the fire," she explained. Sure enough,

he was the strong, handsome, amiable, stupid type. Fortunately, stallions didn't need brains; they were attractive as they were.

"Douse fire!" he said, understanding. "Make water." He jumped over the pen wall, landing with such a thump that Imbri had to jam a dream of an earthquake at the sleeping henchman to prevent him from being alarmed. Of course he was alarmed, but then she modified the dream to show that the earthquake had been weak and brief, and had cracked open the ground in front of him to reveal a treasure chest filled with whatever it was he most desired. The henchman quickly opened the chest, and out sprang a lovely nude nymph. He would remain asleep for a long time!

The day horse walked over to the burning logs, angled his body, and urinated on the flames. Clouds of steamy smoke flared up as the fire hissed angrily. It certainly did not appreciate this treatment!

The new noise disturbed the henchman despite his dream. He started to awaken. This time Imbri sent a mean dream at him, showing the merest suggestion of a basilisk the size of a horse, swinging around to glare at the man. The Mundane immediately squinched his eyes tightly closed; he knew what happened when one traded gazes with a bask! He did not want to wake and see the monster. Imbri let him drift off again, returning to his treasure-chest nymph; Imbri was as relieved as he to see him sleep.

In a moment the fire had sizzled down enough to let the shadows reach out to Imbri. She phased through her hobbles and the wall of the pen. The day horse leaped to follow her.

They ran through the forest. "Come with me to Castle Roogna!" Imbri projected, her filly image smiling gladly and swishing her black tail in friendly fashion.

But the day horse faltered. The handsome centaur image frowned. "Night—tire quickly—creature of day—must give it up." He stumbled. "By night I sleep."

She saw that it was so. "Then we'll hide, so you can rest," she sent.

"You go. I came only to free you," he said, speaking

more clearly now. He might be slow, but he did catch on with practice. "Pretty mare, black like deepest night."

Imbri was flattered and appreciative, though he was only telling the truth. She was as black as deep night because she was a night mare. But any notice by a stallion was a thing to be treasured.

Nonetheless, she did have a mission and had to complete it without delay. "When will I see you again?"

"Come to the baobab at noon," he said. "Nice tree. If I am near, I will be there. Do not betray me to the human kind; I do not wish to be caught and ridden again."

"I'll never betray you, day horse!" she exclaimed in the dream, shocked. "You freed me! I'll always be grateful!"

"Farewell," his dream image said. He turned and walked north as the dreamlet faded out. Imbri saw the brass circlet on his foreleg glint faintly in the moonlight.

"The baobab tree!" Imbri sent after him. She knew of that growth from her dream duties; sometimes human people camped out there, and it was conducive to bad dreams at night, a little like a haunted house. It was at the edge of the Castle Roogna estate, out of sight of the castle but impossible to overlook. She would certainly be there when she had the chance.

Chapter 3. Centycore et Cetera

By midnight Imbri reached Castle Roogna. She skirted it and went to Chameleon's home, which was a large cottage cheese. Imbri had once delivered a dream here to Chameleon's husband Bink; it had been a minor one, for the man did not have much ill on his conscience, but at least she knew her way around these premises despite lacking the seniority required to bring dreams to Kings. She phased through the hard rind and made her way—should that be whey, in this house? she wondered—to Chameleon's bed.

But a stranger occupied that bed. Chameleon, according to the image the Night Stallion had formed, was a crone; this person was a lovely older woman of about fifty. Had she come to the wrong address?

"Where is Chameleon?" Imbri inquired in a pictureless dreamlet. Maybe this woman was visiting, and would know.

"I am Chameleon," the woman replied in the dream.

Imbri stood back and considered. The reply had been direct and honest. The Night Stallion must have made an error, forming the image of some other woman. Imbri had never known him to make an error before, but obviously it was possible.

Something else bothered her. Chameleon was sleeping alone, yet she was a family person. Where were her husband and son?

Imbri projected a dream. It was of herself as another centaur filly, standing beside the bed. "Chameleon, I must give you a message."

The woman looked up. "Oh, am I to have a bad dream? Why do they always come when my family's away?"

"No bad dream," Imbri reassured her. "I am the night mare Imbri, come to be your steed and bear a message for the King. When you wake, I will remain. I will talk to you in your sleep, as now, or in daydreamlets."

"No bad dreams?" The woman seemed slow to understand.

"No bad dreams," Imbri repeated. "But a message for the King."

"The King's not here. You must seek him at Castle Roogna."

"I know. But I can not go to him. I will give you the message to relay to him."

"Me? Repeat a dream?"

"Repeat the message." Imbri was getting impatient; the woman seemed to have very little wit.

"What message?"

"Beware the Horseman."

"Who?"

"The Horseman."

"Is that a centaur?"

"No, he's a man who rides horses."

"But there are no horses in Xanth!"

"There is one now, the day horse. And there are the night mares, like me."

"But then people don't need to fear him. Just horses should fear him."

That might be true; certainly Imbri would never again be careless about the Horseman. But it was irrelevant; she had to get the message through. "That is for the King to decide. You must give him the message."

"What message?"

"Beware the Horseman!" Imbri's image shouted, frustrated.

Chameleon's image looked around nervously. "Where is he?"

What was this? Was the woman a complete idiot? Why had the Night Stallion sent Imbri to such a creature? "The Horseman is west of here. He may be hazardous to the health of Xanth. The King must be warned."

"Oh. When my husband Bink comes home, I'll tell him."

"When will Bink be back?" Imbri inquired patiently.

"Next week. He's up north in Mundania, working out a new trade agreement with Onesti, or something."

"I certainly hope he works on it with honesty," Imbri said. "But next week's too long. We must warn the King tomorrow."

"Oh, I couldn't bother the King! He's seventy years old!"

"But this affects the welfare of Xanth!" Imbri protested, getting frustrated again.

"Yes, Xanth is very important."

"Then you'll warn the King?"

"Warn the King?"

"About the Horseman," the centaur filly said, keeping her tail still and her face straight with an effort.

"But the King is seventy years old!"

Imbri stamped a forefoot angrily, in both her dream form and her real form. "I don't care if he is a hundred and seventy years old! *I* am! He's still got to be warned!"

Chameleon stared at the filly image. "You certainly don't look that old!"

"I am a night mare. We are immortal, at least until we die. I have a soul now, so I can age and breed and die when I'm material, but I never aged before, once I matured. Now, about the King—"

"Maybe my son Dor can tell him."

"Where is your son now?" Imbri asked warily.

"He's south at Centaur Isle, getting the centaurs to organize for possible war. Because Good Magician Humfrey says there may be a Wave. We don't like it when Waves are made. But I don't think the centaurs believe it."

"A Wave?" It was Imbri's turn to be confused. She knew the woman wasn't talking about the ocean.

"The Nextwave," Chameleon clarified unhelpfully.

Imbri let that go. She had seen the Lastwave, but that had been a long time ago. "When will Dor be back here?"

"Tomorrow night. Just in time for the elopement."

Somehow the woman's ingenuous remarks kept making Imbri react stupidly, too. "Elopement?"

Chameleon might not be smart, but she had a good memory. "Dor and Irene—she's King Trent's daughter, a lovely child with the Green Thumb, only it's really her hair that's green—have been engaged for eight years now, a third of their lives. They could never decide on a date. We think Dor's a little afraid of the responsibility of marriage. He's really a very nice boy." Obviously "nice" meant "innocent" in this connection. Imbri was surprised to learn that any innocent males remained in Xanth; perhaps this was merely the fond fancy of a naive mother. "Irene is twenty-three now, and she's getting impatient. She never was a very patient girl." This seemed to mean that the other woman in Chameleon's son's life was not viewed with entire favor, but was tolerated as a necessary evil. In this attitude, Chameleon was absolutely typical of the mothers of sons. "So she's going to come here at night and take Dor away and marry him in an uncivil ceremony, and then it will be done. Everyone will be there!"

So the pleasure of a wedding ceremony overwhelmed the displeasure of turning her son over to an aggressive girl. This, too, was normal, except—

"For an elopement?" Imbri felt more stupid than ever. Was this a human folk custom she had missed? She had understood that elopements were sneak marriages; certainly she had delivered a number of bad dreams relating to that.

"Oh, they'll all be in costume, of course. So Dor won't know, poor thing. Maybe Irene won't know either. It's all very secret. Nobody knows except everybody else."

Imbri realized that she had again been distracted by an irrelevancy and was getting ever more deeply enmeshed in the confusions of Chameleon's outlook. "Two days is too long for my message to wait. The Horseman is within range of Castle Roogna now, spying on the Xanth defenses. Anyway, it seems that Prince Dor will be too busy to pay attention to it. You must go to the King first thing tomorrow morning."

"Oh, I couldn't bother the King. He's—"

"Seventy years old. He still needs to know. The Horseman is dangerous!"

The dream Chameleon looked at the dream Imbri with childlike seriousness. "Why don't *you* tell him, then?"

"I can't. My mission here must be confidential."

Then Imbri paused, startled. Confidential? From whom was the secret of her nature to be kept? The Horseman already knew! He had ridden her and intercepted her message and forced her to tell him everything!

"I'll go tell him right now!" Imbri said, cursing her own foolishness.

"But it's night! The King's asleep!"

"All the better. I'm a night mare."

"Oh. That's all right then. But don't give him any bad dreams. He's a good man."

"I won't." Imbri trotted through the rindwall of the cottage, letting Chameleon lapse into more peaceful slumber. She hurried to Castle Roogna, hurdled the moat with one prodigious leap, and phased through the massive outer wall. This would be no easy castle to take by storm! She passed through the somber, darkened halls and passages, until she came to the royal bedchamber.

The King and Queen had separate apartments. Both were safely asleep. Imbri entered the King's chamber and stood over him, exactly as if she were on dream duty.

Even at seventy, which was old for a mortal man, he was a noble figure of his kind. The lines of his face provided the appearance of wisdom as much as of age. Yet it was clear he was mortal; she detected infirmities of system that would in due course bring him to a natural demise. He had reigned for twenty-five years; perhaps that was enough. Except that if he lacked a competent replacement in Prince Dor . . .

She entered his mind in dream form, this time assuming the likeness of a nymph, bare of breast and innocent of countenance, symbolic of her intention to conceal nothing from him. "King Trent!" she called.

He had been dreaming he was sleeping; now he dreamed he woke. "What are you doing in my bedroom, nymph?" he demanded. "Are you one of my daughter's playmates? Speak, or I will transform you into a flower."

Startled, Imbri did not speak—and suddenly, in the dream, she was a tiger lily. She growled, baring her petals in a grimace.

"All right—I'll give you another chance." King Trent did not make any gesture, but Imbri was back in nymph form. Even in dreams, the King's magic was formidable!

"I bring you a message," she said quickly through the mouth of the nymph. "Beware the Horseman."

"And who is the Horseman—a kind of centaur?"

"No, sir. He is a man who rides horses. He rode me—" She paused, realizing this statement did not make much sense while she was in nymph image. "I am a night mare—"

"Ah, then this is, after all, a dream! I mistook it for reality. My apology."

Imbri was embarrassed that a King should apologize to a dream image. "But it is real! The dream is only to communicate—"

"Really? Then I had better wake."

The King made an effort and woke. Imbri was amazed;

in all her one hundred and fifty years' experience in dream duty, after her youth and apprenticeship, she had not seen anyone do this so readily.

"So you really *are* a mare," King Trent said, studying her in reality. "Not a nymph sent to tempt me into foolish thoughts."

"Yes. Not a nymph," she agreed, projecting a spot dreamlet.

"And you do not fade in my waking presence. Interesting."

"I am spelled to perform day duty," she explained. "To bring my message."

"Which is to beware the Horseman." The King stroked his beard. "I don't believe I know of him. Is he by chance a new Magician?"

"No, sir. I think he is a Mundane. But he is clever and ruthless. He hurt me." She nodded at the scrapes on her flanks.

"You could not phase away from him, mare?"

"Not by day. I am now mortal by day."

"Would this relate to the invasion the Mundanes are supposed to be mounting?"

"I think so, sir. The Horseman has two Mundane henchmen and a Mundane horse."

"Where did you encounter this cruel man?"

"Two hours' trot west of here."

"South of the Gap Chasm?"

"Yes, your Majesty. At Faux Pass."

"That's odd. My scouts should have spotted any crossing of the Chasm, or any sea approach. You are sure of the location?"

"Quite sure. I made a bad misstep there."

"That happens at Faux Pass."

"Yes." Imbri was embarrassed again.

"Then they must have found a way to sneak in." The King pondered a moment. "Ah—I have it. A quarter century ago, Bink and Chameleon and I entered Xanth below the Gap when we departed from the region of the isthmus, far northwest of here. We somenow traversed in perhaps an hour a distance that should have required a day's gallop by your kind. Obviously there is a magic channel under water. The Horseman must have found it and somehow gotten by the kraken weed that guards it. We shall have to close that off, devious though it may be. There are merfolk in that vicinity; I shall notify them to investigate." He smiled. "Meanwhile, a lone man and two henchmen and a Mundane horse should not present too much of a threat to Xanth."

"The horse is not with them any more, your Majesty. He is the day horse who fled his master and helped me escape."

"Then we must reward that horse. Where is he now?"

"He does not want to meet with human folk," she explained. "He is wary of being caught and ridden again."

Again the King smiled. "Then we shall ignore him. True horses are very rare in Xanth, for there is no resident population. He might be regarded as a protected species. That will help him survive in what might otherwise be a hostile land."

King Trent had a marvelous way of solving problems! Imbri was grateful. "I am also to serve as liaison to the gourd—the realm of the Powers of the Night and to the folk of Xanth," Imbri said in another dreamlet, maintaining her nymph image for the purpose. "And I am to be the steed of Chameleon. But I don't know why; she seems not very smart."

"An excellent assignment!" King Trent said. "Evidently you do not properly comprehend Chameleon's nature. She changes day by day, becoming beautiful but stupid, as she is at the moment, then reversing and turning ugly but intelligent. She is alone because of the exigencies of this presently developing crisis, and that is unfortunate, because someone really should be with her at her nadir of intellect. You can be with her and nudge her from danger. In a few days she will become smarter, and in two weeks she will be so smart and ugly you can't stand her. But she is a good woman, overall, and needs a companion in both phases."

"Oh." Now the Night Stallion's assignment made more sense. It also explained his seeming error: he had shown an image of ugly Chameleon, but meanwhile her aspect had changed.

"Return to her now," King Trent said. "I will have a new assignment for you both by morning."

How thoroughly the King took over, once he tackled something! Imbri trotted through the wall and jumped down to the ground outside. Actually, she landed in the moat, but it didn't matter because she was immaterial; she didn't even disturb the moat monsters. Soon she was back with Chameleon, now understanding this woman better. Appearance and intelligence that varied in a monthly cycle—how like a woman!

Imbri checked in with a reassuring dreamlet, then moved back outside to graze on the excellent local grass. She slept while grazing, comfortably, suspecting she would need all her energy the next day.

A tiny golem appeared at the cottage in the morning. "Oh, hello, Grundy," Chameleon said. "Do you want a cookie?"

"Yes," the miniature figure said, accepting the proffered delicacy. It was an armful for him, but he chewed bravely into the rim. "But that's not why I'm here. King Trent says you must ride the night mare to Good Magician Humfrey's castle and ask his advice for this campaign."

"But I couldn't bother the Good Magician!" Chameleon protested. "He's so old nobody knows!"

"The King says this is important. We have a crisis coming up in the Nextwave and we don't want to misplay it. He says Humfrey should see this mare. Get going within the hour."

Imbri snorted. Who was this little nuisance, to order them about?

The golem snorted back—speaking perfect equine. "I'm Grundy the Golem, and I'm on the King's errand, horseface."

"So you can communicate in nonhuman languages!" Imbri neighed. That was quite a talent! She didn't even have to project a dreamlet at him. Still, she didn't like the insulting inflection he had applied to the uninsulting "horseface," so she sent a brief dream of the fires of hell at him.

The golem blanched. "That's some talent you have yourself, mare," he concluded. He departed with dispatch.

Chameleon looked at Imbri. "But I don't know how to ride a horse," she said. She seemed very unsure of herself in her stupid phase, but she was certainly an excellent figure of a woman of her age.

"Use a pillow for a cushion, and I will teach you how," Imbri projected, her dreamlet showing Chameleon seated confidently and somewhat regally on the dream horse's back, her lovely hair flowing down about her.

Chameleon got a pillow and followed instructions. Soon she was precariously perched, her legs dangling awkwardly, her arms rigid. This was an immense contrast to the evil expertise of the Horseman! But Imbri moved carefully, and the woman gradually relaxed. It really was not hard to ride a horse, if the horse was willing.

They moved east through field and forest, toward the Good Magician's castle. Because Imbri had been almost everywhere in Xanth in the course of her century and a half of dream duty, she needed no directions to locate it. She stayed clear of dragons, tangle trees, and similar hazards and reached the castle without untoward event late in the day. Imbri could have covered the distance much faster alone, but Chameleon would have taken much longer by herself, so it was a fair compromise. They had paused to eat along the way and had taken turns napping; Imbri carried the woman carefully while she slept, then had shown her how to guide the snoozing mare away from holes in the ground and other nuisances by the pressure of knees on sides. Chameleon was quite surprised that a creature could walk while sleeping. She was stupid, but she had a sweet personality and followed directions well; she was learning to be a helpful rider.

As the castle came into view, both mare and woman were startled. It was a monstrous circle of stones set within a moat. Each stone was too huge to be moved physically and stood upright. On top were set enormous slabs of rock, so that the whole formed a kind of pavilion. There was no sign of the Good Magician.

"I am not very smart, of course," Chameleon said, "but I don't understand this at all. That megalith looks many centuries old!"

Imbri was reasonably smart, but she was similarly baffled. She had been by this castle several times in the past, and though it had always looked different, it had never been *this* different. "We shall have to go in and look," she projected. "Maybe there is some sign of what happened to the Good Magician."

"Maybe he moved," Chameleon suggested.

They approached the moat. By night Imbri could have hurdled it or trotted across the surface of the water, but now she had to wade and swim, since she did not want to delay unnecessarily.

The moment her hoof touched the water, a fish swam up. It changed into a naked man before them. "Halt! You can't pass here!"

"Oh, dear," Chameleon said.

Imbri recognized the type. "You're a nix," she projected.

The man shifted form again, partway, adopting the tail of a fish. "Well, mare!" he said. "What else would you expect to find guarding a moat?"

"At Castle Roogna there are nice moat monsters," Chameleon said.

"I *am* a moat monster!" the nix declared. "And you can't pass unless you know the password."

"Password?" Chameleon was plainly perplexed. So was Imbri. Why should they be allowed to pass it they knew a word, if their merit was not otherwise apparent? This did not seem to make sense.

Imbri tried to evoke the word from a dream, but the nix was too canny for that. Dreams were aids to communication and often evoked deep feeling, but were not for mind reading.

"We'll just have to cross despite him," Imbri projected privately to Chameleon, with a dream picture of woman and horse forging across the moat while the nix protested helplessly. After all, the creature carried no weapon and was not physically imposing in either its fish or man form. Also, they had the right and the need to cross; they were on the King's business.

"Yes, we must cross," Chameleon agreed. She hiked up her skirt so that it would not get wet, though of course Imbri was likely to sink low enough in the water to wet the woman's legs to the thighs anyway. They were excellent limbs, considering her age. Perhaps even not considering her age. Water would hardly hurt them.

This was not lost on the nix. He whistled lewdly. "Look at those gams!" he exclaimed.

"Ignore him," Imbri said in the dream image, for she saw that the dream girl Chameleon was blushing. It seemed that despite a quarter century of marriage, Chameleon remained fundamentally innocent. That probably accounted for her son's innocence. Imbri found herself liking the woman even more and felt protective toward her. Chameleon was as esthetic emotionally as she was physically, almost too nice to be true.

They plunged into the water. "Nix, nix!" the nix cried. "You shall not pass without the word! I will freeze your tracks!" He pointed—and the water abruptly congealed about Imbri's legs.

Imbri stopped, perforce. She stood knee-deep in ice! The nix did have power to stop her progress.

"What do you think of that, nag?" the nix demanded with insolent satisfaction. He was now back in fish form, able to speak that way, too. "No password, no passing. I told you! Did you think the rule was passé?"

Chameleon fidgeted helplessly, but Imbri struggled to draw one foot and then another from its mooring. Ice splintered as her hooves came free. Soon she stood on the frozen surface and began to walk forward.

"Nix! Nix!" the sprite cried, back in man form, pointing again with a finlike arm. The ice melted instantly, and Imbri dropped into deeper water with a splash. The nix chortled.

Well, then she would wade again. One way or another, she would cross this moat.

The nix froze the water again—and again Imbri struggled to the top. He melted it, plunging her down. This was awkward, but she continued to make progress. The nix could not actually stop her.

Then she reached the deep where she had to swim. The water came almost to the top of her back. Chameleon hiked her skirt up over her waist. "Oh, it tickles!" she protested.

The nix gloated, now faintly resembling a satyr. "Where

does it tickle, wench? *I'll* give you a good tickle, if that's what you like." This caused the dream girl to blush furiously again. But she wouldn't let her dress get wet. Actually, it was a fairly simple outfit in shades of gray, the parts neither matching nor clashing; it was she herself who made it attractive.

"Hey, I never knew a doll could blush that far down," the nix said evilly.

Imbri nosed a splash of water at him, but continued swimming. If the nix remained distracted by the woman's exposure and embarrassment long enough, they would be across. That should embarrass *him*. He certainly deserved it.

Alas, the nix was not that foolish. "Nix, nix!" he cried, pointing again.

This time the freezing was incomplete. The water thickened into cold sludge, but Imbri was able to forge through it. It seemed there was too much volume here to freeze enough to immobilize her submerged body, so the effect was diluted.

"Well, then, nox!" the nix cried angrily. "Nix, nox, paddywox, live the frog alone!"

This nonsense thawed the water, then thinned it farther. Suddenly it was too dilute to support the mare's swimming weight. She sank down over her head.

This was like phasing through solids—with one difference. She could not breathe. The water was now too thin to swim but too thick to breathe, and its composition was wrong.

Imbri's feet found the bottom. This was solid. She turned hastily about and walked the few paces needed to bring her high enough for her head to break the surface. Now she could breathe.

She projected a dreamlet to Chameleon: centaur filly shaking a spray of water out of her hide. "Are you all right, woman?"

"My dress is soaked—I think," Chameleon lamented. "The water isn't very wet."

That was good enough for Imbri. "Take a deep breath, and I will run all the way across the moat on the bottom. With thin water we can do it."

"That's what you think, night nag!" the nix cried, evidently catching part of the dream. He was swimming along, his forepart that of a fish, his hind part that of a man. The water was abruptly fully liquid again. "Try to run through that!"

Imbri realized that it could be dangerous to try. If she swam and the nix vaporized the water, she would sink without a breath and have to turn back. Chameleon could panic and possibly drown. Imbri wasn't certain whether Chameleon could swim, and now was not the time to inquire.

She paused to consider. Alone, she could probably forge through despite the mischievous nix. But with Chameleon, it was harder. Too bad the woman was so stupid; Imbri had to do all the thinking. How could she get them both across with minimum risk?

Then she had a notion. She projected a new dream to Chameleon, a scene of herself in mare form and the woman in woman form, exactly as they were in life. But the nix was there, too, eavesdropping. Whatever they tried, he would foil.

The dream mare projected a dream within the dream to Chameleon. This one bypassed the snooping nix, who did not realize the complex levels available in dream symbolism. In that redistilled dream, Imbri was a woman in black and Chameleon a woman in white. "Trust me," she said to the dream-in-dream girl, who looked slightly startled. "We shall cross—but not the way we seem to. Follow what I say, not what I do. Can you do that?"

The dream-in-dream girl blinked uncertainly. "I'll try, Imbri," she agreed. "That *is* you?"

Oh—it was the human guise that confused her. "Yes. I can take any form in dreams, but I usually am black or wear black, because that's night mare color."

The Chameleons on the three levels of reality, dream, and dream-dream smiled, getting it straight.

Now they returned to focus on the outer dream. "Hang on, Chameleon," the mare cried. In real life Imbri could not physically talk human language, but dreams had different rules. "I'm swimming across now."

"Swimming across," the woman agreed, hiking her skirt

high again. Her limbs were just as shapely in the dream as in reality.

"You'll get your no-no wet!" the nix cried, evilly teasing her.

Chameleon blushed yet again—she seemed to have an excellent supply of blush, as pretty women did—but held her pose. The dream mare moved into deep water, swimming across. The real mare did likewise.

"Nix! Nix!" the sprite cried, caught halfway between fish and man forms. He vaporized the water.

The real mare and woman sank—but the dream pair continued swimming. "It's not too deep here," the dream mare called. "We can run along the bottom and still breathe. In just a moment we'll be across!"

"Hey!" the nix exclaimed angrily. "Nix, nix, I'll nix you!" And he froze the water.

Now the real mare was able to slog upward through the cold slush and get her head and the woman's above water so they could breathe again. She plowed clumsily forward.

But the dream mare was stuck. "I can't move!" that mare cried. "We're frozen in tight!"

"Serves you right, nocturnal nag!" the nix shouted jubilantly. "You can't cross without the password!"

"We must turn back!" the dream mare said despairingly.

"Yes, turn back," dream Chameleon agreed, though she did not seem fully convinced.

"You're doing well," the dream-in-dream Imbri woman figure reassured her on that level.

Meanwhile, the real mare pulled free of the slush and swam on toward the megaliths. Progress was faster as the water cleared.

"We'll never get across!" the dream mare wailed.

"Never!" the dream girl agreed enthusiastically.

But the nix was not completely gullible. "Hey—those are your dream images! Real mares can't talk!" He blinked, orienting on the real-life situation—and discovered how they had tricked him. He had been so busy snooping on the supposedly private dream that he had neglected reality, as Imbri had intended. "Nix! Nix! Nix!" he screamed from a fish mouth set in a human face, hurling a vapor spell. The water thinned about them, dropping them down—but now they were close to the far side, and the moat was becoming shallow.

Imbri galloped up the slope, and her head dipped under water only momentarily. The nix froze the water; the mare scrambled up on top of it, as here in the shallower region the freezing was solid.

"Can I breathe now?" the dream Chameleon pleaded.

"Breathe!" Imbri responded, clambering to shore. They had made it!

Behind them, the nix sank wrathfully into a region of vaporizing ice, his human head set on a fish's body. "You females tricked me!" he muttered. Then, looking at the forming cloud of ice vapor: "I never did believe in sublimation."

"It is the nature of males to be gullible," Imbri agreed in a dreamlet, making a picture of the nix formed as a human being with the head of a fish, wearing a huge dunce cap, while an ice storm swirled about him.

They climbed out of the moat and stood wetly before the stone structure. It was immense. Each vertical stone was the height of an ogre, crudely hewn, dauntingly massive.

They had little time to gawk. A monster came charging along the inner edge of the moat. The creature was horrendous. It had horse-hooves, a lion's legs, elephantine ears, a bear's muzzle, a monstrous mouth, and a branching antler projecting from the middle of its face. "Ho, intruders!" the beast bellowed in the voice of a man. "Flee as well as you can so I may have the pleasure of the hunt!"

Imbri recognized the monster. It was a centycore. This was a creature without mercy; no use to reason with it. They would need either to stop it or to escape it.

Imbri ran. She was a night mare; she could outrun anything. She left the centycore behind immediately.

Chameleon screamed and almost fell off. She was still an inexpert rider, not at all like the cruel Horseman, and could readily be dislodged by a sudden move. Imbri had to slow, letting the poor woman get a better hold on her mane. Then she accelerated again in time to avoid the monster.

Soon she had circled the region enclosed by the moat, being confined—and there was the monster again, facing her from in front. Imbri braked and reversed, angling her body to prevent Chameleon from being thrown off, and took off the other way. But she realized that this was no real escape; she would not be able to concentrate on anything else, such as exploring the megalithic structure and searching for clues to the whereabouts of the Good Magician's castle, until she dealt with the centycore.

She slowed, letting the thing gain, though this terrified Chameleon, who was clinging to Imbri for dear life. Imbri hurled back a dreamlet picture of herself as a harpy hovering low, calling, "What are you doing here, monster?"

"Chasing you, you delectable equine!" the centycore bellowed back, snapping his teeth as punctuation.

Ask a foolish question! "We only came to seek the Good Magician," Imbri sent.

"I don't care what you seek; you will still taste exactly like horsemeat." And the centycore lunged, his antler stabbing forward with ten points.

"Oh, I don't like this!" Chameleon wailed. "I wish my husband Bink were here; nothing too terrible ever happens to him!"

That was surely an exaggeration, but Imbri understood her feeling. She accelerated, putting a little more distance between herself and the predator. How could she nullify the centycore? She knew she couldn't fight it, as it was a magic beast, well able to vanquish anything short of a dragon. Even if she were able to fight it, she could not safely do so while Chameleon rode her; the woman would surely be thrown off and fall prey to the monster.

"Run through a wall!" Chameleon cried, sensing the problem.

"I can't phase through solid things by day," Imbri protested, her dreamlet showing herself as a mare bonking headfirst into a megalithic column and coming to a bone-jarring stop. She felt Chameleon's sympathetic hand pressure, though the accident had been only a dream; the woman tended to take the dreams too literally. "Only at night—and we have at least an hour of day left." It seemed like an eternity, with the centycore pursuing.

But the description of the problem suggested the answer. Suppose they somehow made it prematurely dark? Then

Imbri would be able to phase. For it wasn't night itself, but darkness, that made her recover her full night mare properties; otherwise the Horseman's fire would not have been able to hold her. The Powers of the Night came to whatever night there was, natural or artificial, whatever and whenever it was, for night was nothing but an extensive shadow. Just as day was nothing more than a very large patch of light.

How could they make it dark? Sometimes, Imbri understood, the moon eclipsed the sun, rudely shoving in front of it and blocking it out. But the sun always gave the moon such a scorching on the backside when the cheese did that, that the moon hardly ever did it again soon. There was very little chance of it happening right at this moment; the moon wasn't even near the sun.

Sometimes a big storm blotted out most of the light, turning day to night. But there was no sign of such a storm at the moment. Count that out, too.

There was also smoke. A bad, smoldering blaze could stifle the day for a time. If they could gather the makings of a fire, then start it going—

"Chameleon," Imbri sent in a dreamlet. "If I let you off behind a stone, so the monster doesn't see you, could you make a fire?"

"A fire?" The woman had trouble seeing the relevance, naturally enough.

"To stop the centycore."

"Oh." Chameleon considered. "I do have a few magic matches that I use for cooking. All I have to do is rub them against something rough, and they burst into flame."

"Excellent. Make a big fire—" Imbri projected a sequence in pictures: Chameleon hiding behind a stone column, dashing out when the monster wasn't near, gathering pieces of wood and dry moss and anything else that might blaze. "A big, smoky fire. Keep it between you and the centycore." Actually, the monster could go around the fire to get at the woman, but that wasn't the point. The fire was merely the mechanism to generate smoke.

"I can do that," Chameleon agreed. Imbri accelerated, leaving the centycore puffing behind, veered near a megalithic column, and braked as rapidly as she could without

throwing her rider. Why hadn't she tried a fast decelera-
tion, or bucking, when the Horseman had ridden her? Because she, like a dumb filly, hadn't thought of it. But she
suspected it wouldn't have worked anyway; the man understood horses too well to be deceived or outmaneuvered by
one. Hence his name—the man who had mastered the
horse.

Chameleon dismounted and scurried behind the megalith
while Imbri galloped ostentatiously off, attracting the
monster's baleful attention. It worked; the centycore
snorted after her, never glancing at the woman. It probably
preferred the taste of horsemeat anyway. Imbri was relieved; if the monster had turned immediately on the
woman, there could have been real trouble.

Imbri led the monster a merry chase, keeping tantaliz-
ingly close so as to monopolize its attention. Meanwhile,
Chameleon dashed about, diligently gathering scraps of
wood and armfuls of dry leaves and grass.

In due course the blaze started. A column of smoke
puffed up.

"Ho!" the centycore exclaimed, pausing. "What's this?"

Imbri paused with him, not wanting him to spy the
woman behind the column. "That's a fire, hornface," she
projected. "To burn you up."

"It won't burn me up!" the centycore snorted, the tines
of his antler quivering angrily. "I will put it out!"

"You couldn't touch it," Imbri sent, her dreamlet showing the monster yelping as he got toasted on the rump by a
burning brand.

"So you claim," the centycore muttered, glancing at his
posterior to make sure there was no burning brand being
shoved at it. He approached the flame. Imbri skirted it to
the other side and reached Chameleon, who climbed eagerly on her back. The woman evidently had been afraid,
with excellent reason, but had performed well anyway. That
was worth noting; she might not be smart, but she had
reasonable courage.

The centycore kicked at the fire. A piece of wood flew
out, starting a secondary blaze a short distance away. "You
won't put it out that way, bearsnoot," Imbri projected with
a picture of a burning branch falling on the monster's ant-

ler and getting caught in it. The dream centycore shook his head violently, but the brand only blazed more brightly, toasting his snoot. In a moment the antler began to burn.

"Stop that!" the monster snapped, shaking his antler as if it felt hot.

"You'll burn to pieces!" Imbri dreamed, causing the image's antler to blaze more fiercely. Jets of flame shot out from each point, forming bright patterns in the air as the monster waved its antler about. The patterns shaped into a big word: FIRE.

"Enough!" the centycore screamed. He leaped for the moat and dunked his horn. That doused the dream flame; reality was too strong for it. But Imbri did manage to dream up a subdued fizzle where the points entered the water.

"Hey!" the nix protested, picking up the dream image. He froze the water around the antler, trapping the centycore head-down. The monster roared with a terrible rage and ripped his head free, sending shards of ice flying out. The nix changed to a fish and scooted away, daunted.

Now the centycore scooped icy water toward the fire with his antler. But the fire was too big and too far away; only a few droplets struck it, with furious hissing. Hell had no anger like that of a wetted fire, as Imbri knew from experience.

The centycore considered. Then he scooped up a hornful of muck from the edge of the moat and hurled that toward the fire. There was a tremendous hiss as the blob scored, and a balloon of steam and smoke went up.

"Ha ha, mare, he's putting it out!" the nix called from a safe distance across the moat. Apparently he felt that it was best to join sides with the monster. "I guess that knots your tail!"

"You shut up!" Imbri projected in a dream that encompassed both nix and centycore. "He won't get it all!"

"That's what you think, horsehead!" the nix cried.

Encouraged by this, the monster indulged in a fever of mudslinging. His aim was good; more gouts of smog ballooned out. The fire was furious, but was taking a beating.

"Curses, he's doing it!" Imbri projected with wonderfully poor grace.

Indeed he was. Soon the fire was largely out and smoke suffused the entire region, making them all cough. The light of the sun diminished, for sunrays didn't like smelly smog any better than anyone else did.

Was it dark enough? Imbri wasn't sure. "If this doesn't work, we're finished," she projected privately to Chameleon. "Maybe you should dismount."

"I'll stay with you," the woman said loyally. Imbri chalked up one more point for her character, though she realized it might be fear of the monster that motivated Chameleon as much as support for Imbri.

Now the centycore reoriented on them. "You're next, mareface!" he cried, and charged.

Imbri bolted for the megalith nearest the fire, where the smoke hovered most thickly. The centycore bounded after her. He was sure he had her now.

The mare leaped right into the stone column—and phased through it. Chameleon, in contact with her, did the same. The darkness was deep enough!

The monster, following too closely, smacked headfirst into the column. The collision jammed several points of his antler into the stone, trapping him there. He roared and yanked, but the stone was tougher than the ice had been, and he could not get free. That particular menace had been nullified.

Actually, Imbri now recognized an additional concern she hadn't quite thought of before. She had not been certain she could phase a rider with her. She had brought the ogre out of the gourd, but he had already been in it, his body separate. She had carried the girl Tandy once, but that had been in genuine night. When she phased out of the Horseman's pen, she had left the hobble behind, and it had certainly been in contact with her body. So the precedents were mixed. Apparently she could take someone or something with her if she wanted to, and leave it behind if she chose. It was good to get such details straight; an error could be a lot of trouble.

Now they could explore the center of the stone structure. They moved in cautiously.

There was a rumble, as of a column wobbling in its socket and beginning to crumble. Some sand sifted down from one of the elevated slabs. Both mare and woman looked up nervously. What was happening?

The noises subsided as they stood. Apparently it was a random event, possibly the result of the heat or smoke of the recent fire.

Imbri took another step forward. There was a long, moaning groan to the right, causing their heads to snap about. It was just another massive stone column settling, doing nothing.

Again Imbri stepped forward. The huge rock slab above slipped its support and crunched down toward them.

Imbri leaped backward, whipping her head around and back to catch Chameleon as the woman tried to fall off. The massive stone swung down where the two of them had been the moment before, thudding into the ground with an awesome impact.

"This place is collapsing!" Chameleon cried. "Let's get out of here!"

But Imbri's memory was jogged by something. "Isn't it strange that it should collapse the very moment we enter it, after standing for what seems by the cobwebs and moss to have been centuries?" Actually, cobwebs could form faster than that, but Imbri wasn't concerned about minor details. "This resembles the handiwork of the spriggan," she concluded in the dream.

"Spriggan?"

"Giant ghosts who haunt old castles and megalithic structures. They are destructive in nature; that's why old structures eventually collapse. The spriggan keep shoving at columns and pulling at cross pieces, until there is a collapse."

"But why right now?" Chameleon asked, since Imbri hadn't directly answered her own question. A creature had to make things quite clear for this woman.

"To stop us from proceeding farther. Don't you remember the nature of Magician Humfrey's castle?"

"Oh, yes. I had to ask him a Question once, before I married Bink, and it was just awful getting in! But not like this."

"His castle is different each time a person comes to it. I've seen it on my way to deliver dreams. Never the same."

"Yes, I remember," she agreed. "He must spend a lot of time getting it changed."

"So this is Humfrey's castle *now*. A megalithic structure. We have passed two hazards and are encountering the third—the spriggan. They are preventing us from advancing by shoving the stones down in our path."

"Oh." Chameleon was not entirely reassured. "But we don't have a Question. We're on the King's business."

"Yes, I understand the Good Magician is not supposed to charge for official business. He must not have realized we were coming."

"But he's supposed to know everything!"

"But he's old and absent-minded and set in his ways," Imbri's dream image reminded her. Still, she was not pleased at having to run this gauntlet. "So we must find out how to get past the ghosts," Imbri concluded. "Then we will be able to consult the Magician despite his forgetfulness."

"The ghosts at Castle Roogna are friendly," Chameleon said, evidently not liking the spriggan.

"No doubt. I am supposed to convey greetings from the ghosts of the haunted house in the gourd to one of the ghosts of Castle Roogna. I haven't yet had the opportunity."

"Who?"

"One named Jordan. Do you know him?"

"Not well. He keeps mostly to himself. But I do know Millie, who is not really a ghost any more. They're all pretty nice, I think, except for the six-year-old ghost, who—" She hesitated, not wishing to speak evil of the dead.

"Who is a brat?" Imbri supplied helpfully.

"I suppose. But the others are nice."

"Spriggan are not. They are to nice ghosts as ogres are to elves."

"That's awful!"

Evidently Chameleon was not going to be much help on this one. Imbri skirted the fallen stone and started forward once more. There was another groan, this one to the left. Imbri shied right—and the column there began to crumble threateningly.

"Oh, I don't like this!" Chameleon cried.

Imbri paused. She didn't like this either. But there had to be a way through. There always was. This was the nature of the Good Magician's defenses. He did not like to be bothered by frivolous intrusions, so he set up challenges; only smart, determined, and lucky petitioners could get through. Imbri knew King Trent would not have sent them here if the matter had not been important, so they had to conquer the challenges. Too bad the smoke had dissipated so she could no longer phase them through solid obstacles. That would have made it easy. But already the shadows were lengthening; soon it would be dusk, and that would solve her problem. All she had to do was keep from getting squished under a rock before then. She really would have been smarter to wait for night before trying to enter the castle, but now she was in it and would carry through with marish stubbornness.

She thought about the spriggan. They were distantly related to night mares, being both material and immaterial. In their natural forms they were invisible, but they could solidify their mouths to issue groans, and their hands to shove stones. They never touched living creatures directly, however; contact with warm flesh discombobulated them, and it took them a long time to get recombobulated.

There might be the answer! All Imbri had to do was make the giants show themselves, then advance on them. Maybe.

"I'm going to try something risky," Imbri projected to Chameleon. Her dreamlet showed herself charging directly at a horrendous ghost. "Would you like me to set you down outside the megaliths, where it is safe?"

Chameleon was frightened but firm. "It's not safe. The centycore is there. Maybe he's gotten unstuck from the column. I will stay with you."

Good enough. "Now we must provoke the ghost-giants into showing themselves. When they do, you must act terrified."

A touch of humor penetrated the woman's naiveté. "I will."

Imbri nerved herself and took a step forward. There was an immediate warning groan. She projected a dream to the vicinity of the sound. "You're pretty bold, hiding behind big stones," her dream image said with an expression of contempt. "You wouldn't scare anyone if you were visible."

"Oh, yeah?" the sprig she had addressed responded. "Look at this, mare!"

The ghost took form before her. He was the size of a man, but his arms were huge and hairy, and his face was dominated by two upcurving tusks. "Grooooan!" he groaned.

Chameleon shrieked in presumably simulated terror. But Imbri moved directly toward the ghost.

The sprig, startled, shrank to the size of a midget. Then, catching itself, it expanded to the size of a giant. "Booooo!" it boooooed, shoving at a ceiling stone. The stone budged, sending down a warning shower of sand. Chameleon screamed again. It seemed she didn't like sand in her hair.

But as the mare neared the ghost, the sprig jumped out of the way, avoiding contact. They passed right through, and Imbri knew she and Chameleon had penetrated well in toward the castle.

There was another invisible groan, from another sprig. Imbri charged it, though another column was crumbling. Her ploy worked; the column crashed the other way, not striking her. The ghosts never pulled columns down upon themselves; thus where the spriggan stood was the safest place to be, despite the scary noises they made. All she had to do was keep charging them, and she would be safe.

It worked. Columns and ceiling stones tumbled all around her, but Imbri navigated from the groan to groan and threaded the dangerous maze successfully.

Abruptly they were inside the castle proper.

Chapter 4. Forging the Chain

"Well, hello Chameleon!" the Gorgon said. She was a mature, almost overmature woman, whose impressive proportions were verging on obesity. Life had evidently been too kind to her. Her face was invisible, so that there was no danger from her glance. "And the mare Imbrium, too! Do come in and relax."

"We are here to see Good Magician Humfrey," Chameleon said. "King Trent sent us."

"Of course he did, dear," the Gorgon agreed. "We have been expecting you."

Chameleon blinked. "But you tried to stop us!"

"It's just Humfrey's way. He's such a dear, but he does have his little foibles. Those creatures wouldn't really have hurt you."

Imbri snorted. She was not at all sure of that!

"You both must be hungry," the Gorgon continued blithely. "We have milk and honey and alfalfa and oats in any combination you two may desire."

"Milk and oats," Chameleon said promptly.

"Honey and alfalfa," Imbri projected in a dreamlet.

"Ah, so it is true!" the Gorgon said, pleased. "You really are a night mare! What a cute way of talking!" She led them to the dining room, where she brought out the promised staples. Chameleon's oats were cooked over a little magic flame, then served with the milk and a snitch of honey from Imbri's soaked alfalfa. It was an excellent dinner.

Then they were ushered into the surly presence of Good Magician Humfrey. He had a tiny, cluttered study upstairs, stuffed with old tomes, multicolored bottles, magic mirrors, and assorted unclassifiable artifacts. Humfrey himself hunched over an especially big and ancient volume. He was gnomelike, with enormous Mundane-type spectacles and wrinkles all over his face. He looked exactly as old as he probably just might be. "Well?" he snapped irritably.

"Chameleon and the mare Imbrium are here for advice," the Gorgon said deferentially. "You have them on your calendar."

"I never pay attention to that bit of paper!" the Good Magician grumped. "I'm too busy." But he looked at a chart on the wall. There, in large letters, was the note FAIR & MARE. "Oh, yes, certainly," he grumbled. "Well, let's get on with it."

There was a pause. "The advice," the Gorgon reminded the Magician gently.

"Have they paid the fee?"

"They're on the King's business. No fee."

"What is Xanth coming to?" he mumbled ungraciously. "Too many creatures expecting a free lunch."

"That was dinner," Chameleon said brightly.

Again there was a pause. The Gorgon touched Humfrey's elbow.

He looked up, startled, almost as if he had been dozing. "Of course. Beware the Horseman." His old eyes returned to his book.

"But we've already had that message," Imbri protested in a dreamlet.

Humfrey's brow corrugated yet farther. Such a thing would have been impossible without magic. "Oh? Well, it remains good advice." He cogitated briefly. "Break the chain." He looked at his tome again.

"I don't understand," Chameleon said.

"It isn't necessary to understand Humfrey's Answers," the Gorgon explained. "They are always correct regardless."

Imbri wasn't satisfied. "Don't you folk realize there's a war on?" she projected in an emphatic dream. Her picture showed brutish Mundanes tromping like ogres through the brush, frightening small birds and despoiling the land with sword and fire. The image was taken from her memory of the Lastwave. "We have to find out how to defend Xanth!"

Humfrey looked up again. "Of course I realize! Look at my book!"

They crowded closer to peer at his open tome. There was a map of Xanth with portions marked in color.

"Here is where the Mundanes are invading," Humfrey said, pointing to the northwestern isthmus. "They have not yet penetrated far, but they are well organized and tough and determined, and the auspices are murky. Divination doesn't work very well on Mundanes, because they are nonmagical creatures. But it seems the Nextwave of conquest is upon us. It will be the end of Xanth as we know it, unless we take immediate and effective measures to protect our land."

"The Nextwave!" Chameleon repeated, horrified.

"We knew there would be another Wave sometime," the Gorgon said. "All through the history of Xanth there have been periodic Waves of conquest from Mundania. All human inhabitants derive from one Wave or another, or did until very recently. But each Wave sets Xanth back immeasurably, for the Mundanes are barbaric. They slay whatever they do not understand and they understand very little. If this Wave succeeds in conquering Xanth, it will be a century before things return to normal."

"But how do we stop it?" Chameleon asked.

"I told you," Humfrey snapped. "Break the chain."

Imbri exploded with full night marish ferocity. Storm clouds roiled in her dream image, booming hollowly as they fired out fierce jags of lightning. "This is no time for cute obscurities! We need a straight Answer to a serious problem! Do you have an Answer or don't you?" A jag struck near Humfrey.

Humfrey gazed soberly at her, one hand idly swatting away the jag of lightning, though it was only a dreamlet image. "There are no simplistic Answers to a complex problem. We must labor diligently to piece together the best of all possible courses, or at least the second best, depending on what is available."

The mare backed off. She did realize that some answers could not be simple or clear. Magic often had peculiar applications, and predictive magic was especially tricky, even when Mundanes weren't involved.

"Night nears," the Gorgon said gently. Indeed, the cluttered scrap of a window showed near-blackness outside. "You will be able to travel more freely then. We must let Magician Humfrey labor in peace." She led them to another room, where there was a couch. "You will want to rest first. I will wake you at midnight."

That was good enough. There were sanitary facilities and a pleasant bed of straw. Imbri lay down and slept. She could rest perfectly well on her feet, but suspected the Gorgon would worry about hoofprints and droppings and such, so lying down was best. Actually, there was hardly any place in Xanth that could not be improved by a nice, fertilizer-rich dropping, but human beings tended not to understand that.

A night mare visited her, of course. Imbri recognized her instantly. "Mare Crisium!" she exclaimed in her dream. "How is everything back home?"

"The Dark Horse is worried," Crises said. She, like Imbri, could speak in the human language in the dream state. "He says the menace advances, and you are the only one who can abate it, and you have fallen into the power of the enemy."

"I did, but I escaped," Imbri replied. "I delivered the message to King Trent. Now I'm on a mission for him."

"It is not enough. The King is about to be betrayed. You must tell him to beware the Horseman."

"I told you, I told him that!" Imbri flared.

"You must tell him again."

Imbri changed the subject. "Where's Vapors?" She had a special affinity for both Crises and Vapors, for those two mares had picked up half souls at the time Imbri got hers. But the others had not retained them. Their halves had been replaced by the halves from a demon, cynical and cruel, which gave them a certain competitive edge: their bad dreams were real terrors, and they got the most challenging assignments. Even so, they had not been satisfied and had finally turned the half souls into the central office. So Imbri was now the only night mare with any part of a soul. But still, she felt closer to those other two; they understood the impact a soul could have.

"Vapors is with Chameleon. In a moment the woman will wake screaming; then you both must go and warn the King."

Imbri started to protest, but then Chameleon's scream sounded, and both woman and mare were jolted rudely awake. Instantly Vapors and Crises bolted, leaving only their signature hoofprints. Imbri was saddened; she was now considered a mortal creature, who was not permitted to see a night mare in the waking state. That wrenched at her, for she had spent most of her long life in the profession. How quickly the prerogatives and perquisites of employment were lost, once a creature retired! But that was the price she paid for the chance to see the rainbow.

She went to Chameleon, who clutched at her hysterically. "Oh, it was awful, Imbri! Such a bad dream! Is that really what you used to do?"

"Not that well," Imbri sent, with a tinge of regret. Obviously Mare Vaporum retained the terrifying touch that Imbri had lost. "What did you dream?"

"I dreamed King Trent was close to death, or something almost as awful! We must go right back and warn him!" She was still breathing raggedly, her lovely hair in disarray.

A simple premonition of danger to another person—and the client was in shambles. Imbri realized that she had retired none too soon; she would have had to bring in a fire-breathing sea monster to achieve a similar effect. She was just too softhearted.

"Get on my back, woman," Imbri projected. "We'll ride immediately."

The Gorgon appeared, carrying a lighted candle that illuminated her empty head oddly, showing the snakelets that were her hair from the inside surface. "Midnight," she said. "Time to—oh, I see you're ready. Do come again soon!"

"We will!" Chameleon called, her mood lightening because of the contact with the familiar facelessness of a friend. Then Imbri plunged through the wall and they were off.

This time there was no trouble from the spriggan, centy-core, or nix. Imbri was in her night mare form, phasing through everything, and Chameleon phased with her be-cause that was the nature of night mare magic. They gal-loped in a straight line toward Castle Roogna, passing blithely through trees and rocks and even a sleeping dragon without resistance. Chameleon was pleasantly amazed; she was a good audience for this sort of thing, and that made Imbri's mood improve.

"Oh, no!" Chameleon exclaimed suddenly. "I forgot the elopement!"

That was right—this was the scheduled night for the marriage of Prince Dor. Chameleon was the mother of the victim; of course she wanted to attend. "We can make it," Imbri sent.

"No, we can't," Chameleon said tearfully. "It was to happen at midnight, and we're hours away, and it's past midnight now!"

Imbri hated to have this lovely and innocent woman un-happy. "We can travel faster—but it's a route you may not like."

"Anything!" Chameleon exclaimed. "If we can even catch the end of it—my poor baby boy—I know he'll be so happy!"

Imbri had a certain difficulty following the woman's thought processes this time, but decided Chameleon had mixed feelings about her son and his marriage. Mothers were notorious for that sort of thing. "Then hold on tight and don't be afraid of anything you see." Imbri galloped into a patch of hypnogourds and plunged into a gourd.

It was dark as they phased through the rind and became part of the gourd world. Of course they were *not* part; they were alien visitors who normally would have found access only by looking through a peephole, instead of passing physically through. This was a gray area of magic, possible only because of Imbri's special status as an agent of liaison.

Then they were in a graveyard. "Oh, are we there al-ready?" Chameleon asked. "The zombie cemetery?"

"Not yet," Imbri projected. "Stay on me!" For if the woman ever set foot inside the world of the gourd alone, she would not readily get free. That was the nature of the region of night.

A walking skeleton appeared. It reached for Chameleon, its hollow eye sockets glinting whitely. "Go away!" the woman cried, knocking the bony arm away. "You're no zombie. You're too clean." Startled, the skeleton retreated.

"They are a lot more cautious about visitors since an ogre passed through and intimidated them," Imbri sent. It had taken weeks after the ogre's departure for the skeletons to get themselves properly organized, since their bones had been hopelessly jumbled together. Probably some of them were still wearing the wrong parts.

Imbri charged into the haunted house. A resident ghost loomed, flaring with awesome whiteness at Chameleon. "Are we back at Castle Roogna already?" she asked. "I don't recognize this ghost." Disgusted, the ghost faded out, thinking it had lost its touch. Imbri knew the feeling; there were few things as humiliating as having one's efforts unappreciated when one's business was fear.

Now Imbri shot out the front wall of the house. She galloped along a short walkway, then out through the decorative hedge. She emerged into a bleak moor. The ground became soggy, opening dark mouths to swallow intruders, but the night mare hurdled them handily. The terrors of the World of Night were for others, not herself. She might be retired, but she was not yet that far out of it.

She passed on to a mountain shaped like a burning iceberg, galloping up its slope. Amorphous shapes loomed, reaching for Chameleon with multiple hands and hungry snouts. Misshapen eyes glared.

Now the woman was frightened, for she had had no prior experience with this type of monster. Zombies and ghosts were familiar, but not amorphous monsters. She hunched down and hid her face in Imbri's mane. That was another trait of human folk: they tended to fear the unfamiliar or the unknown, though often it was not as threatening to them as the known.

Then they were out through the rind of another gourd, their shortcut through the World of Night completed. They emerged from a gourd patch much nearer Castle Roogna.

Night mares could travel almost instantly anywhere in Xanth, simply by using the proper gourds. This route was not available to Imbri by day, since she was solid then; fortunately, it was now night.

Chameleon's fright eased as she saw that she was back in the real world of Xanth. "Is that really where you live?" she asked. "Among the horrors?"

"Daytime Xanth seems far more hazardous to me," Imbri projected. "Tangle trees and solid boulders and the Mundanes—those are monsters enough!"

"I suppose so," Chameleon agreed doubtfully. "Are we near the cemetery?"

"Very near." Imbri veered to head directly toward it.

"Wait!" Chameleon cried. "We must go in costume!"

"Costume?" What was this creature thinking of now?

"We must look like zombies so no one will know."

Evidently so. Imbri humored her, since it was difficult to argue with a person of such low intelligence and sweet personality. They stopped, and the woman found stink-vines and ink pots, which she used to make each of them look and smell rotten. Her artistry was reasonably good; Chameleon did indeed resemble a buxom, flesh-loose zombie more than the lovely older woman she really was. Imbri looked like a half-dead nag.

Now they continued to the cemetery, where it lurked in the lee of Castle Roogna. The zombies were up and about in strength. Not many things stirred them, but marriage was in certain ways akin to death in its finality and disillusion. "We conspired with the Zombie Master," Chameleon whispered to one of Imbri's perked furry ears. "He roused his minions for the occasion, though he could not attend himself. One of the zombies is a justice of the peace. I don't know what that is, but it seems he can marry them." She was all excited with anticipation.

Zombies were loosely formed creatures, so naturally would have a justice of the piece, Imbri realized. It was not too great a stretch of the rationale to extend the authority to restore lost pieces of zombie to the union of full creatures of flesh. Marriage, in Xanth, was whatever one made of it, anyway; the real test of it would be the acceptance by the partners in it and by the wider community, rather than any single ceremony.

As they stepped onto the graveyard grounds, things changed. Suddenly the zombies were twice as ghastly as before, dressed in tuxedos and gowns that concealed much of their decay but made the parts that showed or fell off more horrible in contrast. All were standing quietly between the gravestones, facing the largest and dankest crypt at the north end, where an especially revolting zombie stood with a tattered book in his spoiled hands.

A femal zombie came up. Her eyeballs were sunken, and parts of her teeth showed through her worm-decimated cheek. Her low décolletage exposed breasts like rotten melons. "Are you a centaur?" she inquired in a surprisingly normal voice.

"I'm Chameleon, your Majesty," Chameleon said, dismounting, evidently recognizing the voice. "And this is the mare Imbri, who brought me back in time for the wedding. Have we missed anything?"

"Wonderful, Chameleon!" Queen Iris cried, embracing her with a sound like funguses squishing. "Take your place in the front row, by the chancel; you're the mother of the groom, after all. You haven't missed a thing; these events always run late."

"And you're the mother of the bride," Chameleon said, happy at the way this was working out.

The Queen Zombie turned to Imbri, her rotten body rotating at differing velocities. Her illusion was a morbid work of art! "You really are a mare?" she asked. "Yes, I see you are. Since you're not related to the principals, you should stand in back."

"But Imbri's my friend!" Chameleon protested loyally.

"I'll stand in back," Imbri projected quickly. She knew little about human folk ceremonies and much preferred to be out of the way.

"Oh, my, that's interesting magic!" the Queen said. "Almost like my illusion, only yours is all inside the head, or do I mean all in the mind? I didn't know animals could do magic."

"I am a night mare," Imbri clarified.

"Oh, that explains it, of course." The Queen turned away, going to greet other arrivals.

Chameleon went dutifully to the front, while Imbri made her way back. She came to stand between two zombies. It seemed the lucky couple for whom this ceremony was waiting had not yet arrived, so there was time to talk.

"Hello," she projected to the one on the left.

The answer was an awful morass of foulness, resembling a blood pudding riddled with maggots. This was a true zombie, who might have been dead for centuries; she had just glimpsed its actual brain. Imbri was not unduly finicky, for every monster was allowed its own style in Xanth, but she was accustomed to the clean bones of the walking skeletons in the gourd. She tried not to shy away from this person, for that would be impolite, but she did not attempt to communicate with it again.

Imbri tried the figure on the right. "Are you a zombie, too?" she sent tentatively.

This person was alive but startled. "Did you address me, or was I dreaming?"

"Yes," Imbri agreed.

He turned to peer more closely at her. "Are you a person or a horse?"

"Yes."

"I'm afraid I'm not used to this concentration of magic," he said. "I may have made a faux pas."

"No, that's west of here," Imbri corrected him.

"It's true! You are a horse, and you did address me!"

"Yes. I am the night mare Imbrium."

"A literal nightmare? How original! One never knows what to expect next in Xanth! I am Ichabod the Archivist, from what you term Mundania. My friend the centaur Arnolde—he is currently in Mundania, as that's his office, liaison to that region—brought me here so I could do research into the fantastic and, ahem, pursue a nymph or two."

"That is what nymphs are for," Imbri agreed politely. She knew it was a very popular human entertainment. But his reference to Mundania alarmed her; was he one of the enemy?

"Oh, no, I'm no enemy!" Ichabod protested, and Imbri

realized she had forgotten to separate her private thought from the formal dreamlet. She would have to be more careful about that, now that she was among waking people. "Mundania is many things—you might say, all things to all people. It seems Mundania has extremely limited access to Xanth, while Xanth has virtually unlimited access to Mundania. This includes all the historical ages of our world. Therefore Xanth is but an elusive dream to the Mundanes, most of whom do not believe in it at all, while Mundania is a prodigious reality to Xanthians, who are very little interested in it. Am I boring you?"

He was doing that, of course, but Imbri had the equine wit not to say so. "I deal in dreams, and I am elusive, so I am certainly a creature of Xanth."

"Really? You mean you are a dream yourself? You're not really there?" He reached out a hand, tentatively, to touch her shoulder.

"Not exactly." She phased out, and his hand passed through her.

"Fabulous!" he exclaimed. "I must put you in my notebook. You say your name is Imbrium? As in the Sea of Rains on the visible face of the moon? How very intriguing!"

He might be Mundane, but she saw that he was not entirely ignorant. "Yes. They named the Sea of Rains after my grandam, who lived a long time ago. I inherit my signature from her and the title to that portion of the moon." She phased back to solid and stamped a forehoof, making a moonmap imprint with her own name highlighted.

"Oh, marvelous!" Ichabod cried. "I say, would you do that on a sheet of my notebook? I would love to have a direct record!"

Imbri obligingly stamped his page. The map showed up very clearly on the white paper, since of course there was a coating of good, rich, cemetery dirt on her hoof.

"Oh, thank you, thank you!" the Mundane exclaimed, admiring the print. "I have never before encountered a genuine nightmare—not in the flesh, so to speak. It is not every Mundane who receives such an opportunity! If there is any return favor I might possibly do you—"

"Just tell me who is here and how the ceremony is to proceed. I have never attended an elopement."

"I shall be delighted to, though my own understanding is far from perfect. It seems that Prince Dor and Princess Irene—their titles are similar but have different derivations, as he is the designated heir to the throne, while she is merely the daughter of the King—both of whom I met eight years ago in Mundania, are at last to achieve nuptial bliss, or such reasonable facsimile thereof as is practicable."

Imbri realized that Mundanes had a more complex manner of speaking than did real people; she cocked one ear politely and tried to make sense of the convolutions.

"But he seems not yet to be aware of this, and she is supposedly not aware that virtually everyone in Castle Roogna or associated with it is attending. It is supposed to be an uncivil ceremony, performed in the dead of night by a dead man—i.e., a zombie. A most interesting type of creature, incidentally. Queen Iris has cloaked all visitors with illusion—she does have the most marvelous facility for that—so they seem to be zombies, too, and she has mixed them in with the real zombies so that no one not conversant with the ruse is likely to penetrate it. Oh, what a tangled web we weave, when first we practice to deceive! That is a Mundane quotation from—"

He broke off, for there was a stir to the south. Just in time, for he had been about to bore Imbri again. He did seem to have a formidable propensity for dullness. All the zombies, real and fake, hushed, waiting.

The pale moonlight showed a young woman of voluptuous proportion stepping through the fringe of the Castle Roogna orchard, hauling along a handsome young man. "We'll just cut through the zombie graveyard," she was saying. "We're almost there."

"Almost where?" he demanded irritably. "You're being awfully secretive, Irene. I'm tired; I have just come back from Centaur Isle, where I couldn't make much of an impression; I've consulted with King Trent about the Nextwave incursion and how to contain it; and now I just want to go home and sleep."

"You'll have a good sleep very soon, I promise you," Irene said. "A sleep like none before."

A rock chuckled. "It'll be long before you sleep, you poor sucker!" it said.

"Shut up!" Irene hissed at the rock. Then, to Dor: "Come on; we're almost there."

"Almost where?"

"Don't trust her!" the ground said. "It's a trap!"

Irene stamped her foot, hard. "Ooooo!" the ground moaned, hurting.

"I wish you'd just tell me what you're so worked up about," Dor said. "Dragging me out here for no reason—"

"No reason! Hah!" a chunk of deadwood chortled. Irene kicked it into the moat, where there was a brief, wild splashing as a moat monster snapped it up.

"I suppose you do have the right to know," she said as they entered the graveyard. All the guests had abruptly faded into invisibility, thanks to Queen Iris's illusion. "It's an elopement."

"A what?"

"Elopement, idiot!" a tombstone cracked. "Better run before you're lost!"

Irene rapped the stone on the top, and it went quiet. She seemed to have had experience dealing with talking objects. "We're eloping," she said clearly. "I'm taking you secretly away to get married. Then you'll have something nice in bed with you."

"Something nice?" Dor asked, bemused. "You mean you're giving me a pillow?"

This time it was Dor she kicked, as the whole cemetery guffawed evilly. "*Me*, you oaf! Stop teasing me; I know you aren't *that* stupid. I can be very soft and warm when I try."

"Ooooo!" the crypt said in a naughty-naughty voice. "Not many of that kind *here*!"

"But we haven't set the date!" Dor protested.

"That's why we're eloping. We'll be married tonight, before anyone knows. So there won't be any foolishness. The job will be done."

"But—"

She turned and kissed him emphatically. "You have an objection?"

Dor, obviously daunted by the kiss, was silent.

"Marvelous, just marvelous, the way she manages him," Ichabod murmured beside Imbri.

The couple arrived at the crypt. "Zombie justice, where are you?" Irene called.

The officiating zombie appeared, holding his book. Also, slowly, the rest of them phased into dim view, under the continued glow of the moon.

"We're going to be married by a zombie?" Dor demanded weakly. "Won't the union fall apart?"

"Ha. Ha. I have laughed." She shook her head, so that her green hair flounced darkly in the limited light. "It's the only person I could get without alerting Mother," Irene explained. There was a choked snort of mirth from the depths of the audience. Irene looked around and spied the crowd. "Well, all you zombies didn't have to rip yourselves from your graves," she said in a spooks-will-be-spooks manner. "But I suppose some witnesses are in order."

"I didn't know there were this many zombies buried here," Dor said.

"There aren't, you poor stiff," the crypt said. "These are—"

"Quiet!" the Queen Zombie snapped.

Now Irene was suspicious. "That voice is familiar."

"Of course it is, you luscious dummy!" the crypt said. Then a black cloud roiled out of nowhere and emitted a roll of thunder that drowned out whatever other information the crypt disgorged.

"There's something very funny about this," Dor said, squinting at the loud cloud.

Irene reverted to first principles. "What's funny about zombies? They love grim occasions. Let's get on with it."

The zombie magistrate opened his book. A page fell out; the volume was as decrepit as the zombie.

"Oh, how I hate to see a book mistreated," Ichabod breathed beside Imbri.

"Wait a moment," Dor protested. "You tricked me out here, Irene. I didn't agree to get married tonight."

"Oh? Well, I intend to marry someone! Should it be one of these zombies?"

"Now that's a bluff I can call," Dor said.

Irene stood in silent but almost tangible grief. Her shoulders shook. Tears plopped into the sod at her feet. Dor, aided by a touch of the Queen's illusion, assumed a form somewhat like the hinder part of a giant's boot: a first-class heel. "Ah, well—" he mumbled inadequately.

Irene flung her arms about him and planted another kiss that made the audience murmur with envy. Even the zombies seemed moved. When she was through, Dor stood as if numbed, as well he might.

"Classic!" Ichabod whispered. "That girl has absolutely mastered the art!"

The zombie magistrate mumbled something unintelligible. He had no tongue, and he was reading from the pageless book, with empty eyeball sockets.

"I do," Irene said firmly.

The zombie mumbled something else as his nose fell onto the book.

"He does," Irene said, nudging Dor.

The zombie made a final effort, causing several loose teeth to dribble out of his mouth.

"I've got it," Irene said. She produced a ring with an enormous stone that glowed in the moonlight so strongly it seemed to illuminate the graveyard. "Put it on me, Dor. No, not that finger, idiot. *This* one."

Dor fumbled the moonstone onto the designated finger.

"We're married now," Irene said. "Now you can kiss me."

Dor did so, somewhat uncertainly. The audience broke into applause.

The remaining illusion faded, revealing the zombies and people standing throughout the graveyard. Irene's gaze swept across the crowd. "Mother!" she exclaimed indignantly. "This is your mischief!"

"Refreshments are served in the Castle Roogna ballroom," Queen Iris said, controlling a catlike smirk. "Come, dears—mustn't keep the King waiting."

Dor came out of his trance. "You made King Trent fetch refreshments?"

"Of course not, Dor," Queen Iris said. "I supervised that chore myself yesterday. My husband refused to participate in this little charade, the spoilsport. But I know he'll want to congratulate you."

"He should congratulate *me*," Irene said. "*I* landed Dor, after all these years."

"In the whole castle, one honest person," Dor muttered. But he did not seem unhappy. "I knew the King would not betray me."

"Well, you're married now," Queen Iris said. "At last. Now come on in before the food spoils."

The zombies stirred. They liked the notion of spoiled food.

Soon all the living people were across the moat, where sleepy moat monsters made only token growls of protest, and inside Castle Roogna, where food and drink had been set out. Imbri found herself near the beverage table. Since she did not drink human-style drinks, and did not much care for human-style treats, she was satisfied to watch.

Ichabod, still beside her, felt otherwise. "I love to eat," he confided. "It is my inane ambition eventually to become obese." He took a buttercup filled with a sparkling brown liquid. "This looks suitably calorific." He tilted it to his mouth.

As the liquid passed his lips, Ichabod made a funny little jump. Brown fluid splashed over his face. "I say!" he sputtered. "Why did you do that, mare?"

"Do what?" Imbri projected.

"Kick me!"

"I did not kick you!" she protested.

"I distinctly felt a boot in my posterior!" Then he cocked his head, looking at her feet. "But you don't wear boots!"

"If I kicked you, you would have a map of the moon on your rump," Imbri sent.

Ichabod rubbed the affected portion. "True. It must have been an hallucination." He tipped the remaining liquid to his mouth.

Again he jumped. "Someone *did* kick me!" he exclaimed. "But there was no one to do it."

Imbri got a notion. "Let me sniff your drink," she sent. Ichabod held down the cup for her. Imbri sniffed—and felt a slight shove at her tail. "I thought so. This is the rare beverage Boot Rear, distilled from the sap of the shoe-fly tree. It's the drink that gives you a real kick."

"Boot Rear," Ichabod repeated thoughtfully. "I see." He picked up another cup. "Perhaps this differs. It seems effervescent, but colorless." He put it cautiously to his lips, paused, and when no suggestion of a kick manifested, gulped it quickly down.

Shining bars formed about him, enclosing him so tightly that he yelped with discomfort. "Let me out!" he cried.

Imbri quickly put a hoof on a nether bar and used her nose to shove the higher bars apart. In a moment Ichabod was able to squeeze out, his suit torn, abrasions on his body. "I suppose that was the result of the drink, too?" he asked irritably.

Imbri sniffed the empty cup. "Yes. That's Injure Jail, a concoction of incarcerated water," she reported.

"I should have guessed." But the man hadn't given up. He took a third drink, sipped it with extreme caution, paused, took a deeper sip, waited, and finally swallowed the rest. "This is excellent."

Then he fidgeted. He reached inside his jacket and drew out a card. "Where did this come from?" He found another up his sleeve, and a third dropped out of his pant leg.

Imbri sniffed the cup. "No wonder. This is Card Hider," she reported.

"This begins to grow tiresome," Ichabod said. "Imbri, would you do me the immense favor of locating me a safely sedate beverage?"

Imbri obliged, sniffing her way along the table. "Seam Croda," she sent. "Poot Frunch. June Pruice."

"I'll take that last," Ichabod said. "That sounds like my style. I think it is presently June in my section of Mundania."

Chameleon came to join them. "Wasn't that a wonderful wedding?" she asked, delicately mopping her eyes. "I cried real tears." She picked up a drink.

"Wait!" Imbri projected and Ichabod cried together. It was an unclassified beverage.

But Chameleon was already sipping it. It seemed she had to replace the fluid lost through her tears. Then her feet sank into the floor. "Oh, my—I'm afraid I took a Droft Sink!" she exclaimed. "I'm sinking!"

Imbri and Ichabod managed to haul her back to floor level. "I wouldn't want to seem to criticize the Queen, who I am sure put a great deal of attention into this spread of refreshments," Ichabod said. "But in some quarters it might be considered that certain types of practical jokes become, shall we say, tiresome."

Now the Queen herself approached. "Have you taken any of these drinks?" she inquired brightly. She had clothed herself in a fantastically bejeweled royal robe that was perhaps illusory. "I trust you find them truly novel and not to be taken lightly or soon forgotten. I want this occasion to make a real impression on the guests."

Mutely, the three nodded. The drinks were all that the Queen described.

Queen Iris picked one up herself and sipped delicately. Then she spit it out again, indelicately. Her pattern of illusion faltered, revealing a plain housedress in lieu of her robe. "What's this?" she demanded.

"A truly novel beverage that makes a real impression and is not soon forgotten," Ichabod murmured.

"Don't get flip with me, Mundane!" the Queen snapped, a miniature thundercloud forming over her head. "What's in this cup?"

Imbri sniffed. "Drapple Ink," she projected.

"Drapple Ink!" the Queen exclaimed, her gems reforming and glinting furiously. "That's meant for signing official documents indelibly! What's it doing on the refreshment stand?"

Ichabod picked up another cup of Boot Rear. "Perhaps this one is better, your Majesty," he suggested, offering it to her. "It certainly made an impression on me."

The Queen sniffed it. She took a step forward, as if shoved from behind. "That's not what I ordered!" she cried, and now her gems shot little lances of fire. "Some miscreant has switched the drinks! Oh, wait till I get my claws on that chef!"

So Queen Iris had not been responsible for the joke. Chameleon looked relieved.

The Queen paused, turning back. "Oh—Chameleon,"

she called. "I really came to ask if you had seen my husband the King. He doesn't seem to be here. Would you look for him for me, please?"

"Of course, your Majesty," Chameleon agreed. She turned to Imbri. "Will you help me look, please? He might be in a dark room, meditating."

"And we have another message to give him," Imbri reminded her, remembering. "Beware the Horseman, or break the chain."

"If only we knew what chain." Chameleon sighed. "I haven't seen any chains."

"I'll help, too," Ichabod said. "I do love a mystery."

They looked all through the downstairs castle, but could not find the King. "Could he be upstairs, in the library?" Ichabod asked. "That's a very nice room, and he is a literate man."

"Yes, he is often there," Chameleon agreed.

They went upstairs, going to the library. A ghost flitted across the hall, but was gone before Imbri could send a dreamlet to it. If she ever had a moment when she wasn't busy, she would catch up to a ghost and inquire where Jordan was, so she could give him the greeting from the ghosts of the haunted house in the gourd world.

The library door was closed. Ichabod knocked, then called, but received no answer. "I fear he is not in," he opined. "I do not like to enter a private chamber unbidden, but we should check."

The others agreed. Cautiously they opened the door and peeked in. The room was dark and quiet.

"There is a magic lantern that turns on from a button near the door," Chameleon said, fumbling for it. In a moment the lantern glowed, illuminating the room.

There was King Trent, sitting at the table, an open book in front of him.

"Your Majesty!" Chameleon cried. "We have to tell you—"

"Something is wrong," Ichabod said. "He is not moving."

They went to the King. He sat staring ahead, taking no notice of them. This was odd indeed, for King Trent was normally the most alert and courteous person, as men of genuine power tended to be.

Imbri projected a dream to the King's mind. But his mind was blank. "He's gone!" she sent to the others, alarmed. "He has no mind!"

The three stared at one another with growing dismay. Xanth had lost its King.

Chapter 5. Sphinx and Triton

By morning the new order had been established. King Trent had been retired to his bedroom for the duration of his illness, and Prince Dor had assumed the crown and mantle of Kingship and sat momentarily on the throne, making it official. For Dor was the designated heir, and Xanth had to have a King. He had vaulted in one strange night from single Prince to married King.

If there was to be a visible transformation in the young man, it had not yet materialized. He called a meeting of selected creatures after breakfast. The golden crown perched somewhat askew on his head, and the royal robes hung on him awkwardly. These things had been fitted for King Trent, who was a larger man, and it seemed King Dor preferred to wear them unaltered, so that they could be returned when King Trent recovered.

The shadows of Dor's eyes showed that he had not slept. Few of them had; the joy of the elopement had shifted without pause to the horror of involuntary abdication. Indeed, King Trent had lost his mind while the others were celebrating in the zombie graveyard. It was hard not to suspect that the two events were linked in some devious way. The new Queen Irene evidently thought they were; she had lost a father while in the process of gaining a husband.

"We have a crisis here at Castle Roogna," King Dor said, speaking with greater authority than his appearance suggested. Queen Irene stood at his side, poised as if ready to catch him if he fell. Her eyes were dark and red, and not from any artifice of makeup or magic. How well she knew that it was the misfortune of her father that had catapulted her to replace her mother as Queen; this was hardly the way she had wanted it. Former Queen Iris was upstairs with King-emeritus Trent, watching for any trifling signal of intelligence. No one knew what had happened to him, but with the Mundane invasion, they could not wait for his recovery.

The King turned to a blackboard that his ogre friend had harvested from the jungle. On it was a crudely sketched map of Xanth, with the several human folk villages marked, as were Centaur Isle and the great Gap Chasm that severed the peninsula of Xanth but that few people remembered. "The Mundanes have crossed the isthmus," Dor said, pointing to the northwest. "They are bearing south and east, wreaking havoc as they progress. But we don't know what type of Mundanes they are, or how they are armed, or how many there are. King Trent was developing that information, but I don't know all of what he knew. I will consult with the Good Magician Humfrey, but that will take time, as we don't have a magic mirror connecting to his castle at the moment. The one we have is on the blink. We shall try to get it fixed; meanwhile, we're on our own."

That reminded Imbri. "Your Majesty," she sent in a dreamlet. "We have Magician Humfrey's message for the King. In the excitement we forgot—"

"Let's have it," Dor said tiredly.

"It was 'Beware the Horseman'—which we had already told King Trent. And 'Break the chain.' That was his other message."

Dor's brow wrinkled. He had a full head of intermediate-shade hair that was handsome enough when disciplined, but it was now a careless mop. Were it not for the crown, he would have been easy to mistake for some weary traveler. "I don't understand."

"Maybe my father would have understood," Irene murmured. "He could have had dialogue with the Good Magi-

cian. Maybe there's a chain in the armory whose magic will
be released when it is broken."

"Sometimes Humfrey's obscure Answers are more trouble than they are worth," Dor grumbled. "Why can't he
just come out and say what he means?"

"I can perhaps explain that," the Mundane Ichabod said.
"First, he may believe he is speaking plainly, since he
knows so much more than others do. Second, prophecy
tends to negate itself when made too obvious. Therefore it
has to be couched in terms that become comprehensible
only when conditions for fulfillment are proper."

"Maybe so," Dor said. "Or maybe Humfrey is getting too
old to give relevant Answers any more. If we don't find a
chain in the armory, we'll just have to wage this war ourselves. The first thing we have to do is get good, recent
information. I'll have to send a party I can trust to scout
the Mundanes—"

"I'll go," Chameleon said.

King Dor smiled. "Even a King does not order his own
mother into danger. Especially when she is as pretty as
mine." Imbri exchanged a glance with Ichabod, aware that
what Dor really meant was that Chameleon was well into
her stupid phase, a probable disaster on a reconnaissance
mission. "At any rate, I doubt you could travel fast enough
to—"

"I mean with Imbri," Chameleon said. "Anyone is safe
with her."

"Ah, the night mare." Dor considered. "Is it true, mare,
that you can move as fast as thought itself?"

"Yes, King," Imbri replied. "When I use the gourd. But
that's only at night."

"And can you keep my mother safe, even by day?"

"I think so."

King Dor paced the floor, the oversized robe dragging.
"I don't like this. But I've got to have better information,
and my mother is one person I trust absolutely. I think I'd
better send Grundy the Golem along, too, to question the
plants and animals. I'd go myself, to question the stones,
if—"

"You must stay here and rule," Irene said, holding his
arm possessively.

"Yes. I really wish we could include an expert in the party who would know exactly what to look for. It's so important that we know precisely what we're up against. Mundanes are not all alike."

Ichabod coughed. "Your Majesty, I fancy myself something of an expert in Mundane matters, since I am of Mundane persuasion myself. I should be glad to go and identify the invading force for you."

Dor considered. "Ichabod, I have known you for eight years, intermittently. You have done excellent research on the magic of Xanth, and your information has been invaluable when we have needed to research Mundania. You enabled us to locate and rescue King Trent when he was captive in Mundania. I do trust you, and value your information, and know King Trent felt the same. That's why he gave you free acess to all the things of Xanth and allowed you to research in the castle library. But you *are* Mundane; I can not ask you to spy on your own people."

"My people do not ravage and pillage and slaughter wantonly!" Ichabod protested. "Do not judge all Mundanes by the transgressions of a few."

"Those few may be enough to destroy Xanth," King Dor said. "Yet you make a good case. But you would need a steed to keep up with the night mare, and I do not think any of our available creatures are suitable. A centaur might help, but most of them are down at Centaur Isle, organizing for the defense of their Isle. I should know; I just returned from there! So—"

"The day horse might help," Imbri projected.

"The day horse?" King Dor asked.

"I met him in the forest. He was Mundane steed for the Horseman, but he escaped and helped me escape. He doesn't like the Mundanes. He might be willing to carry Ichabod, though, if no bit or spurs were used, if he knew Ichabod was not one of the enemy Mundanes." Imbri twitched her skin where her own sore flanks were healing. "I am to meet him at the baobab tree at noon."

King Dor considered briefly. "Very well. I don't like organizing such an important mission so hastily, but we can't defend Xanth at all unless we get that information. If you meet this day horse, and if he agrees to help, Ichabod can ride him. But you, Mother, will be in charge of the mission. Only please listen to Grundy—"

Chameleon smiled. "I have been stupid since before you were born, Dor. I know how to get along. I will listen to Grundy."

Now the golem appeared. He was as tall as the length of a normal hand and resembled the wood and rag he had originally been fashioned from, though now he was alive. Most people of Xanth had magic talents; he was a talent that had become a person. "We'll get along fine," he said. "I care about Chameleon."

"I know you do," King Dor said.

"I was Dor's guide when he wasn't even a Prince," Grundy said, asserting himself. "I know Chameleon from twenty-five years back. Can't say the same for this nag, though."

Imbri's ears flattened back in ire. She sent a dreamlet of a thousand-toothed monster chomping the golem.

"Then again," Grundy said, shaken as he had been the last time they clashed, "maybe I've met her in my dreams."

Chameleon smiled in an inoffensive way. "Night mares are very scary in dreams, but nice in person."

"Take care of yourselves," King Dor said gravely. He seemed quite different from his petulance and indecision of the prior evening, as if the responsibility of leadership had indeed brought out a new and superior facet of his character. "There is not one of you I would care to lose." He smiled, to show there was a modicum of humor there, though it wasn't really necessary.

"We must say good-bye to Queen Iris," Chameleon said. She led the way upstairs, and Imbri and Grundy followed, not knowing what else to do.

The King's bedroom had become an enormous dark cave, with stony stalactites depending from the domed ceiling and deep shadows shrouding the walls. Muted wailing sounded in the background. Fallen King Trent had the aspect of phenomenal grandeur, while Queen Iris was garbed in the foulest rags. The setting was illusion, courtesy of the Queen's talent, but the sentiment was real.

"I just wanted to say, your Majesty, that we miss the King and will try our best to help," Chameleon said, standing on a rocky escarpment.

Queen Iris looked up. She saw how lovely Chameleon was, and knew what it meant. "Thank you, Chameleon. I'm sure your son will make a good King," she said, speaking slowly and clearly so the woman would understand. Of course there was no assurance that Dor would be able to handle the job, let alone the Mundanes, but this was not the occasion for the expression of such doubts.

"I'm going north now with Mare Imbri and Grundy and Ichabod maybe, to spy on the Mundanes."

"I'm sure you will spy well." Queen Iris's gaze dropped; her politeness was almost exhausted.

"Good-bye, your Majesty," Chameleon said.

The Queen nodded. Then the visitors left the gloomy cave and found the stairs leading down.

They grabbed some supplies, reviewed the map, selected a promising daytime route, and moved out. Imbri galloped ahead to the baobab tree, for it was coming on to noon and she didn't want to miss the day horse. She carried Grundy, who could talk to any living thing and would not seem like a human person. Ichabod and Chameleon followed more slowly on foot.

The baobab was a monstrous tree. It towered above the jungle, its apex visible from far away. The oddest thing about it was the fact that it grew upside down. Its foliage was on the ground, and its tangled roots were in the air. A space around it was clear, for the baobab didn't like to be crowded, and used hostile spells to drive away competitive plants.

Imbri poked her nose in the foliage. Was the day horse here? He hadn't specified which day; he might be elsewhere this noon.

The golem made a windy, whispering sound. The tree replied similarly. "Bao says the horse's waiting inside," Grundy reported.

Imbri nosed her way to the tremendous, bulbous trunk. There was a split in it wide enough to admit a horse. She entered cautiously.

Inside it was like a cathedral, with the dome of the tree rising high above. Wooden walls convoluted down to a tesselated wooden floor. From inside, the tree looked right side up. Perhaps that was illusion.

There in the center stood the handsome day horse, shining white. His mane and tail were silken silver, and his hooves gleamed. His small ears perked forward alertly on either side of his forelock. He was almost the prettiest sight she had seen.

"Now there's a horse you can call a horse," Grundy murmured appreciatively. "No fish-tail, no unicorn-horn, no shady colors, no bad dreams. The Mundanes may not be good for much, but they certainly know how to grow horses!"

Imbri could only agree, despite the golem's obliquely derogatory reference to herself—the implication that Xanth could not grow good horses. The only male of her species she had known before was the Night Stallion, who was her sire. The dark horses had been closely interbred for millennia, but now they seldom bred at all because the relationship was too close. New blood was needed—but what was she thinking of? This was a Mundane horse, not really her kind. Her new solidity was giving her new sorts of reaction.

The day horse made a nicker. "He says come forward so he can see you in the light, black mare," Grundy translated unnecessarily. Of course Imbri understood equine talk! She stepped forward. She hadn't seen the day horse more than fleetingly by day before and was now as skitterish as a colt. The sheer masculinity of him had a terrific impact on her.

"You are lovely as the night," the day horse nickered.

"You are handsome as the day," Imbri nickered back. Oh, what a thrill to interact with such a stallion!

"I just hate to interrupt this touching dialogue," Grundy cut in with a certain zest. "But you do have business, you know."

Imbri sighed. The confounded golem was right. Quickly she projected a dream of explanation, describing what she wanted from the day horse.

He considered. "I don't like going near Mundane human

folk," he said in the dream. "They might capture me again." He stomped his left foot nervously, making the brass circlet on it glint. "Then I would never get away."

Imbri well understood. Once he was tethered, he would not be able to phase away by night, as Imbri could, for he was not magic. Like the Mundane human beings, he was limited to Mundane devices. This was the terrible curse of all Mundanes. *They could not do magic.* Most of them did not even believe in magic, which might be a large part of their problem. Fortunately, their offspring in Xanth soon became magical. That was why the Mundane conquests never lasted more than a generation or so; the intruders stopped being Mundane.

"You don't have to go near them," Grundy said in equine language. "All you have to do is carry Ichabod close enough so *he* can look at them. He's Mundane himself, so he knows—"

"Mundane!" the day horse neighed, his nostril's dilating and white showing around his eyes.

"But he's a tame Mundane," the golem continued. "Loyal to Xanth. He doesn't want to see it despoiled. He likes the wild nymphs too well."

"What does he do with nymphs?" Imbri asked, curious.

"Mostly he just looks at their legs," the golem explained. "He's too old to chase them very fast. I'm not sure he would know what to do with one if he caught her, but he likes to dream. No offense to you, night mare." Grundy was getting more civil as he became better acquainted with her.

"No offense," she sent. "That's not the kind of dream I carry, anyway."

The day horse was shaking his head and scuffling the floor with his hooves. "I don't like Mundane men. I know about them. They can't be trusted."

"Say, that's right!" Grundy said. "You came with them! You can tell us all about them. What time and region of Mundania are they from?"

"Time? Region?" The day horse seemed confused.

"Mundania is all times and all places," Grundy said with assumed patience. "Thousands of years, and more territory than in all Xanth. We need to know when and where you come from so Ichabod can look it up in his moldy tomes and find out how to fight the men."

"I don't know anything about that," the day horse neighed. "All I know is how the Horseman put the bit in my mouth and the spurs to my sides and made me go." Imbri nickered with sympathy; she understood exactly.

"You've got to know!" the golem cried. "How can you spend your whole life among the Mundanes and not know all about them?"

The day horse just looked at him, ears angling back.

Imbri caught on. "Mundane animals are stupid, like Chameleon," she projected to the golem in a private dreamlet. "He never noticed the details of the Mundane society. He was probably kept in a stable and pasture."

"That must be it," Grundy agreed, irked. "He probably couldn't even talk until he came to Xanth." Then he brightened, speaking inside the private dreamlet so that the day horse would not overhear. "At least *he* can't betray us to the Mundanes. He won't understand our mission either."

"Yes," Imbri acknowledged sadly. "He's such a fine-looking animal, but not a creature of Xanth." Not like the Night Stallion, who was every bit as intelligent as a human being. It was really too bad.

They returned their attention directly to the mission. "Somehow we've got to convince you to help," Grundy told the day horse. "Otherwise the Mundane Wave may wash right across Xanth. Then you won't have anywhere to escape to; Mundanes will control everything."

That daunted the creature. "I don't want that!"

"Of course, you might hide from them easier if you took off that brass circlet you wear," the golem said.

The day horse glanced down at his foreleg where the band clasped it. "Oh, no, I couldn't do that!"

"Why not? As long as you wear it, the Horseman knows you're his horse. If you took it off, he might think you were some other horse, especially if you got your coat dyed black."

The day horse communicated slowly and with difficulty, but with certainty. "If I take off the circuit and they catch me, they will know I am a deserter and will butcher me for horsemeat. If I leave it on, they may think I only got lost and will not treat me so bad."

Grundy nodded. "Not a bad effort of logic, for you," he admitted. "So the band represents, ironically—for all that it's brass, not iron—a kind of insurance. Because they believe you're too dumb really to try to escape—and the fact that you don't remove it confirms that belief."

The day horse nodded back. He was not, indeed, quite as stupid as he seemed.

"But if you give Ichabod a ride, and then are later caught by the Mundanes, they will believe that you were captured by the other side and had no choice. You did not return to the Mundanes because the enemy wouldn't let you. That's insurance, too."

The day horse considered. Slowly the sense of it penetrated. "Does this renegade Mundane of yours use spurs?"

"No. Ichabod is an old man who has probably never ridden a horse before in his life. A centaur, maybe, because the centaur archivist Arnolde is his closest friend, but that's not the same. You'd have to step carefully to prevent Ichabod from falling off."

The day horse digested that. Certainly Ichabod did not sound like much of a threat. "No bit?"

"We don't use that sort of thing in Xanth. Creatures carry people only when they choose to. Imbri, here, is giving me a ride because she knows I can't get about the way she can. You don't see any bit in her mouth, do you?"

In the end, the day horse was swayed by the golem's persuasion and agreed to carry Ichabod, on condition that there be no direct contact between him and the Mundanes. "I don't even want to *see* a Mundane," he insisted. "If I saw them, they might see me, and if they see me, they will chase me, and they might catch me."

"You could outrun them!" the golem protested.

"Then they would shoot me with arrows. So I don't want to go near them at all."

"Fair enough," the golem agreed.

They departed the tree, picked up the archivist, and headed north. Sure enough, Ichabod was unsteady on horseback and had to hang on to the day horse's mane to stop from sliding off one side or the other. But gradually he got used to it and relaxed, and the horse relaxed also. The lack of a bit and reins made all the difference. Soon they were able to pick up speed.

Imbri became aware of another aspect of group interaction. She picked up Chameleon without thinking, but realized by the reaction of the day horse that the woman had not been mentioned before. At first the day horse had hesitated; then, when he saw how pretty Chameleon was, he watched her with interest. If it had been Chameleon who had needed the ride, it would have been easier to persuade this animal!

The day horse was a fine runner, making up in brute strength what he lacked in intellect, and Imbri found herself reacting on two levels to him. She liked his body very well, but was turned off by his slow mind. Yet, she reminded herself, she liked Chameleon well enough despite her slowness. Maybe it was that Chameleon was not a potential breeding object.

Yes, there it was. The presence of a fine stallion meant inevitable breeding when Imbri came into season. As a night mare, she had been immortal and ageless and never came into season, or at least not seriously. But as a material animal, she was subject to the material cycle. She would age and eventually die, and so there would be no one to carry on her work and maintain title to her sea of the moon unless she had a foal. Material creatures had to breed, just to maintain their position, and she would breed if she had the opportunity. This was no imposition; she wanted to do it.

But she also wanted to produce a handsome and smart foal. The day horse was handsome but not smart. That boded only half a loaf for the foal. Yet the day horse was probably the only other possible stallion extant in Xanth, in or out of the gourd; without him there would be no breeding at all, unless she searched out one of the winged horses of the mountains. She understood those types hardly ever deigned to associate with earthbound equines, however. That kept the options severely limited and made the decision difficult.

Would there be a decision? When a mare came into season—and this was a cyclical thing not subject to her voluntary control when she was material—any stallion present would breed her. Nature took it out of the province of individual free will, perhaps wisely. Human folk were otherwise; they could breed at any time, and the complexities of their individual natures meant that often they bred at the wrong time, or to the wrong person, or did not breed at all. That probably explained why horses were so much stronger and prettier than human beings. But humans were generally more intelligent, probably because it required a smart man to outsmart and catch a difficult woman, or a smart woman to pick out the best man and get him committed to the burden of a family. The midnight scene in the graveyard had illustrated that! Prince Dor had no doubt played innocent to avoid getting married, but had this time been outmaneuvered. And unless Imbri found a way to control her own breeding, she would have a stupid foal. So if she didn't want that, she would have to place distance between herself and the day horse when her season came on. Fortunately, that would not occur for a couple of weeks; she would have time.

Soon they arrived at the great Gap Chasm, which separated the northern and southern portions of Xanth. Few people knew about the Gap because of the forget-spell on it; it didn't even appear on many maps of Xanth. Since they were on the King's business, they had access to the invisible bridge that spanned it. Most people forgot about the bridge along with the Chasm, but it was there for those who knew how to find it. Imbri, as a night mare, felt very little effect from the forget-spell, so had no trouble.

The day horse, however, was hesitant. "I don't see any bridge," he neighed.

"No one can see the bridge," Imbri projected. In her daydreamlet she made the bridge become visible as a gossamer network of spider-silk cables. In her night dream duty she had not needed to use the bridge, but had known of it and the two others, as well as the devious paths down and through the Gap. She had perfect confidence in all the bridges, and in the charms that kept monsters off the paths, though she would be wary of descending into the Gap when the Gap Dragon was near. No spell ever stopped that monster; it ruled the Chasm deeps. That was another thing normally forgotten, which meant the dragon caught a lot of prey that didn't know it existed—until too late.

"It's all right, day horse," Ichabod said reassuringly. "I have been across it before. I know magic seems incredible to Mundane folk, such as are you and I, but here in Xanth it is every bit as reliable as engineering in our world. I have no fear in crossing."

Encouraged by that, and by now well aware that Ichabod was Mundane yet harmless but not stupid, the day horse followed Imbri out into midair over the Chasm. "Don't worry," Grundy called back. "You can't fall. It has rails on both sides. Except for the center, where a stupid harpy crashed through them and left a blank stretch."

The day horse stumbled, horrified, for he was now approaching the center. The golem laughed.

"It's not true," Imbri projected immediately. "Don't listen to the golem. He has an obnoxious sense of humor."

The day horse recovered his balance. He glared at Grundy, his ears flattening back. He dropped a clod on the bridge, a symbol of his opinion. Grundy had made an enemy, foolishly. It was one of his talents.

They got across without further event and trotted on north. They still had a long way to go, and would not reach the region of the Mundane line this day.

Now the terrain became rougher, for they were traveling cross-country. Northern Xanth was less populated by human folk than was central Xanth, so there were fewer people paths. One good trail led directly to the North Village, where Chameleon's husband Bink had been raised. But they intended to avoid human settlements, to keep their mission secret; the Mundanes surely had spies snooping near the various villages, Ichabod warned. So they went east of the North Village, threading the jungle between it and the vast central zone of Air in the center of northern Xanth.

The jungle thinned to forest, with clusters of everblues, everyellows, and evergreens, and then diminished to wash and scrub. As if to compensate, the ground became rougher. Their trot slowed to a walk, and the walk became labored. Both horses shone with sweat and blew hot blasts from dilated nostrils. Chameleon and Ichabod, unused to such extended travel, were tired and sore, and even the obnoxious golem was quiet, riding in front of Chameleon where he could hang on to Imbri's mane. The trouble with travel was that it was wearing.

In addition, it was hungry business. Horses had to eat a lot, and it was hard to graze while trotting. They would have to stop at the next suitable field and spring they found. But there was no suitable spot here; the land was pretty much barren. Certainly there was no spring on the hillside, and no river.

"Maybe we should cut west, toward the North Village," Grundy said. "Much better terrain there."

"But it would delay us, and perhaps expose our mission," Ichabod protested. "There must be a better alternative."

Imbri reflected. She had not been to this region recently, because there were very few people in it, and therefore few calls for bad dreams. "There are some lakes scattered through this region, with lush vegetation around them, but I can't place them precisely," she projected to the group. "The local plants and animals should know where they are, however." She gave her mane a little shake, waking Grundy, who, it seemed, had had the indecency to nod off during her reflection.

"Huh?" the golem said. "Oh, sure, I can check that." He began questioning the bushes they passed. Soon he found a fruitfly who had been seeded at a lake to the north. "But the fly says to beware the sphinx," the golem reported. "The sphinx got a sunburn and is very irritable this week."

"Beware the sphinx?" Chameleon asked. "I thought we were to beware the Horseman."

"That's good advice!" the day horse neighed. "How often have I felt that monster's spurs!"

"You mean like Imbri's flanks?" the golem asked. "I find it hard to believe anyone would want to poke holes in the hide of a living horse. What kind of a monster is this Horseman?"

The day horse did not like Grundy, but this question mellowed him somewhat. "A human monster."

"Spurs are an indefensible cruelty," Ichabod commented.

"The typical horse will perform to the best of his ability for his rider. Spurs substitute the goad of pain for honest incentive, to the disadvantage of the animal."

The day horse nodded, evidently getting to like the archivist better. There was always something attractive about a well-expressed amplification of one's own opinion.

Imbri agreed emphatically. "And the bit is almost as bad," she sent.

"I don't see any scars on your flanks," Grundy said to the day horse.

"I learned long ago to obey without question," the day horse replied. "He hasn't used the spurs on me in some time; the scars are now so faint as to be invisible. But if he caught me now, after I escaped him, it would be terrible. There would be blood all over my hide."

Imbri visualized bright red blood on the bright white hide and flinched. What horror!

"Surely so." Ichabod nodded. "Man has a very poor record in his treatment of animals. In Xanth it is not as bad, for animals are much better able to defend themselves."

"Dragons are!" Grundy agreed, laughing. "And ant lions and basilisks and harpies."

They were mounting a steep, bald hill that barred their way north. Aggressive carnivorous vines and nettles to east and west made this the best route, laborious as it was. But soon they would be over it and might be able to relax a little going down the other side, where the sweet lake was supposed to be. Imbri and the day horse dug their hooves into the reddish turf, scuffling the sparse dry grass aside. The slope was spongy and warm from the sun.

Suddenly the bank exploded into a bunch of sticks. Chameleon screamed. Both horses reared and plunged to the sides, startled.

"Flying snakes!" Grundy cried. "Fend them off! I recognize this species; they're mean and unreasonable and some of them are poisonous. No use to try to talk to them; they only respect a clout on the snoot."

Chameleon and Ichabod had staffs they had harvested from a forest of general staffs. They had been using these to brush away clinging vines and such. Now they used them in earnest as the snakes darted through the air, jaws gaping. They were not big serpents, but they might be poisonous, as Grundy had warned. Imbri dodged away from them as well as she could, avoiding a green one and a red one, but a yellow one got through and bit her on her left front knee. She reached down with her own teeth and caught it behind the head and tore it loose, but the punctures hurt. She had never had to worry about this sort of thing as a full night mare!

A few moments of vigorous action got them away from the snakes, who could not fly very fast. Air simply was not as good to push against as ground. They resumed plodding up the hill.

"It is strange that both the Night Stallion and the Good Magician provided the same warning," Ichabod reflected aloud. It was one of his annoying habits. He talked a great deal about obscure aspects of situations, boring people. "Since the Horseman is an obvious enemy and perhaps a leader of the invading Mundanes, naturally loyal Xanth citizens should avoid him. Why waste a prophecy belaboring the obvious?"

"I fell into his power anyway," Imbri confessed. "I carried the warning, but I did not recognize the Horseman when I met him. If the day horse hadn't helped me escape—"

"I couldn't stand to see a mare as pretty as you in the power of a man as cruel as that," the day horse said in the community dream Imbri was providing. "I was terribly afraid to come so close to his camp."

"You didn't seem at all afraid," Imbri returned, complimenting him.

"Thank you," the day horse said. "I look bolder than I am, I suppose."

That seemed to be true. The day horse's fear of the invading Mundanes amounted almost to a fetish. Imbri felt he was overreacting. But outside of that, he did look bold, with his brilliant white coat and flaring mane and tail and muscular body. All factors considered, it remained a pleasure being with him.

With a final effort, they crested the red knoll. Now the Land of Xanth spread out around them in a sufficient if not marvelous panoply, like the clothing of an ill-kempt giant. In the distance to the south was the barely visible crevice of the Gap Chasm; to the west was a faint tail of smoke rising from the cookfires of the North Village; to the north—

"A lake!" Ichabod exclaimed happily. "With rich green color around it, surely suitable grazing for the equines and fruits for the unequines. There's our evening campsite!"

So it seemed. "But there's an awful mess of corrugations between us and it," Grundy said.

"I can travel a straight line to it," Imbri sent. "I am used to holding a straight course, regardless of the view, once I know where I'm going."

"Good enough," Grundy said.

Imbri started down the slope, leading the way—and stumbled. She went down headfirst, and Grundy and Chameleon were thrown off. They all went rolling down the rough slope helplessly, until they fetched up in a gully on the side of the knoll.

Grundy picked himself up, shedding red dust and bits of grass. "What happened, horseface?" he demanded grumpily. "Put your foot in it?"

"My knee gave way," Imbri projected, abashed. "That never happened before."

Chameleon righted herself. Even dirty and disheveled, she looked lovely. It was not necessarily true that women grew ugly as they aged; she was the impressive exception. "Is it hurt?" she asked.

Imbri rolled over, got her forefeet placed, and heaved herself up front-first in the manner of her kind. But she immediately collapsed again. The knee would not support her weight under stress.

Chameleon looked at it as she might inspect the scrape on the leg of a child. She was not bright, but that sort of thing did not require intelligence, only motherly concern. "You were bitten!" she exclaimed. "It's all swollen!"

The day horse arrived, picking his way carefully down the slope. "Bitten?" he neighed.

"So those snakes *were* poisonous!" Grundy said. "Why didn't you tell us one got you? We could have held it for interrogation and maybe found the antidote."

"Horses don't complain," Imbri sent. She had never been

bitten before and had not properly appreciated the possible consequence. Her leg had hurt, but she had assumed the pain would ease. It had done so—but the extra strain of the downhill trek had aggravated what she now realized was not a healing but a numbness. Her knee had no staying power.

"I will carry all the people," the day horse offered. "I can handle it."

After a brief consultation, they acceded. The stallion was tired and sweaty, but still whole and strong; he could bear the burden. Chameleon and Grundy joined Ichabod on the day horse's broad back. It was a good thing he was along; the whole party would have been in trouble had it been Imbri alone for transportation.

Now it was up to Imbri to get herself on her feet. She set her good right leg under her and heaved herself up. Now that she wasn't depending on her left knee, it couldn't betray her.

She tried her left leg, but the numbness remained. It was better to hold it clear and hop along on the other three. It was possible to walk, jerkily, slowly, this way.

"Perhaps we could fashion a splint," Ichabod said. "To keep your knee straight so you can at least put weight on it."

That was an apt notion. They scouted around and found a projecting ledge from which several fairly stout poles sprouted. Ichabod dismounted and took hold of one, but though it wiggled crazily under his effort, it did not come loose from the ground.

"Cut it," Grundy said.

Chameleon had a good knife. Where she kept it Imbri wasn't sure, for it had not been evident before, but this suggested the lovely woman was not entirely helpless. She stooped beside the pole, applied her blade, and sawed at the base.

The ground shook. There was a rumble. Chameleon paused, looking askance at the others. "No meaning in a rumble," Grundy said. "Except to get out of here before an earthquake decides to visit."

"Earthquakes don't decide to visit," Ichabod protested. "They are natural, inanimate phenomena—merely the release of stresses developing within or between layers of rock."

There was another rumble, closer and stronger. "Not in Xanth," the golem said. "Here the inanimate has an ornery personality, as is evident when King Dor converses with it. Everything has its own individuality, even a quake."

The archivist had to step about to keep his feet during the second shaking. "There is that," he agreed nervously.

Chameleon sawed again at the pole. Her blade was sharp, but the pole was tough; progress was slow. A gash appeared, from which thick red fluid welled.

"I wonder what kind of plant that is?" Grundy said. He made some noises at it, then shook his head. "It doesn't answer."

"Maybe we can break it off now," Ichabod said, becoming increasingly uneasy. He wrenched the pole around more violently than before.

Suddenly the entire horizontal ridge of poles lifted up. A slit opened in the ground beneath them, revealing a moist, glassy surface crossed by bands of white, brown, and black. It was pretty enough for a polished rock formation.

"That's an eye!" Grundy exclaimed.

Ichabod, hanging from the pole, looked into the monstrous orb, aghast. "What's a hill doing with an eye?" he demanded. "And what am I suspended by?"

"An eyelash," the golem said. "I should have realized. It's alive, but it's not a plant. I was trying to talk to the eyelash of an animal. Naturally it didn't answer; eyelashes don't."

Ichabod dropped to the lower eyelid. One foot jammed accidentally into the eye. The eye blinked; the lid smashed down like a portcullis. The man wrenched out his foot and scrambled away.

"Get on the horse!" Grundy cried. "Get out of here!"

The three of them scrambled aboard the day horse, who moved out rapidly. Imbri hobbled after them.

Suddenly Imbri caught on. "The sphinx!" she broadcast. "This is the sphinx!"

"We were warned to beware of it," Grundy agreed. "As usual, we walked right onto the danger without recognizing it."

The ground shook again and buckled. The monstrous face of the sphinx was opening its mouth. A tremendous bellowing roar came forth in a hurricane blast of air.

"When it pains, it roars!" Grundy cried.

"Oh, for pity's sake!" Ichabod grumbled. "This is no time for idiotic puns."

"Xanth is mostly made of puns," the golem told him. "You have to watch where you put your feet, or you end up stepping on puns."

"Or something," Chameleon said, noting where some horse clods had fallen.

Meanwhile, the day horse was galloping off over the flexing cheek of the monster toward the shoulder. The tremendous sphinx was reclining, its face tilted back, so that the slope was by no means vertical. The pink knoll they had climbed was its sunburned pate. Every hoofprint must have aggravated the monster, but it had not become truly aroused until its eyelash had been attacked.

"Imbri!" Chameleon called from far ahead, realizing that the mare was not maintaining the pace.

"Keep going!" Imbri projected. "I'll follow!"

But she could not follow well on three legs, with the face of the sphinx shaking all over. She lost her footing and rolled toward the mouth, which was now sucking in a gale of breath. She scrambled desperately and managed to avoid it—but then rolled helplessly across the cheek in the wrong direction. Now the mouth was between her and her friends.

She fetched up against another projection. It was the huge, curving outcropping of the ear. Beyond it the face dropped unkindly far to the cracking and shuddering ground.

Imbri decided to stay where she was. At least the ear could not chomp her.

But what about her friends? They could be caught and tromped! They were on the dangerous part of the face.

Then she had a notion. She pumped her dream projection up to maximum strength and sent the sphinx a vision of absolute peace and contentment. Imbri wasn't expert at this sort of dream; all her experience had been with the other kind. But she did have half a soul now, and it was a gentle soul, and it helped her fashion a gentle dream.

Slowly the irritated sphinx calmed. It submitted to the dream of soft, sunny pastures with little sphinxes gamboling on the green. Cool mists wafted across its burning pate. Its eyes closed, broken eyelash and all, and the rumbling diminished.

Carefully Imbri left the cavern of the ear and hobbled back along the huge cheek toward real ground. But her hooves irritated the sunburned skin, resuming the waking process. The monster was not nearly as deeply asleep as it had been before; any little thing could disturb it now. A creature of such mass had considerable inertia, whether heading into sleep or out of it, and at the moment it was almost in balance. She had to retreat to the safe ear.

Unable to depart during daylight, Imbri settled down for a nap herself. She kept the sphinx passive by projecting a nominal sweet dream, just enough to lull it back to sleep when it thought about waking. Fortunately, sphinxes liked to sleep; that was why they were very seldom seen wandering around Xanth. There was a myth about one who had retreated to Mundania to find a suitably quiet place, and who had found a nice warm desert and hunkered down for a nap of several thousand years. The ignorant locals thought it was a statue and knocked off its nose. There would be an awful row when it woke and discovered that . . .

Meanwhile, it was easy for this one to doze off when no one was trotting on its face or blasting off its nose. This was just as well, considering the situation of Imbri's party.

When she woke, it was dark. Now she could move freely. Her bitten leg did not need to support any weight, now that she was able to dematerialize. She got up and galloped through the sphinx's head, where sweet dreams still roamed; her hooves got coated with sugar and honey. She emerged from the other ear and moved on north toward the lake. Soon she found it, trotted across it, and found the camp of the others.

Chameleon was the first to spy her. "Mare Imbri!" she screamed joyfully. "You got away!" She hugged Imbri fiercely, and the mare remained solid for the occasion. It was easy to like Chameleon despite her intellectual handicap, especially at a time like this. No creature except a basilisk would object to being hugged by a person of Chameleon's configuration.

"She wanted to return for you," Grundy said, "but we told her no. All we could have done was get ourselves in trouble and maybe make things worse for you."

"My son the King told me to listen to the golem," Chameleon said apologetically, her lovely face showing her distaste.

"It was best," Imbri agreed in a general dreamlet. "I hid in the sphinx's ear until night, then shifted to immaterial form."

"Your leg seems better," Ichabod observed.

"It isn't. But it's no worse. Maybe it will improve by morning."

They settled down for the remainder of the night. Chameleon, Grundy, and Ichabod slept, while the day horse and night mare grazed on the rich pasturage and snoozed. Imbri had to go solid to crop the grass, but she could phase out while chewing it, and she moved slowly enough so as not to aggravate her knee. And indeed, as the pleasant nocturnal hours passed, the numbness faded and strength returned. She had at last thrown off the lingering effect of the snake's venom.

In the morning, rested, they all were feeling fit. Chameleon stripped and washed in the shallow edge of the lake; Ichabod turned his back self-consciously, but Grundy openly goggled. "Age sure comes gracefully to some folk," he remarked. "But you should see her in her off-phase."

"I have," Ichabod said stiffly. "She has the most remarkably penetrating mind I have encountered."

"And the aspect of the most horrendous hag," the golem said, smirking.

"She merely manifests the properties of all women, with less ambiguity. They all begin lovely and innocent, and end ugly and smart."

"I guess that's why you like looking at nymphs," Grundy retorted. "They don't have minds, so there's nothing to distract you from their important points."

"Oh, I don't look at the points," Ichabod protested. "I look at their legs."

"Why don't you look at Chameleon's legs? They're as good as any and better than most."

"Chameleon is a person and a friend," the archivist said severely.

"Oh, she wouldn't mind." The golem was enjoying himself, needling the man. "Hey, doll, is it all right if Ichabod looks?"

"Silence!" Ichabod hissed, flushing.

"Certainly," Chameleon called back. "I'm under water."

"She was under water all the time!" Ichabod said, catching on as the golem rolled on the ground with mirth. "There was nothing to see!"

Something stirred across the lake. There seemed to be a cave just below water level. Now several heads showed.

"Tritons!" Grundy said. "Stand back from shore; they can be ornery."

Indeed, the mermen approached with elevated tridents. Chameleon tried to rise, then remembered her nakedness and settled back in the water, not smart enough to realize that her modesty could be fatal. Imbri charged back to guard her, and the day horse joined them.

Three tritons drew up just beyond the kicking range of the horses. "Ho! What mischief is this?" one cried. "Do you come to muddy our waters?" His three-pointed spear was poised menacingly.

Imbri broadcast a pacifying dreamlet. She was getting better at this with practice. "We only pass by, meaning no harm," her dream figure of a black mermaid said. "We did not know this lake was occupied by your kind."

Now the triton peered at Chameleon, whose torso he had briefly glimpsed when she started to stand. "That one must have nymphly blood," he remarked appreciatively.

But several mermaids had followed the tritons from the cave. "That's a human woman," one said. "Leave her alone."

The triton grimaced. "I suppose these people are all right. They haven't littered the grounds."

"Say," Grundy asked as the tension eased, "do you folk know the Siren? She settled in a lake somewhere in this general region several years back."

"The half-mer? Sure, she comes by here sometimes. She

can split her tail into legs, so she can cross between lakes when there's no waterway. She married Morris, and they've got a halfling boy like her, part human but okay. Nice people."

"I know the Siren from way back," Grundy said. "And her sister the Gorgon, who married Good Magician Humfrey." He relaxed, seeing the tritons relax. "Where is the Siren now? Maybe we can pay her a visit."

"They live by the water wing," a mermaid said. "I don't think your kind could get there safely. You have to swim, or go through the zone of Fire."

The golem shrugged. "So we can't get there from here. It was a nice thought, anyway."

"Do you know any special hazards north of here?" Imbri asked in another dreamlet.

"Dragons on land, river monsters in the water, man-eating birds in the air—the usual riffraff," the triton said carelessly. "If you got by the sphinx, you can probably handle them."

"Thank you. We'll try to avoid them," Imbri sent, and let the dreamlet fade.

The group organized, once Chameleon had gotten dressed, and trotted north. Imbri had no further trouble with her knee; the toxin had dissipated, leaving no permanent damage, and she carried woman and golem as before.

They kept alert, avoiding the dragons, river monsters, and predator birds, and by evening arrived near the Mundane front. The invaders had penetrated well into Xanth, which shortened the trip; the fleeing animals gave Grundy horrendous reports of their violence. It seemed the Mundanes were using fire and sword to lay waste to anything they could, and were such deadly warriors that even large dragons were getting slain. This did not bode well for the defense of Xanth.

"I think my turn has come," Ichabod said. "I must actually see the soldiers to identify them specifically; there should be details of armor and emblem that will enable me to place them, if not immediately, then when I return to my references. Already I know they are medieval or earlier, since they employ no firearms. That's fortunate."

"Firearms?" Chameleon asked, looking at her own slen-

der limbs as if afraid they would flame up. Her gesture
was touching in its innocence.

"Those are weapons utilizing—something like magic
powder," Ichabod clarified. "Imagine, well, cherry bombs
shot like arrows from tubes. I hope Xanth never encounters
that sort of thing. I wish *my* world had never encountered
it." He looked around. "Suppose I ride Imbri, while Chameleon rides the day horse? I don't believe King Dor intended his mother to expose herself to extreme danger."

"I'm sure he didn't!" Grundy agreed emphatically. "It
was bad enough when she exposed herself to the tritons.
That's why he sent me along."

"To look at his mother bathing?" Ichabod inquired with
a certain faint malice. Grundy got on everyone's nerves.

"Go with the day horse, Chameleon," Grundy said, ignoring the gibe. "We'll spy on the Mundanes and rejoin
you later."

"We?" Ichabod asked, frowning, and the day horse's ears
flattened back. Neither of them was thrilled by the prospect of the golem's company.

"I'm coming with you. I can learn a lot by talking with
the plants and animals—maybe enough to spare you the
natural result of you own heroics."

Ichabod smiled with certain scholarly resignation.
"There is indeed that. I confess to being somewhat of a
Don Quixote at heart."

"Donkey who?" Chameleon asked, blinking.

"Donkey Hotay, to you," the archivist said, smiling obscurely. "It is not spelled the way it sounds, even here in
Xanth. He was an old Don, a Mundane scholar, buried in
his books, exactly as I was before Dor, Irene, Grundy, the
ogre, and Arnolde the Centaur rousted me out of my sine-
cure and opened a literally fantastic new horizon to my
perspective. Don Quixote set himself up as a medieval
knight in armor and rode about the Iberian countryside,
having adventures that were far more significant for him
than for the spectators, just as I am doing now. There was
an encounter with a windmill, a truly classic episode—"

"What kind of bird is that?" Chameleon asked.

"Oh, a windmill is not a bird. It is—"

"We had better get going," Grundy interjected impatiently.

"Yes, indeed," Ichabod agreed. "We shall locate the two of you by asking the plants your location when we return. Do stay out of danger, both of you."

The day horse neighed. "You can be sure of that!" Grundy translated for him.

Chapter 6. The Next Wave

Imbri carried the golem and the Mundane scholar toward the terrible Mundane front. Xanth had not suffered a Wave invasion in a century and a half; this was an awesomely significant event.

"I believe I perceive some tension in you, Imbri," Ichabod said. "Am I imposing on you?"

"I was thinking how long it has been since the Lastwave," Imbri sent. "I was young then, only twenty years old, but I remember it as if it were last year."

"You were there?" Ichabod asked, surprised. "That's right—I forgot that you are one hundred and seventy years old. Since the Lastwave, as I reconstruct it, was one hundred and fifty years ago—" He paused. "I have, of course, researched this historically, but have talked with no eyewitnesses. I would dearly love to have your personal impressions."

"Well, I only saw bits of it at night, on dream duty," Imbri demurred. "The big battles were by day, and I could not go abroad by day then."

"Still, I would be fascinated!" the scholar said. "Your impressions, in the context of historical detail, would help complete the picture."

"Maybe you had better give that context," Grundy said,

getting interested in spite of himself, "so we all know exactly what we're talking about." The golem, of course, had not been around for the Lastwave and hated to admit ignorance on anything.

"Certainly," Ichabod said. Historical detail was dear to his old heart. "My friend Arnolde Centaur provided some considerable information. It seems that the Firstwave of human colonization occurred over a thousand years ago. Before that, there were only the animals and hybrids, such as the centaurs. They have a touching story about the origin of their species—"

"Get on with the recent stuff," Grundy said.

"Um, yes, of course," Ichabod agreed, irritated. "There were a number of Waves, perhaps a dozen, most of them quite brutal, as the Mundanes invaded and ravaged Xanth. After each Wave conquered the land and settled down, the children would turn up with magic talents, becoming true citizens of Xanth. Then in fifty or one hundred years, another Wave would come, destroying much of what the prior Wave had accomplished. Finally, one hundred and fifty years ago, the Lastwave was so savage that the people of Xanth decided to prevent any future invasions. Once things settled down, in about fifteen years, a Magician King adapted a magic stone of great potency to project a deadly shield that destroyed anything crossing through it, and set that shield entirely around Xanth. The shield kept Xanth safe from intrusions for one hundred and ten years, until King Trent, who had spent time in Mundania, assumed power after the demise of the Storm King and abolished the shield. It seemed that mankind had been diminishing in the absence of immigration. So it was better to risk another invasion than to suffer certain extinction of the human species in Xanth by stiflement. Thus for the past quarter century there has been no shield—and now the consequence would seem to be upon us. King Trent refused to reinstate the magic shield, preferring to fight off the invaders, and perhaps with his power of transformation he could have done it. But now—"

"Now King Trent is out of the picture, and King Dor doesn't know how to set up the shield," Grundy finished.

"Anyway, the Mundanes are already inside Xanth, so that's no answer."

"I am not certain it ever was an answer," Ichabod said. "I believe King Trent was correct; there has to be freedom of the border and commerce between Xanth and Mundania. Unfortunately, not all Mundanes come in peace. The Lastwavers, as I understand it, were Mongol Mundanes, of our thirteenth century A.D., circa 1231, if I do not misremember my Asiatic history. They believed they were invading the peninsula of Korea. Today Korea is severed by a line very like the Gap Chasm, with a major city where Castle Roogna is, suggesting a most intriguing parallelism—" He noted Grundy's open yawn and broke off that conjecture. "But that's irrelevant to the present reprise. The Mongols were truly savage conquerors, and I can well understand the Xanthians' decision to have no more of that." He shook his head. "But it was Imbri's impressions I wanted. How did the Mongols look from this side, mare?"

"In the bad dreams I had to deliver, they were savage, flat-faced people," Imbri projected. "They killed all who opposed them, using arrows and swords. They rode horses—all those horses were killed, after the Wave was stopped, because of the terror the people of Xanth had for my kind after that. That was the equine tragedy; horses never intended mischief for Xanth."

"I am sure they didn't," Ichabod said consolingly. "The innocent often suffer most from the rigors of war. That is one of the appalling things about violence."

Imbri was getting to like this man. "Some of the dreams I delivered were to the Lastwavers. We night mares have always been fair and impartial; we deliver our service to all in need, no matter how undeserving. The Wavers suffered fears and sorrows, too, especially when their drive began to falter. They killed animals without compunction or compassion, yet they cared about their own families, left behind in Mundania, and about their comrades-in-arms. They saw Xanth as a terrible magic land, with deadly threats everywhere—"

"Well, of course it is, to Mundanes," Ichabod said. "Yet a person of Xanth would have similar difficulty going about in my own portion of Mundania, particularly if he did not know the patterns of highway traffic. Had I not been protected by my friends when first invited here, I would not have survived long. My first day in Xanth, I almost walked into a nickelpede nest. I thought the nickelpedes were units of currency."

"Xanth natives avoid such things routinely," Grundy said. "But I do remember those metal dragons in your land, shooting smoke out of their tails and carrying people around inside them for hours before digesting them. It was awful! When a person gets into unfamiliar territory, he's in much danger. We walked right onto that sphinx's head, for example—and we had been warned to beware the sphinx."

"And to beware the Horseman," Ichabod added. "And to break the chain. The trouble with these warnings is that we seldom understand them until it is too late."

"I don't even know where the chain is, let alone how to break it," Grundy said. "Fortunately, that's not my worry. King Dor is no doubt pondering that question now. I somehow doubt there is any chain in the Castle Roogna armory."

Ichabod returned to the subject. "Are you saying, Imbri, that you found the Mundane invaders—the Mongols—to be human beings, that is to say, feeling creatures, like the rest of us? You know, I'm fascinated to converse with a person who shared, as it were, the same stage with the Mongols, who were centuries before my time."

"That was the strangest thing about it," Imbri admitted in the dream. "Among themselves, they were perfectly decent creatures. But in battle they thought of people as they did dragons and basilisks and salamanders. They actually liked slaying them."

"It is an unfortunately familiar pattern in Mundania," Ichabod said. "First one group dehumanizes another, then it destroys it. In Xanth no real line between human and creature exists; many animals are better companions than many human folk." He patted Imbri's flank. "And how are we to define the centaurs, who have aspects of both? But Mundania has no recognized magic, so all animals are stupid, unable to speak the language of man. This leads to terrible wrongs. I much prefer Xanth's way."

"Yes, it is handy for communication," the golem agreed. "Here the animals and plants speak different languages, while human folk speak only one. Vice versa in Mundania. So animals don't really speak the language of men; it's just that some have learned it, as you have. No one has ever figured out what enchantment makes all human folk intelligible to each other here, even invading Mundanes. It just seems that the moment any human type steps into Xanth, the language matches."

"There is much remaining to learn about the magic of Xanth," Ichabod said. "I only hope I live long enough to fathom some significant part of it."

Imbri's ears perked forward. She sniffed the breeze. "Mundanes!" she projected.

Instantly the others were alert. Soon they all perceived the smoke of a burning field. "Why do they destroy so wantonly?" Grundy grumbled. "They can't use burned-out land any better than we can."

Ichabod sighed. "I'm afraid I can answer that. The point of such destruction is not to preserve land for one's own use, but to deprive the opponent of its produce, to diminish his capacity for war. Starving creatures can't fight effectively. Since there is magic everywhere in Xanth, and the Mundanes have none, they hurt Xanthians much more than themselves by ruining the land for everyone. It is an unkind but effective ploy."

"We have to stop them," Grundy said.

"Of course. But it will not be easy. We must spy out their nature, then organize to contain them. That is why our mission is so important. A side can not prevail, militarily, without good information about the enemy."

Imbri continued forward, carefully watching for the dread Mundanes. There was a slight wind from the north, whipping the fire south, and small creatures were fleeing it. But fire was hardly unknown in Xanth; fire-breathing dragons, fireflies, firebirds, and salamanders started blazes all the time. So this one would burn out in due course, since rivers and dense, juicy vegetation were all over Xanth and did not ignite well. Possibly the fire would be put out when it irritated a passing storm cloud and got rain

dumped on it. The Land of Xanth put up with many in-
dignities, but once properly aroused, it could find ways of
dealing with nuisances. It seemed to Imbri that the Mundane Nextwavers had just about worn out their presumed
welcome.

The trouble was, to remain downwind of the fire was to
suffer the discomfort of heat and smoke. To cross to the
upwind side was to risk discovery by the enemy. This
scouting was awkward in practice, however necessary it
was in theory.

"This will never work," Ichabod said, coughing, as a curl
of smoke teased him. "I fear we are in an untenable situation. I don't like to counsel delay, but perhaps we should
wait till evening—"

"Wait!" Grundy cut in. "I think I see an errant gust."

Imbri looked. Terns were wheeling to the west, first one
and then another, taking turns in the manner they were
named for. From the way they maneuvered and coasted
and floated in the sky, she could tell the direction of the
wind they rode. It was bearing north. It was indeed an errant gust, going counter to the prevailing wind. Probably it
was a young breeze, not yet ready to settle down and pull
with its elders.

"While the tern is wheeling, I'll not dream of squealing,"
the golem said in singsong. "Know what will happen when
that gust dusts the fire?"

Ichabod, who had been wincing at something he must
have taken as another pun, caught on. "Thick smoke—
back in their faces, blinding them—and can you phase
through it, Imbri?"

"Yes, I can phase through smoke when it's thick
enough," Imbri projected. That was what she had done to
escape the centycore at Magician Humfrey's castle. "But
it's unreliable. When it thins, I'll turn solid again."

"Once we see them clearly, we can depart in utter
haste," Ichabod said. He was now taut with nervousness,
well aware of the danger they faced. "They may have
horses; can you outrun your own kind?"

Imbri considered. "If they're like the day horse, they can
match my pace by day. Not by night."

"Better not risk it," Ichabod said. "We are in no condition to oppose armed men."

"But with the smoke, we won't have to!" Grundy protested.

"Why don't we find a region where they have been, one that has not yet been burned?" Imbri projected. "Grundy can question the grass there and get a description."

"Excellent notion," Ichabod agreed.

"There is that." The golem liked a job that made him important.

The errant gust arrived at the fire. The flames swirled gleefully and reversed their angle, and the smoke poured north. There was dismay among the ranks of the Mundanes as it enveloped them. They coughed and gagged in a minor cacophony.

Imbri picked her way along the edge of the reversed fire, looking for a good route north. Suddenly men rushed out of the smoke, coming south.

"Oops," Grundy said. "A small miscalculation."

Imbri bolted. She ran south—but an arm of the fire had made its way there, and its smoke now came back toward her. It was not thick enough for concealment or phasing, though. She veered east, not wanting to leap through the flames unless she had to—and came up against the Mundanes. They had quickly taken advantage of the change in the wind to overrun this region. They held spears and swords at the ready, and some had bows. There were too many of them to permit escape.

The Mundanes closed on Imbri and her party, carefully. They were a fairly motley bunch, with different types of armor and clothing, but they were evidently disciplined.

"This has the aspect of a mercenary force," Ichabod murmured. "Little better than brigands. Pre-Christian era, European. Gaul or Iberia, I surmise."

"You a Roman or a Punic?" a soldier demanded.

"Roman or Punic!" Ichabod repeated under his breath. "That's it! The Romans used citizen-soldiers, at least at first; later they became, in fact, professional soldiers, landholders in name only. But the Punic forces—that's a contraction of 'Phoenician'—were known to make open and extensive use of mercenaries. Carthage—these would likely be Carthaginian mercenaries, circa 500 to 100 B.C."

"Speak up, old man!" the soldier cried, making a threatening gesture with his sword.

"Oh, I am neither," Ichabod said hastily. Quietly, to Grundy and Imbri, he murmured: "They assume I'm the only intelligent person. I think it best to deceive them, much as I detest the practice of prevarication."

"Yes," Imbri projected. "Grundy can pretend to be a doll, and I will be a stupid animal."

"You don't look like much," the Mundane said. "Where'd you steal the fine horse?"

"I did not steal this horse!" Ichabod protested. "I borrowed her from a friend."

"Well, we'll borrow her from you. Dismount."

"We shouldn't be separated," Imbri sent in a worried dreamlet. She remembered her prior capture by the Horseman and did not relish a repetition of that experience.

"This is not a completely tame animal," Ichabod said. "I ride her without saddle or reins, but she would not behave for a stranger."

The soldier pondered. Evidently he had had experience with half-wild horses. He put his hand on Imbri's shoulder, and she squealed warningly and stomped a forefoot, acting like an undisciplined animal. "All right. You ride her for now. We're taking you to Hasbinbad for interrogation."

Hasbinbad was evidently a leader, for he had a comfortable tent to the rear. He emerged fully armed and armored, with a shaped breastplate, a large, oblong shield, and an impressive helmet. He was a gruffly handsome older man on the stout side. His face was clean, his beard neatly trimmed.

"My troops inform me you were lurking south of our clearance blaze," Hasbinbad remarked. "What were you doing there?"

"You're a true Carthaginian!" Ichabod exclaimed.

"All my life," Hasbinbad agreed with an ironic smile. "Are you a native of this region? I am prepared to offer a fair reward for good information."

Imbri did not trust this urbane Mundane leader. But she had to let Ichabod handle the interview.

"I am a visitor to this land, but I have traveled a fair amount," Ichabod replied carefully. He seemed more intrigued than concerned now. Apparently he liked meeting what were to him historical figures. "I saw your fire and came to investigate—and your ruffians quickly made me captive."

"They are instructed to kill all strange animals and take prisoner any men they encounter," Hasbinbad said. "Strange things have happened since we crossed the Alps and entered Southern Gaul. This is much wilder country than Hispania."

"It certainly is!" Ichabod agreed emphatically. "This would be about the year 210 or 215 B.C., in the Po valley, and—" He paused, and Imbri sent a questioning dream.

"You speak strangely," Hasbinbad said. "Where did you say you were from?"

"Horrors!" Ichabod said to Imbri in the dream. "I am speaking nonsense! I can't refer to pre-Christian dates; these people of course have no notion of their future! And I can't tell him where I'm from, or *when* I'm from; he would think me a lunatic."

"Tell him you are a lunatic from Castle Roogna yesterday," Imbri suggested, not following all of the man's confusion. She had thought it was only Chameleon who became convoluted in her thoughts, but perhaps it was a general human trait.

"From Castle Roogna, in central Xanth," Ichabod said to the Mundane, following the suggestion.

"You are Roman, then?"

Ichabod laughed. "Not at all! This isn't Italy!"

Hasbinbad elevated an eyebrow. He was fairly good at that. "It isn't? Where, then, do you claim it is?"

"Oh, I see. You crossed from Spain to France, then through the Alps to the Po valley—"

"Bringing twelve hundred men and nine elephants to the aid of my leader, Hannibal, who is hard-pressed by the accursed Romans," Hasbinbad finished. "But we have not yet located Hannibal."

"I should think not," Ichabod agreed. "I fear you have lost your way. Hannibal was—is—in Italy, during the Second Punic War, ravaging the Roman Empire. This is, er, present-day Xanth, the land of magic."

"Xanth?"

"This is Xanth," Ichabod repeated. "A different sort of land. No Romans here. No Hannibal either."

"You are saying we do not know how to navigate?"

"Not exactly. I'm sure you followed your route exactly. You must have encountered a discontinuity. It is complicated to explain. Sometimes people step through accidentally and find themselves here. It's generally sheer fluke. It is much easier to leave Xanth than to find it, unless you have magic guidance."

The Carthaginian leader puffed out his cheeks, evidently humoring the crazy man. "How should we find Rome?"

"Turn about, leave Xanth, then turn about again." But then Ichabod reconsidered. "No, perhaps not. You would probably be in some other age and place of Mundania if you went randomly. You have to time it, and that's a rather precise matter. I suppose if you tried several times, until you got it just right—"

"I'll think about it," Hasbinbad said. "This is an interesting land, whatever it is."

"What do you think?" Imbri asked Grundy and Ichabod in a dreamlet. "I distrust this person's motive."

"Yes, he's lying," Grundy said in the dream. In life he was lying on Imbri's shoulder, playing the part of a lifeless doll. "He knows this isn't Rome, or wherever he was going. He's testing you, maybe to see if you're lying to him."

"If you don't find your way to Italy," Ichabod said aloud to the Carthaginian, "Hannibal will not have the reinforcements he needs and will be hard-pressed. We could help you find the way."

"If, as you claim, this is not Italy," Hasbinbad rejoined, "then perhaps it is still ripe for plunder. My troops have had a hard journey and need proper reward. Who governs you?"

"King Trent," Ichabod said. "I mean, King Dor."

"There has been a recent change?" the Mundane asked alertly.

"Uh, yes. But that is no concern of yours."

"Oh, I think it is my concern. What happened to the old King?"

Ichabod obviously was not adept at deception. It was part of the foolish yet endearing nature of the man. "He suffered a mishap. Perhaps he will recover soon."

"Or perhaps King Dor, if he proves competent, will suffer a similar mishap," Hasbinbad murmured.

"He definitely knows something," Imbri sent. With an effort, she kept her ears from flattening back so that she would not give away the fact that she understood the dialogue.

"What can you know of our Kings?" Ichabod demanded, though technically he was not a citizen of Xanth.

Hasbinbad shrugged. "Only that they are mortal, as all men are." He looked meaningfully at Ichabod. "Now what should I do with you, spy? I shall retain your horse, of course, but men are more difficult to manage, and you do not appear to be very good for hard labor."

"We must get out of here!" Ichabod said to Imbri in the dream. The man was getting really worried.

"Do you think your King Window would pay a decent ransom for you?" the Punic leader inquired.

"That's King Dor, not Window," Ichabod muttered. "Ransom is a Mundane concept; he would not pay."

"Then I suppose we'll just have to sacrifice you to Baal Hammon, though he prefers the taste of babies. Even our gods have to go on less succulent rations in the field."

Ichabod tried to run, but Hasbinbad snapped his fingers and Mundane soldiers charged up. They seized Ichabod and dragged him away. Imbri tried to follow, but they threw ropes about her, tying her. Resistance was futile; the Mundanes bristled with weapons.

Imbri was hustled to a pen and left there. Fortunately, the Mundanes did not know her nature and did not realize that the golem was a living creature. The two remained together, but Ichabod was imprisoned separately. "Maybe we can rescue him tonight," Imbri sent in a dream.

"I hope so," Grundy replied. "He's a decent old codger, even if he is Mundane. But that Mundane chief certainly knows more than he's letting on. He knew King Trent was out of the picture. There's a conspiracy of some nefarious sort here, and it's not just the Nextwave conquest."

Then a man approached the pen. "Why, it is the dream horse!" he exclaimed.

Imbri looked at him—and her heart sank down to her hooves. It was the dread Horseman!

"Oh, don't pretend you don't know me, mare," the Horseman said. "I don't know how you managed to escape me before—well, I do know, but don't see how you doused the fire. I was so angry when in the morning I discovered you were gone that I almost slew my henchmen, but then I realized that none of us had really come to terms with the notion of a horse as smart as a person. *My* horse certainly isn't smart! The fool's probably half starving by this time. So I chalked up my experience with you as a lesson in underestimating my opposition, and I shall not do that again." The Horseman grinned with a somewhat feral edge. "I'll make you a deal, mare: tell me the secret of your escape, and I will take you for my own now, sparing you the brutality of the Punics. I'll let you go, once I recapture my regular steed, the day horse. *Him* I can confine, once I have possession. Fair enough?"

"I won't deal with you!" Imbri sent tightly.

"You don't believe I have power here? I am second in command to Hasbinbad and can take what steed I choose. I am a good deal more than a spy."

"I believe you," Imbri sent. "That's why I will not cooperate with you."

"I'm really not such a bad fellow," the man continued persuasively. "I treat my steeds well, once they know their place. All I require is absolute obedience."

"Spurs!" Imbri sent in a dream like a blast of dragonfire.

"Hotter than the breath of Baal, your thought! But I don't use the spurs, once my steed is tame," he argued. "There are no fresh cuts on the hide of the day horse, I'll warrant, unless he got himself caught in one of those prehensile bramble bushes. The ungrateful animal! He'll perish in that jungle alone; he's not smart enough to survive long. So he needs me—and I need him. The Punic horses are lean and tired from their arduous trek over the cold mountains; the best food was reserved for the elephants. I had to subdue a centaur to make my way up here, once the forces of Xanth started closing in on me south of the—I misremember, but I think there was some kind of barrier—"

"The Gap Chasm," Imbri sent, then cursed herself; she should have let him forget it entirely.

"Yes, that. You told the King of my presence, didn't you?"

"Of course I did!" Imbri sent viciously, with the image of two hind feet kicking him in the face.

The Horseman jerked back involuntarily before controlling his reaction to the dreamlet. "So you won't tell me how you doused the fire? Well, I can conjecture. The guard was nodding, and you sent a bad dream at him that he was on fire, so he fetched a bucket of water—something like that? I deeply regret underestimating your talent there."

Now why hadn't Imbri thought of that? She probably *could* have tricked the guard into something like that! Meanwhile, she refused to implicate the day horse, who, it seemed, was one or two iotas smarter than his master credited.

"Still, I can't really fault you for fighting for your side," the Horseman continued. "I am fighting for my side, after all. So let's call it even: I caught you, you escaped, you betrayed me to the Xanth King. But now you have been caught again, and because I appreciate your full spirit and powers, I want you more than ever for my steed. You and I could go far together, Imbri! On the other hand, my friends the Punics would be very interested to know exactly what kind of horse you are, and how to prevent you from escaping at night. Should I tell them?"

Imbri stiffened. He could make her truly captive! That would strand Ichabod and Grundy, too, and leave Chameleon in a very awkward situation, for she was no smarter than the day horse. Grundy might escape, since he continued to play the rag-doll role and the Horseman did not know about him, but what could the tiny man do alone in the jungle of Xanth?

She would have to deal with this horrible man, appalling as the very thought was. She forced her ears up and forward, instead of plastered against her neck the way they wanted to be.

"I see you understand, Imbri," the Horseman said. "You should, as you are the smartest horse I have ever encountered. But you refuse to cooperate. Very well, I am a reasonable man. I am prepared to compromise. I will exchange information for noninformation: you tell me exactly how you escaped before, so I know who or what betrayed me, and I will not provide any part of the information to the Punics. It will all be privileged communication. What will happen will happen."

Imbri was in a quandary. Could she trust the Horseman to keep his word? Was it fair to betray the day horse? What should she do?

"You don't trust me, I can see," the man said. "Indeed, you have no reason to. But trust must begin somewhere, mustn't it? Try me this time, and if I betray you, you are no worse off than otherwise. All you are really gambling is some information that won't change anything now. I simply want to profit from a past mistake. I try never to make the same error twice. Since it profits me nothing if the Punics destroy you and your scholarly friend, I am not gambling much either. We each stand to lose if we do not cooperate, regardless of our opinion of each other. I'd rather have you loose and living, so that there is hope to capture you fairly at some future date. My education for your freedom, no other obligation. I don't see how I can proffer a more equitable deal than that."

"What should I do?" Imbri queried Grundy in a dreamlet.

"This is bad," the golem replied therein. "This character is insidious! He's trying to get you to trust him. That's the first step to making you his steed for real, to convert you to his side and betray Xanth. Think of the damage he could do if he could phase through walls at night on your back! So you can't afford to trust him."

"But if he tells Hasbinbad my nature, I'll be trapped and Ichabod will be sacrificed to Baal Hammon!"

"That's bad, all right," Grundy agreed. "I guess you'll have to go along with him. Just don't trust him! Beware the Horseman!"

Imbri decided she would have to accept the deal. She stood to lose too much otherwise, and her friends would suffer as well, and her mission would be a failure and Xanth would pay the consequence. "The day horse freed me," she sent reluctantly to the Horseman, hating him for what he was making her do.

"Ha! So he was close by all the time? What did he do?"

"He—doused the fire."

"But a horse has no hands! He can't carry water. He—" The Horseman paused. Then he laughed. "Oh, no! He didn't!"

"He did."

"That animal is smarter than I thought, for sure! Must have been the presence of a fine mare that spurred him to his finest performance. He never paid such attention to any ordinary mare, I'm sure. So you ran off with him—but I gather you did not stay with him. Where is he now?"

"I don't have to tell you that!" Imbri sent, simultaneously angry at the way the Horseman had made her reveal a secret and flattered at his assessment of the day horse's opinion of her. Any female was delighted at the notion that an attractive male found her interesting. Even if she wasn't sure she wanted anything to do with him, she still wanted to be considered worthwhile by him. It gave her a certain social advantage.

The Horseman frowned. "No, I suppose you don't. That wasn't part of our deal, this time. But I'm sure that stallion didn't do such a risky favor just from the equine goodness of his heart. Women make fools of men, and mares make fools of stallions! He must have been attracted to you even then, and surely more so now."

Better and better! But Imbri was careful not to react.

"So if you're here, he can't be far distant. You probably see each other often, and maybe travel together. That way you repay him for helping you, and he gets shown where to graze and how to survive on his own in Xanth. That's why I wasn't able to find him, and why he didn't return from sheer hunger and thirst. It was probably just chance that the Punics caught you instead of him."

The man was uncomfortably sharp! Imbri did not respond.

"Very well," the Horseman said. "You have answered my question, perhaps more completely than you intended, and I believe you. I will leave you in peace. We shall surely meet again." He turned and walked away.

Imbri hardly dared relax. "Do you think he will keep his bargain?" she sent to Grundy.

"We'll find out," the golem replied. "I can see why you fear him; he's a keen, mean basilisk of a man! But in his arrogance, he just might be sincere. His perverted standard of honor may mean more to him than the opinion of one mare, and he does hope to use you to locate the day horse. He'll probably try to follow you when you escape. At least he doesn't know about me. I can untie the ropes and scramble out of the pen and probably free you even if they light fires."

"Save that for the last resort," she suggested. "If the Horseman honors his word, for whatever reason, I won't need it."

"But I can go scout out where they have Ichabod," the golem said. "That will facilitate things, so we can act fast when night comes."

"Yes," she agreed, her confidence beginning to recover from the bruising the Horseman had given it. "But we must play dumb until then."

"Oh, sure." But though the golem lay like a limp doll, he used his special skill to interrogate the plants and creatures nearby. There was a blade of grass growing at the edge of the pen that had somehow escaped the attention of whatever horse had been penned here before. Grundy told it that he would have his friend the mare chomp it off flat if it didn't answer his question, and the grass was intimidated. Grundy was forcing it to cooperate the same way the Horseman had used leverage against her. That made her wonder whether there was really any difference between them in ethics, and she was distressed but did not protest.

The blade of grass told Grundy all it knew of the Mundanes of the Nextwave—which was not very much. They had camped here two days ago, and called themselves Punics, though they were mostly recruits from Iberia and Morocco, wherever those places were. Many of them had sore feet from their arduous march through the mountains, so were resting now.

Grundy questioned a spider who had a small web against the wall of the pen. The spider said the Mundanes had carried Mundane lice and fleas along with them, and that these parasites were fairly fat and sassy and made pretty good eating. The spider had made it a point to learn the language of its prey, so as to be able to lure the bugs into its web; thus it had picked up some of the Mundane-bug gossip.

The trek over the mountains had been truly horrendous. It seemed the Mundane seasons were more rigorous than those of Xanth, and the high mountain passes were covered with magic masses of ice called glaciers that made the passage treacherous. The had started with twelve hundred men and nine elephants; they had lost a third of the men and two-thirds of the elephants. Hasbinbad, for payroll reasons (whatever a payroll might be; none of them could guess), refused to acknowledge the missing men. They had also started with two hundred horses, of which only fifty remained, and some of those had run away when they came to Xanth.

"The day horse," Imbri projected.

"Yes, one of a number," Grundy agreed. "The spider doesn't know the horses by name, of course, but that fits the pattern. The day horse was smart for a Mundane animal, so must be doing better than the other escapees. Most of them are probably inside dragons by now."

That saddened Imbri, but she knew it was likely. "What do the soldiers think of Xanth?"

Grundy questioned the spider. "They grumble a lot," he reported in due course. "They have not been paid, so they must plunder. Paid—hey, that must be what the payroll is! What Hasbinbad owes the soldiers! Many of them have died as they blundered into tangle trees, dragon warrens, and monster-infested waters. Some have been transformed to fish because they drank from an enchanted river; the spider got that from a flea who jumped off a man just in time. Others pursued nymphs into the jungle and were never seen again. Perhaps two hundred have been lost to the hazards of Xanth. So now they are proceeding very carefully, and doing better. They have slain several dragons and griffins and roasted and eaten them. But they are nervous about what else may lie ahead."

"Justifiably," Imbri sent. "They have antagonized all creatures of Xanth by their carnage. They should march back out of Xanth before they do any more damage."

"They won't as long as there is plunder to be had," Grundy said. "The spider confirms what we have seen ourselves: these are tough creatures, dragons in human guise, with a cunning and ornery leader. Only force will stop them. That's the way Mundanes are."

"Except for Ichabod," Imbri qualified.

"He's not a real Mundane," the golem said, irked at having been caught in an unwarranted generalization. "He's greedy for information, and his head always was full of fantasy, and he has an eye out for nymphs, too."

A Mundane guard came and dumped an armful of fresh-cut hay into Imbri's pen. Hay was best when properly cured, but naturally the ignorant Mundanes didn't know that, and this was better than nothing. She munched away, like the stupid animal she was supposed to be. Then she snoozed on her feet, patiently awaiting the fall of night.

At dusk, when deepening shadows offered concealment, Grundy the Golem slipped out to scout the region. His ability to converse with all living things enabled him to get information wherever he went.

By the time it was dark enough for Imbri to phase through her confinement and free herself, Grundy was back. "I've found him," he whispered. "I'll show you where." He jumped onto her back—and fell right through her to the ground.

Oops. She was insubstantial. She phased back to solidity, let him mount, then phased out again, taking him with her. Then she followed his directions to find Ichabod.

The scholar was in a separate pen, guarded by an alert swordsman. The area was lighted; Imbri could not safely go in.

"I'll distract the guard," Grundy said. "You go in solid, pick him up, and charge out. It'll be chancy, and they'll be after us—but they can't do a thing when you're phased out."

Imbri was not sanguine about this, but saw no better course. Soon they would discover her absence from her own pen and be after her anyway, so she had to hurry. "Go ahead," she projected. The golem jumped down, turning solid as he left her ambience, and made his way behind the guard.

"Hey, roachface!" Grundy called from a region not far back. His tone was exquisitely insulting.

The man glanced about, but could not spy the hidden golem. "Who's there? Show yourself."

"Go show your own self, snakenose," Grundy replied. Cheap insults were his forte; he was surely enjoying this.

The soldier put his hand on his sword. "Come out, miscreant, or I'll bring you out!"

"You can hardly bring out your own sloppy dank tongue, monstersnoot!" Grundy retorted.

The man whipped out his sword and stalked the sound. He was as vain about his appearance as any true monster, with as little justification. The moment his back was turned, Imbri walked quietly into the pen. "Get ready!" she sent to Ichabod in a dream.

The scholar had been snoozing uncomfortably. Now, in his dream, he reacted with startled gladness. "My hands are tied," he said. "I can't mount."

Imbri applied her teeth to the rope binding his hands and chewed. She had good teeth, and soon crunched through it. But the delay was fatal; the guard turned around and spied them.

"Ho!" he bellowed, charging forward with sword elevated. "Prison break!"

Ichabod jumped onto Imbri's back. She leaped away, avoiding the descending sword. But she remained in the lighted enclosure, still solid, and therefore vulnerable.

Grundy ran up. "Move out, mare!" he cried, leaping to her neck and clutching her mane.

The soldier swung his sword again, clipping a few hairs from her tail. Imbri leaped over the wall of the pen, escaping him.

But the Mundane's cry had roused the camp. Hundreds of torches were converging, lighting the area, preventing

Imbri from phasing out. She had to gallop in the one direction that remained open: east.

"Shoot them down!" a voice commanded. It sounded like Hasbinbad himself.

Arrows sailed toward them. Ichabod jumped and groaned. "I'm hit!"

"Keep going!" Grundy cried. "We're doomed if we stop now!"

Imbri kept going. The torches fell behind. Those soldiers were afoot, not having had time to get to their own horses, so they could not keep the pace. But the pattern of lights was such that she still could not veer south to rejoin Chameleon and the day horse. So she raced on east. As she got beyond the torchlight, she phased into unsolid form, so that the arrows could no longer hurt them, and became invisible to the Mundanes. But they retained a fair notion where she was, and the pursuit continued. Since she was pure black, she tended to disappear in darkness anyway, and they probably assumed this was why they couldn't actually see her. Some of them were now on horses and could keep the equine pace.

But a night mare in dream form could outrun any ordinary equine. Imbri left them behind and ran on into the night, through trees and small hills, getting as far clear as she could.

"How are you doing?" she sent to Ichabod.

There was no answer. She phased back to solid and queried him again, in case he hadn't heard her in the phased-out state. Now she felt the warm blood on her back. The man was losing blood and was unconscious; only the fact that he had no more mass in the phased-out state than Imbri herself did enabled him to remain mounted. He had sunk so far he no longer dreamed. This was worse than she had feared!

"We've got to get magical help for him," the golem said, worried. "Fast, before he sinks entirely. Some healing elixir."

"We don't have any," Imbri sent.

"I know that, mareface!" he snapped. "We'll have to take him to a spring, or to Castle Roogna, where they have some stored."

"Too far. He may be dead before we get there."

"Find a closer place, then!"

"Maybe the Siren has some," Imbri suggested. "She lives in the water wing, and we're not far from it."

"Move!" Grundy said. "Get him there before it's too late! He's no young squirt, you know."

She knew. She moved. She came to the wall that confined the water wing and plunged through. Beyond it was water, a sea of it, with a storm raining thickly down to add to the total. It was one of the seven natural wonders of Xanth, though creatures could not agree just which the seven were. But the water passed through them as Imbri galloped along the surface. She wished there had been a gourd patch handy so that she could use the gourd network in this emergency. But of course there were no gourds in the lake. The water wing was all water.

Fortunately, she was able to travel at maximum velocity across the sea. In a much shorter time than any ordinary horse could manage, she reached the home region of the Siren.

It was night, but the merfolk colony was awake, nightfishing. Several of them had strings of nightfish already. "Where is the Siren?" Imbri sent in a broadband dreamlet.

A mermaid swam up. "Hello, Grundy," she called. "Why do you seek me?"

The golem jumped off Imbri's back, turning solid and splashing into the water, where the buxom creature picked him up. "My friend Ichabod is wounded and dying. My friend the night mare brought him here. Have you any healing elixir?"

"We do," the Siren said. "Carry him to land at the edge of the wing; Morris will bring the elixir."

Imbri trotted to the shore. The Siren got the elixir from her husband, then emerged from the water, her tail splitting into two well-fleshed legs. She sprinkled a few drops on Ichabod.

To Imbri's dismay, there was no immediate effect. "It's not working!" she projected.

"This is a dilute elixir," the Siren explained. "We don't have any really potent springs here in the water wing. They're under the water, you see, so it's hard to capture the essence. But this will work in a few hours—faster, if he can drink some."

They set the unconscious man up and poured a few drops in his mouth. Then Ichabod stirred. His eyes opened and he groaned.

"He lives!" Grundy exclaimed joyfully. "I was really worried about the old codger."

"Get that arrow out of his back!" Morris called from the lake. He was a full merman, so could not go on land. "The healing can't be complete with the arrow in him!"

That was obvious; they had been so concerned about the bleeding that they had not paid attention to the wound. But this remained a problem. The arrow was barbed, and they could not dislodge it without inflicting terrible new pain and damage that might kill the man despite the elixir. Magic did have its limits.

"Maybe if you phase it out—" Grundy suggested.

Imbri tried this. She took the shaft of the arrow in her teeth, then phased into insubstantiality and backed away. The arrow phased with her, and the spaced-out head of it moved without resistance through the man's body until it was free. She hurled the arrow away, gratified; she had removed it without hurting Ichabod at all!

Now the gaping wound started visibly healing. All they had to do was wait.

In half an hour, Ichabod was whole once more. "I hope I never have to go through that particular experience again!" he said. "Thank you, lovely maiden, for your timely help."

The Siren smiled, pleased. She was middle-aged, and evidently appreciated being called a maiden.

"She's no maiden," Grundy said, with his customary etiquette. "She's the Siren."

"The Siren?" Ichabod asked, growing if anything more interested. "But does she lure sailors to their doom?"

"Not any more," the Siren said with a frown. "A centaur smashed my magic dulcimer, and that depleted my power."

"Oh." Ichabod pondered. "You know, if you had your power again, you could do a lot of good for Xanth. You could lure the Mundanes—"

"I really don't want to harm people, not even Mundanes," she said. "I'm a family woman now. Here is my son Cyrus." She introduced a small boy who smiled shyly, then dived into the lake, his legs changing in mid-dive to the tail of a triton.

"Nobody likes killing, of course," Ichabod said. "But perhaps you could lure them to some isolated island in waters infested by sea monsters so that they could not do anyone any harm."

"Yes, that would be all right," she agreed. "Or lure them to my sister the Gorgon, who could change them to stone. Such statues can be restored with the right magic, or when returned to Mundania, where the spell would be broken, so it's not quite the same as death." She shrugged. "But I fear my power is gone forever, as only the Good Magician knows how to restore the instrument, and he wouldn't do it even if I were willing to pay his fee of one year's service. So it really doesn't matter. I think I'm much happier now than I ever was when I had my power, frankly." But she looked pensive, as if aware of the enormous ability she had lost.

Ichabod spread his hands. "One can never tell. I am on good terms with Good Magician Humfrey, having provided him with a number of excellent Mundane research tomes, and perhaps I can broach the matter. I suspect you have just saved me at least a year of life by your assistance. At any rate, I certainly appreciate what you did for me." He turned to Imbri. "And you and Grundy, of course. Now we really must rejoin Chameleon."

He was right. The night was passing entirely too rapidly. They bade farewell to the Siren and the friendly merfolk and headed southwest. They had to get out of the water wing before Imbri turned solid again, for she could not gallop across the water by day.

They made it through the perpetual storm at the edge of the water wing and out into normal Xanth terrain before the sun rose. Imbri invoked her person-locating sense, which she had used during her decades of dream duty to find the sleepers on her list, and oriented on Chameleon. The Night Stallion had always provided the addresses of the sleepers as part of the labeling on their dreams, but she could tune in on people she knew well and who were thinking of her. At least she hoped so; she had not tried it when the location of the person was unknown.

It worked. In this manner they caught up to Chameleon and the day horse. The woman was sleeping in a cushion bush, while the horse grazed nearby. Apparently they had scouted the area and made sure it was safe. Chameleon seemed to have a good sense for safety, despite her stupidity. Of course, while no place in Xanth was completely safe, many were safe enough for those who understood them. A Mundane in this area would probably have fallen prey to a patch of carnivorous grass or a tangle tree or the small water dragon in the nearby river; Xanth natives avoided these things without even thinking about them. Perhaps it was the complex of dangers here that made it safe from Mundanes.

Chameleon woke as they approached. "Oh, I'm so glad you're safe!" she exclaimed. "I had a night mare visit—I thought at first it was you, Imbri, but it wasn't—with a horrible dream about Ichabod getting badly wounded. I'm so glad to see it wasn't true!"

"It was true," Ichabod said. "That's why our return was delayed."

"We got caught by the Mundanes," Grundy said.

"Oh, now I remember; that was in the dream, too. How perfectly awful!"

The day horse approached, ears perking up. "How glad I am to have had this horse near," Chameleon said, patting him on a muscular shoulder, and the day horse nickered. Obviously he liked Chameleon, as did all people who knew her in her lovely phase.

"We were using the smoke of that brush fire for cover, but the wind shifted," the golem continued. "They surrounded us. We talked to their leader, Hasbinbad the Punic. Then the Horseman came—"

The day horse snorted.

"I tell you he was there," Grundy insisted. "Said he forced a centaur to carry him north, since things got hot near Castle Roogna. We don't know what happened to the henchmen Imbri told us about; maybe a dragon got them. Good riddance! He wanted to know how Imbri escaped from him before—"

"And I had to tell him," Imbri sent apologetically. "He promised to let us go, and I think he kept his word."

"If he kept his word, it was only because he had no reason to keep you there!" the day horse insisted in the dream Imbri provided. "I know that man! He never does anything for anyone unless he stands to gain!"

"Well, he did let us go," Grundy said. "Maybe it was a plot to follow us back to you. But we foiled that! We went through the water wing to see the Siren and get Ichabod healed, and the Mundanes couldn't follow. So maybe we outsmarted the Horseman after all."

"I doubt it," the day horse said in the dream. "He has levels and levels of cunning. He probably wanted to let you go, for some devious reason of his own. Maybe he knew the Mundanes wouldn't let him have Imbri for himself, so he saw to it they couldn't keep her either. He's like that. He spites people in subtle ways so the mischief can't be traced to him. He wants everything his own way. But he surely knows just about where we are now. We must flee south immediately."

"That's for sure," Grundy agreed. "We've got our information; we know who the Mundanes are. Now we have to get it to King Dor as fast as we can, so he can figure out how to break up the Wave."

That made sense. Imbri was amazed at the expressiveness of the day horse, who hardly seemed stupid at all now. His points about the Horseman were well taken. But if the man had wanted them free, knowing they would go straight to King Dor, what was his rationale? He was an enemy who would only suffer if the King organized a good defense. Something important was missing, and it made her uneasy.

They set off south. Chameleon was satisified to continue riding the day horse, so they left it the way it was. All day they galloped, avoiding the problems of the journey up, and made such good progress that by nightfall they had crossed the invisible bridge and were back at Castle Roogna.

The day horse, wary of populated places, begged off entering the castle itself. "People tend to want to catch me and pen me," he explained in equine language that Grundy translated for the nonequines.

Chameleon was sympathetic. "I understand," she said. "The Mundanes penned Imbri." She dismounted, then threw her arms about the horse's sweaty neck, giving him an affectionate hug. "Thank you so much, day horse!" She kissed his right ear.

Horses did not blush, but this one tried. He wiggled his ear, snorted, and scuffled the ground with a forefoot. He flicked his tail violently, though there were no flies near. Then he turned on two hooves and trotted away, seeking his own place to graze and rest.

"It's easy to like a pretty woman," Grundy remarked somewhat wistfully. "Even if you are a horse."

And easy for a mare to like such a horse, Imbri thought to herself. He was such a beautiful, nice, helpful animal. If only he were smarter!

Chapter 7. The First Battle

King Dor was waiting for them. He listened gravely to their report, making careful note of the numbers and armament of the enemy as Ichabod reported them. Imbri was amazed to discover how observant the Mundane scholar had been; he had noted everything relevant, and was able to fill in from his wide background information. It seemed Xanth now knew more about the Mundanes than the Mundanes knew about Xanth.

"The Carthaginian mercenaries were—are—redoubtable fighters," Ichabod concluded. "They had excellent leadership, and were accustomed to carrying on on their own with very little support from the home city. They dominated the western half of the Mediterranean Sea, and even the Romans were unable, generally, to match them in battle." He broke off. "But I wander too far afield, as is my wont. My point is that these are formidable foemen who are prone to feed captives to their bloodthirsty god Baal Hammon. You must not give them any quarter. I dislike advocating violence, but I see no peaceful way to abate this particular menace. Fortunately, they have no weapons with which you are unfamiliar, except perhaps that of treachery."

Dor shook his head heavily. He seemed to have aged in the three days Imbri's party had been away, though he had caught up on his sleep. "I had hoped it would be otherwise, but a Wave is a Wave. We shall fight with what resources we have. So there are about six hundred Nextwavers remaining, armed with swords, spears, and bows. This is too great a number for us to handle by ordinary means. I have marshaled the old troops of King Trent's former army, but I am skeptical about their combat readiness. What we really need is the help of some of Xanth's more ferocious animals, such as the dragons. In Xanth's past they have been known to help us out of bad situations. But so far, this time, they have rejected my overtures. I think they might have been more positive toward King Trent, as his power is more compelling than mine. The dragons seem to feel that if men wish to kill men, this will make things easier for dragons."

"Wait till the Nextwavers ravage Dragon Land," Grundy muttered. "Then the beasts will take notice."

"That may be too late for us," Dor said. "In any event, it is not just the dragons. The goblins, who really are more manlike than beastlike, told our messenger to go soak his snoot."

"The goblins don't want to get drafted for war," Imbri sent, remembering the last bad dream she had processed.

King Dor concentrated on a map of Xanth before him. "We expect the Mundanes to drive for Castle Roogna first. That is where the Mundane city of Rome is in the land they thought they were invading, so naturally they see it as the target. Unfortunately, they are correct; if they conquer or destroy Castle Roogna, Xanth will have no central focus for resistance. Dragon land and Goblin land are in central Xanth; if the Nextwave flows down the west coast, it will miss those regions. So the dragons and goblins are not worrying. Since the main human regions are in the west, we must bear the brunt." He ran a hand over his hair, which seemed already to be thinning. "I wish King Trent were well; he has the tactical ability to handle this sort of thing."

There it was again. Even King Dor lacked confidence in his ability. The loss of King Trent had been a terrible blow to Xanth—as it seemed the enemy leader Hasbinbad was well aware. The Horseman had done a good reconnaissance.

"The Gap Chasm will stop them," Grundy said.

"It may, if we take down the magic bridges. I don't want to do that except as a last resort. Those bridges are hard to restore. Good Magician Humfrey supervised the installation of the main one, and he's not young any more."

"He never was young," Grundy said. "I think he was born a wrinkled, hairless gnome. But you do have a point. I think the Gorgon pretty well runs his castle now. I'm not sure I'd trust a bridge whose construction he supervised today."

"So I shall lead King Trent's old army to intercept the Mundanes north of the Gap—"

"Not you, Dor!" Chameleon exclaimed, alarmed.

"But, Mother, I'm the King!" he protested somewhat querulously. "It's my job to lead the troops."

"It's your job to govern Xanth," Grundy said. "If you go foolishly out to battle and get yourself killed, where is Xanth then?"

"But—"

"Listen to them, your Majesty," a voice said from the doorway. It was Queen Iris, garbed in black. "I know what it is like to be halfway widowed; I don't want my daughter to learn."

Dor smiled wanly. "I'll try to hang on to my life. I'll stay out of the actual battle. But I must be there with the troops. I can not do less than that."

As anticipated, the Nextwave flowed down the western side of Xanth, avoiding the deadly central region and the monsteriferous coastal region. The Horseman, obviously, had scouted out their best route—the enchanted path that trade parties used to reach the isthmus that was the only access to Mundania. Now that enchantment was helping the enemy force to drive directly for Castle Roogna.

Most creatures of Xanth thought of the historic Waves as sheer ravening hordes of Mundanes, and the current Wave resembled that notion closely enough. But it was evident that this force had considerable expertise supporting its violence. The Mundanes were quickly learning how to handle the hazards of Xanth and how to use beneficial magic.

The quiet North Village had to be evacuated hastily before the Wave swamped it, and the centaur village south of it was similarly abandoned. These local centaurs were less prudish about magic talents than were those of distant Centaur Isle and were quite helpful to the human Villagers, carrying the aged and infirm. In return, the human folk used their magic talents to facilitate the travel of the centaurs, conjuring food and tools as needed. It was a fine cooperative effort. Imbri knew that Dor's paternal grandparents lived in the North Village, and the sire and dam of Chet and Chem Centaur lived in the centaur settlement, so this effort was important to those who were at Castle Roogna in a personal as well as a tactical sense. Faces were turning grim at the notion of handing these areas over to the enemy, but it was a necessary evil.

Queen Iris was deputized by King Dor to supervise the evacuation of those regions. She spent day and night in the bedroom with unconscious King Trent, using her enormous powers of illusion on behalf of the welfare of Xanth in the manner King Trent would have asked her to. She projected her image to every household of the Village, warning each person of the danger and making sure that person left. Iris could actually perceive these people, and they could perceive her; to that extent her illusory images were real. It was indeed difficult to ascertain exactly where illusion left off and reality began. She spoke calmly but certainly, making sure that important belongings were taken and that nothing of possible advantage to the Mundanes was left behind.

Because she could also perceive the progress of the Wave, though this was at the fringe of her range, the people had the confidence to evacuate in an orderly manner, not rushing wastefully, while also not delaying overlong.

But the Queen was working too hard. Her use of illusion at such range was like a horse galloping cross-country; it required a lot of concentration and energy. Iris would not rest herself at night, insisting on checking and rechecking every detail. Her illusion-figures were blurring. Iris was no longer in the flush of youth; she was as old as King Trent. This enormous effort without respite was apt to put her into a state no better than that of Trent.

Finally King Dor sent Imbri in to her, carrying a basket of food and drink, with instructions to make the Queen take a needed break. King Dor did not feel right about giving orders to his mother-in-law, which was why he asked Imbri to handle it. His reason for choosing her was seemingly superficial—her ability to project dreams resembled the Queen's ability to project illusions. Perhaps there would be rapport. Imbri was glad to try.

Imbri entered the bedroom and set the basket down, releasing the strap she had held in her teeth. "Queen Iris, I have brought refreshment," she sent. "You must eat and drink."

Iris paused in her labor of illusion. "Don't try to fool me, mare," she snapped. "There's sleep potion in that beverage."

"So there is," Imbri agreed. "Your daughter put it in. But she says she will watch her father while you rest, if you are willing."

"Her place is with her husband, the new King," Iris said, softening. "I know she loves her father. She doesn't have to prove it to me."

"Please—take the rest. The Villagers can travel now without you, and your talent may be needed later. There are people in charge like Dor's grandfather Roland, of the Council of Elders, and Chester and Cherie Centaur, who tutored King Dor in literacy and martial art. They can handle it now."

"In fact, Irene loves Trent more than she loves me," Iris grumbled. But she ate the cake and drank the coconut milk provided, and allowed herself to get sleepy. "*You* watch the King," she said. "And don't send me any bad dreams! I have more than enough already."

"No bad dreams," Imbri agreed.

But she did send the Queen a good dream, of the Villagers and centaurs arriving safely south of the Gap Chasm and finding temporary homes in other villages and on other ranges.

"Don't try to fool me!" Queen Iris said in her sleep, catching on. "I deliver illusions to others; I prefer reality for myself."

"You are brave," Imbri sent.

"I'll have none of your false flattery either!" the Queen retorted, threatening to wake up.

"I didn't say you were nice," Imbri said in the dream, taking the form of an older woman, one with whom the Queen might be comfortable. "I said you were brave."

"It takes no courage to project pictures to others; you should know that."

"To seek reality," Imbri clarified. "I send my images inside the minds of others, rather than outside, as you do, but I, too, prefer to know the truth, which may not be at all like a dream. Many people do prefer illusion, however."

"I appreciate your effort," the Queen said. "You're trying to keep me asleep, and I suppose I do need it. I can't serve Xanth well if I am overtired." Then she brought herself up short. "Xanth? Whom am I fooling? I said I sought reality, but this is illusion! I never cared for the welfare of Xanth! I always wanted to rule it, which is an entirely different matter. But no Queen is permitted to rule Xanth, no matter what her talent."

"Ichabod says Xanth is a medieval Kingdom," Imbri's image said. "He thinks that eventually it will progress to equal rights for women."

"Is the King all right?"

Was this a deliberate shifting of subject, or merely the meandering of an overtired mind? Imbri checked King Trent. "He is unchanged."

"Do you know, I only married him so I could be Queen. If one can not rule, the next best thing is to be married to the one who does. It was a marriage of convenience; we never fooled each other that there was love between us. He had to marry because the Council of Elders who made him King required it; he married me so as to eliminate Magician-level dissension."

"But surely—" Imbri started to protest.

"I have my faults, and they are gross ones, but I was never a hypocrite," the Queen insisted. "I craved power more than anything else, and Trent craved power, too. But he did not want to remarry, and when he saw he had to, he refused to marry for love. So he made the deal with me, as I was unlovable. That was perhaps almost as potent an asset as my magic; if his dead Mundane wife was watching, she would have known I was not capable of replacing her in his esteem. He was, in fact, punishing himself. I knew it—but the truth is, I wasn't looking for love either. So I was happy to prostitute myself for the appearance of power and distinction—though it wasn't prostitution in any literal sense. He had no physical desire for me."

Imbri was embarrassed by these revelations, but knew the Queen was unwinding in her sleep. Long-buried truths were bubbling to the surface. It was best not to interfere. "Horses don't look for love either," she said. "Just companionship and offspring and good pasturage."

The Queen laughed. "How well you define it, night mare! That was what I sought, in addition to power. And King Trent gave me all those things, in his fashion; I can not complain. He was known in his youth as the Evil Magician, but he was in fact a good man. Is a good man."

"And a good King," Imbri agreed. "I understand this is the best age of Xanth since King Roogna's time."

"True. King Roogna fought off the Fourth or Fifth Wave, I misremember which, and ushered in the golden age of Xanth. He built this fine castle. We call the present the silver age, but I suspect it is as gold as the other was." She paused reflectively. "It is strange how things work out. I married Trent from contempt, thinking to use him to achieve subtle power for myself. But he was stronger and better than I thought, and instead of dominating him, I was dominated by him. And strangest of all, I discovered I liked it. I could have loved him . . . but the one love of his life died before he returned to Xanth. He had had a son, too. Some alien disease took them both; he never spoke about it. He would have felt guilty if he ever loved again. So he was true to his design, while I was not. How I envied that unknown, deceased Mundane woman!"

"But you have a child by him!" Imbri protested.

"That signifies less than it might," the Queen said. "Xanth needed an heir, in case there should be no Magician when Trent died. Someone to fill in, to occupy Castle Roogna until a Magician showed up. So Trent had to come to me. He was so disturbed by it that I had to invoke my illusion to make it appear to be two other people, not him and me. *That* was how we conceived Irene."

Imbri was shocked. "A mating of convenience?"

"Again you phrase it aptly. It was real for me, but not for him; he was only doing his duty. But after Irene came—not even a Sorceress, and not male, a double failure—I think there was no conflict there. He could love another child, for it is possible for a man to have several children without denying any of them. The girl was no threat to his memory of his son. He loved Irene. And sometimes, I think, he almost loved the mother of Irene."

"Surely so!"

"And now he is gone, or temporarily incapacitated—that is one illusion I must cling to!—and I can play the role I am supposed to: that of the grieving, loyal wife. Because it is true. A marriage of convenience turned secretly real—for me, at least. And I can do what I can for the good of Xanth, because that is what *he* would be doing, and now I can only realize myself through him." She grimaced. "I, the original feminist! How utter was my fall, the worse because it is unrecognized."

"I don't see that as a fall," Imbri said.

"You are a mare." But the Queen smiled, accepting the comfort. "I would give anything to have him back, on any basis, or to join him in his ensorcellment. But it seems that is not my decision to make, any more than any of the other crucial decisions of my life have been."

Queen Iris sank then into a deeper sleep, and Imbri let her descend below the threshold of dreams, gaining her precious rest. Imbri had not suspected the depth and nature of Iris's feeling and had not sought such knowledge, but was glad she had learned of it. Truly, human folk were more complex than equine folk!

In the same period of a few days, King Dor's hastily marshaled and outfitted army prepared to meet the enemy onslaught. Everyone knew that King Trent could have organized an effective campaign—but King Trent was sadly out of it. People lacked confidence in Dor—but he was the only King Xanth had. Was he enough?

Dor accompanied the army north, along with his private bodyguard composed of long-term boyhood friends. He rode Chet Centaur, who was armed with a fine bow, spear, and sword, and who could magically convert boulders to pebbles, a process he called calculus. Chet's sister Chem was along, too, for her magic talent of map projection was invaluable for charting the positions of Xanth and Next-wave troops. Chem carried Grundy the Golem, whose ability to converse with living creatures complemented King Dor's ability to talk with inanimate things; together they could amass a lot of information in a hurry. Smash the Ogre also came. He now resembled a large, somewhat brutish man, for he was half man by birth. But when the occasion required, he could still manifest as the most fearsome of ogres. Since he could not readily keep pace with the centaurs afoot in man form, Imbri served as his steed. She knew Smash from the time he had visited the world of the gourd. He had terrorized the walking skeletons, but had been gentle with her, and in a devious manner she owed her half soul to him.

Of course, Imbri knew Chem in an even closer manner. It was half of the centaur filly's soul she had. This was the first time Imbri had encountered her since that exchange.

They trotted side by side, following King Dor and Chet. Chem was a pretty brown creature with flowing hair and tail and a slender, well-formed human upper torso. Imbri liked her, of course, but felt guilty about the soul. So as they moved, she conversed by dream privately with the filly.

"Do you remember me, Chem? I have half your soul."

"I remember. You helped us escape the Void. Without

you, we would have been doomed, for nothing except night mares can travel out of that awful hole. Now you are helping Chameleon, aren't you?"

"She doesn't like battle, but wants to safeguard her son Dor, so she delegated me to carry the ogre. I think that makes sense, in her fashion."

"Yes, I know. My folks wanted me to stay at Castle Roogna with the wives—Queen Iris, Queen Irene, Chameleon, and Smash's wife Tandy, who is as nice a girl as I know. But I'm not married, and I don't feel quite at home with the wifely types. They live mostly for their males."

Imbri remembered her conversation with Queen Iris. "They seem to like it that way."

"I can't see it. So I persuaded King Dor he needed me at the front."

Imbri's mental image of another female centaur laughed. She liked this creature better than ever! "Now that I'm a day mare, I suppose I should return your soul—"

"No, it was a fair exchange, as these things go," Chem said. "As I said, without your help, and the help of those other two night mares, Crises and Vapors—without them, Smash, Tandy, and I would not have been able to resume our normal lives. My half soul is regenerating nicely now, and I hope your half soul is doing the same."

"It may be," Imbri said. "I don't know how to judge. I was always a soulless creature before."

"Some of the best creatures are soulless," Chem said. "I don't know why souls should be limited to human and part-human creatures. Some dragons are more worthy than some Mundanes." Her gaze flicked to Imbri's rider. "And even some ogres are good people."

"I caught that!" Grundy exclaimed. "They're talking about you, Smash, in dreams."

"And why not?" Smash inquired mildly. "They're friends of mine."

"Aw, you don't even think like an ogre any more. You're no fun," the golem complained. The others laughed.

"And there may be some reason for you to have that half soul," Chem concluded privately in Imbri's dream. "Often these things turn out to have greater meaning or direction than we at first appreciate. I like to think that someday my shared soul will help you as greatly as your assistance helped me. Obviously it won't rescue you from the Void, but—"

They spied a harpy sitting on a branch of a pepper tree. The marching troops had skirted this tree generously, so as not to catch the sneezes. The harpy seemed to be immune, perhaps because she was already fouled up with dirt. "Hey, birdbrain!" Grundy called in his usual winning manner. "How about doing some aerial reconnaissance for us?"

"For you?" the harpy screeched indignantly. She had the head and breasts of a woman and the wings and body of a buzzard. This one was fairly young; were it not for the caked grime, her face and form might have been tolerable. "Why should I do anything for your ilk, you blankety blank?"

Imbri and Chem stiffened, the latter's delicate shell-pink ears reddening, and Smash turned his head, for the blanks had not been exactly blank. Harpies were as foul of mouth as they were of body, and that was about the limit of foulness in Xanth.

"For the greater good of Xanth, fowlmouth," Grundy called back, being the fastest to recover from the verbal horror that had spewed like festering garbage from the harpy's mouth. Indeed, he seemed to be mentally filing the terms for future use, though there were few if any occasions where he might safely do so. "To help stop the invading Mundanes from ravaging everything."

"The greater good of Xanth can go blank up a blankety blank, sidewise," the harpy retorted. "It's no blankety doubleblank to me."

Again it took a moment for the terminology to clear. Even the pepper tree was turning red. If there was one thing harpies were good at, it was bad language.

"There will also be a lot of carrion after the battle," Grundy said. "Gooey, gooky corpses steaming in the sun, swelling and popping open, guts strewn about—"

The harpy's eyes lighted with dismal fires. "Oh, slurp!" she exclaimed. "It makes me unbearably hungry!"

"I thought it might," Grundy said smugly. Strangely enough, no one else looked hungry. "All you have to do is fly by the enemy positions and report where they are and how many—"

"That's too much blank blank work!"

"Spiked eyeballs, chopped livers, severed feet—"

"I'll do it!" the harpy screeched, licking her dirty lips. She launched from the tree, stirring up a huge cloud of pepper, and flapped heavily north.

"But the Mundanes may shoot her down with an arrow," Chem protested without much conviction.

"The smell will keep them beyond arrow range," Grundy said facetiously. It occurred to Imbri, however, that he might be right; it took some time to get used to harpy scent.

Now they came to the Gap Chasm and proceeded across. This was the only visible two-way bridge, so was the most used; it would have to be the first to go if the Mundane Wave got this far.

The Gap Dragon was present; it raged and reached upward, but the Gap was too deep to make this a serious threat. "Go choke on your own tail, steamsnoot!" Grundy called down to it, and dropped a cherry bomb he had plucked carefully from the Castle Roogna orchard tree. The dragon snapped at it and swallowed it whole. There was a muffled boom as the bomb detonated, and smoke shot out of the dragon's ears. But it seemed to make no difference; the monster still raged and pursued them. The Gap Dragon was tough; no doubt about it!

By the time they were across, the harpy was back. "There are about three hundred of them," she reported. "They're headed toward the nickelpede crevices. I don't like that; the nickels don't leave anything behind worth eating."

Chem concentrated, and her magic map formed. It showed the nickelpede crevices, a minor network of cracks in the ground. "Where exactly are the Mundanes?" she asked.

The harpy gave her the specifics, and Chem plotted them on her map. Then the harpy flew off, explaining that she had trouble with the smell of the human folk. Now they had a clear notion of the disposition of the enemy troops. "But there are only three hundred of them here,"

Chem remarked. "That suggests they are holding back half their force, perhaps as a reserve."

They drew abreast of King Dor to advise him. "Yes, we'll try to drive them into the nickelpede crevices," he agreed. "If they take cover there, they'll regret it."

But Dor's troops were out of condition and not young; their average age was near fifty. Progress was slow. They would not reach the Mundane Wave before it cleared the nickelpede region. Such a fine opportunity lost!

"We shall have to establish our position and wait for them," King Dor decided. "As I recall, there's a love spring north of the Gap—"

"There is," Chem agreed, projecting her map. "Right here." She pointed to the spot. "We're already past it, and the path by it is one-way; we can't reach it from here."

"That's fine; I don't want to reach it. I want to avoid it. I don't want my troops drinking from it."

Grundy laughed. "That's for sure! But maybe if we fetched some of that water for the Mundanes, they'd immediately breed with any female creature they saw—"

"No," Dor said. "That's not funny, Grundy. We won't fight that way."

The golem scowled. "You can be sure the Mundanes would fight that way! They have no civilized scruples. That's what makes them so tough."

"But we do have civilized scruples," King Dor said. "Perhaps that is what distinguishes us from the Mundanes. We shall maintain that distinction."

"Yes, your Majesty," the golem agreed with disgust.

"What other difficult aspects are there between us and the Nextwave?" King Dor asked Chem.

"There's a river that changes anyone who drinks from it into a fish," she answered, pointing it out on the map. "From what Ichabod said, I think they've encountered an arm of that river farther north, but they may not realize it's the same. And over here is the Peace Forest, where people become so peaceful they simply lie down and sleep forever—"

"That won't give the Mundanes any trouble," Grundy said. "They're not peaceful at all!"

"But we should keep our troops clear of it," King Dor

said. "And the river. We'll have to find a safe supply of water. Anything else?"

"Just the nickelpedes," Chem answered. "But the Mundanes will be past that region and the peace pines. The river is probably where we'll meet them."

King Dor sighed. "So be it. I hope we can stop them without too much bloodshed."

No one replied. Imbri knew they shared one major concern: did this young, untried King have what it took to halt the devastating incursion of a Mundane Wave of conquest? They would know the answer all too soon.

To the gratified surprise of all, King Dor did seem to know what he was doing. He ranged his troops along the river, having them dig trenches and throw up embankments with brush piled up in front so that the archers could sight on the enemy without exposing themselves. He had the spearmen ranged in front of the archers, to protect them from charging enemy troops, and the swordsmen in front of the spearmen. "Do not break formation until your captains give the order," King Dor concluded. "They outnumber us; they may try a false retreat, to draw us out, so they can fall on us in the open. Beware! Do not assume that those who lack magic are not dangerous."

The men chuckled. They were all former Mundanes and lacked magic themselves. The King had paid them a kind of compliment.

Now they just had to wait for the arrival of the enemy. The harpy, eager for the spoils of battle, continued her spy overflights, so everyone knew the Mundanes were not trying anything fancy. They were marching straight down the main path, without any attempt at secrecy. They had no advance scouts and sent no detachments out to flank a potential enemy force. In this respect they were indeed merely a horde charging down the route of least resistance, at greatest speed. Their progress was marked by flame and smoke; they left mainly ashes in their path. The North Village was gone, and it would be long before the centaur range was green again.

Imbri hurt, thinking of all that wanton destruction of excellent pasture. Yet she could understand the Mundanes' rationale; the fire destroyed the unknown threats of magic and routed hiding magic creatures, making the Mundanes feel more secure.

"I don't trust this," Chet Centaur said. "Either they're criminally careless or they have no respect at all for the opposition. Or it's a ruse of some sort. Where are the rest of their troops?"

"Maybe they plan to take Castle Roogna before we know they're coming," King Dor said, perplexed. "Mundanes are unsubtle folk, but we can't afford to underestimate them. All I want is to stop them today. If they have to forage in their own burned-out territory, they'll soon be hungry."

"And thirsty," Grundy added, eyeing the river.

"I suppose transformation is kinder than slaughter," King Dor agreed with a sigh. "Certainly King Trent believed that it was."

It was late in the afternoon when the Nextwave arrived. The motley crew forged up to the river, not even noticing the embankments beyond it. There was no action by Dor's army; his captains would give the attack order only on his signal. Imbri was much impressed; the young King had amazing grasp of the strategy of battle. It was almost as if he had fought Mundanes before—and of course that was impossible, as there had been no Wave in his lifetime, or in the lifetimes of his parents or grandparents. Only Imbri herself had ever seen a Wave surge into Xanth, as far as she knew, though maybe Good Magician Humfrey was old enough. Well, there were the zombies and ghosts, who had existed in their ageless manner for centuries, but they didn't really count.

The first Mundanes threw themselves down beside the river and slurped up the sparkling water. They converted instantly to fish, who leaped and flipped with amazement and discomfort until they splashed into the water and disappeared.

The standing Wavers stared. But they were not completely dull; very soon they caught on to the nature of the enchantment, realizing that this was the same river they had encountered before. Immediately they cried the alarm to their companions.

Some of these were skeptical. They had not seen the

transformations of their leading comrades, and suspected some crude Mundane practical joke was being played to aggravate their thirst. So one dropped down to guzzle water—and turned into another fish while all were watching.

That did it. Guards were posted along the river to warn the others, and the Mundane losses were cut. Perhaps a dozen had become fish; the great majority remained.

The Mundanes pushed on past the river, obviously wanting to find a better place to camp for the night. Then they spied the barricades.

"We should give them fair warning," King Dor said.

"Fair warning!" Grundy expostulated. "You're crazy!" Then the golem looked abashed, remembering to whom he was talking. "Figuratively speaking, your Majesty."

"Opinion noted," King Dor remarked dryly, and in that moment he reminded Imbri of King Trent. "Imbri, can you project a warning dream that far?"

"It would have to be very diffuse and weak," she sent. "They would probably shrug it off as of no consequence."

King Dor nodded. He spoke to the leader of the Xanth army. "Ask for a volunteer to stand up and warn the Mundanes not to proceed farther."

"I'll do it myself, sir," the man said, saluting. He was a balding, fattening, middle-aged man, but he had done good work organizing the troops and handling the logistics of feeding and moving so large a force—one hundred men—on such short notice.

The man lumbered down the back slope of the hill on which King Dor was situated, so as not to give away the King's location. He circled to the rear of the barricade and mounted a convenient boulder. Then he cupped his mouth with his hands and shouted with excellent military volume: "Mundanes! Halt!"

The leading Mundanes looked up, then shrugged and marched on, ignoring him.

"Halt, or we attack!" the Xanth leader cried.

The leading Mundane brought his bow about, whipped an arrow out of his quiver, and shot it at the Xanth general. The other Mundanes charged toward him.

"Well, we tried," King Dor said regretfully. He signaled

the general, who had dodged the first arrow and now was taking cover behind the boulder.

The general gave the order. The Xanth archers sent their first shafts flying. Most of them missed, either because the archers were long out of practice or because their hearts weren't in it. For over two decades they had opposed monsters, not men, or indulged in elaborate war games whose relation to actual warfare was questionable. One arrow did strike a Mundane, more or less by accident.

"Blood!" the harpy screeched hungrily.

The Mundanes finally realized they were under attack. They retreated across the river, protecting their bodies with their shields. A couple of them tripped as they stepped backward through the water, fell, gulped, and became fish.

Now the Mundanes were angry, as perhaps they had reason to be. They lined up along the river and shot off a volley of arrows. But these did not have much effect, because of the embankments and brush that protected the Xanth troops.

Then Hasbinbad, the Carthaginian leader, appeared at the front, splendidly armed and armored in the grand Punic tradition. He was a considerable contrast to the motley assortment of archers and spearmen he commanded. Imbri could not overhear his words, but the effect on the Mundanes was immediate. They formed into a phalanx, shields overlapping, and marched back across the river. The Xanth defenders were astonished, but a few of them knew of this type of formation, and word quickly spread. The Mundanes were now virtually impervious to arrows.

But the Xanth commander knew about this sort of thing. At his orders, crews of strong men heaved at boulders that had been scouted and loosened earlier, starting them rolling grandly down the slope. One crunched directly toward the phalanx. The Mundanes saw it coming and scattered, their formation broken. That threat had been abated.

Maybe the Nextwave would be contained, Imbri thought. They had to pass this spot to get to Castle Roogna, and they weren't making headway yet. Soon night would fall, and the nocturnal creatures would emerge, forcing the enemy to seek cover.

But the Mundanes who remained beyond the river had

been busy. They had a big fire going—they certainly liked to burn things!—and now were poking their arrows into it. Were they destroying their weapons? That did not seem to make much sense!

Then they stood and fired their burning arrows at the brush barriers of the defenders. "Trouble!" Chet Centaur muttered. "We should have anticipated this."

Trouble indeed! The dry brush blazed up quickly, destroying the cover. Men ran to push out the burning sections, but during this distraction the entire Mundane army charged in a mass. The Xanth archers sent their arrows more seriously now, bringing down a numbe' of the enemy, but this was only a token. Soon the Mundanes were storming the barricades, brandishing their weapons, and the Xanth troops were fleeing in terror. A rout was in the making.

"I won't put up with this!" King Dor cried. "Take me there, Chet!"

"But you could be killed!" the centaur protested.

"I have faced death before," the King said seriously. "If you don't carry me, I'll go afoot."

Chet grimaced, then drew his sword and galloped forward. "Idiocy!" Chem muttered, taking her coil of rope and pacing her brother, carrying the golem. Imbri agreed with her—and bore Smash right behind them. One thing was certain, there were no cowards in the King's bodyguard, but plenty of fools.

They charged to the burning barricades, where the Mundanes were making their way through. Suddenly the flames began talking, as the King exerted his talent. "I'm going to destroy you, Mundane!" one cried as it licked close. "I'll really burn you up!"

A number of Mundanes whirled, startled. "Yes, you, armorface!" the flame taunted. "I'll scorch the skin off your rear and boil you in your own fat! Beware my heat!"

Some Mundanes hastily retreated, but others leaped out the near side. They closed on the King's party. "Get him!" one cried. "That's their King!"

But now Smash the Ogre went into action. He swelled up monstrously, bursting out of his human trousers, until he was twice the height and six times the mass of a man.

He no longer sat astride Imbri; he stood over her. He roared, and the blast of his breath blew the leaves off the nearest trees and bushes and shook the clouds in their orbits. He ripped a small tree from the ground and swung it in a great arc that wiped a swath clear of enemy personnel. It seemed the Mundanes had not before encountered an angry ogre; they would be more careful in the future.

King Dor and Chet trotted on, and where they went the ground yelled threats at the Mundanes, and the stones made crunching noises as if a giant were tromping near, and dry sticks rattled as if poisonous. The Mundanes were continuously distracted, and more of them retreated in disarray. Any who sought to attack Dor were balked by the sword and rope of the two centaurs, and many of the rest were terrified by the charging ogre. The Punics seemed daunted as much by the strangeness of this new opposition as by its ferocity.

The Xanth troops rallied and came back into the fray. Blood had been shed; now they knew for certain that this was serious business. Long-neglected skills returned in strength. Soon the Mundanes were routed, fleeing across the river and north as dusk came. King Dor called off the chase, not wanting to risk combat at night.

The harpy had her heart's desire: there were some fifty Mundane corpses left on the battlefield. But there were also twenty Xanth dead and twice that number wounded. The brief action had been mutually devastating. This was every bit as bad as the terrible dreams Imbri had delivered during the campaign of the Lastwave! Still, it was a technical victory for the home team, and the pain of the losses was overbalanced by the satisfaction of successfully turning back the Nextwave.

"This is internecine warfare," Chet said. "It does great harm to both sides. I wish there were some more amicable way to deal with this problem."

"It isn't ended," King Dor said. "They'll return tomorrow, and they still outnumber us. We have barely forty men in fighting condition. We must set up new boulders and make a rampart that is impervious to fire. We'll haul up supplies of river water, which no one must drink, and drill on targets for bow and arrow accuracy. We can hold them if we work at it, but it still will not be easy."

"And if we hold them for another day or so," Chem added, "they should lose interest in fighting and gain interest in feeding themselves. Then it may be possible to negotiate an end to hostilities, and the Wave will be over."

Imbri hoped it would be that easy. She had a deep distrust of the Mundanes and knew how devious they could be.

The troops were allowed to eat and sleep in shifts, while others labored all night on the defenses. The walking wounded were encouraged to walk south, back across the bridge over the Gap, as this was safer than remaining for tomorrow's renewed battle. If the Mundanes were hurting as badly as the Xanthians, they would not renew the attack, but that was uncertain.

The two centaurs, the golem, the ogre, and Imbri ranged themselves about King Dor's tent and slept by turns also. There was no trouble; evidently the Mundanes were no more eager to fight by night than were the Xanthians.

"Did you notice," Chet said at one point, apparently having cogitated on the events of the day, "there are no Mundane horses here? They must all be with their reserves."

Imbri hadn't noticed, but realized it was true. She should have been the first to make that observation! If the Punics had wanted to move rapidly, why hadn't they used their horses? "Maybe they did not have enough horses for every man," she sent, "and could not take time to let the horses graze, so could not use them here. An all-horse mounted party would have been too small to capture Castle Roogna. But surely those horses will be used later."

"Quite possible," Chet agreed. "But I also wonder whether the missing horses and the missing men can be doing an encirclement, planning to attack where we least expect, while our attention and all our troops are concentrated here."

"We had better tell the King in the morning," Imbri sent. "He will want to set a special guard about Castle Roogna in case the Mundanes do try that! Fifty horses and riders could take Castle Roogna if our forces were elsewhere."

Reassured that they had anticipated the Mundane ploy, they relaxed.

The Mundanes, amazingly, attacked again at dawn. They formed another phalanx, this time maneuvering skillfully to avoid the rolling boulders.

"Your Majesty!" Grundy called. "The enemy is attacking!"

There was no response from the tent. Chet swept the flap aside and they all peered in.

King Dor lay still, his eyes staring upward. But he was not awake.

Chet drew the King to a sitting posture. Dor breathed, but did not respond. His eyes continued staring.

Imbri flicked a dream at him and encountered only blankness.

"He has gone the way of King Trent!" Chem exclaimed, horrified.

After that, it was disaster. The Mundanes rapidly overran the Xanth defenses. The surviving home troops fled, and this time there was no one to rally them. The centaurs tied the King to Imbri's back, then guarded her as she carried their fallen leader back to Castle Roogna. Seeming victory had become disaster.

And what would they tell Queen Irene, Dor's brand-new wife and widow?

Chapter 8. The Zombie Master

"Somehow I knew it," Irene said. "A nightmare told me Dor would not come back." She was dressed in black. "I blotted the dream from my mind, thinking to escape the prophecy, but when I saw your party coming, I remembered." She looked at King Dor, suppressing her expression of grief for the moment. "Take him to the King's chamber."

They took King Dor up to join King Trent, and Irene remained there. There was nothing more to say to her at the moment.

"Who is the next King?" Grundy asked. "It has to be a Magician."

"That would be the Zombie Master," Chet said. "Magician Humfrey is too old, and he doesn't participate in contemporary politics. When King Trent was lost in Mundania eight years ago and King Dor had to go look for him, the Zombie Master reigned for a couple of weeks quite competently. When there was a quarrel, he would send a zombie to break it up; pretty soon there were very few quarrels." Chet smiled knowingly.

"But the Zombie Master is off in the southern unexplored territory," Chem protested. "He likes his privacy. I don't even have him on my map."

"And the magic mirror's still out of commission," Grundy said. "We can't call him."

"We should have had that mirror fixed long ago," Chem muttered. "But it seemed like such a chore when we didn't have any emergency."

"Life is ever thus," Chet said. "We've got to reach him. He's got to be King again, at least until King Dor gets better, and he'll have to stop the Nextwave from crossing the Gap Chasm."

"Dor's not getting better," Grundy said. "Queen Iris tried everything to bring King Trent around, but the healer says it's an ensorcellment, not an illness, and we don't know the counterspell."

"I can reach the Zombie Master," Imbri projected. "I have been to his castle before, delivering dreams to his wife."

"His wife is Millie the Ghost!" Chet protested. "Surely she doesn't have bad dreams!"

"She worries about the mischief her children may get into," Imbri sent.

"Now that's worth worrying about!" Chem agreed. "They visited Castle Roogna some years back, and I'm not sure the place has recovered yet. Those twins must drive even the zombies to distraction!"

"We have to get news to the Magician that the onus has fallen on him again," Grundy said. "He won't believe Imbri alone. He doesn't know her, and will think it's just another bad dream."

"He'll believe Irene," Chet said. "But I don't know whether she—"

"She's all broken up right now," Chem said. "I don't think she can handle it."

"There's Chameleon," Chet said. "But she's lost her son—"

Chem shook her head. "There's more to Chameleon than shows. But she's not yet out of her pretty phase. That means—"

"We all know what that means!" Grundy cut in. "But maybe it's better for her to be busy while her husband is away in Mundania."

"Cynically put," Chem said. "Still, we could ask her. The need is pressing."

They asked her. Chameleon, pale from reaction to her son's sudden fate, nevertheless did not hesitate. "I'll go."

Just like that, Imbri and Chameleon were traveling again, this time without other companions. They had delayed three hours until nightfall, for that was the night mare's best traveling time, and with the gourds, the distance did not matter. Imbri filled up on hay and oats, and Chameleon forced herself to eat, too, preparing herself for the excursion.

At dusk they went out, going to the nearest patch of hypnogourds. As darkness thickened, Imbri phased through the peephole and galloped across another segment of the gourd world. She regretted she couldn't stop to check in with the Night Stallion and report on her recent activities. But he surely knew, and he could send another night mare to contact her any time he needed to.

The gourds ushered any ordinary peeper into a continuing tour, locked to the particular person. If someone broke eye contact, he reverted immediately to the world of Xanth, but if he looked into any gourd again, he would find himself exactly where he left off. Imbri was not bound by that; she was passing strictly from one gourd to another, and the terrain was incidental. But she was carrying Chameleon, and this influenced the landscape; they were in the region they had left before—the burning iceberg.

But the amorphous entities that reached for Chameleon no longer frightened her. "I have lost my son," she said simply. "What worse can the likes of you do to me?"

Imbri realized that the woman was smarter than she had been. She was also less lovely, though still quite good-looking for her age. Every day made a difference with her, and several days had passed since their last journey together.

The amorphous shapes gaped and grabbed, but were helpless against the woman's disdain. Also, Imbri and her rider were not completely solid here; nothing in the gourd could touch them physically.

Imbri galloped on over the iceberg and down the far slope. Now they came to the stonemasons' region. The stonemasons were made of stone, and worked with wood and metal and flesh, as was reasonable. Some were fashioning a fancy backdrop set painted with horrendous fleshly monsters, the stage scenery for some of the worst dreams. There was, of course, no sense wasting effort bringing in real monsters when they weren't going to be used; the pictures were just as good in this case.

Chameleon stared at these with dull curiosity. "Why do they work so hard to make dreams people don't like?" she asked.

"If people didn't suffer bad dreams, they would never improve their ways or prepare for emergencies," Imbri explained. "The dreams scare them into behaving better and warn them about possible calamities. There's a lot of evil in people, waiting to take over unless they are always on guard against it."

"Oh. Like not fixing the magic mirror."

Well, that was close enough. Probably a warning dream should have been sent about that, but of course it was hard for the Night Stallion to keep up with every minor detail of a crisis. People did have to do some things on their own initiative, after all.

They moved on past the stonemasons and into a region of boiling mud. Green and purple masses of it burst out in messy bubbles, and bilious yellow currents flowed between them. Imbri's hooves didn't even splash, however; she didn't need a mud bath. "What's this for?"

"This is the very best throwing-mud," Imbri explained. "It is impossible to hurl a glob of it without getting almost as much on yourself as on your target. Most people, after a messy experience with this, start to mend their ways."

"Most?"

"A few are addicted to mud. They wallow in it constantly."

"They can't have many friends."

"That's the funny thing! They have almost as many friends as the clean people. The trouble is, the friends are all the same kind of people."

"But who would want that kind of friend?"

"Nobody. That's the beauty of it."

Chameleon smiled. She was definitely getting smarter.

They raced on through a tangle of carnivorous vines and out another peephole. They were back in Xanth proper, in sight of the Zombie Master's new castle.

It looked just about the way an edifice constructed by

zombies should look. The stones were slimy green and crumbling; the wood was wormy and rotten. The hinges on the door and the bars on the windows were so badly rusted and corroded they were hardly useful or even recognizable. The moat was a putrid pool of gray gunk.

"This is certainly the place," Chameleon remarked.

Imbri picked her way through the surrounding gravesites and across the bedraggled drawbridge. She remained phased out, so that she had virtually no weight; otherwise it could have been a risky crossing.

A zombie guard met them at the main entrance. "Halsh!" it cried, losing part of its decayed epiglottis in the effort of breath and speech.

"Oh, I never liked zombies very well," Chameleon said. But she nerved herself to respond to the thing. "We came to see the Zombie Master. It's urgent."

"Thish waa," the zombie said. It turned, dropping a piece of its arm on the ground. Zombies had the ability to lose material continually without losing mass; it was part of their magic.

They followed it into the castle. Once they got past the decrepit outer wall, an amazing change occurred. The stone became firm and clear and the wood solid and polished. Healthy curtains draped the hall. There was no further sign of rot.

"Millie must have laid down the law," Chameleon murmured. "He has his way outside, she has it her way inside. A good compromise, the kind men and women often arrive at."

"Eh?" something inquired.

They both looked. A huge human ear had sprouted from the wall, and a mouth opened to the side.

Chameleon laughed. "Tell your mother she has visitors, Hi," she said.

Imbri remembered now: the Zombie Master had twin children, eleven years old, named Hiatus and Lacuna.

"Then sign in, dummy," the lips said.

There ahead of them was a big guest book. Chameleon dismounted, going to the book. "Oh, see who has signed in before!" she exclaimed. "Satan, Lucifer, Gabriel, Jack the Ripper, King Roogna—"

"Lacky's talent is changing print," Imbri reminded her in a dreamlet.

"Oh, of course; I remember," Chameleon said. She signed the book, watching to make sure her signature didn't change to something awful. Then Imbri set her right forehoof on the page, imprinting her signature-map of the moon, with MARE IMBRIUM highlighted.

"Chameleon! I'm so glad to see you again!" It was Millie, no longer a ghost. Her talent was sex appeal, and, like Chameleon, she remained true to her nature as she matured. She was now about eight hundred and forty years old, with only the forty really counting, and looked as pretty as her visitor.

The two women hugged each other. "It's been so long!" Chameleon exclaimed. "Hasn't it been eight years since you visited Castle Roogna?"

"And then only because Jonathan had to be King for a while. That was simply awful! He doesn't like indulging in politics."

Chameleon sobered. "I have bad news for you, Millie."

Millie looked at her, quickly turning serious herself. "You came on business!"

"Terrible business. I apologize."

"The King—"

"Is ill. Too ill to rule."

"Your son Dor—"

"Is similarly ill."

"Chameleon, that's horrible! But—"

"The Zombie Master must be King now, as he was before, until the crisis is past."

Millie looked stricken. "King Trent—he was getting old—we knew that sometime he would—but your son is in his prime—"

"He was ensorcelled."

Millie stared at her for a long moment. Then her face began losing its cohesion, as if she were becoming a ghost again. "I was Dor's governess! I always liked him—and he rescued Jonathan for me. He fetched the elixir that made Jonathan whole. And in doing that, he gave me back my happiness. I really owe him everything. How could something like that happen to him?"

"He got married. Then he was King. Then he won a battle against the Nextwave. Then he—"

"Oh, Chameleon!" Millie cried, horror-stricken.

Now at last Chameleon collapsed, her burden shared. "My son! What will I do without my son? I was ready to, to let him be married, but this—he's almost dead!" She was crying openly now.

Millie embraced her again, joining her in tears. "Oh, I know what it is to be almost dead! Oh, Chameleon, I'm so sorry!"

Imbri did not wish sorrow on anyone; that was part of what had made her lose her effectiveness on dream duty. It seemed she had been thrust into a reality with horrors worse than those of dreams. She had worried about Chameleon's lack of reaction to Dor's loss. Now she realized that Chameleon had come to the right place; Millie the Ghost had known Dor almost as closely as his mother had. Shared grief was easier to bear than isolated grief.

A man appeared in the far doorway. He was of middle age, dourly handsome, and wearing a black suit. He was the Zombie Master, the Magician from Xanth's past.

"You are a night mare," the Zombie Master said to Imbri. "I am familiar with your kind. Speak to me in your fashion."

Imbri realized that it would be some time before the women were able to communicate intelligibly. Quickly she sent a dream that summarized the situation, showing pictures of Kings Trent and Dor lying mindlessly on beds in Castle Roogna, with the grieving widows sitting beside them. Xanth needed a new King.

"I had hoped this type of crisis would not come again," the Zombie Master said gravely. "I have seen prior Waves, in life and death. This one must be abated. I will go with you to Castle Roogna tonight. Chameleon can remain here with my family."

"But you must bring your zombies!" Imbri sent.

"I fear there is no time for that. At any rate, most of them are already at Castle Roogna. They will have to do the job."

"But how will Chameleon get home, when—?"

"We have Magician Humfrey's magic carpet here, on

loan but never returned. She can use that when she is ready. But she will be more comfortable here for the time being, I believe."

"I don't know—" Imbri demurred.

"If what you tell me is true, I am now King Pro Tem. Balk me not, mare."

That was the truth. King Jonathan the Zombie Master bade farewell to his wife and children, then mounted Imbri, who trotted out into the night. She returned to the gourd patch, warned the Zombie Master not to be alarmed at what he might perceive, and dived in.

This time they entered Phantom Land. The phantoms swooped in, howling.

"Say, haven't I seen you before?" the Zombie Master asked, looking directly at one phantom. The thing paused, startled.

"They are trying to scare you," Imbri sent.

"Naturally. I am in the same business." He concentrated on the phantom. "Beside Specter Lake, about seven hundred years ago. I was the zombie Jonathan, keeping company with a ghost. You—"

The phantom brightened, literally. It remembered.

"But that was in Xanth," the Zombie Master continued. "How did you get in here?"

The phantom made a gesture of holding an object and of looking closely at it.

"Oh—you peeped into a gourd," the Zombie Master said. "And got trapped inside."

The phantom nodded.

"But I suppose one place is as good as another for your kind," the Zombie Master concluded. "You can operate here as readily as in Xanth, and you have companions of your own kind. And the useful occupation of acting in cautionary dreams."

The phantom made a gesture of appreciative agreement. Someone understood! Then it moved on, evidently having business elsewhere. Dreams were too important to be delayed by social meetings.

Imbri moved on also. She should have known that the Magician would not be frightened by routine horrors!

They passed through a region of spinning nebulae, avoiding the brightest and hottest of them. Then on into a forest so thick with giant spiders that Imbri had to weave between their legs to get through. Then on out the peephole of a gourd near Castle Roogna, and to the castle itself.

"You certainly have an efficient mode of travel," the Zombie Master remarked.

The two widows were grieving by the two Kings, dry-eyed and sleepless, exactly as Imbri had shown them in her dream for the new King. Imbri brought the Zombie Master right into the bedroom where both Kings lay like corpses, side by side.

The Zombie Master dismounted and approached. "This ascension is not of my choosing," he said to the women. "Allow me to verify their condition. Perhaps they can be revived."

He put his hand on Dor's forehead. "He does not respond to my power. He is not dead."

"No, not dead," Irene agreed in a whisper. "Ensorcelled."

"Of course. We shall track down the source of that ensorcellment," the Zombie Master said. "Magician Humfrey surely can do that. But at the moment we must stop the advance of the Nextwave, about which the good mare Imbri has kindly informed me. I have fought a Wave before, in my prior life; my zombies alone are not sufficient, but, abetted by a formidable natural barrier such as—what is it, something that crosses Xanth—"

"The Gap Chasm," Irene said. "You moved too far from it, so have almost forgotten it because of the forget-spell on it."

"Just so. The Gap Chasm. My zombies can guard the bridges and destroy them if necessary. I shall need a lieutenant who is familiar with Castle Roogna and the recent events. I can not afford to waste time updating myself about recent changes in the castle."

"Grundy the Golem," Irene said. "And Ichabod the Mundane; he knows all about the enemy. And Chet and Chem Centaur. And, of course, Mare Imbri."

"Indeed," the Magician agreed dourly, and left the room. Imbri followed.

Soon there was another council of war. Grundy and Ichabod reported all relevant details of their spy mission, and Chet Centaur gave the details of the battle with the Punics and the manner in which King Dor had been enchanted.

The Zombie Master pondered. "There seems to be a pattern here," he remarked. "In each case the King was alone, though seemingly well guarded. In each case the enchantment occurred by night. I suspect we have a nocturnal enemy who can strike at a moderate distance, or who is able to pass guards unobserved. Whom do we know who could do that?"

"A night mare," Imbri said in a general dreamlet. "My kind can become insubstantial and invisible by night and can project dreams from a small distance. But we can't ensorcell."

"A night mare," the King repeated, removing the crown. It fitted him well enough, but he evidently was not comfortable with such trappings and preferred to dispense with them. "Could there be a renegade, one with special powers?"

"I know of no renegade among residents of the gourd," Imbri sent. "The Night Stallion has special powers—but he is loyal to Xanth and never leaves the gourd. All other dark horses lack mental powers, other than dream projection, and regular horses lack even that. There are only the Mundane horses anyway, completely unmagical."

"There's the day horse," Grundy said. "But he's stupid."

"Not completely stupid," Imbri sent. "He seems smarter as he becomes accustomed to our ways. Still, I don't see how he could be the sorcerer, even if he had night power. Twice he helped us against the Mundanes. He freed me from the Horseman and carried Chameleon on the spy mission."

"I did not mean to implicate horses," the Zombie Master said. "Could some other creature develop similar powers?"

Chet shrugged. The gesture started at his human shoulders and rippled down along his equine forepart. "Anything is possible. Perhaps a variant of a basilisk, who stuns instead of kills. Or a groupie-fish, stealing souls. Obviously *some* creature or person can destroy Kings."

"One smart enough to recognize a King, since they're the only ones taken," Grundy put in.

"Precisely," the Zombie Master said. "And I am surely the next target. There is one thing you should know about me: I was a zombie for eight hundred years. I was restored to life by a special elixir Dor obtained, and I owe him an eternal debt of gratitude. I retain the power to animate myself as a zombie, should I suffer an untimely demise. So if the mysterious enemy should strike me down and I die, you must locate my zombie and question it. Perhaps the identity of the mysterious enchanter will be revealed."

They all nodded sober agreement. What a grim way to locate an enemy!

"Now I must rouse the Castle Roogna guardian zombies and march them tonight to the Chasm. It is surely our only chance to get there before the Nextwave does. Timing is critical."

"The zombies are already mostly roused," Grundy said. "Dor and Irene got married less than a week ago in the zombie graveyard."

"That would rouse them," the Zombie Master agreed with a gaunt smile. "Zombies love weddings and similar morbidities. Now I must go organize them into an army. The rest of you get some sleep. Report to the Chasm at dawn, armed. I may need some of you living folk to be captains, as zombies do not think too well." He left the room, going to gather his forces.

"Captain of a zombie troop!" Grundy said. "Well, why not? Zombies aren't bad people, once you get used to the smell."

Imbri remembered the brief dream contact she had had with one zombie at the wedding: maggoty blood pudding. Zombies might not be bad people, but they were hardly pleasant companions. Still, as warriors against the Mundanes, the zombies had definite promise.

At dawn, imperfectly rested, they reported as directed. The King had already ranged his zombies along the Chasm and behind trees. The Mundanes could cross only where the bridges were, and since one bridge was one-way from south to north and another was invisible, the third was the obvious choice. It was visible and solid, with a well-worn path to it.

The Mundanes had had a full intervening day to regroup and travel, and they had not wasted it. At midmorning they arrived at the Gap Chasm, following the main path. They had evidently learned that straying from the path was to invite assorted and awful hazards. The wilderness of Xanth had ways to enforce its strictures.

Immediately the zombies closed on them, throwing chunks of rotting flesh and fragments of bone in lieu of missiles.

The Nextwavers reacted exactly as they were supposed to. They screamed and retreated in confusion. Mundanes were prejudiced against zombies, as they were against ghosts, ghouls, vampires, werewolves, and similarly innocent creatures, and tended to avoid physical contact with them.

Then Hasbinbad appeared, gesticulating. Again he rallied his errant army. The potency of a good leader was manifest; the motley crew became a determined force. The Mundanes began attacking the zombies, shooting arrows into them. Naturally the arrows had no effect; they could not kill what was already dead. Other Mundanes hacked at the zombies with their swords. This was more effective, for Zombies could not function well without limbs or heads.

But the Mundane's aversion to the zombies handicapped them, and many living men were brought down by the walking dead. Soon the ground was littered with bones and flesh, fresh-dead mixed with un-dead.

Now Hasbinbad led a charge to the main bridge. His surviving men followed in a hastily formed phalanx, their overlapping shields brushing aside the zombies. The Mundanes were winning the battle.

"We have to deal with that leader," the Zombie Master muttered. "Without him, they are nothing; with him, they will prevail."

Imbri had to agree: leadership made all the difference. Had King Trent remained active, the Wave would not have gotten this far. King Dor, too, had been winning. How could Xanth defend itself when it kept losing its leaders just as they got the hang of it?

A picked squad of zombies guarded the bridge. These were zombie animals, more formidable than zombie people.

Hasbinbad came up against a zombie wyvern. The small dragon was in bad condition, even for its kind, and shed scales and flesh with every motion. The Mundane chief hacked at its snout with his sword. The snout exploded like a rotten log; teeth, tongue, nostrils, and eyeballs showered down around the Mundanes. Then the wyvern fought back, exhaling a belch of fire. The fire was as decrepit as the creature, drooling out greenishly and licking at Hasbinbad's feet. It was hot, though; the Mundane danced back out of the way with a green hotfoot.

When the gasp of fire faded, the Nextwaver advanced again. He lopped off the rest of the wyvern's head. Ears, brains, and tonsils flew up in slices, showering the Mundanes again. But the bare neck thrust forward, jamming into Hasbinbad's face, squirting candy-striped pus, forcing him to retreat a second time.

Again the man struck. Vertebrae, muscles, and stringy nerves flung out, festooning the Waver's sword arm. But still the man pressed forward—and received a faceful of watery blood that pumped out of the truncated torso. He shook himself off as if not quite believing this was happening, wiped the gook out of his eyes with the back of his left fist, then slashed some more, heedless of the guts and tatters of skin that burst out and wrapped about his body. He now resembled a zombie himself.

"That Mundane is determined," the Zombie Master remarked.

"He's the one who brought them through the snow-covered Mundane mountains of Halp," Grundy said. "From Ghoul to Hitaly. He's one smart, ruthless cuss."

A zombie ant lion pounced at the Mundane leader. This was a relatively new zombie, not very far decayed. The lion-head roared, showing excellent teeth, and the ant-body had six healthy legs and a stinger. The creature was alert to the strikes of the sword, dodging out of the way. Few zombies had any sense of self-preservation; even Hasbinbad recognized this as unusual.

Another Mundane emerged from the phalanx, aiming an arrow at the ant lion. But three zombie goblins charged at him, grabbing for his legs.

Then the other Mundanes got into the action. Soon they had dispatched the ant lion and goblins, together with zombie frogs, rabbits, and a watery-eyed hydraulic ram. As the ram fell into the Gap, the gore- and rot-strewn men stood at the very edge of the bridge.

On the bridge, however, was a zombie python, buttressed by zombie roaches, a zombie flying fish, and a zombie cockatrice. The Mundanes concentrated on the python, apparently not recognizing the genuinely dangerous monster, the cock. Hasbinbad tackled the snake's head, distracting it so that two other Mundanes could skirt it and start across the bridge.

"That chief's valor has just preserved his life," the Zombie Master murmured.

The two Wavers on the bridge trod diligently on the roaches, which popped and squished with assorted ghastly sounds, depending on their state of preservation. The Wavers swished their swords at the flying fish, who darted around their heads, squirting mouthfuls of stagnant water. Then the first Mundane came face to snoot with the cockatrice.

There was a moment's pause before the Mundane dissolved into green goop and slurped off the bridge. A living cockatrice could convert a living creature to a corpse by the mere force of its gaze, but a zombie cockatrice lacked full power. Instead it halfway melted creatures to muscle rot.

The second Mundane charged the little monster—and he, too, melted into putrescence and plopped into the Chasm. There was a choking sound from below; the Gap Dragon had arrived on the scene and snapped up the gob. Now the poor dragon had mild indigestion.

"Avert your gaze! Use your shields!" Hasbinbad bawled, so loudly that Imbri heard it all the way across the Chasm.

One brave Nextwaver obliged. The man pulled his helmet over his eyes, raised his shield, and edged out onto the bridge, guided by the guardrails. Listening to yelled instructions from his leader, he oriented on the cockatrice and finally used the bottom edge of his shield to sweep the little monster off the bridge.

The cockatrice fell, and the Gap Dragon had recovered enough to snap it up. There was a gulp, then a kind of stifled belch. Now the dragon had a real pain in the gut.

"I don't like this at all," the Zombie Master muttered. "Those Nextwavers are too strong for us. We may be forced to destroy the bridge."

"I can bring them down singly as they cross," Chet said, holding his bow ready.

The Zombie Master considered. "It seems worth a try, though I am skeptical of its eventual success. There are quite a number of Mundanes who have not yet seen battle; the bridge is too small a compass. We have held them so far only because they can not bring their full force to bear, but they will surely overwhelm us before long."

Hasbinbad had by now dispatched the zombie serpent. Now the Nextwave started across the bridge, single file.

Chet nocked an arrow, aimed, and let fly. The shaft arced across the gulf, then thunked into the face of the leading Mundane. The man collapsed and fell into the Chasm.

The second Nextwaver elevated his shield to protect his face. The centaur's second arrow struck him on the exposed thigh. The man screamed, lost his balance, and fell.

The third Nextwaver held his shield low, but waited until the centaur aimed, watching closely. When the arrow flew at his head, he used his shield to intercept it—and got caught by Chet's second arrow, aimed at his leg.

In this manner, Chet methodically dispatched six Mundanes, using as many arrows on each as were necessary to do the job. Then he ran out of arrows.

Now the Mundanes double-timed across the bridge, one after the other. They had taken the unavoidable losses and finally were charging to victory. Their depth of numbers, so feared by the Zombie Master, was taking effect.

"The bridge!" the Zombie Master snapped.

Chet brought out his sword and hacked at the cables that supported the bridge. They severed, but the walk held, so he chopped into that, too.

"Hold!" the first Mundane bawled, seeing what was happening. Of course Chet continued desperately chopping. Chem swung her rope, looping the first Mundane just before he reached solid ground, and yanked him off the walkway.

Still the tough planks of the bridge resisted Chet's sword. This was a job for an axe, and they had none. Imbri wished that Smash the Ogre were here—but he had been delegated to defend Castle Roogna itself, in case of complete disaster, since the palace guard of zombies was no longer there. The Zombie Master had been warned about the missing reserve force of Mundanes, which might even now be circling to take Castle Roogna from the rear. The ogre was also on the lookout for who ever or whatever lurked in the vicinity, enchanting the Kings. So it was a necessary post, and Smash could not be spared for action farther afield.

The next Nextwaver leaped across the opening crevice in the bridge—only to be met by the Zombie Master's own sword. Stabbed neatly through the heart, he died, falling headlong on the ground.

The Zombie Master bent to touch the dead man—and this Mundane revived. He stood up, blood dripping from his chest. "Master!" he rasped.

"Guard this bridge," the Zombie Master ordered him. "Let no living creature pass."

The new zombie faced the Chasm, sword in hand, while Chet continued chopping. As the next Mundane came across, the zombie drove fiercely at him with that sword.

"Hey!" the next one cried. "You're on *our* side!"

"No more," the zombie Mundane grunted, and slashed again. The other warrior danced aside, startled—and stepped off the bridge.

Now at last Chet got through the final board. The weight of the crossing soldiers snapped the remaining tie. The bridge pulled away from its mooring and flopped down into the Gap Chasm. Screaming, a dozen Mundanes fell with it.

Hasbinbad stood at the far side. "That won't stop me!" he bawled. "I'll cross anyway and wipe you out! You're finished, King Zombie!"

Imbri swished her tail in fury, but the Zombie Master turned away. "My proper business is reanimating the dead, not killing the living," he said. "I have been responsible for destroying more lives this day than ever elsewhere in my life. I concede the necessity but detest the reality. Pray that the Chasm holds them back, sparing us further malice."

"We'll have to watch them, though," Grundy said. "To be sure. I don't trust Hasbinbad."

"My minions will watch." The Zombie Master walked away from the Chasm. "But we shall be near to reinforce them, until we know the Nextwavers have given up."

Imbri looked back. Hasbinbad the Carthaginian still stood at the brink of the Chasm, yelling and shaking his fist. ". . . take you out, too, Zombie King!" his voice came faintly. "Just like the Transformer and Firetalk Kings . . ."

So the attacks on the Kings were definitely connected to the Mundane invasion! But *how*? Until they had the answer, they could not even take reasonable precautions against it.

They found a tent in the forest near the Chasm that a large tent caterpillar had left. This was the very best natural shelter available, fashioned of the finest silk; tent caterpillars made themselves very comfortable before they magically transformed themselves to winged form and took off. The King retired for necessary sleep, as he had not rested the prior night. Chet and Grundy stood guard by the tent, beating a path around it in a circle, watching for any possible sign of intrusion, while Chem galloped back toward Castle Roogna with news of the battle.

Imbri found a forest glade close by that had good pasturage. She grazed and slept, for it had been long since she had eaten and rested properly, and this constant physical existence was wearing. No wonder the material creatures soon aged and died; they simply wore out!

After an hour's munching and cogitation—grazing was always the best time to chew on concepts, between snoozes—Imbri became aware of the approach of another animal. It was the day horse. She nickered to him gladly, discovering that she had missed him these past two hectic days. "Where have you been?" she projected.

"Staying well away from the Mundanes," he replied in

the dream. "They have been coming south, frightening me; I think they are chasing me down."

"You're beautiful, but not bold," she informed him. "We had two battles with them, and have halted them only at the Gap Chasm."

"I know. I heard the clamor. Have you really stopped them?"

"I think so. We cut the main bridge across the Chasm, and they don't know about the invisible bridge to the east. If they try to climb down through the Gap, the Gap Dragon will get them. They've already lost about forty more men today."

"Xanth won't be safe until all of them are gone, especially the Horseman."

Imbri remembered the double warning to beware the Horseman, and understood the horse's personal concern. She had felt those spurs herself! Still, she wasn't sure he was the worst threat. For one thing, there had been no sign of him among the Mundanes recently; he must be with the reserve force, way up in northern Xanth, so was no present threat. "Especially Hasbinbad, too," she amended.

"He's just a brute man. He drives straight ahead and hacks away at anything. But the Horseman is devious and clever; he is the true leader and your real enemy."

The day horse certainly was hung up on that! "But we haven't seen him since we escaped the Punics."

"That means he's up to something. Until you nullify him, you'll never sleep securely."

Imbri didn't argue further. If the Night Stallion and Good Magician Humfrey both felt the Horseman was the real danger, he probably was. But in what way? That wasn't clear at all. What could even the smartest, least scrupulous Mundane do to harm a Kingdom of magic?

They grazed together for an hour. Then, as night came on, the day horse departed, traveling south, away from the Mundanes, seeking his safe haven. Imbri snorted indulgently to herself. He was excellent company, but he had his idiosyncracies. The Mundanes couldn't get him as long as they were north of the Chasm. And if they came south of it by some infernal miracle, all he had to do was run; no man afoot could gain on a healthy horse, and the trees of the jungle would block an attack by bows and arrows.

Imbri returned to the Zombie Master's tent at night, phasing through trees and hillocks. She found Grundy alert; he spotted her the moment she returned to material form. "You don't catch me sleeping on the job, mare!" he said, smirking. "Though if you stayed invisible, I'd have a problem. I'll admit that much."

"Perhaps I should maintain invisible guard," Imbri sent.

"No, you have to graze and rest yourself," the golem said, perhaps not wanting to share the honor of guarding the King.

"I could check invisibly every hour or so."

"Well—" Then Grundy had a notion. "Could I go with you when you do?"

"Certainly. You would be invisible, too."

"Goody! Let's check now."

Imbri let him jump on her back. Then she phased out of sight and walked through the tent wall. The Zombie Master was sleeping peacefully. Imbri sent a dream into his mind. "Hello, your Majesty," she said in her dream form, this time a reasonably well-preserved female zombie. "It's only Mare Imbrium. Are you comfortable?"

"Quite comfortable, thank you, mare," the King replied. "Except that I miss my family. Do you think you could put them in this dream?"

"Certainly," Imbri said, her zombie image shedding a hank of moldy hair in approved fashion. She concentrated, and in a moment Millie the Ghost appeared, somewhat faintly, but quite beautiful, radiating sex appeal.

"Oh, Jonathan!" Millie said. "I love you so much!" She opened her arms to him.

"Now this is what I call a good dream!" the Zombie Master exclaimed, encompassing her. Their love had endured the eight hundred years while he was a zombie and she a ghost; evidently the flesh had not weakened it. Imbri, having recently made the transition to mortality herself, could understand this better than she might have before she left dream duty. There was a special intensity to physical existence that insubstantial creatures could not experience.

Then an eye popped open in the nearby wall. Print appeared beside it. MUSH! MUSH! YUCK!

"Go to your room, children!" the Zombie Master snapped. "Go make your own dreams!"

Cowed, the eye and print faded. The Zombie Master kissed his wife, who responded passionately. If there was one thing Millie was really good at, it was passion.

Then the Magician's eyes went blank. He froze in place.

"Jonathan," Millie asked, alarmed, "what's the matter?"

But the Zombie Master did not respond. He simply stood there, staring through her.

Imbri was abruptly out of the dream—for there was no longer a mind to receive it. "He's been taken!" she sent to Grundy. "Right while he was dreaming!"

"But no one's here but us!" the golem protested. "Imbri, you didn't—?"

"No! I don't do that to people! I *can't*. And wouldn't if I could. This was not the work of any night mare. I would have recognized any who came, and none came, anyway!"

"I'll investigate this," Grundy said. "Make us solid, quickly."

She materialized, there in the tent. Grundy jumped down. He made a whispering, rustling sound, talking to a patch of grass within the tent. "The grass didn't see anything," he said.

"Maybe outside the tent—"

Grundy lifted up the flap and scrambled out. Imbri phased through the wall and trotted to Chet. "The King's been ensorcelled!" she sent to the centaur. "Just now!"

"But Grundy was on guard!" he cried, snapping alert.

"So was I. But the King went from right under my nose—in the middle of a dream I sent!"

"Hey, I've got it!" Grundy cried from the tent area. "This tree says there was a man here a moment ago. He climbed in the tree, then jumped down and ran away."

Chet galloped over to the golem. "Who was it? Anyone we know?"

"The tree can't identify him," Grundy said. "All men look alike to trees. Anyway, it was dark, and he seems to be a stranger to this glade. He could be anyone, Xanthian or Mundane."

"He must be Xanthian," Imbri sent. "Obviously he has magic: he threw a spell to blank out the King, then ran away."

"Why didn't it blank us out, too?" Grundy asked.

"We weren't material. The spell must have passed right through us."

"Or it was aimed specifically at the King, as the other spells were," Chet said. "I agree; it has to be Xanthian. Someone with the power to cloud men's minds. A traitor among us, taking out our Kings in the midst of a crisis so we can't organize a good defense against the Nextwave."

"Exactly as Hasbinbad threatened," Imbri sent. "This is no coincidence; this is enemy action."

Grundy was pursuing the trail, questioning grass, bushes, and trees. But soon the path crossed a rocky region that led into a river, and was lost. "King Dor could have handled this; he talks to the inanimate. But—"

"But King Dor has already been taken," Chet finished. "Oh, we're in terrible trouble! What will we say to the others?"

"The truth," Grundy said. "We were watching the King, instead of the surroundings, and we got skunked. We need a new King—again."

"I'll go!" Imbri sent. "I can reach Castle Roogna quickly. The Queens must be told."

"Take me with you," Grundy said, leaping onto her back. "Chet, you notify the zombies. They'll have to defend the Gap Chasm as well as they can without their master."

"Yes," the centaur agreed. "I fear the Punics will pass the Chasm. But we should have a few days to prepare for their next onslaught." He looked at the fallen King. "And I'll carry him back to Castle Roogna."

This was becoming almost commonplace, this disposition of the Kings of Xanth! Imbri felt the shock, but not as hard as it had been when King Trent and King Dor were taken.

Imbri phased out and charged through the night toward the nearest gourd patch. She knew the location of most of the hypnogourds of Xanth, since the night mares used them for exits. "Brace yourself for a strange environment," she warned the golem.

"It can't be worse than what we know now in Xanth," Grundy muttered.

Imbri feared he was right. The Kings were being taken faster now; where would it end? How could the loyal defenders of Xanth stop it, when the sorcery could happen right while they were watching?

Chapter 9. Good King Humfrey

Queen Iris met them at Castle Roogna. "Somehow I knew it," she said. "Every time we get our defense going well, we lose our King. I have been mourning for my husband when I should have been protecting his successors. You two go directly to Good Magician Humfrey; he must be the next King. Don't let him put you off; the old curmudgeon can't refuse this time! I'll send word to Millie the Ghost, if a regular night mare hasn't beaten me to it, and will organize things here at the castle. Tell Humfrey this is pre-emptive; he's the last male Magician of Xanth and must assume the office immediately, and no gnomish grumbling."

Imbri realized that the old Queen still had considerable spirit and competence. Now that the crisis was deepening, she was putting aside her personal grief and shock to do what needed to be done. She was providing some leadership during the vacuum. Grundy had commented with innocent malice on the uselessness of the Queen, whom King Trent had married mainly out of courtesy; now Imbri knew directly that there was much more to it than that. Queen Iris's grief was genuine, but so was her mettle.

Fortunately, Imbri's century and a half of night labors had inured her somewhat to busy nights. The golem remounted and they galloped for the Good Magician's castle.

She used the same gourd patches she had taken with Chameleon, but her rider was different and so the gourd terrain differed. This time they charged through a region of carnivorous clouds that reached for them with funnel-shaped, whirling, sucking snouts and turbulent gusts. They whistled with rage when unable to consume this seeming prey. Clouds tended to be vocally expressive.

Then there was a forest of animate trees whose branches clutched at them and whose leaves slurped hungrily, but these, too, failed. Finally they threaded through a field of striking weapons—swords, clubs, and spears moving with random viciousness, nooses tightening, and metallic magic tubes belching fire, noise, and fragments. Yet again they passed through safely, for Imbri was long familiar with this region. The world of the gourd had to supply everything that was required for bad dreams, and weapons were prominent.

"This is a fun scene you have in your gourd," Grundy remarked, relaxing once he realized they were safely through.

They emerged near the Good Magician's castle and charged through its walls and into its halls. Humfrey was in his study, as usual poring over a huge tome. He looked up glumly as Imbri and Grundy materialized. "So it has come at last to this," he muttered. "For a century I have avoided the onerous aspect of politics, and now you folk have bungled me into a corner."

"Yes, sir," Grundy said. The golem was halfway respectful, for Humfrey had enabled him to become real, long ago when he had been unreal. Also, Humfrey was about to come into considerably more power. "You have to bite the bullet and be King."

"Xanth has no bullets," Humfrey grumped. "That's a Mundane anachronism." He scowled as his old eyes scanned a shelf on which sat a row of magic bullets, giving him the lie. "I'm not the last Magician of Xanth, you know."

"Arnolde Centaur doesn't count," Grundy said. "His talent only works outside Xanth, and anyway, he's not human."

"Both arguments are specious. His turn will come. But first must come Bink; he will be King after me."

"Bink?" the golem cried incredulously. "Dor's father? He has no magic at all! King Trent had to cancel the rule of magic for citizenship, just so Bink could stay in Xanth."

"Bink is a Magician," Humfrey insisted. "Possibly the most potent one alive. For the first quarter century of his life, no one knew it; for the second quarter, only a select few knew it. Now all Xanth must know it, for Xanth needs him. Bear that in your ugly little mind, golem, for you will have to pass the word. Perhaps Bink will break the chain."

"Breaking the chain!" Imbri sent. "That's your advice for saving Xanth from the Nextwave!"

"Yes, indeed," Humfrey agreed. "But it is proving hard to do. I shall not succeed, and I am unable to prophesy beyond my own doom. But I think Bink is the one most likely to break it—or perhaps his wife will."

Golem and mare exchanged a glance. Had the Good Magician lost what few wits remained to him?

The Gorgon appeared in the doorway. A heavy opaque veil covered her face completely. "I have packed your spells and your lunch, my love," she murmured.

"And my socks?" Humfrey snapped. "What about my spare socks?"

"Those, too," she said. "I might forget a spell, but never something as important as your spare socks." She smiled wryly under the veil and set a tied bag before him on the desk.

"Not on the open tome!" he exclaimed. "You'll muss the pages!"

The Gorgon moved the bag to the side of the book. Then she dropped to her knees before Humfrey. "Oh, my lord, must you go into this thing? Can't you rule from here?"

"What's this 'my love, my lord' business?" Grundy demanded. "The Gorgon kneels to no one!"

Humfrey picked up the bag. "What must be must be," he said. "So it is written—there." He jammed a gnarled finger on the open page of the tome.

Imbri looked. The book said: IT IS NOT FOR THE GOOD MAGICIAN TO BREAK THE CHAIN.

The Gorgon's veil was darkening as moisture soaked through it. Imbri was amazed; could this fearsome creature be crying? "My lord, I implore you—at least let me come with you, to petrify your enemies!"

Grundy looked at her with sudden, horrified understanding. "To petrify—and she wears a concealing veil she wouldn't need for an invisible face. The Gorgon's been loosed!"

"Her power must not be loosed prematurely," Humfrey said. "Not till the King of Xanth so directs, or it will be wasted and Xanth will fall. She must fetch her sister for the time when the two of them are needed."

"But how will we know?" the Gorgon demanded. "You restored the Siren's dulcimer and have it waiting for her here. But we may not even *have* a King of Xanth, let alone one who knows what to direct!"

"Someone will know," Humfrey said. "Mare Imbrium, I must borrow you until I recover my flying carpet. Golem, you must baby-sit this castle until the girls return."

"Me? But—"

"Or until need calls you elsewhere."

"What need?" the golem asked, baffled.

"You will know when it manifests." Humfrey cocked a forefinger at the miniature man. "Do not diddle with my books. And leave my spells bottled."

"But suppose I'm thirsty?"

"Some of those bottled spells would turn you into a giant—"

"A giant!" the golem exclaimed happily.

"—purple bugbear," the Gorgon concluded, and the golem's excitement faded.

The Magician climbed onto Imbri, using a corner of his desk as a stepping block. He was small, old, and infirm, and Imbri was afraid he would fall. Then he hauled up the heavy bag of spells and almost did fall as it overbalanced him. "I'd better use a fixative spell," he muttered. He opened the bag and rummaged in it. He brought out a bottle, worked out the cork, and spilled a plaid drop.

A plaid banshee formed and sailed out through the ceiling with a trailing wail.

"Wrong bottle," the Gorgon said, standing. "Here, let me get it." She reached into the bag and drew forth a white bottle. She popped the cork and spilled out a drop. Immediately it expanded into a white bubble that floated toward Imbri and the Magician, overlapped them, and shrank suddenly about them, cementing Humfrey and his bag firmly to the mare's back.

"You see, you do need me," the Gorgon said. "I know where every spell is packed."

"Stay," Humfrey said, as if addressing a puppy. "Move out, mare."

Imbri moved out, phasing through the wall and leaping down to the ground beyond the moat. In her insubstantial state, such leaps were safe.

They were on their way to Castle Roogna, but Imbri was dissatisfied. "Why didn't you let her be with you?" she sent reprovingly to the Magician. "The Gorgon really seems to care for you."

"Of course she cares for me, the idiot!" Humfrey snapped. "She's a better wife than I deserve. Always was."

"But then—"

"Because I don't want her to see me wash out," he said. "A man my age has few points of pride, and my doom will be ignominious."

That seemed to cover it. Humfrey loved the Gorgon; his way of showing it was subtle. Still, Imbri had a question. "If you know you will fail, and are only going to your doom, why do you go at all?"

"To buy time and allow my successor to return from Mundania," Humfrey replied. "Xanth must have a King, a Magician King, and Bink is the next. But he is in Mundania. Without a King, Xanth will fall to the Nextwave."

"But to go to your death—"

"It is not death, precisely," Humfrey said. "But since I can not be sure it will not in due course become death, I do not care to temporize. My wife will perform better if not handicapped by hope. I have locked up hope."

"That is a cruel mechanism," Imbri sent, shuddering as they entered the eye of a gourd.

"No more cruel than the dreams of night mares," he retorted.

The raw material of those bad dreams now surrounded them. Mirrors loomed before them, distorting their reflections, so that Humfrey resembled now a goblin, now a squat ghoul, now an imp, while Imbri passed through stages of bovine, ursine, and caprine resemblances. They entered a region of paper, where nothing existed that was not formed of painted paper, and the birds and animals were folded paper.

"This is fascinating," Humfrey said. "But I have more immediate business. Mare, I mean to unriddle the identity of the hidden enemy before he takes me out. I will record his name on a magic slate and hide it in a bottle he can not find. You must salvage that bottle and recover that Answer so that my successor may have it."

"You are the Magician of Information," Imbri sent. "How is it you do not know the Answer?"

"Some knowledge is self-destructive," Humfrey replied. "Some Answers I could fathom, but my fathoming would cause the situation to change, perhaps creating uglier Questions than the ones answered. But mainly, I can not accurately foretell a future of which I am an integral part, and the discovery of the identity of the ensorceller is in that future. Answers might seem valid but be false, because of my conflict of interest."

Imbri could not quite understand that, but decided it probably made humanish sense. After all, the Good Magician was supposed to know.

They emerged from the gourd in the patch nearest to Castle Roogna and trotted toward the castle. Dawn was threatening, for Imbri's travels did take a certain amount of time. But she phased through the stone ramparts and delivered the Good Magician to the throne room, where Queen Iris awaited him.

"Excellent," she said. "The resources of this castle and of Xanth are at your disposal, Good King Humfrey."

"Naturally," Humfrey grumped. "Just let me dismount."

But he was unable to dismount, for the adhesion spell held him securely on Imbri's back. He had to fish in his bag for an antidote. He did not get it right the first time, instead releasing a flock of green doves, then a fat book

titled Mundane Fatuities; remarking that that had been lost
for some years and would now be useful for entertainment
reading, which was probably why the Gorgon had packed
it, he then brought out a rolled pair of polka-dot socks. The
Gorgon had indeed remembered! Finally he found the antidote and was free to return to his own two feet.

"Now let's review the situation," King Humfrey said.
"We've lost five Kings, with five to go—"

"What?" Queen Iris asked, startled.

"Five Kings," he repeated, irritated.

"What five?"

"Bink, Humfrey, Jonathan—"

"You're counting backward," Queen Iris said. "And you
and Bink haven't been lost yet—" She paused. "Bink?"

"I just told you, Iris!" Humfrey snapped.

"It was me you told, Magician," Imbri sent hastily.
"Bink is to succeed you as King."

"Same thing. You're both females. How can I remember
you apart? Now, the essential thing is to beware the Horseman and break the chain. Bink is the one most likely to—"

"But Bink has no magic!" Queen Iris protested.

"Stop interrupting, woman!" Humfrey snapped.

The Queen's notorious ire rose. Her standard evocation
of temper, black thunderclouds, boiled in the background,
split by jags of lightning. This was impressive, since they
were inside the castle. Imbri liked to generate similar
storms when she herself was angry, but hers remained
within the dreamer's mind. "Whom do you suppose you are
addressing, gnome?"

"*King* Gnome," Humfrey corrected, reaching into his
bag. He withdrew a vial, removed the cork, and shook out
a drop that scintillated at the lip of the container. As it fell,
the drop exploded in heat and light. The Queen's storm
cloud sizzled and shrank as if being fried in a hot pan, and
the lightning jags drooped limply. The Queen's display of
temper subsided. The Magician had made his point. He
had destroyed illusion.

"King Gnome," she repeated sullenly.

"The nature of Bink's talent is this," Humfrey said. "He
can not be harmed by magic. Since the Mundanes represent

a nonmagical menace, he may not be able to stop them—but he may be able to break the chain of lost Kings—"

"The chain of lost Kings!" Queen Iris exclaimed. "*That* was what you meant!"

"And thereby provide essential continuity of government for Xanth. Given that, the Mundane menace can be contained."

The Good Magician paused. When Queen Iris saw that he had finished, she ventured another question. "Why wasn't Bink's magic known before? He should have been King by now—"

"If it had been generally known that he was secure from the threats of magic, his enemies would have turned to nonmagical means to harm him," Humfrey explained. "Therefore his magic would betray him after all. So it protected him by protecting itself from revelation, making his immunity from magical harm seem coincidental. Only King Trent knew the secret, and he protected it rigorously, lest Bink's talent turn against him as a magical enemy. For Bink's magic is powerful indeed, however subtle its manifestation; in fifty years of his life, nothing magical has ever harmed him, though often it seemed to, or was aborted only by apparent coincidence. I myself was unable to fathom his secret."

"But obviously you know it now!" the Queen protested.

"I was able to penetrate it when he went to Mundania," Humfrey said smugly. "That temporarily nullified his power. I knew he had magic all along; I simply had not known its nature. But even after I ascertained this, I couldn't tell anyone. Until now, when he is away again—and must be recognized as the legitimate heir to the throne of Xanth."

"He shall be recognized," Queen Iris said grimly. "But how can there be five more Kings after him if he is to break the chain of Kings?"

"That detail is unclear to me," the Good Magician confessed. "Yet my references suggest it is so."

"How can there be five more Kings when there are no more Magicians in Xanth?" the Queen persisted.

"There is one more—Magician Arnolde," Humfrey said. "But he's a centaur!"

"Still a Magician."

"But his magic operates only beyond Xanth. Inside Xanth he has no power!"

"The law of Xanth does not specify what type of magic a Magician must have or where it should operate," Humfrey reminded her. "After Bink, Arnolde will be King."

"And after Arnolde?"

Humfrey spread his hands. "I would like to know that myself, but my references were opaque. If the full chain of future Kings were known, our hidden enemy might nullify them in advance; paradox preserves the secret."

Queen Iris shrugged. She evidently suspected Humfrey was getting senile, but didn't want to say it. "What can I do to help save Xanth, your Majesty?"

"Bide your time, woman. Acclaim each King as he comes. When the chain is broken, you will have your reward. The single thing you most desire."

"I've been biding my time while three Kings have been lost!" she exclaimed. Then, as an afterthought: "What single thing?"

"You don't know?"

"I asked, didn't I?"

"I don't remember. Whatever it is, you'll get it. Maybe before the chain breaks. Meanwhile, these are difficult times." Humfrey yawned. "Now let me sleep; later in the day I must bait my trap." He sighed. "Too bad it won't be effective." He reached into his bag again, brought out a small, folded wallet, and unfolded it lengthwise and breadthwise again and again, until it became a small folding cot. He lay down on this and commenced snoring.

Queen Iris shook her head. "Difficult times indeed!" she repeated. "They don't make Kings the way they used to. Humfrey always was the most annoying man."

There was a noise outside as the sun came up. Queen Iris walked to the largest window and opened it. The magic carpet sailed in and landed neatly on the floor. Chameleon was on it, slightly less pretty than before. "I just had to come," she said apologetically. "My husband is due home from Mundania tonight, and I have to be here to meet him."

Queen Iris greeted her with open arms. Imbri noted that

human women did a lot more hugging than did other creatures. "My dear, I have a lot to tell you, not much of it good." They moved into another room.

Imbri went down and out to the deserted zombie graveyard to graze and sleep on her feet. The best grazing was always around graves. She knew Magician King Humfrey would summon her when he needed her.

At noon Good King Humfrey summoned her back to the castle. "Carry me to the baobab tree," he said. "I shall set my trap there."

The baobab! That was where she had gone to meet the day horse! Would he be there today?

Chameleon appeared. "Your Majesty—may I go now to meet my husband? I want to be sure he does not blunder into the Mundanes, who are between him and here."

"He's due in the isthmus tonight," Humfrey said. Now that he was King, he did not seem at all vague or confused, though he remained stooped by age. "Imbri will fetch him then, when she can travel swiftly and safely."

"But I want to go with her," Chameleon said. "I've lost my King, my son, and my friend the Zombie Master; I must see to my husband myself."

Humfrey considered. "Perhaps this is wise. The Night Stallion believes you are important in coming events. There will be much to prepare Bink for, in the short time remaining to him. But you will need another steed. Arnolde will be with him, but the centaur will be tired; he is almost as old as I am, you know."

Imbri, of course, was older than either. But night mares were eternal. "The day horse!" she sent. "He helped before. He meets me at the baobab tree. He can be the second steed."

Humfrey's brow wrinkled even more than normal. "The day horse? I have not researched that one. Is he magic?"

"No, he's an escaped Mundane horse," Chameleon explained. "He is very nice. He would be an excellent companion."

The Magician shrugged. "As you wish." He loaded himself and his bag of tricks onto Imbri and spelled the works into place.

"We'll be back for you tonight!" Imbri sent in a dreamlet to Chameleon. Then she headed off, carefully using the doors and stairs, since this was solid day.

She trotted out to the baobab. She did not see the day horse—but of course he would hide from the Magician, being very shy of strangers. "Day horse!" Imbri sent. "It is all right! This is Good Magician King Humfrey."

The day horse came out from behind the upside-down tree. "He's not Mundane?" he asked within the dreamlet.

"Far from it! He's a great Magician. He knows everything."

The day horse stepped back, alarmed.

"Not everything," Humfrey grumped. "Only what I choose to research—and I haven't researched Mundane horses and don't have time now. Come on—we have to set up my spells."

The day horse hesitantly followed them inside. Humfrey spelled himself free of Imbri's back, then began setting out his devices. Bottles and vials and packages and books emerged from his bag in bewildering number and variety, until the volume of them was obviously more than the bag could have enclosed. Naturally the Magician used a magic bag that held an impossible amount.

"What are these things for?" Imbri asked in a dreamlet, her equine curiosity getting the better of her. She wasn't sure the Magician would deign to answer.

"It's best that you know," he said, surprising her. "First, I need to keep informed of the progress of the Nextwavers. Therefore I shall release these Spy I's." He opened a metallic container by rolling up its top on a kind of key. This seemed like an absolutely senseless way to package anything, but of course the Good Magician had his own ways of doing things. Inside were packed a score of white eyeballs. He shook the can, and several popped out and hovered in the air uncertainly.

"Go peek at the Gap Chasm," he directed them. "Snoop on the Mundanes. Set up a regular schedule of reports."

The balls flew off in a line. "Eye Spy!" they whistled as they departed.

Now Humfrey brought out a bundle of paper-thin doll cutouts. "I must also lure them to this spot so as not to endanger Castle Roogna," he said. He untied the string binding the cutouts, and the first ones began peeling off. As they did, they expanded and filled out. Hair unstuck itself and billowed about the head-sections; breasts popped forward from the upper torso-frames, and legs rounded from the lower portions. The dolls became floating, air-filled nymphs, lovely in the manner of their kind, but fundamentally empty. They hovered, bounced, and jiggled expectantly.

"Follow the Spy I's," Humfrey directed them. "Put on your airs on the return trip, staying just ahead of those who pursue you. Any of you who get caught are apt to get punctured." He smiled obscurely.

Silently the nymph shapes flew away.

"But if the Mundanes come here, they'll attack you!" Imbri sent protestingly.

"Naturally," Humfrey agreed. "And I shall destroy them with my remaining spells." He seemed to have forgotten his earlier remark about his plans being doomed to failure. He reached in the bag again and drew forth a wet-looking loop of substance. "Now pay attention, mare, in case I need your help, though obviously I won't need it." He held up the loop. "This is the River Elba, conveniently coiled." He hung it on his right arm, demonstrating its convenience. "It says 'Able was I ere I saw elbow,' close enough. If you untie the cord binding it, Elba will be unbound and will flood out the region. Do not free the river unless you have the enemy in a floodable region."

The day horse snorted. Humfrey's nose wrinkled. "You doubt me, horse? Note this." He took hold of a single strand of the loop and broke it where it passed under the binding cord. This enabled him to separate the strand from the main loop. He tossed it at the day horse.

The loop-strand expanded in midair, becoming a torrent of water. The day horse was soaked. The water splashed down his legs to his hooves and flowed on out of the baobab tree, tapering off as its volume diminished. It was indeed part of a fairly substantial river.

"Well, you did snort!" Imbri sent mirthfully. The day horse shook himself, not particularly pleased. He did not snort again.

Humfrey brought out a box. Lettering across the top spelled PANDORA. "My secret weapon, more potent than any other. Pandora was a charming girl who really didn't want to give this up," he said, smiling with an ancient memory. "But I knew she'd open it if I didn't get it out of her hands." He set the box down.

Imbri wondered what the Good Magician's relationship with Pandora had been, and what had happened to the girl. Probably she had died of old age long ago. What was in that box? Imbri experienced an intense female curiosity, but decided not to inquire. She would surely find out in due course.

"Box of quarterpedes," the Magician said, setting out another item.

"Quarterpedes?" Imbri sent inquiringly.

"Very rare cousins of the nickelpedes," Humfrey explained. "They are five times as bad. They gouge out two bits at a time."

Imbri had no further curiosity about that. Nickelpedes were ferocious little creatures, five times as fierce as centipedes. Anything worse than that was too dangerous to loose upon Xanth. It was a doomsday weapon.

"Dirty looks," Humfrey said, setting out a biliously swirling bottle. "Jumping beans. Enormous squash." Other items appeared.

"Isn't a squash something to eat?" the day horse ventured within the dream Imbri maintained for him on standby.

"This one is to your Mundane vegetables as a hypnogourd is to a pumpkin," the Good Magician said with a certain relish. "Which is not to say that the pumpkin does not have its place. I remember a pumpkin carriage a young woman used—or was that a glass slipper? At any rate, this particular vegetable is not edible. It likes to squash things."

The day horse twitched his white ears, obviously impressed.

"Now here is the higher power armament," Humfrey said, bringing out a small book. "Herein are listed selected Words of Power. Anyone can use them to excellent effect. Of course, it is necessary to pronounce them correctly." He continued setting out items, humming to himself.

"What do you think?" Imbri asked the day horse in the dream. "Can Magician Humfrey stop the Mundanes?"

"Yes," the animal answered, awed.

"Can he stop the Horseman?" she persisted, though she was not yet clear what threat the Horseman represented, aside from his position as second in command to Hasbinbad.

The day horse backed up a few steps, skitterishly. "No, I don't think so."

"But the Horseman can't put spurs to the Good Magician!"

"Stay clear of the Horseman!" the day horse insisted, breathing harder.

Obviously some element of this puzzle was missing. Imbri had glimpsed only a part of the Good Magician's array of spells, but was satisfied that they could quickly ruin an army. Humfrey, like the preceding Kings, was stronger than anticipated. Yet the day horse thought the Horseman could prevail.

The first Spy I returned. "What have you glimpsed?" Humfrey asked it.

The seeing eyeball hovered before a wall. It projected a beam of light. Where the light struck the wall, a magic picture appeared. It showed the Mundanes using ropes to lower themselves down the wall of the Chasm. Some men were already down; these were using drawn swords and spears to fend off the Gap Dragon. A number of them were lying in blood on the ground of the Chasm floor, but the dragon was suffering, too. Some of its scales were missing, and it was limping. As more Mundanes joined the first ones, the dragon would suffer more.

Humfrey, Imbri, and the day horse watched, fascinated, as the procession of Spy I balls constantly updated the newsreel report. The tough Mundanes drove the Gap Dragon back until at last the poor thing turned a battered tail and fled. Imbri had known of the activities of the Gap Dragon and its predecessors for all her life; it was a merciless monster who destroyed all those creatures misfortunate enough to blunder into the Chasm. But now she felt sorry for the monster. The Mundanes were worse.

As the afternoon declined, the Mundanes crossed the

bottom of the Chasm and set their ropes for climbing the south wall. A few zombies remained to guard the Chasm; they flung down the ropes, preventing any anchorage from being achieved. Mundane archers ranged along the north side to shoot arrows at the zombies. These scored, but of course did not have any significant effect. But the arrows trailed cords that dangled down into the Chasm. The Wavers below grabbed the ends and yanked the zombies down. Then they chopped the zombies into pieces too small to continue fighting. The Punics had certainly gotten over their initial horror of the un-dead!

Now the Mundanes flung anchors up and, when the ropes were firmly caught, hauled themselves up hand over hand. The process was time-consuming but inevitable. By nightfall the entire Punic army, as much as remained of it, would be on the south bank of the Gap. Xanth's greatest natural barrier had been conquered by the enemy.

Humfrey made a note. "Two hundred and five surviving Mundanes," he said. "A number of those are wounded. No horses or elephants. More than enough to swamp Castle Roogna. But my bag of tricks can accommodate them. The problem will be the other band of Nextwavers who remain in northern Xanth—the reserves. We have no such reserves."

"The other band remains north?" Imbri asked. She had been afraid they were circling south.

"You did not suppose that six hundred troops could dwindle to two hundred merely by marching down the length of Xanth?" the Magician inquired curtly, missing the point. "Hasbinbad wisely divided his forces. The Horseman commands the reserve contingent, though he seems to have delegated the routine to a lieutenant. That is the force we must fear, for it is whole and fresh, while our defense has been decimated. They have been using their horses to carry messengers back and forth, so the second force knows what happens to the first, and where and of what nature the hazards of Xanth are. These are experienced troops, tough and cunning."

The Good Magician's talent for information was manifesting, Imbri realized. Humfrey had an excellent grasp of the tactical situation. Why, then, was he so certain he would not survive the encounter? Why was he so carefully explaining things to her? She knew this was not his nature. Normally the Good Magician was very tight with his information. It was as if he thought *she* would have to invoke many of these spells, or show someone else how to do it. That belief of his, if such it was, was unnerving.

The Spy I balls showed the Nextwavers making camp and foraging for food and drink. They were catching on to the bounties of Xanth and now, instead of burning out the region, they were hammering out chocolate chips from an outcropping of chocolithic rock and tapping beer-barrel trees for flagons of foaming natural brew, to which they seemed to be quite partial.

"The nymphs travel slower than the I balls," Humfrey remarked. "I had thought they would lead the Wavers here tonight, but it will be noon tomorrow before they arrive. My error; I misread my prophecy." He frowned. "I'm not quite as young as I used to be. I'm making foolish mistakes. That must be why I'm doomed to ignoble failure."

"But, your Majesty!" Imbri protested in a dreamlet. "You have an excellent program of defense! When you bring the Punics here and loose your spells against them—"

Humfrey shook his head. "Don't try to flatter an old curmudgeon, mare! You're a few years older than I am! Certainly my program is good; I researched it years ago from a tome describing how best to wash out Waves. But I am about to make a single colossal, egregious, flagrant, and appalling oversight whose disastrousness is exceeded only by its irony."

"What oversight?" Imbri asked, concerned.

"I am going to overlook the single most phenomenal flaw in my plan—the one that completely nullifies all the rest. It is ironic because it is a flaw that I would readily have perceived in my younger years, when I was more alert than I am now."

"But surely if you know there is a flaw—"

"I'm too dull and corroded to find it now," he said. "I have cudgeled my ailing brain, but I can not detect it. The thing is so obvious any fool could see it—except me. That is my undoing. That is why I forbade my wife, the lovely Gorgon, to accompany me. I am ashamed to have any human being witness my final folly. And I charge you, you animals, not to embarrass me after my failure by blabbing the truth in this respect. Just tell the world that I did my best and it wasn't sufficient."

"But *I* can't see the flaw either!" Imbri protested.

"Because you are blinded by your own marish folly," he said. "At least you will have a chance to redeem yours, at the cost of great heartbreak."

"What folly is this?" she asked, curiosity warring with distress.

"If I knew that, it would provide the key to my own folly," he said. "Swear to me now that you will protect my guilty secret when finally you fathom it."

Disturbed, Imbri yielded to his entreaty. "I so swear," she sent. Then she put it to the day horse, in a separate dreamlet.

He, too, swore. "No one shall know his folly from me."

Humfrey smiled grimly. "At least I salvage that foolish fragment from the yawning abyss of my indignity." He lifted a small bag. "Here is another potent weapon—the bag of wind. Loose it when only enemy troops are near, for it is dangerous to all. Brace yourself well, lest you, too, be blown away." Then he looked at the magic sundial on his wrist, which showed him the time even when no sun was shining. "Ooops—it is time for you to go pick up Chameleon. Then you will have to teach your stallion friend how to remain in contact with you while you phase through the World of Night, lest he get lost forever in the gourd. Go to it, hoofmates."

"Hoofmates!" Imbri was startled and embarrassed by the appellation. But the fact was, she did like the day horse, and knew that it showed, and soon she would be coming into season. If she did not wish to mate with him, she would have to come to a decision and take action soon. Human females could be choosy and difficult about mating and usually were; mares had no such option. If she were near the stallion at the key time, she would mate. The day horse, obviously, was aware of that, which was one reason he was indulging her by assisting in activities of little interest to him, such as the Good Magician's setting up of spells.

The day horse was looking at her curiously. Imbri fought back her half-guilty thoughts, perked her ears up straight, and formed a dream for him to step into, one with innocent open pasture for a background and absolutely clear of any suggestion of mating. She doubted she was fooling him, but had to maintain the pretense.

But his curiosity was unrelated. "Phase through the night?" he asked in the dreamlet.

"Oh, I forgot to ask you," she sent, relieved. "Will you come with me again, to carry Ambassador Bink home from the isthmus? He is to be the next King of Xanth, so must be brought safely past the Mundanes."

"The Mundanes!" he reacted, alarmed.

"They won't see us in the night," she sent reassuringly. "I want to carry his wife Chameleon there to meet him, so we need another steed."

"Chameleon!" he said gladly. "She is a nice woman."

"You seem to like her better than me!" Imbri snorted, her dream mare turning green with jealousy.

"Well, she *is* human, therefore a creature of power—"

He really had an obsession about human beings, whether negative or positive! In the dream, Imbri shifted to human form—jet-black skin, a firm, high bosom, and with a regal flow of hair from her head. "How do you like me now?" she demanded.

He snorted with mirth. "I like you better equine. I can't touch a dream girl."

"That's what you think!" she said, her dream form striding lithely forward.

"You're wasting time," Humfrey snapped. "Save your flirtations for the journey. There's a war on."

The dreamlet puffed into confused vapor. Imbri was glad horses couldn't blush; otherwise she would now be solid red. She had indeed been flirting, when she had resolved not to; the presence of a handsome male brought out this aspect of her nature.

She walked somewhat stiffly out of the baobab tree. There was a small spring beside it; she went to it and drank deeply, knowing it might be long before she drank again. Water was very important to horses! Especially when they were burning with embarrassment. Also, she was giving the day horse time to come join her. She was sure he would, though his own equine dignity required that he not seem eager. After all, he was a stallion, and stallions did not leap to the bidding of mere mares.

In a moment, to her relief, he did emerge. He, too, took a long drink. In this subtle way he had committed himself to the journey; he had taken the first step.

She set off for Castle Roogna, and the day horse paced her. He was truly magnificent in the lessening light, his white coat standing out bravely, while her black coat made her almost invisible. Truly, they were like day and night! It was as if he epitomized the male of any species, bright and bold, while she was the essence of the female, dark and hidden.

He glanced sidelong at her, perking his ears forward, and she knew he was giving her the horselaugh inside. She had certainly been making a foolish filly of herself, parading in the dream as a woman! She was indeed somewhat smitten with the stallion, the first she had known who was not her sire, and knew she would not flee him when the season came upon her and would not retreat to some far, inaccessible region before that time to avoid the compulsion of nature. Far region? She had only to step into any gourd! But would not. He knew it, too, and knew she knew. No artifice for equines!

"The World of Night?" he inquired in neightalk, for she had shut down the dreams.

She relented and opened her dream to him. "I can enable creatures in direct contact with me to phase through objects at night and to use the gourd bypass for rapid travel. But it is dangerous, for there are spooky things within the world of the gourd. You may not want to risk it."

"And if I don't," he asked cannily, "where will you be when you come in season?"

She hadn't thought of it quite that way, at least not consciously. Of course she had a certain leverage of her own! Any normal mares in Xanth were in the hands of the Mundanes, so he couldn't chance that, and no other night mare was accessible. He was the only male—but she was the only female. Stallions did not govern the times for mating, but they were always interested. Naturally he would seek to please her, even at some inconvenience to himself. He did not know her cycle; for all he knew, she might come into season tomorrow. He had to stay close to her when opportunity came, lest he miss it.

So she could be difficult and choosy, too, in the manner of the human women! She could turn her favor on and off capriciously, driving the male to distraction. That promised to be fun—except that she really did have important business to attend to. She had to fetch Bink to Castle Roogna before Good King Humfrey made his abysmal blooper and wiped out, so Bink could be King and take over the campaign before the Nextwave swamped the last bastion of Xanth. How important her participation had become!

"My season is not yet," she returned. Of course that did not answer his question; she was not about to yield her newfound advantage by committing herself prematurely. "I must train you in continuous contact now, while some light remains. Then we'll use the gourds to go to the isthmus with Chameleon during darkness."

"I like the sound of this," he nickered.

So did she, actually. Horses were not as free about bodily contact as human beings were, but they did indulge in it. "You must remain touching me continuously, for my phase-magic extends only to those in contact with me. We must match strides exactly so we can run together without separating."

"Like this?" he asked in the dream, and in the flesh he moved over until his side squeezed against her. His flesh was soft and warm and firm; he had a nice, smooth coat and excellent musculature that made contact a pleasure.

"Like this," she agreed, feeling guilty again for enjoying the sensation so much. What was there about pleasure that so readily inspired guilt? She had associated with human beings so much, recently, that she was starting to react in the same confused way they did!

Imbri and the day horse walked in contact, then shifted together to a trot. Now the beats of their eight hooves become two, as one front hoof and one rear hoof struck the ground together for each of them. BEAT-BEAT, BEAT-BEAT! There was something very fulfilling about such a cadence, and even more pleasant about matching cadences; the measured fall of hooves was the very essence of equine nature.

Then, all too soon, Castle Roogna hove into view. The day horse sheered away, breaking contact. "I'll not go there!" he snorted, his abiding fear of human places taking over.

Imbri sighed, but understood. "I will bring her out. You wait here." It was a good place for a horse to wait, for the castle orchards had extremely lush grass.

She left him grazing and trotted on into the castle. Chameleon was waiting, eager to join her husband. It was a feeling Imbri was coming to understand much better, now that she had a male interest of her own.

Chameleon seemed to have become less pretty, even in the few hours of this day, and now was hardly out of the ordinary in appearance. But Imbri knew she was correspondingly smarter. Maybe she wanted to meet Bink before she lost too much of her charm; it was a natural enough concern. A human woman without charm was the least fortunate of creatures.

The woman mounted and they moved out. The day horse was waiting, grazing dangerously near a pinapple tree that he evidently didn't recognize. Darkness was closing, but still his white hide showed up clearly.

"Oh, I'm so glad to see you, day horse!" Chameleon exclaimed with girlish enthusiasm.

The horse lifted his head, startled. He breathed hard, half snorting.

Imbri caught on. "This is Chameleon," she sent to him. "She changes each day, getting less pretty, more intelligent. You saw her several days ago, in her most beautiful stage—but she really is the same woman."

"Of course I am the same woman," Chameleon said. "You and I stayed in the forest while Imbri and Grundy and Ichabod encountered the Nextwavers and Hasbinbad and the Horseman. We had such a nice time together."

The day horse softened, allowing himself to be persuaded. His ears perked forward. Chameleon stroked his nose. Now he was sure of her. He nickered.

"But I am different in my fashion," Chameleon acknowledged. "Not as pretty—and I will become less pretty yet, until you can't stand me at all. I also have a sharp tongue when I'm smart, as women do; nobody can stand me then."

The day horse snorted. He would not be that fickle, surely, he thought.

"You'll see," Chameleon said sadly. "The stupidest thing a woman can do is to be too smart. Give it another week, maybe less. If you can tolerate me then, I'll gladly ride with you again."

They trotted toward the nearest gourd patch. Chameleon became nervous. "Will we be passing the place where . . . ?" She trailed off, unable to finish.

"We will not pass the place where your son was taken," Imbri sent in a gentle dream that could not entirely eschew the horror connection. Chameleon was standing up well; perhaps Millie the Ghost had talked with her and put things in perspective. Millie had eight hundred years' perspective! But as Chameleon became more intelligent, Dor's loss would strike her more profoundly. That was probably another reason she wanted to rejoin her husband—especially since he was now in line to become King himself. She was not going to be absent when the second of the two men in her life was in peril.

As if to distract herself from the looming grief, Chameleon chatted innocently enough to the day horse. "Back when I was young, I lived in a village on the north edge of the Gap Chasm, and I had a separate name for each phase of my cycle. I was Wynn when I was pretty, and Dee when I was normal, and Fanchon when I was ugly. The villagers knew how it was and treated me like three different people, and that made it easier. But though they all liked Wynn—especially the young men!—and half of them liked Dee, nobody could stand Fanchon. Since anyone who married me would get all three, I was doomed to spinsterhood. Then I met Bink, who seemed like such a nice man, though he lacked magic, and I thought that if I didn't let him find out my nature . . . I was foolish, but I had an excuse, as I was stupid at the time. Wynn was the first me he encountered. So I thought maybe I could find a spell to make me normal all the time. Good Magician Humfrey told me no spell would do it, but that all I had to do was go to Mundania, and when my magic faded I would be Dee, permanently. So I tried, but somehow things got tangled up, and in the end Bink liked me as I was, so he unspinstered me." She laughed. "No spell for Chameleon! I didn't need magic, just the right man."

And if she lost Bink, Imbri thought gloomily, she would be in deep, deep trouble.

They arrived at the gourd patch. "Now get in step and in contact with me," Imbri sent to the day horse. "Do not heed anything you see within the gourd. If you break contact, you are lost."

The day horse moved close, but Chameleon's right leg got in his way. "I'll ride sidesaddle," she said, shifting her posture though there was no saddle. She was quicker to catch on to both problem and solution than she would have been before. "And I'll hold on to a strand of the day horse's mane, to be sure there's contact." She caught his mane, which was conveniently on the left side, while Imbri's was on the right. "Oh, it's like silk!" she exclaimed.

This was a gross exaggeration; his mane was more like flexible white wires, beautiful but tough. The mane and tail of a horse were designed by nature to swing about and slap flies stingingly, and were effective in that capacity. But the day horse nickered appreciatively. He had liked Chameleon in her pretty-stupid guise; he seemed to like her better in her neutral state. She was, certainly, a nice if ordinary woman now.

They matched step and plunged into the gourd. Obviously the day horse was no coward about new experiences; it was only strange people he was wary of. The green rind passed by them; then they were in a region of massive wooden gears that turned slowly and ground exceeding fine. Now the day horse snorted with alarm, but maintained contact with Imbri. Together they charged between the gears, Imbri directing their progress through a continuing dreamlet. She showed an image of the gourdscape, with a dotted yellow line marking their route. She ran just to the left of that line, he to the right. It worked well enough, for she was familiar with this region, as she was with all of the gourd.

"What are these wheels for?" Chameleon asked. She had visited the gourd before, so was no longer frightened.

"They measure out the time for every event in every dream," Imbri explained. "There are hundreds of people and creatures having thousands of dreams every night; if the length and placement of each dream were not precise, there would be overlapping and gaps and fuzziness. Each night mare has a schedule; she must deliver each dream on time. These gears measure out those times more accurately than any living creature could do. Even so, there are many small jumps and discontinuities in dreams, as the timing and placements get slightly out of synch."

"Thousands of dreams each night," Chameleon breathed, awed. "I never realized there was such precision behind the few little dreams I have!"

"You have dreams all night," Imbri returned. "But most of them you forget by morning. Most of them are probably good dreams, for you are a good person; those ones emanate from another source. The true day mares are invisible horses who carry the daydreams and the pleasant night dreams; they don't keep good accounts and don't seem to mind if their dreams are misplaced or forgotten. They are happy, careless creatures." She realized she might be unfairly condemning the day shift, perhaps from ignorance; the day mares were probably quite decent when one knew them. "Still, their time slots have to be allocated, and they must be integrated with the serious dreams we working mares deliver. The coordination is complex."

"I just never knew there was so much inside the gourd!" Chameleon said.

"Few people do," Imbri sent. "They assume things just happen coincidentally. There is very little coincidence in Xanth. It is a term used to hide our ignorance of the true causes of things."

On they went through the labyrinth of grinding gears, leaping over small ones, skirting big ones, and jumping through holes in the hollow ones. The gears were all different colors and turned at different rates, in a bewildering array.

At last they came to a new region. This was watery, and huge fishlike shapes swam through it. Loan sharks and card sharks and poor fish crowded the channels, powering toward the team of horses, then banking off with a great threshing of flukes. No one in the gourd could touch a night mare or her companions; any who did would answer to the Night Stallion, and he was not a forgiving creature. These fish were denizens of the gourd and could be dispatched to inclement assignments, such as desert duty— most unpleasant for a fish. All who molested night mares had long since gone to the most hellish spots, with the hoofprints of the Dark Horse branding their posterior regions forever. Nevertheless, the fish could bluff, and this they were doing now.

The travelers came to a third region. Here coruscating beams of light sliced crisscross in every direction plus one. Some were burning red, scorching what they touched; others were searing white, vaporizing their objects. Black ones turned things frigidly cold; green ones made them sprout leaves.

"Oh, I know what these are for!" Chameleon exclaimed. "They make things hot or cold or bright or dull or clean or dirty or anything!" She was certainly getting smarter.

"Yes," Imbri agreed, discovering new interest in these things that were long familiar to her. "If Xanth dreams were left to themselves, they would be horribly bland. They have to be touched up so that there is good contrast. A great deal of art goes into dreams to make them properly effective."

"Then why do we forget most of them?" Chameleon asked. "It seems like such a waste!"

"You don't really forget them," Imbri qualified. "They remain in your experience, the same as does every tree you see every day, every bug you hear buzzing, and every gust of breeze your body feels. All of these things influence your character, and so do the dreams."

"It's amazing!" Chameleon said, shaking her head. "There is so much more to life than I thought. I wonder if the Mundanes have similar things to influence their characters?"

"I doubt it," Imbri sent. "After all, look at how brutish and bad they are. If they had proper dreams, they wouldn't degenerate like that."

Now they reached another rind and burst out of the gourd. They were in the isthmus of Xanth, the narrow corridor of land that led to Mundania. This was where Bink and Arnolde would be arriving, having completed another diplomatic mission. Imbri and the day horse separated; it really was easier to run separately. "You came through that very well," Imbri complimented him.

"I just concentrated on my running," he replied tightly in the dream. "I knew if I looked about too much, I'd lose my step and get separated."

They entered a plain, where the flat, hard ground was illuminated by the faint light of the waning moon and running was excellent. Imbri loved to run and knew the day horse did, too; horses had been created to do most of the quality running in Xanth. She tried to imagine the bad dreams being carried by lumbering dragons, and suffered a titillation of mirth. No, it had to be done by true night mares!

Then a shape appeared in the moonlight, like a low-flying cloud. It was flat on the bottom and lumpy on top. It swooped toward them.

Imbri phased into intangibility, protecting herself and her rider from hostile action. "Hide!" she sent to the day horse.

But a voice from the cloud hailed them. "Imbri! Chameleon! It's me—Grundy the Golem!"

So it was. Imbri phased back. "Whatever are you doing here?" she sent indignantly. "You're supposed to be watching King Humfrey's castle while the Gorgon is away."

"Emergency," he said, coasting down beside them. "I used one of Humfrey's bottled spells to summon the magic carpet and buzz right over here. You certainly move fast! I tore through the night so swiftly that I've got shatters of cloud on me! Glad I caught you in time."

"In time for what?" Chameleon asked.

Suddenly the golem was oddly diffident. "Well, you have to know, before—"

"What's that?" Imbri projected—and as she touched Grundy's mind, she became aware of a maelstrom within it. The golem was generating his own bad images!

"I had to tell you—about the Good Magician. I activated

a magic mirror—all it took was the right anti-glitch spell; it could have been done any time before, and we could have had good communications—I got the spell from a book the Gorgon left for me in case I needed magic for an emergency—and tuned him in, or tried to—"

"Have the Mundanes attacked already?" Chameleon asked, worried.

"No, not exactly. Yes, I guess so. That is, it's a matter of definition. He's gone."

"What?" Chameleon's confusion was Imbri's, too. "You mean the Good Magician left the baobab tree?"

"No, he's there. But not there."

"I don't—"

"Humfrey's been taken!" Grundy cried.

"No!" Chameleon protested. "It's too soon!"

"He's gone, just like the others. Staring into nothing! Bink has to be King right now! That's why I had to reach you, before the Mundanes get to the baobab tree and wipe out all the bottled spells or use them against us!"

Chameleon put her hand to her eyes, stricken. "Already! I won't have my husband at all, any more than Irene had Dor!"

"Bink can take the carpet!" Grundy said. "He's got to get to Castle Roogna right away!"

"No," Chameleon demurred. "Bink knows nothing about being King. He has to be prepared."

"There's no time! The Mundanes will be marching in the morning, and we're halfway through the night now!"

"Imbri and I will bring him back," she said firmly. "We'll prepare him on the way. We'll catch him up on all the recent details he's missed by being away. By the time he arrives, he will be ready. I hope."

Grundy shook his little head dolefully. "You're the Queen now, you know. But if Xanth has no King when the Mundanes reach Castle Roogna—"

"Xanth will have a King," Chameleon said.

"On your head be it," the golem muttered.

Chapter 10. Magic Tricks

The Good Magician's prophecy of the moment of Bink's arrival in Xanth was accurate. In the early wee hours of the morning, Bink and Arnolde walked out of drear Mundania. Chameleon ran to embrace her husband, while Imbri and the day horse exchanged diffident glances with the centaur. Grundy performed introductions.

"You're just the way I like you, Dee," Bink remarked after their kiss. He was a fairly solid, graying man who had been physically powerful in his youth. Imbri remembered him now; she had on occasion brought him bad dreams.

"Dee?" Grundy asked.

Bink smiled, confirming what Chameleon had already told the others. "My changeable wife has a private name for each phase. Dee is ordinary, not too much of anything. I don't know why I pay attention to her." He kissed her again.

Arnolde was an old, bespectacled centaur who seemed out of place in the forest. He was by training and temperament an archivist, like his friend Ichabod, one who filed books and papers in obscure chambers, for what purpose no one understood. But he was also a Magician, his talent being the formation of an aisle of magic wherever he went, even in the most alien reaches of Mundania. This greatly facilitated contact and trade with that backward region. He had no apparent magic in Xanth itself, which was why his status had been unknown for most of his life. In this respect he resembled Bink, and the two males seemed to enjoy each other's company.

"Might I inquire the reason for this welcoming party?" Arnolde asked. "We expected to sleep the rest of the night here at the fringe of Xanth, then take two more days to travel south to the North Village."

"Ha!" Grundy said. "There *is* no—"

"Please," Chameleon said, interrupting the golem. "I must tell him in my own way."

"But Humfrey told *me* to tell him!" Grundy protested competitively.

The centaur interceded benignly. "May I suggest a compromise? Let the golem make one statement; then Chameleon can tell the rest in her own manner."

Chameleon smiled fleetingly. "That seems fair."

"Okay," Grundy grudged. "Bink, you're King. You have to get back to Castle Roogna right away. You can use the magic carpet; it will get you there in an hour."

"King!" Bink exclaimed. "What happened to King Trent? I'm not in line to be King of Xanth!"

"King Trent is ill," Chameleon said.

"Then our son Dor should take over."

"Dor is ill, too," she said very gently.

Bink paused, his face freezing. "How ill?"

"Too ill to be King," she replied. "It is an enchantment. We have not yet found the countercharm."

"Surely Good Magician Humfrey can—" Bink saw her grave expression. "Him, too? The same enchantment?"

"And the Zombie Master. But Humfrey told us that you are, in fact, a Magician who can not be harmed by magic, and that you have the best chance to break the chain of lost Kings, though he feared you would not. You must be King and stop the Mundanes—"

"The Mundanes! What's this?"

"The Nextwave invasion," Grundy put in.

Bink laughed mirthlessly. "I see there is indeed much for me to catch up on. Is the magic carpet big enough for two? You and I, Chameleon, could—"

"No," Grundy said. "It won't support two full-sized people; it's a single-seater model. And you can't take two days riding south. You'd get there after Castle Roogna falls to the Mundanes, and anyway, the main bridge across the Gap is down, and Wavers are all over the place, and—"

"I won't let you go alone!" Chameleon protested, showing some fire. She was not nearly as accommodating to the notions of others as she had been in her lovely stage. "I've lost my son, so soon after he was married. I won't let it happen to you!"

"But Xanth must have a King," Bink said. "Though I'm incompetent in any such activity, I must try to do my duty. How else can I get there in time?"

"Imbri can take you," Chameleon declared with sudden inspiration. "She's a night mare; she can get you there by morning—and she can tell you everything you need to know and help you manage. That way you'll be properly prepared."

"I find this mostly incomprehensible," Bink said. "But I'm sure you know best, Dee. I had had another kind of meeting with you in mind—"

"So did I," she said bravely. "By the time I catch up with you, I'll be well on toward ugly."

"You are never ugly to me," he said with a certain gallantry. But he could not quite conceal his disappointment. He had been some time away from her, and obviously she was a woman who needed to be appreciated at the right time.

"Go with Imbri," she said. "The rest of us will follow at our own pace."

They embraced again. "Can the rest of you travel safely?" Bink asked as he went to Imbri.

"Oh, sure," Grundy said. "The day horse knows how to stay clear of Mundanes, and I've got the flying carpet for emergencies. I'll ride Arnolde and keep him out of mischief."

"Indubitably," the centaur said, smiling wryly.

"I've got to fill you in on everything before I fly back to Humfrey's castle," Grundy continued. "You'll be King after Bink, Arnolde."

Chameleon frowned. "Grundy, you are a perfect marvel of diplomacy," she said with gentle irony.

"I know it," the golem agreed smugly.

Bink mounted Imbri and waved farewell to his wife. Imbri could tell by the way he sat that he had had some experience riding animals, unlike his wife. The centaurs probably accounted for that. Bink had traveled to Mundania many times, and perhaps had encountered Mundane horses there, too.

Imbri sent a dream of sad parting to the others, seeing them as a pretty picture—the old centaur appaloosa carrying the golem, and the magnificent white stallion bearing the sad woman. Yet it was true that Arnolde, too, needed to be updated in detail for when he would be King. If nothing else, he would need time to ponder whom to designate as his successor, since things tended to move too rapidly for the Council of Elders to deliberate and decide.

Imbri set off for the nearest gourd patch. "What's this about my son Dor getting married?" Bink asked her.

Imbri sent him a small dream showing the elopement wedding in the zombie graveyard. She followed that with their discovery of the fate of King Trent. The dream became a full-fledged narrative, so that Bink hardly noticed when they plunged into the gourd and charged through the maelstrom of the raw stuff of real dreams. By the time they emerged from the gourd near Castle Roogna, Bink had become acquainted with everything relevant that Imbri knew.

"You are some mare, Imbri!" he said as the castle came into sight. They were just in time; dawn was threatening; had it arrived while they were in the gourd, they would have been trapped within the World of Night for the day. Imbri's night powers existed only at night, as always.

They entered the castle. Queen Iris met them. "Thank fate you're here, Bink; we just discovered King Humfrey has been taken. You—"

"I am King," Bink said with surprising certainty. He had assimilated Imbri's information readily and now was taking hold in a much firmer fashion than Imbri had expected. Bink had been a kind of nonperson in Xanth, considered to be a man without magic and therefore held in a certain veiled contempt; that contempt had been undeserved. Imbri suspected that even Grundy and Chameleon and the day horse expected little of Bink; already it was evident that he would surprise them. Xanth's recent Kings had not lasted long, but each had shown competence and courage in the crisis. Yet how long could this continue, in the face of the terrible enchantment that persisted in striking each King down?

They went to the room where the enchanted Kings were laid out. The Zombie Master and Good Magician Humfrey had been added to the collection. Chet and Chem Centaur had evidently been out to the baobab tree and carried in the latest victim.

Irene remained by her husband. She looked up. "Bink!" she said, rising and going to him. "Did you know that he—we—"

Bink put his arm around her. "The mare Imbri told me everything. Congratulations! I'm only sorry you did not have more time together."

"We had no time at all!" she complained, making a moue. "The Kingship monopolized him. Then he was ensorcelled." She choked off, her eyes flicking toward her supine husband.

"Somehow we'll find the counterspell," Bink said reassuringly.

"They say you—that it can't happen to you—"

"It seems my secret is out at last. Your father knew it always. That is why he sent me on some of the most awkward magical investigations. But I am not invulnerable; the Mundanes represent as much of a threat to me as to anyone else. But perhaps I can deal with this mysterious enemy who has enchanted these four Kings. I shall go immediately to the baobab tree and try to use Humfrey's bag of tricks to stop the Nextwave."

"You seem remarkably well informed," Queen Iris remarked.

"Yes. Only a man of my talent can safely use Humfrey's spells. Only those spells can stop the Mundanes at this point—which, of course, is the reason Humfrey was ensorcelled before he could use them. *I* will use them, and I want that enchanter to come to me. His magic won't work—and then I'll be able to identify him. That's why Humfrey thought I might break the chain of enchantments—if I can prevent the Mundanes from taking me out physically."

"Then it is victory or real death for you," Irene said.

"Yes, of course. This is why Magician Humfrey could not foresee my future; my talent prevents him, and neither he nor I can handle the Mundane element as a matter of divination." He paused. "It is odd, however, that he, the most knowledgeable of men, was taken out by enchantment, not by a Mundane weapon."

"He knew it was coming," Imbri sent. "He said he was overlooking something important, perhaps because he couldn't foresee his own future." That was as much as she could impart without abridging her promise not to reveal the ignominious nature of the Good Magician's fall—though it did not seem ignominious to her. Obviously the enemy enchanter had waited till Humfrey was alone, then struck stealthily. The shame should attach to the enchanter, not to Humfrey.

"Take me there," Bink told her. "And the rest of you—let it be known that I am alone at the baobab tree. I want the enemy enchanter to get the news." He looked down at his enchanted son. "I will set things right for you, Dor. I promise. And for the others who so bravely served. The enchanter shall undo his mischief." Bink's hand touched the hilt of the sword he wore with a certain ominous significance. Imbri had not thought of him as a man of violence, but she realized now that he would not hesitate to do whatever he felt was required to accomplish his purpose.

Imbri took him to the baobab. Chem Centaur was there, guarding the Good Magician's spells. Everything seemed undisturbed.

"How was he found?" King Bink asked.

"He was sitting on the floor here, holding this bottle," Chem said, picking up a small red one. "He must have been setting it up with the others when—"

"Thank you," Bink said, taking the bottle. "You may trot back to Castle Roogna—no, just one moment." He popped the cork.

Red vapor swirled out. "Horseman!" the Good Magician's voice whispered. Then the vapor dissipated, leaving silence.

"He bottled his own voice!" Chem exclaimed.

"Now we know who enchanted him," Bink said. "The

Horseman. Humfrey promised to tell us who, and he did—just before he was taken himself."

"Beware the Horseman!" Imbri sent in a nervous dreamlet. "That was his earlier warning!"

"It suggests the Horseman is near," Bink said. "That is what I want. He will come to me when I am alone." He waved Chem away. "Humfrey was true to his promise. He has produced the key information. Go inform the others. I think we are on the way to breaking the chain. At least we now know the meaning of the two prophecies. We know whom to stop and why."

"I don't like this," Chem said, but she trotted obediently out of the tree.

"I remember when she was a foal," Bink remarked. "Cute little thing, always making mental maps of the surroundings. She's certainly a fine-looking filly now!" He turned to Imbri. "I said I would be alone, but I wasn't thinking of you. I hope you don't mind remaining, though I know you fear the Horseman."

"I don't fear the Horseman," Imbri protested. "It's the day horse who fears him. If that horrible man comes near me, I'll put a hind hoof in his face and leave my signature on the inside of his skull."

"Good enough," the King agreed with a grim smile. "But it may be better to leave him to me, as he is obviously no Mundane, and you may be vulnerable to his magic. What does he look like?"

Imbri projected a dream picture of the Horseman. She was shaking with abrupt rage. Of course the man was no Mundane! He had deliberately deceived her so she would not know in what manner he was a threat to Xanth. And she had allowed herself to be fooled! This was the sort of indignity Humfrey must have felt, overlooking the obvious.

"That's very good, Imbri. You have a nice talent there. If you weren't a night mare, it would be a double talent—dream projection and the ability to dematerialize at night. But I suppose both are really part of your nature, not considered talents at all." He shook his head. "Magic is funny stuff; I have never been certain of its ramifications. Whenever I understand it, some new aspect appears, and I realize that I don't understand it at all."

Imbri found herself liking this man in much the way she liked his wife Chameleon. He was a nice person, no snob, intelligent and practical, with a certain unpretentious honesty. "Magic seems natural enough to me," she ventured. "What is so hard to understand about it?"

"For one thing, the distribution and definition of magic talents," he said. "For centuries we men believed that all creatures either had magic talents or were themselves magical. Thus men *did* magic, while dragons *were* magic. Then we discovered that some centaurs could do magic, too. So we have a magical species performing magic, fudging the definition. Now we have you night mares bridging the definition also. If we assume you are natural horses who possess magic talent, we run afoul of the double-talent problem, for only one talent goes to any one person. We had thought every talent was different, but then we discovered the curse fiends, who all have the same talent—but at least that does not violate the one-talent-per-person limit. But you—"

"I see the problem," she agreed. "All night mares can phase out and project dreams. Maybe a creature *can* have two talents."

"Or a magical creature, who phases through objects at night, can have the single talent of sending dreams," he said. "We can make it fit our present definitions—barely—but the suspicion remains that someday we will discover some form of magic that does not. Consider this Horseman: he's obviously a man with the ability to ensorcell other men. That's not remarkable in itself; my father Roland can stun people, and, of course, King Trent transformed them. But how does the Horseman get around so handily without being observed? Does he have a second talent, perhaps similar to yours of the night? We don't know, but must be prepared for that possibility."

"Now I understand your doubt," she said. "Magic is more complicated than I thought."

"I would like you to review your knowledge of the whereabouts of the Horseman each time a King was enchanted," Bink continued. "Obviously he was there to do his foul deed, but he has also been associated with the Mundanes when they were far distant. The manner of his travel may give us some hint how to balk him. He must be a man of Xanth, helping the Mundanes for personal advantage. Evidently they made him second in command in exchange for his help, but he does not help them too much. He let you escape them, knowing you were helping Xanth, and that would have the effect of evening the contest and making his service more valuable."

"The rogue!" Imbri sent emphatically, with the image of the moon colliding violently with the sun and showering Xanth with fragments of burning cheese. "If the Mundanes and Xanthians destroy each other, he can take over himself!"

"Such is the way of rogues," King Bink agreed. "His power is to banish the minds of people, but it may not be inherent in him. Perhaps he has a bottle full of minds, the same way Good Magician Humfrey has bottles of everything else. Maybe it is the bottle that does the magic, sucking in the Kings. But surely he had to approach his victims to do this. We must not assume we know the precise nature of his magic."

Imbri concentrated. She had actually met the Horseman only twice—once near Castle Roogna, just before King Trent was taken, and once in Hasbinbad's camp in northern Xanth. She had not seen him when King Dor was taken, or when the Zombie Master went, though it was obvious in retrospect that he had been the man in the tree.

"So he could have been there with the Mundane army, then," Bink said. "The Mundanes were not far away, just across the river, while King Dor slept. You did not see the Horseman because he was hiding, skulking around, waiting for his chance."

Imbri had to agree. In the confused situation of the battlefield, it would have been easy to sneak up close to the King's tent at night.

"And the next time, the Zombie Master was in the field, too," King Bink persisted.

Imbri reviewed the scene for him, showing how the Zombie Master had been sleeping, enjoying a dream Imbri had brought him. How Grundy had tracked a man to a river and lost him, after the King had been taken.

"So we know he does not have to touch his victim physically," Bink concluded. "He can be a short distance away, perhaps out of sight. That's an important point—no direct visual contact needed. He could have come here to this tree and hidden in a recess; perhaps he was here when you were and simply waited until Magician Humfrey was alone. It could have happened soon after you departed. How many more of Humfrey's spells have been set out since then?"

This was a most methodical approach! Imbri studied the bottles and boxes, trying to remember how many had been out of the bag before. "Not many more," she said.

"The Horseman wouldn't have had reason to travel far in the night," Bink continued. "Though I doubt he remained here in the tree. For one thing, he did not disturb Humfrey's spells. Not even the bottle that named him— surely a prime target! He must have been nervous about discovery and not delayed one moment after doing his deed. That suggests he can not enchant someone who is on guard, or perhaps can take only one person at a time, so must catch his victim alone and may be vulnerable for a period thereafter. So he left quickly, lest someone else arrive on the scene. Smash the Ogre's little wife Tandy is like that; once she stuns someone with a tantrum, she can not do so again for some time."

Again Imbri had to agree. It made her nervous to think that the dread Horseman lurked close by. By daylight she could not dematerialize, and that increased her nervousness.

"You surely need to rest and graze, Imbri," Bink said. "Go out and relax, but check on me every hour or so. The pseudonymphs aren't due to bring the Mundanes here until noon. I think the Horseman will try to strike before then, for he surely knows these spells of Humfrey's are dangerous to his allies, the Mundanes. If I have miscalculated in any way, I'll need you to carry the message to Castle Roogna."

Imbri nodded, both reassured and worried. King Bink was several times the man she had first taken him for—but it seemed that the Horseman was similarly more devious. She went out to graze, but the grass didn't taste very good. She watched for the possible approach of the Horseman, fearing that he would somehow sneak past unobserved, as it seemed he had done before. The Horseman had been making fools of them all so far!

Every hour she checked, but King Bink was all right. Noon came, and all remained well. Imbri was almost disappointed; she certainly wished no ill to the King, but she hated this tension of waiting. Suppose Bink were not invulnerable to the enchantment? Or suppose the Horseman wanted to reduce the force of Mundanes some more, keeping the sides even, so planned to let King Bink fight a while, using the spells, before taking him out? Or had the Horseman already tried and failed, unbeknownst to them? Where did things really stand?

Right on schedule, the first of the floating nymphs arrived, hotly pursued by a slavering Mundane.

Imbri had relayed all she had learned about the Good Magician's spells. Now Bink picked up one of the unidentified ones. "Stand well clear, Imbri," he warned. "This spell will not hurt me, but it might hurt you. I'm going to experiment while I'm not hard-pressed. I can still use my sword if a single Mundane comes at me. When too many come, I'll draw on the heavy stuff."

Imbri stood back. It seemed to her he was taking a considerable risk—but she realized that he was immune to magical danger and knew it, so could afford to gamble in a way no other person dared. This was safer for him than trying to take on all the Mundanes physically! Perhaps that was another reason Good Magician Humfrey had publicized Bink's secret talent. Bink was the only one who could safely play with unknown killer-spells, so had to be the one to succeed Humfrey himself and had to use those spells when no friends were close enough to be hurt by them. It was amazing how carefully Humfrey had planned every detail, his own failure included.

The nymph floated up, looking devastatingly winsome by human standards. Imbri had seen the creatures as they were first inflating, dead white and bulging. The night air must have done them good, for now there was color and bounce to match the buoyancy, and intricate little jiggles in private places as they moved. No wonder the Mundane was in sweaty pursuit!

Now the Mundane spied King Bink. "Oh, no, you don't! She's mine!" he cried, drawing his sword. "I chased that divine dream half the night and day!"

"In all fairness, I must tell you two things," Bink said. "First, the nymph is not real. She is a shape from a spell, with no mind at all—"

"I don't care where she's from or how smart she is!" the Mundane said, licking his brute lips. "I'm going to give her the time of my life—right after I get rid of you." He advanced, sword poised.

"Second, I am holding the spell of a Magician," Bink continued, backing off. "It may hurt you or even kill you, if—"

The Mundane leaped, his sword swinging viciously. Bink popped the cork on the vial, pointing the opening at him.

A green fireball shot out, expanding as it moved. It was head-sized as it struck the Mundane in the chest.

The man screamed. The fire burned into his chest with terrible ferocity, consuming it. In a moment the Mundane fell, his chest mostly missing.

Bink stared, looking faint. "Humfrey wasn't playing idle games," he whispered. "He was set to destroy the enemy army!"

Imbri agreed. That had been one deadly weapon! "But it was a choice between the enemy or you," she sent in a supportive dreamlet, glad she had taken the advice to stand well clear. "He tried to kill you when you tried to be reasonable with him."

"Yes. I have steeled myself to that," Bink said. "Still, the stomach is weak. I have seldom killed before, and most Mundanes are not like him. They can be quite civilized . . . though I admit this one wasn't."

Already a second pseudonymph was coming, leading another brute Mundane. Bink snatched up another vial. "Halt, Mundane!" he cried. "I have slain your companion!"

"Then I'll slay you!" the Mundane cried. He carried a bow; now he brought out an arrow and nocked it, taking aim.

Bink opened and pointed the vial, as he had the first. Something sailed out of it as the arrow flew toward him. The arrow struck the object and went astray, missing Bink's head by the span of a hand and plunking into the wall behind him.

Imbri looked at the thing skewered on the shaft of the arrow. It was a bean sandwich. The Mundane had just shot Humfrey's lunch.

The Mundane stared for a moment. Then he emitted a great bellow of a laugh. "You're fulla beans!"

Bink took a third vial. As the Mundane drew another arrow and aimed, Bink pointed and opened it.

This time smoke issued from the container. It shaped into a huge face. The face laughed. "Ho ho ho!" it roared. It was laughing gas.

But the Mundane's sense of humor was limited to laughter at others, not at himself. He shot an arrow through the face at Bink, barely missing. He drew a third. Imbri grew more nervous; these spells were not doing the job reliably.

Bink gave up on the spells for the moment. He ducked through the smoke, drawing his sword, and charged at the Mundane.

The Mundane, realizing that his bow was useless at close quarters, hastily drew his own sword. The two met in personal combat—but the Mundane was much younger and faster.

Imbri stepped forward, knowing she could not stand by and let the King be killed. But as the laughing gas dissipated, a third Mundane appeared, carrying a spear. He closed on the other two people, seeking an opening to dispatch the King.

Imbri charged across, spun about, and flung out a kick with her two hind legs. This caught the spearman in the chest and smashed him back. Imbri knew she had either killed the man or hurt him so badly he would not fight again for a long time. She now had blood on her hooves.

She turned again to help Bink, but he had dispatched his opponent. It seemed he knew how to handle a sword; his skill had bested the Mundane speed.

But already three more Mundanes were entering the tree, weapons drawn. Now the Punic army was arriving in force! Pseudonymphs floated all about, dancing just out of the grasp of the men, jiggling remarkably, causing the Punics to become more aggressive than ever.

"I have to return to magic," King Bink said. "I can't take on the whole Nextwave with my lone sword!" He glanced at the one Imbri had dispatched. "And I can't ask you to risk your hide, either. But it's no longer safe for you to stand away from me; soon there'll be many more Mundanes. So you had better stay close to me; that way the magic is less likely to backlash against you, and may protect you exactly as it protects me."

Imbri did not see that the magic had helped the King much. Protection against being harmed by magic was not the same as being protected by magic. But she agreed; she would be better able to help him if she were close. She could carry him out of the tree if the Mundanes became overwhelming.

Bink picked up a package and tore it open. A score of large rubber bands fell out. Now at last he showed some ire. "What good are these?"

Imbri touched one with her hoof. Instantly it climbed up her foot and tightened about her ankle. It hurt; she had to lift her foot to her teeth to rip it off. Then it tried to clasp her nose.

"Oho!" Bink exclaimed. He stooped to pick one up. It writhed in his hand, but could not manage to close on his wrist. He flipped it at the nearest Mundane.

The band slid over the man's head and constricted about his neck. Suddenly he was choking, turning purple in the face.

"A weapon indeed!" Bink said. He flipped two more chokers at the other Mundanes. One looped about a man's arms, binding him awkwardly; the other caught its man around the waist, squeezing his gut. The bands might be small and harmless when Bink handled them, but were savage when they touched any other flesh!

More Mundanes appeared. Bink tossed the rest of the chokers, then picked up another vial. A knife flew from it, transfixing the Punic. But more was needed, so Bink opened a large, wide-mouthed bottle.

The bottle did not eject anything. Instead it expanded rapidly, until it was big enough to admit a man standing upright. On its side were printed the mystic words CAVE

CANEM. Imbri wasn't sure what that signified, but it seemed vaguely threatening.

"So it's a cave," Bink said. "Maybe it will serve. Hey, nymphs—fly in here!" He pointed to the opaque glass cave.

Obligingly, the buoyant nymphs flew inside. The Mundanes who were able charged in after them. Six men disappeared into the cave.

There was a horrendous growling deep inside, and a medley of screams. Imbri, startled, projected in an inquiring dreamlet—and discovered that the minds of the Mundanes had become truly animalistic, like those of vicious dogs.

"The cave of canines," Bink said. "Remarkable device!"

"Beware of the cave!" Imbri agreed. She didn't like canines; they tended to nip at equine heels and were difficult to tag with swift kicks.

Before long, the glass cave overflowed. Mundanes spilled back out, doggedly running on four feet, yelping. Their faces looked more canine than human, though Imbri wasn't sure this was very much of a change. The dogfaces scrambled out of the tree, tails between their legs.

Tails? Imbri looked again—but too late. The creatures were gone.

Still the Mundane menace grew. The rest of their army seemed to have arrived in more or less of a mass, and individual vials were not enough. Some men were distracted by the fleeing canines, and some appeared to have been bitten by those, but there were too many intact Mundanes to stop.

"Time for the ultimate measures," King Bink said. "Stand by to carry me to safety, Imbri; this may be worse than we anticipated."

Imbri stood by. Bink lifted the bag of winds and started to untie it.

A huge Mundane charged at the King, slashing downward with his sword. He missed Bink, who had alertly dodged, but scored on the bound river. The tie was severed cleanly.

Instantly the coil sprang outward as the water was released. The floor flooded, the liquid getting deeper moment by moment. There was a lot of fluid in a river! The

Mundanes cursed as their feet were washed out from under them. The one trying to attack the King was dumped and carried away by the torrent.

Then the string tying the mouth of the windbag came loose. The winds roared out of confinement. They swirled around the chamber of the baobab tree and whipped the surface of the rising water into froth. It became hard to stand, and not much fun to breathe.

Imbri tried to find King Bink, but he had been swept by the swirl, along with the Mundanes. Apparently the river, once released, had become a nonmagical force, so could act on him. Perhaps it was merely moving him without hurting him. No two-footed creature could keep on its feet in this! That was yet another inherent human liability—lack of a sufficient number of feet on the ground. Imbri did not care to gamble that Bink would not drown.

No—as she reviewed what she had been told of his talent, she decided he would not drown, because that fate would have been set up by magic—after all, the river had been magically bound—and therefore his drowning forbidden. But there were Mundanes mixed in that soup with him, and one of them certainly might hurt him, since they had been trying to do that regardless of magic. So her help was definitely needed.

She forged through the frothing water, squinting her eyes against the whirling wind. She did not know in what direction the wind wanted to go, because here in the tree it was still looking for the exit. She found the King. He was holding on to the edge of the Canem Cave. She nudged him, and he shifted his grip to her. He was carrying something that hampered him, but Imbri floated up under him and got him halfway clear of the violent torrent.

Now she half swam, half drifted with the current, moving out of the tree. Mundanes were also being carried along, burdened by their weapons and armor, gasping and drowning in the River Elba. Humfrey had prophesied correctly; able were they ere they saw Elba. She wasn't sure she had the phrasing quite right, but certainly the elements from coil and bag were devastating an army.

Outside the tree, the tide diminished. Imbri found her footing and forged toward higher ground. A few Mundanes were doing likewise. At last Imbri stood on an elevated ridge overgrown with quaking aspen; the timid trees were fluttering with apprehension as the water surged toward their roots. "Are you all right?" she sent to King Bink.

"Tired and waterlogged," he replied. "But whole. However, the battle is not yet over." For more Mundanes were straggling up to the ridge.

"We can outrun them," Imbri sent.

"No. They would only reorganize and march on Castle Roogna, where the women are. It has neither human nor zombie defenses any more. The ogre is there, but he can not be in all places at once. I don't want our loved ones subject to the will of the Punics, treated like pseudonymphs. I must deal with the enemy here, now; I shall not return to Castle Roogna until the threat has been entirely abated."

Imbri could appreciate his sentiment and admire his courage. But Bink was only one man against what appeared to be about twenty surviving Mundanes. He was fifty years old, which was getting along, physically, for a male of his species. He was likely to get himself killed—and his prospective successor, Arnolde Centaur, was still far away. Yet Bink was the King, and his decision counted.

"I see you have doubts," he said, smiling grimly. "You are a sensible mare. But I am not yet entirely dependent on my own resources. I salvaged the Good Magician's book of Words of Power."

"I hope they are good ones," she sent. "Here come two Mundanes!"

King Bink opened the book as the Mundanes approached him, spears poised. He fixed on the first one. "Oops—I don't know how to pronounce it," he said.

"Try several ways!" Imbri sent, for behind the two spearmen other Mundanes were coming, just as ugly and determined. One thing about these Punic mercenaries—they never gave up! If the King didn't use magic to protect himself, the nonmagical assault of the enemy would quickly finish him.

"SCHNEZL!" Bink read aloud, with a short E.

Nothing happened. The Mundanes drew nigh.

"SCHNEZL!" he repeated, this time using a long E.

The two Mundanes broke into uncontrollable sneezing. Their eyes watered, their breath got short, and they doubled over in nasal convulsions, trying vainly to blow their lungs out through their noses. Their buttons popped off, their belts snapped, and their eyes bugged in and out. They dropped their spears and staggered into the murky water, still firing out achoos. The other Mundanes paused in wonder and admiration at the cannonade. It seemed the King had pronounced the Word correctly the second time. Even Imbri felt an urge to sneeze, but she hastily suppressed it and stood closer to Bink. That helped; he did seem to have an ambience of immunity.

"Odd," Bink remarked. "The print has faded from the page. That Word is no longer written there."

"It must be a one-shot spell," Imbri sent. "How many more do you have?"

Bink flipped through the pages of the book. "There must be hundreds here."

"That should be enough." She was relieved.

Another Waver was charging up, sword swinging. Bink read the next Word. "AmnSHA!" he cried, accenting the second syllable.

The Mundane did not sneeze. He continued charging.

"AMNsha!" Bink repeated, this time accenting the first syllable.

Still the Mundane came, seemingly unaffected.

"AMNSHA!" Bink cried, with no accenting and hardly more than one syllable. And ducked as the man's sword whistled at his head. The blow missed.

The Mundane stopped and turned. He looked perplexed. "What am I doing here?" he asked. "Who are you? Who am I?"

"The Word made him lose his memory!" Imbri sent in a pleased dreamlet. "Too bad all the remaining Mundanes weren't within range of it!"

"Good thing you were in contact with me so it didn't catch you," King Bink responded. "Humfrey would have made better use of it and harmlessly abated the entire Mundane threat. My son Dor reported a similar use of a forget-spell eight hundred years ago at the Gap Chasm."

That was another mystic reference to something Dor obviously could not have been involved in. Maybe it was a memory of a dream. "We had better deal with the Mundane," Imbri reminded him in a dreamlet.

King Bink addressed the soldier. "You are an immigrant to the Land of Xanth. You will find a good homestead and a willing nymph, and will settle down to be a productive citizen. Congratulations."

"Yeah, sure," the man said, dazed. He lumbered off in search of his homestead.

But three more Mundanes were coming, and these did not look at all forgetful. The last Word had faded from the page. Bink turned the leaf and read the next one. "SKONK!"

There was a sudden terrible odor. The stench spread out from the sound of the Word, forming a bilious cloud that drifted in the path of the enemy soldiers. Unheeding, they charged into it. They had learned to be concerned about tangible magic, but to ignore mists and apparitions.

Immediately they scattered, coughing and holding their noses. They had received the brunt of the stench, though the peripheral wash was enough to make Imbri gag. That was bad, because horses were unable to regurgitate. A coincidental drift of wind had carried the mist away from the King, so he did not suffer. Coincidental?

The three Mundanes plunged into the water, trying to wash away the smell. A murk of pollution spread out from them, and small fish fled the region. It seemed it would take a long time for the men to cleanse themselves.

Yet another Mundane was attacking as the fog dissipated. This one paused just beyond it, fitting an arrow to his bow.

The King consulted the book. "KROKK!" he yelled at the bowman.

The Mundane changed form. His jaw extended into a greenish snout bulging with teeth. His limbs shrank into squat, clawed extremities. His torso sprouted scales. Unable to hold on to his bow or maintain his balance, he fell forward, belly-flopping on the ground with a loud whomp. He scrambled to the water and paddled away, propelling himself with increasing efficiency by means of a massive green tail that sprouted from his hind part.

"He turned into a gator," Bink remarked, impressed. "I didn't know the Good Magician had any transformation spells."

"He collected all kinds of information," Imbri sent. "Many people owed him favors for his services, and he knew exactly where to find useful bits of magic. He's been accumulating things for over a century. Once I brought him a bad dream about a box of quarterpedes, and he promptly woke and fetched it from the place the dream identified it. I didn't even know what they were and had forgotten the matter until that box turned up in his collection of spells in the baobab tree. He never missed a trick."

"I should have rescued that box," Bink said regretfully. "Maybe when the water subsides—"

Another Mundane charged. He swung a battle-axe with hideous intent. Bink quickly glanced at the book again. "BANSH!" he cried.

The Mundane disappeared, axe and all. These were certainly useful spells, when they worked!

But about a dozen Punics remained on the ridge. They now formed into an organized company and advanced slowly on the King. This was a more serious threat.

Bink leafed through the book, looking for a suitable Word. "If only there were definitions given!" he complained.

A spear sailed at the King. "Dodge!" Imbri sent.

Bink dodged. But the spear caught the open book and knocked it out of his hand. He regained his balance and dived for it, but the volume fell in the water. The crockagator forged up and snapped the book into its big mouth with an evil chuckle, carrying it away. The King had been abruptly deprived of his magic defense by nonmagical means. True, the crock had been magically transformed— but an untransformed Mundane could have done the same thing.

"But see!" he cried, stooping to pick up a floating bottle. It was yellow and warty and somewhat misshapen. "Isn't this the one containing the enormous squash?"

"I believe it is," Imbri agreed. It seemed Bink's talent was helping him compensate for the loss of the remaining Words. Maybe he wasn't being harmed, but just shifted to a more profitable mode, as the Words were highly variable in effect.

"I'll use this; you check the water for any other bottles." King Bink popped the cork, then hurled the bottle at the Mundane formation. The thing grew enormously, as was its nature, until it popped down on top of several Mundanes and squashed them flat.

Imbri found another bottle and fished it out with her teeth. She got some water in her mouth, and it still reeked of Skonk, but that was a necessary penalty. She brought the bottle to the King as the remaining Mundanes skirted the squash and advanced. He opened the bottle immediately and pointed it at the enemy.

A series of specks floated out from it. These expanded, becoming balls. On each ball a face formed, scowling awfully. One directed its glare at Imbri—and suddenly she was coated with grime.

"Oh, I see," the King said. "This is a bottle of dirty looks. Let's get them aimed properly." He reached out and turned each ball so that it faced the Mundanes.

The results were less than devastating, but more than inconvenient. The Punics turned dirty, their clothing badly soiled, their faces and arms gunked with grease and mud and sand. But they had been pretty dirty to begin with, so this was only an acceleration of a natural trend. They hacked and spit, trying to clear filth from their mouths. One aimed an arrow at King Bink, but the slime on his bow was such that the weapon twisted in his hand, fouling his shot. Another tried to draw a knife, but it was stuck in its holster, fastened by dirt and corrosion.

Imbri found two more bottles. One turned out to contain jumping beans. They bounded all over, peppering the Mundanes annoyingly; one man was blinded as the beans happened to score on his eyes, while another got one up his nose. That put him in immediate difficulty, since his nose bobbled about in response to the bean's continued jumping.

But six determined Punics remained, closing in on the King. The odds were still moderately prohibitive.

Bink opened the last bottle. A host of spooks sailed out. "Go get 'em!" the King ordered, and the spooks went after the Punics.

There ensued a fierce little battle. The spooks were supernatural creatures with vaporously trailing nether sections but strong clawed hands and grotesque faces. They
pounced on the Mundanes, biting off noses, gouging for
livers, and wringing necks. This was a reasonably pointless
exercise, as spooks could not digest these tidbits, but old
instincts died hard, and the Mundanes did find the approach somewhat disquieting. They fought back with
swords and spears, lopping off limbs and transfixing faces.
Blood flowed, ichor oozed, and bodies soon littered the
ground.

As the sun dipped low, getting clear of the sky before
night caught it, the mêlée subsided. All the spooks were
gone; one Mundane remained standing.

It was Hasbinbad, the Punic leader, the toughest cus-
tomer of them all.

"So you are the King of Xanth," Hasbinbad said.
"You're a better Magician than I took you for. I knew the
Transformer King was deadly dangerous, and I discovered
the Thing-Talking King was tough, too; I certainly wanted
no further part of the Zombie King, who turned my own
dead against me, and the Information King knew entirely
too much. But you had the reputation of possessing no
magic, so I figured you'd be safe." He shrugged with grim
good nature. "We all do make mistakes. I should have
taken you out, too, to promote the Centaur King, who I
know has no magic power in Xanth."

"You appear to know a great deal about Xanth and the
nature of our government," King Bink said.

"And you know a great deal about Mundania, as you
term the real world," Hasbinbad rejoined. "Men of age and
experience do master the essentials rapidly. It is essential to
survival in this business. When we first entered Xanth, I
thought it was Italy, but when a roc-bird carried away one
of my precious remaining elephants, I realized that something unusual was afoot. So I sent out my spies and in due
course learned much of what I needed. I realized very soon
that we would have to have magic to fight magic, so the
deal we made with the Horseman was fortuitous. This is a
better empire than Rome, and I intend to conquer it and
become the eleventh King of this siege."

"You will have to deal with the fifth King first," Bink said.

"I intend to. All my committed army is gone, but so is all your magic. Now you must meet me my way, man to man, Mundane fashion. After I dispatch you, I shall return to my reserve force and conquer Xanth without further significant resistance." He advanced, sword ready.

Imbri moved to intercept the Mundane. One swift kick would—

"No," King Bink said. "This is my responsibility. I have borrowed Humfrey's bag of tricks; now it is time I do my own work. You stand clear." He drew his sword.

"Well spoken," Hasbinbad said, unimpressed. He held his own sword casually, obviously not unduly alarmed by the caliber of the opposition. He was, after all, well armored, while King Bink was not, and the Punic was sure of his own skill with the weapon. He was a man of war, while the man of Xanth was a recently drafted King, no warrior.

"There remains one detail you may have overlooked," Bink said, and now his expression was anything but amiable. "One of those Kings you had eliminated by the Horseman was my son." The sword glinted as he stalked the Mundane.

"Ah, your son," the Punic said, taken aback. "Then you have a blood motive." He scowled. "Yet it remains to be seen how much that counts against skill."

The two came together. Hasbinbad swung his blade; Bink countered expertly. "Ah, I see you have learned your craft after all," the Mundane said, becoming impressed. He made a feint, but failed to draw the King out of position.

Then Bink attacked, slicing at the Punic's left arm where the armor did not cover it. Hasbinbad countered, but still got nicked. "First blood!" he exclaimed, and parried with a vicious stroke of his own that did not score.

Bink's lack of armor now showed as an advantage, for there was no extra weight on him to tire him, and his skill was great enough to make armor unnecessary. He pressed Hasbinbad methodically, forcing the man to take defensive measures.

Then the Mundane drew back. "It grows dark," he

panted. "I do not like to fight at night. I call for truce till dawn."

Imbri was alarmed. The Mundane was trying to gain time to recover his strength!

Bink shrugged. He had been among Mundanes, so was familiar with their odd customs. "Truce till dawn," he agreed.

Imbri swished her tail in frustration. This was surely folly!

Hasbinbad sheathed his sword and looked about. "I'm hungry," he said. "Want to trade some Mundane travel rations for some good grog? You natives know how to find free-growing juice without getting zapped by a tree, don't you?"

"Yes," Bink agreed.

"I don't like this," Imbri sent in a dreamlet. "That man is not to be trusted. The tide is receding; you can get away from him for the night."

"And risk losing track of him?" King Bink asked in the dream. "He still has half an army up north, and we have no means to stop it if it is competently led. I must deal with the leader now and not let him get away."

"You are honest; he is not. You must not trust him," Imbri urged.

"I know his nature," Bink returned gently.

"Are you conversing with the dream mare?" Hasbinbad inquired. "I'd like to have a steed like that myself. When we captured her up north, I did not know her nature; I'll not make that error again."

"This man knows entirely too much!" Imbri sent urgently. "Your Majesty, he is dangerous!"

"I will keep an eye on him," Bink promised. "You can travel readily at night; go inform the ladies at Castle Roogna of the developments of this day. This war is not over; we must raise new forces to deal with the second Mundane army."

He was the King; she had to obey. With severe misgivings, Imbri phased into nonmateriality and trotted across the ebbing water toward Castle Roogna. As she left, she heard Hasbinbad inquire: "Just who is to be King after the centaur? I thought you were out of Magicians. I inquire purely as a matter of professional curiosity."

"I am not in a position to know," Bink replied. "If I live, there will be no other Kings; if I die, I will not find out. How is it you know as much as we do about these matters?"

Hasbinbad laughed. If he answered, the words were lost in the distance as Imbri moved away. But both questions bothered her: how *did* the Punic know and, after Arnolde, who *would* be King? It seemed that both Xanth and Mundane forces accepted the prophecy that there would be ten Kings before the siege ended. But as was often the case, the specific unfolding of that prophecy was shrouded in alarming mystery.

Chapter 11. Centaur Input

Imbri reached Castle Roogna quickly, for the baobab tree was not far from it. She could readily have brought the King back here, had he been willing to come. But he was determined to finish the action his way and maybe he was right. Hasbinbad would be much more dangerous at the head of his second army than he was alone.

The women were alert and worried. Tandy, the ogre's wife, had moved into the castle, as it seemed she did not like being left alone while Smash guarded it. Now that Imbri had seen first hand—technically, it was first hoof, but the human folk would not understand that—the determination and savagery of the Mundanes, she was sure that one ogre was not enough to stop a siege of the castle. Quickly Imbri projected a broad dream that summarized the events of the day, so that they all understood it.

Irene shook her head with sad resignation. Like her

mother, she had recovered equilibrium after initial grief. This did not mean that she missed her husband and father less, but that she realized she had to do what she could to prevent the Kingdom of Xanth from being entirely destroyed. Her grief would keep; now was the time to fight. "Bink will not come back," she said. "He is too good a man; that's his fatal fault. I love him as I love my father, but I know him. He has never yielded to reasonable odds; he always follows his course, no matter what it costs. There is something of that quality in Dor, too . . ."

"And a great deal of it in Smash!" Tandy added. She was a girlishly small young woman, dark-haired and cute, hardly the type Imbri would have thought would be attracted to an ogre. But Imbri had interacted with her passingly before, and knew that she needed a really strong husband to protect her from the attentions of a demon. Certainly Smash was strong.

"Do you think we should prepare for the next King?" Queen Iris asked gently.

Imbri did not answer.

"I think so," Queen Irene agreed.

"Then we must impose on Imbri yet again to contact the centaurs," Iris said. She turned back to the mare. "Bink should have come back to organize things; since he did not, we women are forced to do what we can. If a centaur is to be our next King, the folk of Centaur Isle must be advised. They have resisted active participation in this campaign— foolishly, I think. Maybe they'll support one of their own in a way they declined to do for a human King." She sounded bitter.

"Not necessarily," Irene said. "They frown on magic talents in sapient species. They exiled Arnolde when his talent became known. They might treat him worse than a man."

"They exiled a centaur with magic. A centaur King of Xanth could be another matter. If we make the situation quite clear, they should come around. We know they are organized and ready; all they have to do is march."

"Make it clear?" Imbri sent in a query.

"That if they do not support us now, with all our faults as they perceive them, they will have to deal with our successors, the Punics. They have run afoul of Mundanes before, historically; I doubt they will relish the prospect."

"I'll go," Imbri sent. "I'll tell them tonight."

She set off, galloping south. She worried about King Bink, but knew he did not want her to return till morning; his peculiar sense of honor required him to win or lose his battle alone. So the best thing she could do was this, to help prepare Xanth for the next King. This was the stuff of which bad dreams were made; her duties had not changed as much as she had supposed!

The southern wilds of Xanth raced by, replete with garden-variety monsters and monstrous gardens. She had seldom been here because it was thinly populated, and thus few people needed dreams delivered. Now she was passing near the castle of the Zombie Master—

On an impulse she swerved. Millie the Ghost and her two children would be there alone, perhaps not even knowing the Zombie Master was ensorcelled. She had to stop by and say something, though there was little she could do.

She reached the castle, hurdled the gooky moat, penetrated the decrepit wall, and trotted into the clean main hall, where Millie was reading from a book titled *Weird Mundane Tales* to the children by the eerie glow of a magic lantern. All looked up as she entered.

"Imbri!" Millie exclaimed gladly.

"I just wanted to be sure you knew—" Imbri projected, but could not continue.

"We know," Millie said. "No one told us, but we knew when Chameleon left that it would soon be our turn. The chain has not yet been broken."

"You are taking it very well," Imbri sent.

"I was a ghost and Jonathan a zombie for eight hundred years," Millie said. "We have had a lot of experience with death and have learned to be patient. Jonathan has not returned as a zombie, so I know he isn't really dead. When the chain is broken, he will return." She had excellent perspective!

"Bink is King now, and after him will come Arnolde Centaur. Then there may be four more Kings before the chain is finally broken—but we don't know who they may be, for Xanth is out of Magicians."

"Who enchanted the Kings?" Millie asked. "Do you know yet?"

"The Horseman. King Humfrey named him, before he . . . The Punic Hasbinbad pretty much confirmed it."

"Is the Horseman a Magician?"

That made Imbri pause, horrified. "If he's a Magician, he might claim the throne of Xanth!"

"That was my thought," Millie said. "He helps the Mundanes conquer Xanth, then assumes the throne as the last Magician, ending the chain. By Xanth law, we would have to accept him."

"This is terrible!" Imbri projected. "He may be encouraging us to fight the Mundanes; then if he becomes King, he'll start ensorcelling the Mundane leaders so they can't fight any more. He is playing both sides against each other so that he can take over in the end. Beware the Horseman—the chain leads to him!"

"Unless we somehow break it before then," Millie said. She hugged her two children close to her, preventing them from becoming too frightened.

"I am going to Centaur Isle to ask them to support Arnolde when he is King," Imbri sent. "Maybe this will help convince them."

"Let's hope so," Millie said. "Don't let me detain you, Imbri; this is too important. But I do thank you for stopping by."

Imbri turned to go—and discovered an eye in the floor looking up at her, and a print where her hind feet had been, reading: THIS IS A HORSE'S REAR. The children were up to their usual tricks. She stepped over the eye and print and walked on through the wall.

She raced on south, glad she had made the side trip. As it happened, she had gained a valuable if horrible new insight in the process. She had known before that the Horseman was playing his own game, but had not thought of the consequence of his being recognized as Xanth's only surviving Magician. He could accomplish his fell purpose—if they didn't break that chain first. Reality was becoming even more like a bad dream.

It was a long way to the southern tip of Xanth. She had

forgotten how much time it would take. It was midnight by the time she arrived. Then she remembered: she should have used the gourds! Her distraction had been such that she had never thought of the obvious!

That reminded her of Good King Humfrey's shame. What obvious thing had he overlooked that should so mortify him before the fact? The Horseman had sneaked up on him, true—but that had happened to every King of Xanth so far.

The centaurs of the Isle were mostly asleep. Imbri had to locate their leader quickly. She projected a dream to the mind of the first sleeper she encountered, a middle-aged female. "Who is your leader?"

"Why, everyone knows that," the centauress said. "Gerome, Elder of the Isle."

"Thank you."

"Since when does a dream thank a person?"

"Anything can happen in a dream."

Now Imbri used her night mare person-locating sense and homed in on Gerome. This centaur was old, his hair and coat beginning to turn gray. She shaped her dream carefully and sent it in to him.

In this dream, she was a female centaur, of middle age and dark of hide. "Elder Gerome, I bring important news," she began.

"Ah, you would be the night mare from Castle Roogna," he said, unsurprised. "We have been expecting you."

Obviously the centaur community had its own sources of information. Centaurs did employ magic; they just didn't like to recognize it in themselves. Those centaurs who developed magic talents were exiled; thus all the ones around Castle Roogna were not welcome here at the Isle. Yet this was the principal bastion of the species and this was where the real help had to come from. "Do you know, then, that Xanth is under attack by the Nextwave of Mundanes?"

"Of course."

"And that one of the human folk called the Horseman has been taking the minds of our Kings—Trent, Dor, the Zombie Master, Humfrey, and maybe Bink?" Imbri didn't really believe that last, but preferred to think of it that way rather than of death at the foul hands of Hasbinbad.

"Bink?"

"He is a human Magician whose talent has been concealed until recently."

"That is in order, then."

"But after him, the King of Xanth will have to be Arnolde Centaur."

"Now that is problematical," Gerome said. "We do not accept—"

"If we do not stop the Nextwave, it will conquer us, as have Waves of the past. You centaurs know what it is like when a new Wave rules Xanth."

Gerome sighed. "We do indeed! Better the obscenity we know than the one we may experience. Very well; we shall treat Arnolde as we might a human King, and answer his call if it comes."

"The Mundanes could overwhelm Castle Roogna before your force arrives," Imbri pointed out. "It would be better to march to Castle Roogna now, to be there at need."

Gerome shook his head. "We dislike this, but acknowledge the merit of the notion. We shall dispatch a contingent by raft in the morning. It will take two days for us to make port near Castle Roogna, and half a day to march inland. Will your forces be able to fend off the Wave until then?"

"Probably," Imbri replied in the dream. "Half the Mundane army has been destroyed; the other half should take two or three days to reach Castle Roogna."

"Very well. You have our guarantee. But there is a price."

"A price?"

"We have *de facto* local autonomy. We want it to become openly recognized by the government of Xanth, henceforth and for all time."

"If Arnolde becomes King, I'm sure he will grant you that."

"See that he does," Gerome said sternly.

That was that. Centaurs were creatures of honor, so she knew they would act as promised. Imbri withdrew from the centaur Elder's dream and let him sleep in peace. But she set a hoofprint in the dirt of his doorway so that he would remember her when he woke.

She trotted out, looking for a gourd patch. But there turned out to be none on the Isle; it seemed the centaurs had methodically stamped them out because of their devastating hypnotic magic. That was understandable but inconvenient. She would have known about this, had this been her beat for dream duty. Now she had either to spend time looking for a gourd on the wild mainland or to race for home directly.

She decided on the latter course. It took more time, but was less frustrating. She raced straight north, through trees and mountains, over lakes and bogs, under low-hanging clouds and the nose of a sleeping dragon, and up to Castle Roogna just as dawn sleepily cracked open an eye. It was good to race flatout for this distance; it made her feel young again.

Inside the castle, she gave her report. "They are sending a detachment, but they want autonomy."

"We can't make that decision," Queen Irene said. She was on duty while her mother slept, awaiting Chameleon's return. "Only the King can do that."

"It's time for me to rejoin King Bink anyway," Imbri sent. If he still lives, she thought nervously.

"Yes. He is my husband's father," Irene said. "Bring him back here, however you find him." She had aged rapidly in the past few days and looked more like her mother. Her eyes were deeply shadowed and there were lines forming about her face. She had the reputation of being a beautiful and well-developed girl; both qualities were waning now. Continued crisis was not being kind to her.

Imbri was tired, but she couldn't take time to rest. She trotted on out toward the baobab tree.

King Bink was not there, of course; he had left when the river flooded it out. Now there were only scattered Mundane bodies, forest debris, drying layers of mud, and occasional bottles. Imbri checked one of these, but found it was open, the cork lost, whatever had resided in it wasted, the penalty of the flood. The water was gone, but it would be long before the region recovered.

She made her way to the ridge that had been an island yesterday evening. She found the remnants of a camfire, with two empty T-cups from a T-tree and pots from a pot pie. Bink and Hasbinbad had eaten together. Then what?

Imbri checked for footprints. She sniffed the ground. She listened. She had acute equine senses. She picked up a trail of sorts.

King Bink had located a pillow bush and slept there. But Hasbinbad's traces came there, too. They were fresher; he had come later. The footprints were not straightforward, not those of one who came openly; they were depressed too much on the toes, scuffling too little sand. A sneak approach.

A sneak attack at night, before dawn. Both men gone. Imbri did not like this. Had the Punic leader treacherously . . . ?

But there was no blood. No sign of violence. Hasbinbad had sneaked up—but Bink had not been caught. He had moved away from his bed before that time, perhaps leaving a mock-up of himself behind.

Hasbinbad, it seemed, had attempted treachery, but Bink had anticipated him. The King had indeed been alert and understood the nature of his opponent. Imbri, working it out, was relieved. But what had happened then?

She quested and found two trails in the night. Bink following Hasbinbad. The wronged pursuing the guilty. The truce had been violated, relieving the King of any further need to be trusting, and now the fight had resumed in earnest. Bink had shown himself to be stronger in direct combat, yet had held back for what he deemed to be ethical reasons, without being naive. Hasbinbad had blundered tactically as well as ethically, and sacrificed any respite he might otherwise have claimed.

Imbri followed the trail with difficulty, knowing that she was losing headway. Bink and Hasbinbad had evidently moved rapidly in the predawn hour; Imbri was moving slowly, lest she lose the subtle traces. This was not ideal tracking terrain; there were rocky patches and boggy patches and the crisscrossing tracks of foraging animals, obscuring the human prints.

Her eye caught something in a hollow to the side. Imbri detoured briefly to investigate. It was a corked vial, containing yellowish vapor or fluid. Another of Magician Humfrey's spells, borne here by the transient tide, unbroken. What should she do with it? She did not want to leave it, but would have to carry it in her mouth. That would be awkward, especially if she happened to chew on it and break the glass. Suppose it was an ifrit? Still, there were many dangers in Xanth, and she might need the help of a spell. So she picked it up and carried it carefully with her lips.

The trail seemed interminable. Hours passed as the two men's traces bore north. Imbri was sure now: Hasbinbad wanted to get away, having found King Bink too much for him. The Punic was trying to rejoin his other army, the one nominally commanded by the Horseman, so he could lead another and more devastating thrust at Castle Roogna. The first army had eliminated the opposition; the second would complete the conquest.

There was a hiss. A flying snake was orienting on Imbri, feeling that its territory had been invaded. This was one of the wingless kind that levitated by pure magic, wriggling through the invisible columns of the air. It was a large one, twice Imbri's own length, and poisonous saliva glistened on its fangs. Probably Hasbinbad's passage had roused it, but Bink's presence had balked it. If magic could not harm the King, how could a magical creature? Bink could go anywhere in Xanth with perfect safety as long as he remained careful about nonmagical hazards. Perhaps, ironically, Hasbinbad had been protected by Bink's ambience, as Imbri herself had been protected when she stood close to him. Now it was her misfortune to encounter the serpent fully roused and by day, when she was vulnerable. Yet she could not detour around its territory; she would never be able to locate the fading trail again in time to do any good.

She hesitated, but the snake did not. It hissed and launched itself at her, jaws gaping. Involuntarily, Imbri bared her teeth, bracing for battle—and cracked the vial she had forgotten she held. Immediately she spit it out— but a trickle of fluid fell on her tongue. It was not yellow—that turned out to be the color of the glass—but colorless, and also tasteless. Plain water?

The snake struck, burying its fangs in her neck. Disaster! Imbri felt the poison numbing her, spreading outward much faster than had been the case when she had been bitten on the knee before. This was a larger, more deadly snake. How she hated snakes!

Imbri flung her head and lifted a forehoof, lashing at the snake's body, knocking it to the ground. The reptile hissed and struck at her again, but she stomped its head into the ground, killing it. The thing had been foolish to attack a fighting mare; horses knew how to deal with serpents. But Imbri herself had been critically slow, owing to fatigue and the distraction of the breaking bottle; otherwise the fangs would not have scored.

Now she assessed her situation. She had been bitten, but she was massive enough so that the poison might dilute to a nonfatal level by the time it spread through her body. If it happened to be a poor bite, and if this happened to be a mildly toxic variety of snake instead of a supertoxic one, she would survive. But she would certainly suffer, and would probably lose the trail.

Yet she didn't feel too bad. The numbness was constricting, retreating back around the puncture. Was her body fighting it off? How was that possible? She had no special immunity; in fact, her condition should have been aggravated by the weapon released from the vial. Too bad it hadn't destroyed the snake!

Weapon? Imbri licked her lips, detecting a faint aftertaste. That was no weapon; that was healing elixir! No wonder she was not suffering; she had blundered into the universal restorative, the one thing that could counter the snake's bite and restore her waning energy. She had had the luck of King Bink!

Luck? In Bink's case it wasn't luck; it was his magic talent. She knew now that it had operated in some extremely devious ways to protect both his health and his anonymity all the prior years of his life. It could not be limited to his direct personal experiences; it had to extend back to affect whatever magic threatened him indirectly. Suppose he was in trouble, and magic was responsible—how would his talent counter the danger by seeming coincidence?

It could arrange to have the vial of elixir float conveniently near, for him to discover when the snake attacked. But the snake had not attacked him; it couldn't, because his magic prevented it more directly. So why the elixir, unused?

This could be operating on a more subtle level. Bink was threatened by a Mundane person—yet in the ambience of magic that was Xanth, Hasbinbad almost had to have had the benefit of some magic, because no one could avoid it here. So in a devious fashion, the threat against Bink was also magical, and therefore his talent would act to protect him against it. But extremely subtly, for this was a borderline case.

His talent just might arrange to have magical help come to him, to protect him from the Mundane. Maybe he would need healing elixir to abate a wound inflicted by Hasbinbad, so here it was. Imbri herself had become a tool of the King's magic, and was being deviously protected by that magic so she could fulfill her mission.

She checked the ground. By an amazing chance, the bottom section of the vial had dropped upright and nestled in the grass, containing some fluid.

Chance?

Imbri found the loose cork, picked it up delicately with her teeth, and set it in the ragged new neck of the vial. She tamped it carefully with her nose. It just fit, sealing in the precious fluid. There was no room remaining inside the truncated container for more than a few drops, but that didn't matter. The amount would be sufficient for its purpose, whatever and whenever that was. She had what King Bink would need.

She moved on, carrying the vial again, feeling more confident. She made better progress, and the trail began to warm. Still, she had a fair amount of time to make up.

It was midafternoon by the time she followed the trail to the Gap Chasm. Here there was a change. There were signs of a scuffle, and some blood soaked the ground, but there were no people.

She sniffed, explored, and formulated a scenario: Hasbinbad had, naturally enough, forgotten the Gap Chasm. Most people did. He had been suddenly balked, and King

Bink had caught up. There had been a desperate fight, with one of them wounded—and one of them had fallen into the Chasm.

Anxiously she sniffed in widening half-spirals, since the Chasm was too deep at this point to show any sign of the victim within it, assuming the Gap Dragon had not already cleaned up the mess. Which man had survived? It should be the King, according to her revised theory of his magic—but she was not sure her theory was correct.

She found a trail leading away. Joy! It had the smell of Bink! There was blood on it, and the prints dragged, but the King had won the final contest. He was the lone survivor of this encounter with the Wave.

She followed it on to the west. Bink must be going to intersect the path to the invisible bridge across the Chasm so he could follow it safely back the other way to Castle Roogna. The path was charmed against monsters; Bink might not need that protection, but still, a path was easier to follow than the untracked wilderness, especially when a person was tired and hurt.

Imbri speeded up, no longer sniffing out the specific traces. Now she knew where he was going; she would catch up, administer the healing elixir, and give him a swift ride home. Maybe there had been yet another level to his power: it had preserved her from the flying snake so she could come and help him now, apart from the elixir, by becoming his steed. All would be well; King Bink had survived his campaign and should have centaur support for the next one. The centaurs were excellent archers; if they lined up on the south edge of the Gap, the Mundanes would never get across!

As she neared the invisible bridge, in the last hour of the day, she spied a figure. It was the King, resting on the ground. She neighed a greeting.

But as she came to him, her joy turned to horror. Bink was sitting unmoving, staring at the ground, in a puddle of blood from a wound in his chest. Was he dead?

Quickly she crunched through the piece of vial and smeared the dripping elixir across his wound with her nose. Instantly the gash healed and turned healthy, and the King's color improved. But still he did not respond to her presence, and when she sent him a dreamlet, she found his mind blank.

"But it can't happen to you!" she wailed protestingly in the dream, assuming the image of a weeping willow tree in deep distress. "You are the one person who can not be harmed by magic!"

Yet the fact belied the logic. King Bink had defeated one enemy physically, only to fall prey to the other magically. He had, after all, been taken by the Horseman.

It was night by the time she got him to Castle Roogna, draped across her back. A man might mount an unconscious horse, but it was another matter for a horse to cause an unconscious man to mount.

Arnolde and Chameleon had arrived fortuitously within the hour. The centaur had given her a ride, after the day horse had tired from the night's hard travel. Day horses were not night mares; they had to proceed carefully through darkness, instead of phasing through the vagaries of the terrain. The stallion had stopped at the brink of the Gap Chasm, too nervous to trust the one-way bridge.

"The one-way bridge?" Imbri sent, perplexed. "It is one-way north; how could you use it south?"

"We had to," Arnolde explained. "We knew the main bridge was out."

The answer was simple: Queen Iris had seen them coming, using an illusory magic mirror, and had sent old Crombie the soldier and his visiting daughter Tandy out to meet them. Tandy's husband the ogre had offered to go and hurl the folk across the Chasm, but they declined his helpful notion by pointing out that he was needed to guard Castle Roogna from surprise attack. Tandy had crossed first, making the bridge real before her, stopping just shy of the north anchor. Crombie had stopped just off the south end, keeping the bridge real between himself and his daughter. Arnolde and Chameleon had crossed safely while it was thus anchored. Had Grundy remained with them, they could have used the magic carpet to ferry across, one by one, but the golem had long since flown back to the Good Magician's castle to keep watch until the Gorgon returned with her sister the Siren. Actually, Arnolde confessed, he would hardly have trusted his mass to a carpet designed for human weight. Once the travelers had crossed, Crombie and Tandy had jumped to land at either end, letting the bridge fade. Tandy would walk around to the invisible bridge and return to Castle Roogna later in the night. The day horse, professing to be too tired to go farther, had settled in place to graze and sleep. They had not argued with him; Mundane creatures did tend to be nervous about things they could not see, and he had not wanted to admit his fear of the bridge.

"But Xanth isn't safe at night!" Imbri protested. She was displeased at the day horse's recalcitrance; he was a big, strong animal who should have been able to carry Tandy to the other bridge before retiring. He would have done so for Chameleon, or if Imbri herself had been along. But, of course, Mundane animals were neither the magical nor the social equals of Xanth animals; this was a reminder of that fact. It was useless to be angry at a Mundane creature for not being Xanthian.

"She is the wife of an ogre, and the path is enchanted; even a tangle tree would hesitate to bother her," Queen Iris said, a trifle grimly.

Imbri remembered how Smash the Ogre had torn up the Mundanes in combat. No one with any sense would antagonize an ogre! The Mundanes who had penetrated to this region had all been dispatched. So it was true: Tandy should be safe enough.

But that was the only light note. King Bink had been taken, and Xanth had a new King. Chameleon now had both a son and a husband to mourn. The grief that the Horseman had brought to Xanth in the name of his ambition for power!

"This development was not, unfortunately, unanticipated," Arnolde Centaur said in his didactic way as Queen Iris broached the matter of the crown. "As an archivist, I am conversant with the protocols. Xanth must have a Magician King. It is not specified that the King must be a man."

"He can be a centaur," Queen Iris agreed. "The framers of Xanth law did not anticipate a centaur Magician."

"Perhaps not," King Arnolde agreed. "They may also

have overlooked the mischief wrought by the Horseman. That was not precisely my meaning, however. Where is the Council of Elders of human Xanth?"

"Roland is here," Queen Iris said. "Bink's father, Dor's grandfather. He is old and failing, but retains his mind. He was rousted from his home at the North Village when the Mundanes pillaged it. He can speak for the Elders, I'm sure."

"I must talk to him immediately."

They brought Roland, for the King had spoken. Roland was King Trent's age, still sturdy and erect, but he moved slowly and his sight was fading. In the years of relative calm during King Trent's rule, the Council of Elders had had little to do and had become pretty much ceremonial. Roland retained his magic, however; he could freeze a person in place.

"Roland, I have in mind a certain interpretation or series of interpretations of Xanth law," Arnolde said. "I would like your endorsement of these."

"Interpretations of law!" Queen Iris protested. "Why waste your time on such nonsense when there is a crisis that may topple Xanth?"

Arnolde merely gazed at her, flicking his tail tolerantly.

". . . your Majesty," she amended, embarrassed. "I apologize for my intemperate outburst."

"You shall have an answer in due course," the Centaur King said gently. "Roland?"

The old man's eyes brightened. This sounded like a challenge! "What is your interpretation, King Arnolde?"

Imbri noted how careful these people were being with titles, in this way affirming the strength and continuity of the Kingship, so vital to the preservation of Xanth.

"Xanth must have a King who is a Magician," the centaur said. "The definition of the term 'Magician' is obscure; I interpret it to mean a person whose magic talent is more potent by an order of magnitude than that of most people. This is, of course, a relative matter; in the absence of the strongest talents, the most potent of the remaining talents must assume the mantle."

"Agreed," Roland said.

"Thus, in the present circumstance, your own talent be-comes—"

"Oh, no, you don't!" Roland protested vigorously. "I see the need to promote new talents to Magician status for the sake of the continuing succession of Kings, and I endorse that solution. But I am too old to assume the rigors of the crown!"

How very clever, Imbri thought. Of course Xanth would find its remaining Kings by this simple device! What a fine perception Arnolde had, and how well he was applying it to the solution of the crisis. It was certainly important that a person be designated to follow Arnolde as King, since Humfrey's prophecy indicated four Kings would follow the centaur. If Arnolde lost his position before attending to that matter, there would be chaos.

"Well, then, the talents of younger people. Irene, for ex-ample, should now be ranked a Sorceress, since her magic is certainly beyond the average, and our top talents are gone."

"True," Roland said. "I have privately felt she should have been diagnosed a Sorceress before; certainly her rela-tive talent qualifies her now. But this will not profit the Kingdom, since she is a woman."

Queen Irene was upstairs with Chameleon and their un-fortunate husbands; otherwise, Imbri knew, she would have been quite interested in the turn this dialogue had taken. Queen Iris, however, was reacting with amazed pleasure.

"In what way is the power of a Sorceress inferior to that of a Magician?" Arnolde inquired rhetorically.

"No way!" Queen Iris put in. This had been a peeve of hers for decades.

"No way," Roland echoed with a smile.

"Then we agree that the distinction is merely cosmetic," Arnolde said. "A Sorceress is, in fact, a female Magician."

"True," Roland acknowledged. "A Magician. The termi-nology is inconsequential, a lingering prejudice carrying across from prior times."

"Prejudice," Arnolde said. "Now *there* is a problematical concept. My kind is prejudiced against certain forms of magic; I have experienced that onus myself. Your kind is prejudiced against women."

"By no means," Roland objected. "We value and respect and protect our women."

"Yet you systematically discriminate against them."

"We do not—"

"Certainly you do!" Iris put in vehemently under her breath.

"I stand corrected," the centaur said with an obscure smile. "There is no legal distinction between the human sexes in Xanth."

"Well—" Roland said. He seemed to have caught on to something that Imbri and the Queen had not.

"Then you see no reason," Arnolde continued, "why a woman could not, were she in other necessary respects qualified, assume the throne of Xanth?"

Queen Iris stopped breathing. Imbri, now discovering the thrust of the Centaur King's progression, suffered a dreamlet of a cherry bomb exploding in realization. What an audacious attack on the problem!

Roland squinted at the centaur obliquely. He half chuckled. "You are surely aware that the throne of Xanth is by ancient custom reserved for Kings."

"I am aware. Yet does that custom anywhere define the term 'King' as necessarily male?"

"I have no specific recollection of such a definition," Roland replied. "I presume custom utilizes the masculine definition or designation for convenience, carrying no further onus. I suppose, technically, an otherwise qualified female could become King."

"I am so glad your perception concurs with mine," Arnolde said. Both men understood that they had just played out a charade of convenience, knowing the crisis of Xanth. "Then with the presumed approval of the Elders, I hereby, in my capacity and authority as King of Xanth, designate the line of succession to this office to include henceforth male and female Magicians." The centaur swung to focus through his spectacles on Queen Iris. "Specifically, the Magician Iris to follow me, and her daughter the Magician Irene to follow her, should new Kings of Xanth be required before this present crisis is resolved."

Again Roland smiled. "I concur. I believe I speak for the Council of Elders."

Queen Iris breathed again. Her face was flushed. A small array of fireworks exploded soundlessly in the air around them: her illusion giving vent to her suppressed emotion. She, together with all her sex, had just been at one stroke enfranchised. "One could get to like you, Centaur King."

Arnolde shrugged. "Your husband has always been kind to me. He provided me with a gratifying position when my own species cast me out. You yourself have always treated me with courtesy. But it is logic that dictates my decision, rather than gratitude. An imbalance has been corrected."

"Yes, your Majesty," she breathed, her eyes shining. In that moment Queen Iris resembled a beautiful young woman, like her daughter, and Imbri was not certain this was entirely illusion.

Arnolde turned to Imbri. "Now I must have a conference with you, good mare. I realize you are tired—"

"So are you, your Majesty," Imbri sent.

"Then let us handle this expeditiously so we both can rest before my brethren arrive."

"Of course," Imbri agreed, wondering what he had in mind. The play of his intellect had already dazzled her, and she knew he would be an excellent King, even though he could perform no magic in Xanth.

They retired to a separate chamber for a private conversation. Imbri wondered why Arnolde should wish to exclude the others, such as Queen Iris, who surely needed to be kept advised of official business.

"Does it strike you as odd that King Bink, who was immune to harm by magic, should nevertheless fall prey to the spell of the Horseman?"

"Yes!" Imbri agreed. "He should have been invulnerable! He believed he was! His talent was working with marvelous subtlety and precision. He wanted the Horseman to approach him, believing that—"

"Yet he evidently was not immune," Arnolde said. "Why should this be?"

"He was very tired after fighting Hasbinbad and getting wounded and dragging himself almost to the bridge path. Maybe his talent had been weakened."

"I question that. His talent was one of the strongest known in Xanth, though it *wasn't* known."

"Yet it failed to protect him from magical harm—"

"There is my point. Could it be that Bink was not actually harmed?"

Imbri glanced toward the room where the Kings were lyng. "I don't understand. He *was* ensorcelled."

"You assume the enchantment was harmful. Suppose it was not? In that event, Bink would not be proof against it."

"But—" Imbri could not continue the thought.

"Let me approach the matter from another perspective," Arnolde said. "It strikes me that the symptoms of these ensorcelled Kings are very like the trance inspired by the hypnogourd."

"Yes!" Imbri agreed, surprised. "But there is no gourd."

"Now suppose the Horseman has the talent to form a line-of-sight connection magically between any two places," the centaur said. "Such as the eye of a King and the peephole of a gourd. Would that account for the observed effect?"

Imbri was astonished. "Yes, I think it would!"

"Then I suspect we know where to look for the missing Kings," Arnolde concluded. "Would you be willing to do that?"

"Of course!" Imbri sent, chagrined that she had not seen this obvious connection before.

"Rest, then. When you are ready, you may return to the gourd and investigate. Only you can do this."

"I must do it now!" Imbri sent. "If the Kings are there—"

"We still would not know how to get them out," the Centaur King finished. "We must be wary of exaggerating the importance of this notion, which perhaps is fallacious. This is why I have not mentioned it to the grieving relatives. I do not wish to deceive them with false expectations."

Imbri understood. "I shall say nothing to them until we know. Still, I must find out. I can rest after I know and after I report to you." She started out, using the door so as not to appear too excited to the others.

"That is very nice of you," Arnolde said.

Imbri almost bumped into the Mundane archivist, Ichabod, who was on his way in. He had evidently been sum-

moned to the King's presence for another conference. Imbri understood why; Ichabod was Arnolde's closest friend
in Xanth, possessing similar qualities of intellect and personality, together with his comprehensive knowledge of
Mundanes. He would be an excellent person to discuss
prospects with, since he could be far more objective about
Xanth matters than the regular citizens of Xanth could.
She sent him a dreamlet of friendly greeting, and Ichabod
patted her on the flank in passing.

Imbri found the nearest gourd patch and dived into the
World of Night. Because she was alone, there were no spe-
cial effects. She trotted directly to the pasture of the Night
Stallion.

He was waiting for her. "It's high time you checked in,
you idiotic mare!" he snorted in an irate dream, the breeze
of his breath causing the lush grass to curl and shrivel.
"You were supposed to serve as liaison!"

"King Arnolde sent me," she replied, intimidated. "A lot
has happened recently, and he—"

"Out with it, mare! Ask!"

"Have the lost Kings of Xanth—?"

"Right this way." The Stallion walked through a wall
that abruptly appeared in the pasture, and she followed.

They came into a palatial, human-style chamber. There
were all the Kings. King Trent was playing poker with
Good Magician Humfrey and the Zombie Master. King
Dor was chatting with the furniture, and King Bink, a recent arrival, was asleep on a couch.

"They're all right!" Imbri projected, gratified. "Right
here in the gourd! Why didn't you send another night mare
out to advise us?"

"It is not permitted," the Stallion replied. "To tell the
future is apt to negate it, likewise to divulge what can not
be known through natural channels. You were the designated channel; it had to flow through you. There was no
other way to handle this situation without supernatural in-
terference, so I had to stand aside and let it proceed undisturbed. All I could safely do was try to warn Xanth about
the Horseman."

Imbri snorted. "That didn't make much difference!"

"Precisely. The future was not spoiled, because people seldom believe the truth about it. It shall not be spoiled, though critical revelations remain to be unveiled. Now that a King of Xanth has figured out the riddle of the Kings, that information is no longer privileged. Perhaps he will figure out the rest in time to save Xanth. I leave you to it." He paused, giving Imbri a meaningful stare. "Still, beware the Horseman."

"I *am* wary of him!" Imbri protested. But the Night Stallion walked back through the wall and was gone, leaving her with the uncomfortable feeling that she was missing something vital, as she had done before. Yet what more could she do except watch out for the Horseman and not trust him at all?

The three Kings quickly concluded their poker game— the Magician of Information, naturally, seemed to be well ahead, and had a pile of oysters, bucksaws, and wilting lettuce to show for it—and turned to Imbri. "How goes it Xanthside?" King Trent inquired politely, as if this were a routine social call.

"Your Majesty," Imbri sent, still halfway overwhelmed by this discovery of the lost Kings. "Do you want the whole story?"

"No. Only since Bink was taken. We know it to that point."

Imbri sent out a dream that showed her search for King Bink, their return to Castle Roogna, the ascension of Arnolde Centaur, and his solution of the riddle of Kings and designation of Queen Iris and Queen Irene as the next Kings.

"Marvelous!" the Zombie Master exclaimed. "That is one sensible centaur!"

"That accounts for two Kings to follow him," Humfrey said. "But there is supposed to be a line of ten. Who are the other two?"

King Dor joined them. "The Dark Horse knows," he said. "But he won't tell."

"He is right not to tell," the Zombie Master said. "We must figure it out for ourselves. Only then can we break the chain and finally save Xanth."

"Is there no way to get you back to Xanth?" Imbri asked.

"Not while the Horseman is free," Humfrey answered. "I believe the only way to stop him from enchanting people is to end his life—but even he may not be able to reverse a line of sight he has made. It seems to be a limited talent, one-way, like the one-way bridge across the Chasm. He is not Magician caliber."

"Yet what mischief he causes!" the Zombie Master exclaimed. "As long as a single gourd exists, his power remains. Perhaps we are lucky he did not strike years ago."

"He probably did not know about the gourds," Humfrey said. "Many people don't."

"The gourds!" Imbri sent, appalled. "*I* told him about the gourds, or at least about the World of Night. He thought the gourd was merely an oddity, but after he knew its nature—*I* showed him how to imprison the Kings!"

"This is the nature of prophecy," King Trent said philosophically. "You carried the message, but did not understand the nature of the threat. None of us did. You are no more culpable than the rest of us. You have certainly done good work since, and your Night Stallion seems to feel that you hold the key to the final salvation of Xanth."

"Me!" Imbri sent, astonished.

"But we do not know in what way," Good Magician Humfrey said. "This is an aspect of information that has been denied to me, along with the specific nature of my own colossal folly. Perhaps it is simply in your position as liaison. I dare say the wives will be pleased to know we remember them."

Dor laughed. "Mine may say good riddance! I certainly didn't pay her much attention after we married."

"She won't sulk long," King Trent said. "My daughter is a creature of femalishly mercurial temperament, like my wife." Then he did a double take. "My wife! I referred to Queen Iris!"

Humfrey elevated an eyebrow. "After a quarter century, it's about time, Trent. You can't live in the past forever."

Imbri remembered how King Trent had loved his Mundane wife, not the Queen, and the sorrow this had brought to Iris.

"It may be a bit late for such a revelation, but yes, it is true. It is time to relate to the present, without renouncing the past. Iris has been worthy." King Trent returned his attention to Imbri. "Please convey that message, Mare Imbri."

Imbri was happy to agree. Then she turned to Humfrey. "How did the Horseman get you and Bink?" she asked the Good Magician. "You recognized him, so should have known how to stop him, and Bink is supposed to be immune from hostile magic."

"That was perhaps part of my blunder," Humfrey said. "I paid so much attention to setting up my spells that I did not see him enter the tree. Suddenly he was standing there. I only had time to whisper his identity before he zapped me. Had I been alert, as I should have been, I could have had a Word of Power ready—" He shook his head, ashamed.

"When did he come?" Imbri asked.

"As I said, I was not paying attention, but I would guess very soon after you and the day horse left. He must have been lurking in hiding, waiting his chance to catch me alone. The cunning knave!"

"And Bink—how did he—?"

"Bink was not harmed by the magic," Humfrey replied, confirming the centaur's diagnosis. "He was only sent to a new awareness, as were the rest of us. We find our present company quite compatible. Therefore his talent was not operative."

Except to the extent of preserving her to rescue Bink's body, Imbri realized. The protective talent had a narrow definition of Bink's welfare; he was in actual physical danger while he was King, and in none thereafter. So it did make sense, though Xanth itself suffered. At least his banishment to the gourd had enabled his successor Arnolde to solve the riddle.

"How can I help?" Imbri asked.

"Just what you plan," the Zombie Master told her. "Liaison. Bear news to the wives. Perhaps we shall have useful advice on the conduct of the war. Tell whatever King is current to request our input if he desires it."

"Or she," Imbri sent. "Queen Iris will be the next King."

The Kings exchanged glances. "We are no longer in direct touch with the situation," Humfrey said. "Perhaps it is best to leave the matter of governance to the centaur; he seems remarkably competent."

"Send my love to my mother and my wife," Dor said sadly. He formed a wan smile. "I'll convey the message to my father myself," he added, glancing at the sleeping Bink.

Imbri bade farewell to the five Kings and set off again for the real world.

She arrived at Castle Roogna near midnight. Some of the people were awake, some asleep. It made no practical difference; she broadcast her glad dream to all. "The Kings are all in the gourd! They are well! They send their love!"

Those who were awake crowded close; those who were asleep woke abruptly. In a moment Imbri was the center of attention. She dispensed all the messages, including King Trent's to the Queen.

Iris seemed stricken. "He said that?" she asked, unbelieving.

"That it is time to live in the present, and you are his wife," Imbri repeated.

"Oh, Mother!" Irene cried, going to Queen Iris and embracing her. "You have become part of the family!" It seemed a strange comment, but Imbri understood its meaning. The tragedy of Xanth was bringing its incidental benefits. Imbri retreated to the castle gardens, where she relaxed, grazed, and slept, catching up on about two days' activity.

Tandy returned safely in the night and was reunited with her ogre husband, who had been pacing the grounds worriedly, idly tearing weed-trees out of the ground and squeezing them into balls of pressed wood. It was a nervous mannerism of his. But all seemed reasonably well for the moment.

In due course the centaur contingent landed, having made excellent time, and Imbri went to lead them in to Castle Roogna. She had thought Chem or Chet would prefer to do it, since they were centaurs, but this was not the case. Chet and Chem were magic-talented centaurs, and

the conventional centaurs would not associate voluntarily
with their ilk. Chet had actually visited Centaur Isle once;
but though he had been treated with courtesy, he had soon
gotten the underlying message and had never visited again.
In certain respects the separation between magic and non-
magic centaurs was greater than that between Xanth human beings and Mundanes. Thus Imbri, no centaur at all,
was a better choice; she could keep the pace, she knew the
way, and they didn't care if she had magic. In fact, they
held her kind in a certain muted awe, since a mare had
been the dam of their species. They revered true horses,
while not being unrealistic about their properties.

She met them at the beach. The centaurs used magic-
propelled rafts that were seaworthy and quite stout. They
certainly weren't shy about the use of magic in its proper
place. There were exactly fifty of them, all fine, healthy
warriors with shining weapons and armor. Imbri wondered
whether fifty were enough to handle three hundred Mundanes, however.

"We are centaurs," their leader said proudly, as if that
made the question irrelevant. He did not deign to introduce
himself. The arrogance of these warriors was unconscious,
and she did not allow it to disturb her. She led the contingent to Castle Roogna by nightfall.

"Thanks to the very kind and competent assistance of
Ichabod and Queen Iris," Arnolde reported, "we have located the second Mundane army. He analyzed their likely
course, and her illusion can project her image briefly to
almost any region of Xanth, so that she can see the enemy." It seemed that Queen Iris was going all-out to help
the Centaur King, being quite grateful to him on more than
one count. "The Horseman is with them, south of the Ogre-
fen-Ogre Fen. We do not know how he reached them so
rapidly. He did have two days to travel, which would be
enough for a healthy and able man who knew the route—
but he must have crossed some of the wildest terrain of
Xanth to get there. I checked it on Chem's map; there are
flies, dragons, goblins, griffins, and ogres, as well as virtually impassable natural regions. I must confess I am at a
loss even to conjecture how he managed it."

Imbri shared his confusion. She had been to those regions of Xanth and knew how difficult they were. The Lord of the Flies took his office seriously and was apt to have intruders stung to death, and the other creatures were no less militant. "He must have used his talent to stop any hostile creatures, and maybe to cow a griffin into transporting him. He is a very efficient rider; he can tame anything with his reins and spurs." Oh, yes, she knew!

"That must be it. At least he is no present threat to us here." Arnolde did not comment on the implication that the Horseman believed the Centaur King would be ineffective, therefore was not worth sending to the gourd. Imbri suspected the Horseman had made a bad mistake there.

The centaurs of the Isle contingent declined to enter Castle Roogna. They camped in the gardens, foraging for fruit from the orchard and pitching small tents. They did not need these for themselves so much as for their supplies. "Tell us where the Mundanes are," their leader said coldly. "We shall march there in the morning and dispatch them."

Imbri showed him the enemy location in a dreamlet map, since Chem was not encouraged to approach with her more detailed magic map. The prejudice of the Centaur Isle centaurs against their talented brethren was implacable.

"They are in ogre territory?" he asked, surprised. "The ogres of the fen are wild and hostile; how could mere Mundanes have bested them?"

"These are very tough Mundanes," Imbri explained. "They beat back the Gap Dragon in the Chasm."

"The what in the where?"

It was that forget-spell operating again. "A ferocious monster in a crevice," she sent.

The centaur was unimpressed. "Any of us could do that. More likely the Mundanes made a deal with the ogres, promising them plunder if they joined the invasion."

"Such deals occur," Imbri agreed, determined not to be antagonized. "Such as the promise of autonomy—"

"Are you attempting humor, mare?" he demanded coldly. It seemed the centaurs' reverence for horses had limits. King Arnolde had immediately granted the Isle centaurs local autonomy, remarking that it made no practical difference, but they did not express overt appreciation. Certainly this particular centaur remained prickly!

"Of course not," Imbri demurred, keeping her ears forward and her tail still. She was getting better at such discipline. Social politics made her master new things. "I merely fear that we may be up against more than Mundanes. When the human King of Xanth sought help from the other creatures, most expressed indifference, feeling that it was a human-folk war, not theirs. So there could be a tacit understanding with the Mundanes, in which the Punic army is allowed to pass through monster territory without impediment, provided no damage is done in passing. It is also possible that some animals chose to ally themselves with the Mundanes. In fact, their current leader, the Horseman, did that; he is a Xanthian turncoat."

The centaur spat to the side, contemptuous of any kind of turncoat. "We'll handle it," he decided, with what she hoped was not an unwarranted confidence. "Now leave us; we shall march at dawn."

Imbri retreated to the castle. Chameleon was up and alert now, less pretty and more potent mentally, restored from her grief by the news that her husband and son were well, if enchanted. "Imbri—do you think you could carry a person into the gourd to visit the Kings?"

Imbri paused, considering. "I suppose I could. I hadn't thought of it. Mostly it is only the spirit of a person that goes into the gourd, but I have been carrying people through on the way to far places. I could take you to see your family."

"Oh, I don't mean me, though I certainly would have been tempted in my other phase. I mean Irene."

"Irene?"

"She and Dor were married just before he became King and had to master the rigors of Kingship and take over the campaign against the Mundanes and go to battle. He never had a moment to himself unless he was sleeping. So she was widowed, as it were, almost before she was married."

Oh. Imbri had a little trouble getting adapted to the woman's more intelligent thought processes, for she had been acclimated to the slow, pretty version. But it was true. There had been no wedding night. Imbri knew that sort of thing was important to human people. It was like coming into season and being walled off from the stallion. "I will take her to him," Imbri agreed. "Tonight, before anything else happens."

Chameleon fetched Irene. "Dear, Imbri has somewhere to take you."

The girl shook her head. "I can't leave Dor. You know that. If anything happened to his body, he would never be able to return."

She didn't know! It was to be a surprise.

"I really think you should go, Irene," Chameleon said. "It will do you good to leave the castle for a while. Things may get harder later. I will watch Dor for you."

Irene sighed. She could not refuse Dor's mother the chance to sit by his body. "You're probably right. Very well, I'll take a ride. This time." She mounted Imbri, and they set off.

It was not yet dark, so Imbri took her time, circling the centaur camp and going to the gourd patch indirectly. She could not safely enter the gourd until night.

"Do you know, it *is* good to get out," Irene confessed, looking about. "I haven't ridden a night mare before. Do you really phase through trees and boulders?"

"I really do, at night," Imbri sent, but did not amplify.

"I've been meaning to thank you for all you have done," Irene continued, brightening as the mood of the evening infused her. "You have taken Chameleon everywhere and made things so much easier for Dor."

"We all must do what we can." This reminded Imbri that she was supposed in some way to hold the key to the salvation of Xanth. If only her role were clearer! All she could do now was continue from hour to hour, trying to improve things in little ways. Was that enough? She doubted it.

"Yes," the girl agreed. "All I've been able to do is sit and wait. I curse myself for a fool; I had so many years I could have married Dor and I just waited, thinking it was a sort of game. Now that it's too late, I realize—" She stopped, and Imbri knew she was stifling tears.

There was no point in deception. "I am taking you to him now," Imbri sent.

"Now? But—"

"Inside the gourd. With your father and the other Kings. A visit. But you must return with me before dawn, or you, too, will be trapped in the world of the gourd."

"I can go there? For a few hours?" Comprehension was coming.

"For a few hours," Imbri agreed.

"And I will be real? I mean, I'll seem solid, or the Kings will? Not just diffuse spirits?"

"Yes. Some creatures are there in spirit, some in body. When I enter the gourd, my magic accommodates; it is all right. No one except a night mare can travel physically in and out of the gourd—except those in contact with a phased-out night mare."

"Then by all means, let's go!" Irene exclaimed, gladdening.

Now it was dark. Imbri came to the gourd patch and plunged into the nearest ripe peephole. The rind passed behind them; they then phased through another wall and into the graveyard, where skeletons roamed. One skeleton waved to Imbri in greeting; then she trotted on into the chamber the Night Stallion had reserved for the visiting Kings.

The Kings were alert and waiting, having somehow anticipated this visit. "Irene!" King Dor cried happily.

Irene greeted her father and Dor's father, then turned to Dor. She frowned attractively. "You can't skip out this time!" she said. "We started our marriage in a graveyard, and we'll consummate it in a graveyard."

"The skeletons wouldn't like that," he murmured.

"The skeletons don't have to participate." But she yielded to the extent of allowing Imbri to show them to a private chamber filled with pillows. As Imbri left, they had a full-scale pillow fight going.

Imbri now retired to the graveyard for some good grazing. One of the graves began to shake and settle, but she squealed warningly at it and it desisted. Imbri did not take any guff from graves, just grass.

Well before dawn, Xanthside—dawn never came to the World of Night, naturally—she returned to the chamber of Kings. Dor and Irene were there, talking with the others, looking happy. A number of pillows were scattered about; it seemed the pillow fight had spread, as conflicts tended to. Everyone appeared satisfied.

Irene looked up and saw the mare. "Oh, it's time to go, or Mother will know what mischief I was up to!" she exclaimed. She brushed a pillow feather from her hair, gave King Dor a final kiss, and went to Imbri.

They moved on out, emerging from the gourd before the sun climbed from its own nocturnal hiding place. The sun was afraid of the dark, so never appeared before day came. "Oh, Imbri!" Irene exclaimed. "You've made it so nice, considering . . ."

Considering that the Kings were still prisoners and Xanth was still under siege by the Mundanes. Imbri understood. This had been no more than an interlude. "We must rescue the Kings soon," Imbri sent. "Before their bodies suffer too much from hunger."

"Yes," Irene agreed. "We have to capture the Horseman—soon."

They returned to Castle Roogna. King Arnolde was alert. "Are you rested, Imbri?" he inquired.

Imbri replied that she was; the cemetery verdure was marvelously rich, and her hours of quiet grazing and sleep within the familiar gourd had restored her to full vitality. Perhaps, too, her part in facilitating Irene's reunion with her father and husband had buoyed her half spirit. She was only sorry she had missed the pillow fight.

"Then I must ask you to lead the centaurs to the Mundanes," the King said. "They are not conversant with the specific route, and we don't want them to fall prey to avoidable hazards. I would do it myself, or have Chet or Chem do it, but—"

Imbri understood. The Centaur Isle troops still refused to deal directly with the obscenely talented centaurs. She couldn't approve of their attitude, but knew that there were few creatures as stubborn as centaurs. It was best to accommodate them without raising the issue; they were, after all, here to save Xanth from the ravage of the Nextwave. "I will take them there," she agreed. "Where exactly are the Mundanes now?"

"They are proceeding south, skirting the regions of Fire

and Earth, passing the land of the goblins. We sent news to the goblins of the Mundane threat, and they promised to organize for defense, but we're not sure they've gotten beyond the draft-notice stage. We don't even know whether we can trust them. It is difficult to intimidate goblins, but the Mundanes are extremely tough. In past centuries goblins were a worse menace than Mundanes, but they were more numerous and violent then. Chem says she knows one of them, a female named Goldy who possesses a magic wand—but I prefer caution."

Imbri went to join the centaurs, who were organizing efficiently for the march. At dawn their tent stables were folded and packed away.

Imbri led them north along the path to the invisible bridge across the Gap. They were amazed; they had no prior knowledge of this immense Chasm, thanks to the forget-spell on it. They trotted in single file across the bridge and soon were able to regroup on the north side.

Guided by her memory of the map Chem had formed for her before she left, Imbri led the centaurs through the land of the flies; they had suitable insect repellent and knew how to cut through the flypaper that marked the border. The flies buzzed angrily, but could not get close; the repellent caused them to bounce away, no matter how determinedly they charged.

The centaurs were able travelers, and progress was swift. Imbri led them to the fringe of the dragons' territory. "Do not menace the dragons," she sent in a general dreamlet. "I will explain to them." And when the first dragon came, she sent it an explanatory dream, showing brute human folk fighting half-human folk, both of whom might turn against reptile folk at the slightest pretext. The dragon retreated. Dragons were cautious about armed manlike creatures, especially in this number. They had experienced the depradations of magic-talented men and knew how well centaurs could fight. It was better to be patriotic and let the war party cross in peace.

Still, there were pauses along the way, for centaurs had to eat and lacked the ability to graze. More and more it was apparent to Imbri that any deviation from the straight equine form was a liability. The centaurs had to consume

huge amounts of food to maintain their equine bodies, but
it all had to be funneled through their inadequate human
mouths. Fortunately, they had brought concentrated supplies along, but it remained inefficient business.

The route was not straightforward. Between the dragon
country and the goblin country there was a jagged mountain range, projecting west into the region of earthquakes;
they had to skirt the mountains closely to avoid getting
shaken up.

It was there, in the late afternoon, that the Mundanes
ambushed them. Imbri cursed herself for not anticipating
this—but of course she was not a mind reader, so could not
discover their nefarious plots. She only projected dreams
and communicated with people by putting herself into
those dreams. Had she known the Mundanes were close—
but she had not known. She *should* have known, though.
She realized this now, for the Mundanes had been marching south; naturally the centaur contingent would encounter them south of the location King Arnolde had described.

The centaurs fought back bravely, but were caught. The
Mundanes rolled boulders down the near slope of the
mountain, forcing the centaurs to retreat into the region of
earthquakes. That was disaster, for the ground cracked
open with demoniac vigor and swallowed a number of
them whole. The carnage was awful. In moments only ten
centaurs remained, charging back out of the trap. Most of
them had been wiped out before they could even organize
for defense.

But as soon as the centaurs were clear, they halted, consulted, and moved slowly back toward the Mundanes.
"What are you doing?" Imbri demanded in a dreamlet.

"Now we have sprung the trap; we shall destroy the enemy," a centaur replied.

"But there are several hundred Mundanes, protected by
the terrain! You'll be slaughtered exactly as your companions were!"

The stubborn creatures ignored her. Weapons ready,
they advanced to battle.

"This is folly!" Imbri projected, sending a background
image of an army of centaurs being washed away by the
tide of a mighty ocean. "At least wait until darkness; then

you can set an ambush of your own. At night I will be able to scout out the enemy positions—"

They walked on, stiff-backed, refusing to be dissuaded from their set course by marish logic. Centaurs were supposed to be very intelligent, but they simply did not readily take advice from lesser creatures.

Imbri hung back, knowing she could not afford to throw away her life with theirs. She had to admire the centaurs' courage in adversity, but also had to disassociate herself from it. She had to return to Castle Roogna to report on the disaster, in case Queen Iris had not picked it up by means of her illusion.

Yet Imbri remained for a while, hoping the centaurs would become sensible. They did not; as the Mundanes gathered and charged to attack the centaur remnant, the ten stalwart creatures exchanged terse commands and brought their bows to bear. There were now twenty times as many enemy warriors on the field as centaurs, and more men in reserve; obviously the Punics believed this was a simple mop-up operation.

It was not. For all their folly, the centaurs were well-trained fighting creatures, with excellent armor and weapons, who now knew exactly what they faced. Their unexcelled archery counted heavily. In a moment ten arrows were launched together, and ten Mundanes were skewered by shafts through their eyes. Even as they fell, another volley of arrows was aloft, and ten more went down. Every single centaur arrow counted; no target was missed or struck by more than a single arrow and no Mundane armor was touched. In the face of marksmanship like this, armor was useless. Imbri was amazed.

The Mundanes, belatedly realizing that they faced real opposition, hastily formed into a phalanx, their shields overlapping protectively. Still, they had to peek between the shields to see their way—and through these crevices passed the uncannily accurate arrows. The leading Mundanes continued to fall, and none who fell rose again. Now Imbri realized that Chet, a young centaur, had not yet fully mastered his marksmanship; otherwise he would have needed no more than a single arrow per Mundane when he had opposed them on the Chasm bridge. What an exhibition this was!

But once committed to this course of battle on the field, the Punics were as stubborn as the centaurs. They maintained their phalanx, stepping over their fallen comrades, and closed on the centaurs. More of them fell, of course, but the rest pressed on. By this time the centaurs' arrows were running out. It was coming to sword conflict—and the Mundanes still outnumbered the centaurs ten to one.

Had all fifty centaurs avoided the ambush, Imbri realized, they could have destroyed the entire Mundane army without a loss. Their confidence had not been misplaced. Of course, the Mundanes would not have met them on the open field if they had been aware of the marksmanship they faced, so it might have been more even. As it was, the centaur disaster had been followed by the Punic disaster; forty centaurs and a hundred Mundanes were dead. And there might still be a good fight—but the centaurs would surely lose, for swords were not as distant and clean as arrows. Imbri turned and galloped away, feeling like a coward but knowing this was what she had to do.

A goblin stepped out before her, waving his stubby arms. Imbri screeched to a halt. "Who are you?" she sent.

"I am Stunk," he said. "You brought me a bad dream once—and then it came true. I got drafted. I should have fled Goblin Land when I had the chance."

After a moment, Imbri remembered. Her last delivery— the one that had shown her inadequacy for the job. "But the goblins didn't fight!"

"All we did was guard our mountain holes," he agreed. "But Goldy, girlfriend of a chief, sent me to intercept you. She says some of her friends are on the human side, so she wants to help—but she's the only one who will. So if the folk at Castle Roogna need her, come and get her. She does have the magic wand and a lot of courage."

"I will relay the message," Imbri sent.

Stunk saluted, and Imbri flicked her tail in response. The goblin turned north, while she continued south. Apparently getting drafted was not nearly as bad in life as in a dream. Of course, it was Stunk's fortune that the goblins had avoided actual combat with the Mundanes.

Night closed. She located a gourd patch and plunged into a peephole. It was too bad she couldn't use this avenue by day; she might conceivably have been able to fetch help for the centaurs in time to do them some good. But if she could not use the hypnogourds by day, at least they could not harm her as they did other creatures. She was a denizen of the gourd world, immune to its effect; but it was pointless to approach a gourd when she couldn't use it.

The Horseman, she remembered—he had actually used the gourd to eliminate the Kings. So if he tried to wield his talent on her, he would fail, and she could destroy him. That, too, was good to know, because she did want to destroy him.

She galloped through the familiar reaches of the dream world. It occurred to her that she could report to the five prisoned Kings on the way and perhaps receive their advice to relay to King Arnolde. She was supposed to serve as liaison, after all. So she detoured toward that section. She wondered briefly whether it would be possible for her to carry one or more of the Kings out, to rejoin his natural body. She had done that for Smash the Ogre once. But she realized immediately that she could not, because she did not know the specific channel that had brought each King into the gourd. Any King she brought out would continue to exist as a phantom; his body would remain inert. There was nothing but frustration to be gained by that. She had to locate the particular channel that connected the Kings to a particular gourd; only the Horseman knew that key. Naturally he would not give that information simply for the asking.

She entered the chamber of the Kings—and skidded to a halt, appalled.

"Yes, it is I," Arnolde said. "I, too, have now been taken."

Imbri projected a flickering dreamlet, stammering out her news of the fate of the centaurs. This was worse even than that, since the Horseman was still taking out the Kings as fast as they could be replaced. She had thought the Horseman was with the Mundane army, but evidently he hadn't stayed there long.

"It seems that every time a King shows competence,"

King Trent said, "the Horseman takes him out. At such time as Xanth enthrones an incompetent King, he will surely be allowed to remain until the enemy is victorious. Meanwhile, Imbri, kindly do us the favor of informing my wife, the Sorceress Iris, that she is now King."

"Queen . . ." Imbri sent, numbed.

"King," he repeated firmly. "Xanth has no ruling Queens."

"With my apologies for misjudging the location of the Horseman," Arnolde added. "I told Iris to sleep, since there was no present menace to me. Evidently I was mistaken."

Evidently so, Imbri had to agree. She nodded and trotted on out, feeling heavy-hoofed. When would it end?

Chapter 12. King Queen

She reached Castle Roogna, unconscious of the intervening journey. The palace staff was sleeping, including the Queens.

Imbri approached Queen Iris and sent her a significant dream: "King Arnolde has been taken; you must assume the Kingship, your Majesty."

"What? Arnolde was quite alert a moment ago!" Iris protested.

"You have slept some time, King Iris."

"King Iris!" the Queen exclaimed, wrenching herself awake. She lurched to her feet and stumbled to the King's apartment. "King Centaur, I just had a bad dream—"

She stopped. Arnolde stood there, staring blankly.

"It's true!" Iris whispered, appalled. "Oh, we should have guarded him more closely!"

"I met him in the gourd," Imbri sent. "He agreed you

must be King now. King Trent said it, too. And I have bad news to report to the King."

Iris leaned against the wall as if feeling faint. She was no young woman, and recent events had not improved her health. Only her iron will to carry on as a Queen should had kept her going. "All my life I have longed to rule Xanth. Now that it is upon me, I dread it. Always before I had the security of knowing that no matter how strong my desire, it would never be fulfilled. Women don't really want all the things they long for. All they really want is to long and be longed for. Oh, whatever will I do, Imbri? I'm too old and set in my ways to handle a dream turned so horribly real!"

"You will fight the Mundanes, King Iris," Imbri sent, feeling sympathy for the woman's predicament.

The King's feminine visage hardened. "How right you are, mare! If there's one thing I am good at, it is tormenting men. Those Mundanes will rue the day they invaded Xanth! And the Horseman—when I find him—"

"Stay away from him, your Majesty!" Imbri pleaded. "Until we unriddle the secret avenue of his power, no King dare approach him."

"But I don't need to do it physically! I can use my illusion on him."

Imbri was doubtful, but let that aspect rest. "He may be close to Castle Roogna," she sent. "We thought he was up in Goblin Land . . ."

"He *was* in Goblin Land!" King Iris cried. "I saw him myself only yesterday!"

"But he must have been here to take out King Arnolde."

"Then he found a way to travel quickly. He's probably back with his army by now. I can verify that soon enough." She took a deep breath. "Meanwhile, let's have your full report on the war situation. If I am to do this job, I'll do it properly. After it is over, I shall be womanishly weak, my foolish hunger for power having been expiated, but I can't afford that at the moment."

Imbri gave the report to her, then retired to the garden pasture on the King's order and grazed and rested. She liked running all over Xanth, but it did fatigue her, and she wished it wasn't always because of a new crisis.

In the morning King Iris had her program ready. She had devised a very large array of illusory monsters, which she set in ambush within the dragons' terrain, awaiting the Mundanes' southward progress. The real dragons took one look at the VLA and retreated to their burrows, wanting none of it.

In midmorning the Punic army appeared, still two hundred strong, marching in disciplined formations. Imbri saw that a number of the soldiers were ones who had not participated in the battle with the centaurs; apparently about fifty had held back or been on boulder-rolling duty; these had filled in for the additional fifty the centaurs had wiped out in the final hand-to-hand struggle. An army of three hundred fifty—slightly larger than the Xanth intelligence estimate had thought—had been reduced to somewhat better than half its original size in the course of that single encounter. If only she, Imbri, had been alert to the ambush, so that all fifty centaurs could have fought effectively! But major errors were the basic stuff of war.

King Iris had somehow gotten the magic mirror to work again, perhaps by enhancing its illusion with her own, and focused it on the Mundane army, so Imbri and the others were able to watch the next engagement. An audience was very important for Iris; her sorcery of illusion operated only for the perceiver.

First to pounce were two braces of sphinxes. Each had the head and breast of a man or woman, the body and tail of a lion, and the wings of a giant bird. The females were five times the height of a normal man, the males larger. All four monsters spread their wings as they leaped into the air and uttered harsh screams of aggression.

The Mundanes scattered, understandably. A number of them charged into the bordering zone of Air and were blown away by the perpetual winds there. Some took refuge in the burrow of a local dragon; there was a loud gulping sound, followed by the smacking of lips and a satisfied plume of smoke. Then there was a windy burp, and pieces of Mundane armor flew out of the burrow. Most of the remaining soldiers simply backed up, shields elevated, awaiting the onslaught. They certainly weren't cowards.

The sphinxes sheered off as if deciding the odds were not proper. Of course the real reason was that the illusion would lose effect if the Mundanes ascertained its nature. No illusion could harm a person directly; he had to hurt himself by his reaction to it. If the sphinxes charged through the soldiers and revealed themselves as nothing, the game would be over.

After the sphinxes came the big birds, the rocs. The sky darkened as six of these monsters glided down, casting monstrous shadows. The two remaining Mundane elephants spooked and fled headlong back north, trumpeting in terror; they knew the sort of prey rocs liked to carry off. That set off most of the remaining horses, who stampeded north, too. It would be long before many of these were recovered, if any could be rounded up unscathed.

"Now that's the way illusion should operate," Queen Irene murmured appreciatively. "They'll make slower progress with most of their animals gone."

Each roc held a big bag, and as they passed over the Mundanes they dropped these bags. The bags burst as they struck the ground, releasing yellow vapor that looked poisonous. Bushes and trees within its ambience seemed to shrivel and wilt and turn black, and phantom figures in the likeness of Mundanes gagged and staggered and fell in twisted fashion to the ground.

Imbri made a whinny of admiration for the sheer versatility of the King's performance; she would have been terrified if she faced that apparent threat. She heard someone cough, as if breathing the awful gas. If the illusion had that effect on these viewers, who knew it for what it was and who were not even in it, how much worse it must be for the superstitious Mundanes in the thick of it! Maybe it was possible after all, to wipe out the enemy without touching it physically.

The Punics reeled back, afraid to let the yellow vapor overtake them. Their leader came forward—the Horseman, riding a fine brown horse. Naturally that man had prevented his steed from spooking. Imbri was startled; this meant he *was* with this army and not lurking around Castle Roogna. How had he traveled so fast? He had to have magical means—a carpet, perhaps, or some renegade person of Xanth who enabled him to do it. Someone who could make him fly—but that did not seem likely. The mystery deepened unpleasantly.

The Horseman yelled at the troops, then strode forward into the fog. It did not hurt him. They rallied and stood up to it—and of course it did not hurt them either. The bluff had been called.

After that, the Mundanes ignored the splendid illusions King Iris threw at them. They marched south, toward the Gap Chasm, and it seemed nothing she could do would stop them. But Imbri knew the King wasn't finished. "There's more than one type of illusion," Iris said grimly.

By late afternoon the Punic army was approaching the Gap. It was making excellent time, because no creature of Xanth opposed it and the Horseman obviously had mapped out a good route. But King Iris made the Chasm appear to be farther south than it was. Then she sent a herd of raindeer trotting across the spot where the real Chasm had been blocked out, bringing a small rainstorm with them. Illusion worked both ways: to make something nonexistent take form, and to make something that was there disappear. This combination was marvelously effective. Little bolts of lightning speared out from the rainstorm, and there were boomlets of thunder. Iris was a real artist in her fashion. One might disbelieve the storm—but overlook the nonexistence of the ground it rained on. Water from that storm was coursing over that ground, beginning to flood it. There were even reflections in that water.

The Mundanes, jaded by the displays of the day, charged past the nonexistent deer, right on into the nonexistent storm, across the nonexistent ground—and fell, screaming, into the very real Gap Chasm. The Horseman had forgotten about it, naturally enough, and the Mundanes had never known of it.

The Horseman quickly called a halt and regrouped the Mundanes—but he had lost another thirty men. He was down to a hundred and fifty now, and obviously not at all pleased. He reined his horse before the illusion and shook his braceleted fist.

Imbri was privately glad to see the man had not caught the day horse. He must have pre-empted this one from a lesser officer. Could he have ridden the brown horse to Castle Roogna and back in the night? It seemed unlikely; the horse was too fresh. But since the Mundanes had retained a number of horses, before the Queen spooked them away, he certainly might have used one of those for his purpose, though the best routes for hoofed creatures were not necessarily the shortest ones and certainly not the safest. The best shortcuts were ones only something like a man could take. So there still seemed to be no perfect answer. Yet the major mystery was not how he traveled, but how to abate the enchantment on the six Kings.

"Is that so, you Mundane oaf!" King Iris demanded, in response to the Horseman's fist-shaking gesture. "You can't threaten me, horsehead! I'll use my illusion to chip away your entire army before it reaches Castle Roogna!" And she formed the image of a raspberry bush, which made a rude noise at him.

Contemptuously, the Horseman guided his horse right through the illusion—and smacked into the ironwood tree that Iris had covered up by the raspberry. His horse stumbled, and the Horseman was thrown headlong. He took a rolling breakfall in the dirt and came to rest unhurt but disheveled and furious.

"Oh, Mother, that wasn't nice!" Irene chortled.

King Iris formed the image of her own face there before the fallen man, smirking at him. She could see him through the eyes of her illusion.

The Horseman saw her. He made a swooping gesture with his two hands—and suddenly the illusion vanished.

Queen Irene glanced at her mother, alarmed. "What's the—" Then she screamed.

Now it was evident to them all: King Iris had taunted the dread enemy—and had been taken by his magic.

After a shocked pause, Imbri sent a dreamlet to the girl: "What is your program, King Irene?"

Irene spluttered. "I'm not—I can't—"

"King Arnolde decreed you a Sorceress, therefore a Magician, therefore in the line of succession, and he named

you to be the eighth King of Xanth. You must now assume
the office and carry on during this crisis. Xanth needs you,
your Majesty. At least we know your mother is safe in the
gourd."

The girl's wavering chin firmed. "Yes, she is with my
father now, perhaps for the first time. As long as we protect her body. But the moment those Mundanes get inside
this castle, all is lost. They will slay the bodies of our
Kings, and then our people will be forever in the gourd, or
worse. Our situation is desperate, for we no longer have
magic that can strike down the enemy from a distance."
She paused, glancing around the room. "Who will be King
after me?"

"Humfrey said there would be ten Kings during this
siege," Imbri reminded her. "But you are the last Magician. We can't let the Horseman claim the throne by default. I think you'll have to designate your successor from
among the lesser talents, just in case."

King Irene nodded. She turned herself about, surveying
the people in the room a second time. Chameleon was helping Crombie the old soldier move King Iris to the chamber
where the six previous Kings were kept; she would be the
seventh.

"Chameleon," Irene said.

The woman paused. Imbri had to do another mental ad-
justment, for Chameleon was now far removed from her
prettiness of the past. It would have been unkind to call her
ugly, but that was the direction in which she was going.
"Yes, your Majesty?" Even her words had harshened.

"You will be King Number Nine," Irene said clearly.

"What?" Chameleon used her free hand to brush a strag-
gle of hair back from an ear that should have remained
covered.

"You are the mother of a King and the wife of a King
and you're just coming into your smart phase. We are out
of Magicians; now we have to go with intelligence. King
Arnolde showed what could be done with intelligence; he
clarified the line of succession and located the lost Kings. He
did more to help Xanth than any magic could have done.
You will be smarter yet. Maybe you will be able to solve
the riddle of the Horseman before—" She shrugged.

"Before he becomes the tenth King," Chameleon said. She was much faster to pick up on other people's thoughts now, after her initial surprise at being designated a prospective King.

Imbri found this steady progression a remarkable thing. She knew Chameleon was the same woman, but most of the identifying traits of the one she had carried north to spy on the Mundanes were now gone. She liked the other Chameleon better.

Tandy went to take Chameleon's place, helping Crombie conduct the former female King to the resting chamber. Chameleon returned to talk with Irene. "I see your logic," Chameleon said. "I am no Sorceress, and there are many people in Xanth with stronger magic than mine, but I believe you are correct. What we most require is not magic, but intelligence—and that, for a time, I can provide." She smiled lopsidedly, knowing better than anyone that if she retained the office of King too long, Xanth would be in an extremely sad state. She would have to wrap up the job during the nadir of her appearance, for there was no intellect to match hers then. "I shall see that the Horseman is not the tenth King, whatever else I do or do not accomplish." She did not bother to argue the unlikelihood of Irene's getting taken; they both knew that this was inevitable as the prophesied chain continued to its end. "But in case you face the Horseman directly, King Irene—"

Irene's brow furrowed. "I'm not sure I follow your implication."

"You are a lovely young woman. He might attempt to legitimize his takeover by taking you in another fashion."

Irene flushed. "I'd kill him!" Then she tilted her head, reconsidering slightly. "I'll kill him anyway, if I get the chance. I owe him for my father, my mother, my husband—"

Again Chameleon smiled. How different this expression was from the one her lovely version had shown. This was a cold, calculating, awful thing. "I am not questioning your personal loyalty to Xanth. I am merely suggesting that it might occur to him to try. It is the kind of thing that occurs to men when they encounter young women of your description. If you could discipline yourself enough to seem to accept his interest, at least until you fathomed his secret—"

Slowly Irene's smile matched that of the older woman. The strangest thing was that it was no prettier on Irene's face than on Chameleon's. Imbri saw, and understood, and was repelled. Human women well knew the advantage they had over human men and used it ruthlessly. What an ugly way to try to save Xanth! Yet if it came to that extreme, was there any better way? What was justified in war? Imbri wasn't sure. Maybe there was no proper answer to this type of question.

Now King Irene went to work organizing her campaign. The magic mirror showed the Mundanes camping for the night; at least there were several campfires. The rest was darkness. If the Punics resumed their march at dawn, it would take them at least two hours to reach the invisible bridge—obviously the Horseman knew about it—and longer to get to Castle Roogna.

Irene turned to Imbri. "The bridge—could you kick that out tonight?"

"I could try," Imbri sent. "But I would run the risk of falling into the Gap, since I can't use a lever or an axe, and would have to stand on the bridge in material form to kick at its supports. This sort of work really requires human hands and tools." It galled her to admit that there was something a human folk person was better at than an equine person, but in this very limited respect it was so.

"I will go with you," Chameleon said. "I'm not strong, but I'm good at that sort of challenge. I have a sharp knife that should cut through the strands."

"But—" King Irene protested.

"There is no danger from the Mundanes by night," Chameleon reminded her. "And none from Xanth monsters when I'm on the enchanted path or on the night mare. If we can take down that bridge quickly, the Nextwave will be stalled at least another day, navigating the Chasm, and we shall be much better able to defend Castle Roogna."

"But if I should be taken during your absence—"

"I'll return promptly. I promise."

The girl spread her hands. "You are correct, of course. I'm afraid to be alone with this responsibility, but that's a luxury I can't afford. Unlike my mother, I never even imagined being King. I shall set up a collection of plants to defend this castle, but I won't make them grow until you are safely back inside."

Chameleon mounted Imbri, and they took off through the wall and headed for the local gourd patch.

"I have another task for you," Chameleon said when they were alone. "I do not believe that either the Gap or Irene's plants can stop the Mundanes for long, and we'll never eliminate the Horseman unless we first trap him and prevent his escape. This will require a lure he can't resist, and some desperate measures on our part."

"I want to kill the Horseman if I find him," Imbri sent. "I'm not sure he'll tell us how to nullify his enchantment. He deceived me once, but he will never trick me like that again." She swished her tail, smashing imaginary flies.

"He is extremely elusive, and I think I know why," Chameleon said. "It would be quite unfortunate if I am wrong—and I'm not yet at my peak of intelligence, so I may be—therefore I will not voice my suspicion. But if I am right, he will take King Irene, and he will also take me, immediately following. He will suppose that will make him the tenth King, the chain complete, but we can prevent that by acting first. There must be one more King of Xanth designated, one he can't send to the gourd. That is the King who can finally break the chain."

"Yes, Magician Humfrey's prophecy makes the tenth monarch vital," Imbri agreed, diving into a gourd. Neither of them paid attention to the gourd world, which now seemed commonplace, being absorbed in their conversation. "But who is it to be? Anyone you select can be enchanted."

"Anyone but one," Chameleon said.

"Who?"

"You."

Imbri veered into the wall of the City of Brass, one of the subdivisions of the gourd, where the brassies labored on metallic aspects of bad dreams. Of course the brass wall didn't hurt her, as it was insubstantial in her present state, but by the time she straightened out, she had startled several of the laboring brass folk. "Who?"

"Who are you looking for?" a brassie man inquired, thinking she was addressing him.

Embarrassed, Imbri covered by naming the one brassie she knew of who had seen the real world. "Blythe."

"You're in the wrong building," the brassie man said. "She's in B-Four."

"Tell her I may need her help soon," Imbri sent, realizing that she might turn this blunder to advantage. Blythe Brassie just might be able to help in the crisis of Xanth. "Right now I'm on my way elsewhere."

"Yes, carrying garbage to the dump," another brassie remarked, eying Chameleon.

Imbri hastily trotted on through another wall, feeling an unequine burning in her ears. "The brass folk are very insensitive," she sent to Chameleon. "They have no souls and no soft tissues."

"I am used to this sort of thing," Chameleon said. "People assume that because I am ugly I must be bad, and they treat me that way, then find confirmation when I do not react with delight. If they approached me in my off-phase the way they do when I'm pretty, they would find me easy enough to get along with."

There was much truth in that, Imbri was sure. She remembered how Smash the Ogre had been considered brutish and violent because of his size and appearance, when in fact he was a most decent creature. People tended to become what others deemed them to be. Perhaps that was another aspect of the magic of Xanth.

Chameleon resumed her discussion. "I am designating you to be the final King of Xanth, Imbri. If I am correct, and I hope I am, you are the only one who can do it. This is the real reason the Night Stallion sent you out into the day. He knew what he was not permitted to tell, so he did what he could to save Xanth by making it possible. It was a course requiring much grief, including Good Magician Humfrey's shame, but the only likely way to save Xanth. You are the key. You must be the tenth King."

"But I'm a horse!"

"Yes, I had noticed. Are you any less a creature of Xanth?"

Imbri snorted. "I think I liked you better when you were beautiful, and not just because of your appearance."

"Everyone does. But on certain rare occasions, intelligence is more valuable to a woman than beauty."

"Oh, of course! I didn't mean—"

"I will be beautiful again, Imbri. I can not afford to remain King then; I would defeat Xanth through sheer stupidity. If the Horseman had the intelligence to banish Irene and keep me in power, he could certainly work his will during my other phase. I must provoke the crisis now, while I have the wit to handle it. Things may move quite rapidly once I return to Castle Roogna. Just you be ready to do your part, mare."

"I don't understand this at all!" Imbri sent in a dreamlet of darkly roiling nebulosities. "You aren't even King yet, but you talk of getting banished to the gourd. If you designate me King, no citizen of Xanth would accept it."

"They won't need to," Chameleon said. "I would explain more thoroughly, but I fear that would disrupt the prophecy. You must tell no one of this—until the time. Meanwhile, after we take down the bridge, you must go and fetch help for Irene's plants. The throne of Xanth has come at last to women; it behooves the women to defend it with greater efficacy than the men did. Go fetch the Siren and the Gorgon from Magician Humfrey's castle and locate Goldy Goblin; we'll need their talents for the final confrontation."

"But if I go there, how will you get back to Castle Roogna?" Imbri had never dreamed such an office would come to her, and as a night mare, she had dreamed a great deal, but did belatedly see the logic of it. She was immune to the Horseman's power, so could stop him in a way no other creature could. But practical details of organization remained. "At least I must take you back there before—"

"We shall see what works out," Chameleon said enigmatically. That was another annoying aspect of her intelligence; obviously there was a lot Imbri was missing.

They plunged out of the gourd near the bridge and galloped to the brink of the Chasm. But there was a problem. The Mundanes had set guards there. Imbri faded back into the dark forest, before the enemy spied her, and halted. "What now? I could approach invisibly, but would have to materialize to attack the bridge."

Chameleon considered, tapping her fingers idly against Imbri's mane. "We'll have to get rid of them. I'll devise a slingshot, and you can power it. Make sure I don't grab the wrong kind of vine."

They quested quickly through the jungle, locating several large elastic bands, which they harvested and tied to firm ironwood trunks, making a huge sling. Chameleon set a big stone in the net, and Imbri drew it back with all the weight of her body. Chameleon had fixed a temporary kind of harness from vines to make this possible.

Following Chameleon's directions, Imbri adjusted her position until the slingshot was aimed right at the Mundanes. At Chameleon's command she phased out, releasing the bands, and the rock hurtled up and across.

It scored a perfect hit on the near side of the bridge, sweeping the two Mundane guards into the Chasm. Chameleon knew exactly what she was doing in this phase! The two of them hurried across and discovered that the stone had also ripped away the bridge. The job was done already!

Two more Mundanes stood across the Chasm. They nocked arrows to strings—but Chameleon jumped on Imbri, and Imbri phased out again, and the arrows passed harmlessly through them. Nevertheless, they retreated from the Chasm, so that there would be no threat.

They heard a noise from the west. "A centaur's coming!" Imbri sent.

"No, I suspect it's a horse."

Indeed, in a moment the white day horse appeared. Imbri projected a dreamlet of greeting to his mind.

"Is the bridge still there?" he asked worriedly. "I heard a crash, so came running. The best grazing is south, but I have a good hiding place on the other side, and it's getting late."

"No bridge," Imbri sent. "We just took it out. You couldn't have used it anyway; the Mundanes had set guards on it."

"The Mundanes!" his dream figure cried. "I understood they were way up north!"

"That was yesterday. Now they are here. Tomorrow they'll be crossing the Chasm, and the day after that they'll be at Castle Roogna."

"I must flee!"

"If I understand his reactions correctly," Chameleon said, "you have informed him of the proximity of the Punic army, and he wants to get away from here."

"Yes," Imbri agreed. "He is very nervous about Mundanes. I can expand the dream to include you so you can talk to him directly—"

"No, don't bother. When I was fair and stupid, I felt at home with the normal equine intellect; now that palls. But I do need transportation. Tell him I shall be the next King of Xanth, the ninth, and ask him if he would like to carry me back to Castle Roogna. That's on his way south, away from the enemy."

Imbri did as she was bidden. "That's Chameleon?" the day horse asked, amazed. The night was dark, since it was no longer a good phase of the moon, but his excellent equine night vision showed him her appearance well enough. "I know she changes, but this creature is ugly, even for the human kind!"

"But she's the same inside," Imbri sent to both.

"The hell I am!" Chameleon snapped.

"And she's going to be Queen of Xanth?" the day horse asked, daunted.

"King of Xanth." Imbri did not have the nerve to say who would follow Chameleon in that office.

The day horse shrugged. "She's ugly, but I liked her once and can carry her, if there are no Mundanes there."

"There are none," Imbri reassured him. "Even Ichabod retired to a human village, after Arnolde the Centaur King got taken out. There are only women inside Castle Roogna now, with King Irene."

The day horse snorted acquiescently. Women were no threat to him. Chameleon mounted, and they set off at a gallop for Castle Roogna.

Imbri headed for Magician Humfrey's castle, via the gourd. As she traversed a fraction of the night world, she wondered idly how Chameleon had guessed she would find convenient transportation back. The woman was hideously smart in her proper phase, but this smacked of prophecy.

Soon she reached the Magician's castle and trotted across its moat and through its wall. "Grundy!" she sent in a general dreamlet. "Is the Gorgon back yet? Tell her not to look at me!"

"I am back," the Gorgon replied in the dream. "The golem returned not long ago to Castle Roogna to help fight the final battle. I am thoroughly veiled. Just let me wake up, and I will introduce you to my sister the Siren and Goldy Goblin, who also returned with me."

So the goblin girl had been serious about helping! "Don't wake up," Imbri sent. "You surely need your sleep, and I already know the Siren. I will talk to you all in one dream." She expanded the dream to include the others, now that she knew their identity.

"Oh, you are the night mare Smash the Ogre knew!" Goldy exclaimed as she saw Imbri. "The Siren told me about you. You carried Smash from the Void."

"Well, not exactly," Imbri demurred, somehow flattered. "But I did help and I received half of Chem Centaur's soul for the service. That enabled me to go dayside."

"I know how that is," the goblin girl said. "The ogre arranged for me to have this magic wand, and that gave me great power among my kind. Soon I will marry a goblin chief. I was down in the mines, picking out a trousseau of precious metals, or I would have come to help the centaurs fight the Mundanes. I didn't know until too late, so I sent a messenger who may not have reached you—"

"He reached me," Imbri sent.

"Then the Gorgon picked me up before I heard from him. *Now* I'm ready." She waved her wand in the dream, and objects flew about, touched by its power of levitation.

"Magician Humfrey told me to fetch my sister," the Gorgon explained. "And she told me that we should gather some of her other friends, so we tried. But Fireoak the Hamadryad can't leave her tree for such a risky venture, and John the fairy is expecting offspring—I don't think you know these people anyway—and we couldn't reach

Blythe Brassie, and have still to get the word to others like Chem and Tandy—"

"Chem and Tandy are already at Castle Roogna," Imbri sent, flashing an image of the castle in the background. "And I can fetch Blythe any time if she wants to come. She expressed interest before, and I left a message at the City of Brass for her to be ready."

"It would be so nice to get together again," the Siren said. "And to see the ogre again, too; he made it all possible."

"Chameleon asked me to fetch help to defend Castle Roogna," Imbri sent. "I can take you there one at a time."

"No, we'll use the magic carpet," the Gorgon said. "We used a bottled conjure-spell to send the golem back, so we saved the carpet. We can start in the morning and keep whistling it back until all three of us are there. Will that be time enough?"

"It should be," Imbri agreed. "We expect the Mundanes there in two days. King Irene will grow plants to stop them—"

"King Irene!" the Gorgon exclaimed. "What happened to the Centaur King?"

Imbri quickly updated them on recent developments. "So Chameleon will be the next King," she concluded.

"This is moving almost too swiftly for me," the Siren said. "We've got to stop losing our Kings!"

"And stop the Nextwave army," the Gorgon added. "I believe I can do much of that myself, if I can get a good look at them."

"Yes," Imbri agreed. "Take care that no Xanth defenders are near."

The Gorgon nodded. "We certainly shall. You go fetch Blythe; we'll meet you at Castle Roogna."

Imbri let them lapse back into dreamless sleep. She trotted out and to the gourd patch and soon was back at the City of Brass.

All the brassies of Blythe's block were frozen into statue form, which was normal for them when at rest. Imbri pressed the activation button with her nose and they came to life. "Will you come with me to the real world, Blythe?"

Imbri asked the pretty brassie girl. "Your friends have asked for you, and you did mention to me—"

"I'd love to!" Blythe exclaimed. "It's a strange place out there, with all its living things, but I liked the ogre and the girls."

"I'll have to clear it with the Night Stallion," Imbri sent. "But I think it will be all right."

Blythe mounted her, and they made an arrangement to have the brassie building turned off again after they departed it, then went on to check on the seven Kings.

Imbri received a shock. Now there were nine Kings. Both Irene and Chameleon had been taken.

"Now it is up to you, King Mare," Chameleon said. "Only you can stop the Horseman."

"But how did he get to you?" Imbri asked, flustered. Chameleon had warned that things might proceed rapidly, but this was hardly to be assimilated.

Chameleon smiled unpleasantly. "I brought him inside Castle Roogna. My plan worked perfectly."

"You what?"

"I confirmed my suspicion and lured him into the trap, using myself as bait. The moment he was inside, we sent all other living occupants of the castle outside, and King Irene grew the plants she had set out, and they quietly confined him to the castle while he was occupied with us." She made that nasty smile again. "For a while he somehow thought Irene found him handsome, but when he realized she was only stalling for time for her plants to complete their growth, he banished her to the gourd. Then I assumed the crown and told him we knew his secret and would never let him escape the castle, and of course he banished me, too. So my tenure as King was very brief: no more than two minutes. He was very angry about being outwitted, particularly by one he had regarded as stupid."

"But he never met you before!" Imbri protested. "You were in the forest with the day horse when Grundy and Ichabod and I met him!"

"Not precisely. Now you must go and dispatch him, and that will not be easy," Chameleon concluded.

"It will be easy!" Imbri sent. "I will gladly kick that monster to death!"

Chameleon shook her head. "No, not easy at all. You can't kill him."

"Certainly I can, King Chameleon!" Imbri sent hotly.

"Because it may be that only he can abate the enchantment he has put all of us under. You must first make him free us—and he won't do that voluntarily."

Of course that was true; they had been over it before. Imbri was letting her equine temper run away with her. "But I can still kick him into submission. Before I finish, he'll be glad to tell me all." But uncertainty was gnawing at her.

"Not so," Good Magician King Humfrey said. "There is an aspect we may have neglected to clarify."

"You see," Chameleon continued, "he is the offspring of a stallion and a human woman. The result of a liaison at a love spring. That's why he calls himself the Horseman. He is a crossbreed, like the centaurs."

"Like the centaurs?" Imbri asked, confused. "But he's a man!"

"He is a werehorse."

Slowly the terrible realization came across Imbri. "The—day horse?"

"The same. His mind could occupy two forms, each one quite natural to him. No one suspected, because no such creature has manifested in recent times."

"Why didn't you tell me?" Imbri sent, appalled. "All this time I—he—"

"I realize that was cruel," Chameleon said. "But I was not quite sure. If I were wrong, I would have maligned a good and innocent animal. If I were right, it would have been dangerous to inform you, because your reaction could have alerted him and made him avoid our trap. So I had to deceive you, and I regret that."

"All the time, with us—the Horseman!"

"Whose magic talent is to connect a line of sight between any two places—such as a human eye and the peephole of a gourd, as we surmised. That is how he enchanted all of us. But if you try to kick him, he will change into his horse form—and he is more powerful than you."

"Not by night!" Imbri protested. But she remained appalled. She had thought the day horse was her friend! Now she remembered how the animal had always been in the general vicinity of the Horseman. Certainly this had been so when she had first encountered both of them, the one purporting to be fleeing the other. What a cunning camouflage—and she had been completely deceived. The horse had even freed her from captivity by the man—how could she suspect they were the same? Then, when she, Grundy, and Ichabod had spied on the Mundane army, while Chameleon slept, the Horseman had appeared in the Mundane camp. And the Horseman's uncanny ability to travel— naturally he had used his stallion form to gallop in hours what might have taken his human form days, while the man form could navigate the special passes and shortcuts that might have balked the animal form. The best of both forms! As the day horse, pretending to be stupid, he had learned the secrets of Xanth—the invisible bridge, the projected lines of Kings—and they had thought him their ally and had told him everything!

Now, too, she understood the shame of the Good Magician. The day horse had been there when Humfrey had set out his spells and explained them to her! Humfrey could have enchanted the Horseman at any time, had he realized what was in retrospect so obvious. Instead he had allowed himself to be caught in that moment when Imbri had been outside, waiting for the day horse to follow; the stallion had changed to the Horseman, ensorcelled the Magician, changed back, and run with Imbri. If Humfrey was mortified, what, then, of Imbri herself. She had indeed been marishly stupid.

It all fitted so neatly together now. She was sickened. It had taken Chameleon, in her nasty smart phase, to put all the clues together and arrive at the proper conclusion. The Horseman, perhaps becoming contemptuous of his opposition, had been fooled himself. Naturally he had gone with her into Castle Roogna; there was his chance to eliminate the last two Kings expeditiously and take over.

They were all standing there, waiting for Imbri to come to terms with it. King Dor had his arm around King Irene, and both looked pretty well satisfied to be together again. King Trent had taken the hand of King Iris, a seemingly minor gesture of quarter-century significance. All nine Kings appeared to be well enough off here, for the time being—but their bodies were in Castle Roogna, at the mercy of their enemy, the Horseman. They had figured out the truth, and that was essential, but the end of this crisis was hardly certain yet.

"Best of fortune, King Imbri," King Trent said solemnly. "Xanth is depending on you."

Now Imbri appreciated the full magnitude of the challenge. The tenth King *had* to break the chain—and she was that King.

Chapter 13. Breaking the Chain

There was no trouble about getting Blythe Brassie released for real-world duty; the Night Stallion had been waiting for the request. Imbri and the brassie girl arrived at Castle Roogna before dawn.

The Gorgon, the Siren, and Goldy Goblin were already there. So were Chem Centaur and Tandy and her ogre husband Smash, who had been faithfully guarding the castle throughout. Other people and creatures had been sent to neighboring villages for their own safety, since it was now known this would be a battle site. The old soldier Crombie had been persuaded by his daughter to march with the others, to protect them on the journey and point the way if any got lost. The truth was, he was no longer in condition to fight Mundanes, but he had indomitable pride. The Siren had organized these things with the tact and sensitivity she possessed.

Blythe was joyed to meet the others. Old friends greeted one another enthusiastically. Then they sobered, knowing that the difficult time was soon to come. Marching from the Gap was one enemy; within the castle was another. Both had to be dealt with—by this pitifully frail-seeming group of females and a single ogre.

"And one golem," Grundy pointed out with grim pride. Obviously he had not departed with the others, though he should have. What he could do to help wasn't clear at the moment, but he was ready to do it.

They looked at Imbri, who suddenly realized it was now her place to give directives, for she was King. "Rest, eat," she sent in a slightly shaky dreamlet. "We don't expect the Mundanes until another day. You'll know what to do."

Imbri faced the castle, a dark silhouette against a sky thinking about brightening. "And I know what I must do first!"

The castle was imposing in a strange new way, as she gradually made out the details. It was almost entirely overgrown by vegetation. Tangle trees braced against its walls, and carnivorous grass sprouted from the crannies. Animate vines dangled from the parapets. Kraken weeds sprouted from the moat, making the normal moat monsters uneasy. King Irene was gone, but her magic remained, and it did indeed seem to be of Magician caliber.

There was no easy way any person could pass in or out of that place. The Horseman certainly was trapped, for a tangler would as quickly gobble a horse as a man. The plants could not invade the interior of the castle, for that was protected by assorted spells that had been in place for centuries, but they certainly lurked for anything outside. Imbri had to enter the castle now, before dawn, or she would not be able to do so until nightfall. Only her immaterial state could pass those savage plants! Chameleon and Irene had certainly set their trap well, and done as much for Xanth in their brief tenures as Kings as any of the prior Kings had.

There was a sound from the north. Chet Centaur came galloping, his fine body sweating from the effort. Imbri marveled at how different the results of crossbreeding could be—a fine centaur on one hoof, the awful Horseman on the other.

"The Mundanes are coming! The Mundanes are coming!" Chet exclaimed breathlessly.

"But we took down the bridge!" Imbri protested.

"I know it. I checked as well as I could without being seen by them. Apparently they sent a man across right after you left. It happened so fast the Gap Dragon didn't have time to get there—though I'm not sure that poor monster is eager to encounter Mundanes again! The man hauled the invisible bridge back up—it's netlike, you know—and tied it in place, and they marched across it at night. Now their vanguard is upon us! I would have discovered it earlier, but I was checking other trails."

"You were on routine night patrol, not expecting anything," Grundy said. "We all knew the one place they would not cross was at the broken bridge. Or thought we knew."

"We have all underestimated the Mundanes," the Siren said. "That's why the war has gone so badly for us. We keep thinking that people without magic can't be much of a threat. That's not true at all; in fact, such people are the most ruthless and depraved, perhaps because of that lack, so are doubly dangerous."

Imbri realized that the Siren, who had been deprived of her own magic talent for more than twenty years, was in a position to appreciate the deleterious social effects of loss of magic. She was a good woman and had survived and perhaps even improved herself during that hiatus, but lesser people could readily do worse.

Imbri, like the others, had made another serious miscalculation. She had assumed that the Mundanes would remain camped for the night, then forge across the Gap Chasm by day in the manner the other army had crossed a few days before, and camp again on the south side. They had outsmarted her, advancing cleverly and rapidly to rejoin their trapped leader. Now the consequence of this misjudgment was apparent; the siege was on before the defense was ready.

The Horseman would have to wait. Imbri had a battle to organize. The Nextwave could not be allowed to capture Castle Roogna, the last solid symbol of Xanth independence, or to rescue the Horseman. If she went inside to deal with him, she would be trapped there by daylight, unable to phase through walls and plants, and thus be unable to deal with the army outside. She might kill the Horseman but lose the battle, so that Xanth would have nothing at all except barbarians overrunning it. Even a bad leader was probably better than none at all. If she dealt first with the Mundanes, the Horseman would remain trapped, and she could deal with him at her leisure.

But that wasn't a perfect answer. Suppose the Horseman got angry and started killing the bodies of the Kings? Could she afford to risk that? Imbri wavered again. The burden of decision making was heavy, for a mistake affected the welfare of many other creatures, and perhaps the entire Kingdom.

"Don't worry," the Siren said, divining her thought. "The Horseman won't hurt the Kings. He is holding them hostage. He knows we could send in a flight of harpies or other deadly creatures to wipe him out, if we weren't concerned about our own people in there. Meanwhile, the Kings are no threat to him. He has everything to gain by taking good care of them—until the Mundanes win this battle and free him. If the Mundanes lose, he'll try to use the Kings as bargaining chips to win his own freedom."

That made sense, Imbri hoped. "We must organize quickly," she sent. "The Gorgon must be where only the enemy can see her, but not where they can shoot arrows at her."

"Fear not," the Gorgon said. "I will remove my veil only in the presence of a Mundane. I can hide behind a tree and peek out—"

"But the others will see what happens to the first," the Siren said. "The Mundanes are very quick to perceive and act against threats to their welfare. But I can help. Magician Humfrey restored my magic dulcimer before he became King; I have it now, and my power has returned. Let me lure them—"

"First we must get all Xanth males clear of the area," Imbri sent.

"Aw, we know about the Gorgon," Grundy protested. "We won't look her in the puss."

"All males must be clear," Imbri insisted. "Beyond hear-

ing, so you won't be lured in by the Siren. You go out and
warn them, in the name of the King. Get far away and
don't return until one of us finds you and tells you it's
safe."

"Oops—Smash went on another patrol through the jungle," Tandy said. "To make sure no Mundanes were sneak-
ing in from any other directions."

"We have to do it, golem," Chet said. "She's the King
Mare. And she's right. We must warn everyone as fast as
we can, catching any stragglers and getting well away from
here ourselves. We can intercept Smash and warn him
off."

"We'll give you as much time as possible," Imbri sent.
"This is a battle only females can fight, because they are
immune to the Siren's song." She turned quickly to the Siren. "That's right, isn't it?"

"That's right," the Siren agreed. "My power is related to
that of Millie the Ghost—projected sex appeal. I suppose a
male Siren could summon females."

"That would serve them right!" Grundy exclaimed. The
Gorgon turned toward him, lifting one hand to her veil.
Hastily he mounted Chet, and they galloped off while the
Siren chuckled. The Gorgon would not really have lifted
that veil!

Imbri remained uneasy. They certainly had an excellent
weapon, or combination of weapons, in these two sisters,
since the Mundane army was all male. If only they had
had more time to work out a really solid defense!

In hurried moments, they set up a crude arrangement,
the best they could manage with the disadvantage of their
situation. As the sun hauled itself up out of the forest to
the east, singeing the leaves of the adjacent trees, the head
of the Mundane column marched upon the castle. Light
glinted from the Punic shields and helmets as the dread
Wave crested a ridge.

Chem Centaur concealed herself in a hollow old beer-
barrel tree and projected a large map of what she saw. This
identified the position of all the Mundanes in the area in a
way that every defender could see. The Punics could see it,
too—but no Xanth positions were marked on it, so it didn't

help the enemy. The Mundanes peered about, trying to spot the origin of the map, but there were a hundred fat old trees in the vicinity, none of whom cared to help the enemy, and many other features of the terrain to baffle the intruders. So the Mundanes spread out, poking their spears at each tree and getting peppered by supposedly accidental falls of deadwood. Soon they would discover the right one.

But Goldy Goblin, using the projected map for orientation, waved her magic wand. A Mundane flew up in the air, involuntarily, with a startled cry. He sailed in a high arc over the jungle, then plunged, screaming, out of sight.

The Mundanes oriented on this new menace, for the moment forgetting the map. They located Goldy, perched high in a you-call-yptus tree. They shot arrows at her, but the tree called out a warning, as was its nature, and moved its branches to intercept them.

The Mundanes stared, thinking this another coincidence, blaming the movement on the wind. But as the breeze died, and the tree kept balking their shots, they realized that it, too, was a combatant. All the trees around Castle Roogna could move, within reasonable limits, and they were guardians of the castle. But they could not do much unless the Mundanes came within reach, and the enemy soldiers were careful to stay clear.

The Mundanes charged the yptus tree. Goldy used her wand to loft another and another over the jungle and into the nearest lake, where hungry goozlegizzard monsters lurked, but there were too many for her to stop. They reached the base of the tree and started climbing.

Then Blythe Brassie went into action. She was perched on a lower branch and had a basket of cherry bombs harvested from the local cherry tree. She dropped these singly on each ascending helmet. The bombs detonated as they struck, splattering cherry juice in the enemy faces and making the helmets clang. The climbing Mundanes fell out of the tree and out of the fight.

The other Mundanes shot arrows at Blythe. They were so close that the tree's branches were unable to react fast enough to protect her. But the arrows clanged off her brass body harmlessly. Well, almost harmlessly; each one left a

dent, and she was very sensitive about dents. Furious, she
hurled more cherries at the archers, blasting them out.

Angered in turn, the Punics formed a kind of phalanx,
overlapping their shields above their heads, so the cherry
bombs had little effect, and marching to the base of the
tree. Then they used their swords to hack at the trunk.

"OooOooO!" the tree groaned with a sound like that of
wind sighing through its branches. It certainly was hurting.

Blythe dropped down on the top of the phalanx and
knelt to locate crevices. Through these she squeezed more
cherry bombs. The explosions in the confined space of the
formation caused the overlapping shields to jump and fall
apart. Smoke poured out, assisted by the coughing and
hacking of the people inside the enclosure. Blythe lost her
perch and fell down into the phalanx.

Now the Punics whose bodies remained intact grabbed
the brassie girl. Blythe struggled, but they were too many
and too strong for her. "Look what we've got here!" one
gloated. "A golden nymph."

"We know what to do with that kind!" another exclaimed. "Hold her arms and legs—"

Imbri, seeing this from deeper in the jungle, galloped
across to where the Siren hid. "They've got Blythe!" she
sent the moment she came within range. "They're chopping
Goldy's tree! Now it's time for you!"

The Siren nodded. She put her hands to her dulcimer
and began to play. Music sprang out magically, filling the
air. Then she sang. Her voice merged oddly with the notes
of the instrument, forming an unusual but compelling melody. The magic was not entirely in the dulcimer and not
entirely in her voice, but together the two formed a powerful enchantment. The sound floated out over the battlefield, suffusing the environment.

The Mundane men reacted in quite a different manner
than the Xanth females. The soldiers straightened up, listening, pausing in whatever they were doing. Some had arrows nocked to strings; some were chopping at the you-call
tree; some were advancing on the castle; and some were
holding Blythe Brassie spread-eagled, preparing for some
heinous male act. All froze a moment, then turned an·

faced the music. Blythe, battered and dented but otherwise
undaunted, dropped to the ground; the men had no further
interest in her.

There was no formation now, only a somnambulistic
shuffling toward the unseen Siren. For almost twenty-five
years the merwoman's power had been blunted by the loss
of her magic instrument; now it burst forth again in its
fantastic compulsion. The Mundane men crowded toward
the source of the sound, jostling one another discourteously.
They clogged like drifting garbage at the narrow entrance
to the glade where the Siren sang and shoved blindly to
enter—and of course got shoved back. Everything about
the Mundanes was brutish. But slowly the clog cleared,
and they funneled in.

Beside the Siren stood the Gorgon. As each man approached, she lifted aside her veil and looked him in the
face. He turned instantly to stone, a statue in place. The
man following him was not concerned; he simply went
around and was in turn converted to stone.

Imbri watched from behind the Gorgon, which was the
safest place to be. The Siren's power operated only on men,
but the Gorgon's worked on anyone or any creature. The
combination of Siren and Gorgon was deadly potent. At
this rate, the entire Mundane army would soon be stoned.

Then Imbri's acute equine ears heard a distant call. "Imbri! Trouble!" It was from one of the girls; what was the
matter?

Imbri left the garden of statues, careful never to face the
Gorgon, though she knew the Gorgon would cover her face
the moment any friendly party turned toward her. A night
mare might be immune to the Horseman's enchantment,
but not to the Gorgon's, which was of a different nature.
Imbri galloped on past the heedless Punics.

It was Tandy who was calling. She had been on peripheral duty, watching out for unexpected developments,
and she had found one, to her horror. "It's my own husband!" she exclaimed as Imbri joined her. "Smash! He
 e missed Chet and Grundy and not gotten the
 o flee! So he came in to report! Now he's caught
 n's song, and I can't stop him!"
 the ogre was tromping along behind the Mun-

danes, orienting on the hidden glade, captive to the melody. Smash stood twice the height of any of the men and weighed about six times as much; no ordinary person could stop him physically. In addition, he had his magic ogre strength, making him much more dangerous than his size suggested; he could crush rock with his bare hands and squeeze juice from trees. A giant could hardly have stopped him; certainly it was beyond the power of a person Tandy's size.

Imbri tried. "Smash!" she sent in an urgent daydream. "You are caught by the song of the Siren! Block it out, or you will face the Gorgon!"

"Me know; me go," the ogre agreed, reverting to his dull ogrish manner, though his human ancestry gave him intelligence. He tromped on. A couple of objects were clutched in his hamhands.

The lure certainly was powerful! Imbri realized she could not stop Smash. She galloped back to the glade, sending a dream to the Gorgon: "Do not petrify me, friend! I'm coming into sight!"

The Gorgon veiled her face, and Imbri approached her safely, albeit feeling shaky in all four knees. She stopped behind the devastating woman, and the Gorgon resumed flashing at Mundanes, petrifying each in place. The glade was now crowded with statues, and the Siren and the Gorgon had to keep backing away to make room for more. These two were destroying an army that had marched the length of the wilderness of Xanth, cowed griffins and goblins and dragons, and made refugees of whole Xanthian communities. It was surely ironic that the end of the Nextwave should be brought about by two middle-aged and fairly gentle married women.

"The ogre is approaching, and I can not dissuade him," Imbri sent. "Siren, you will have to cease singing for long enough to free him. I'll send him far away; then you can resume."

"But that will also free the Mundanes!" the Siren protested in the dream.

"I know. But the Gorgon can continue petrifying them. They won't know they should flee. The ogre can move very fast; it won't be long."

"As you wish." The Siren stopped singing and playing. "Actually, my fingers are getting tired; I haven't done this in a long time." She flexed them, working the fatigue out, getting limber for the next siege of playing.

"Smash!" Imbri sent to the ogre in a strong long-range dream. "Flee to the jungle as fast as you can! Get out of range of the Siren's voice so you won't get stoned!" She accompanied her words with a picture of the Gorgon petrifying men, including one ogre who was converting slowly to an ugly statue.

"Me flee!" the ogre agreed. "Me leave spells, she use well." He set something on the ground, turned about, picked up Tandy, and charged away, shaking the earth with his tread.

"You, too, Chem!" Imbri sent, realizing that the centaur's map was no longer necessary. "Get away from here and see if you can find other help, in case we should need it. Maybe some of the monsters of the jungle—"

"They're staying out of it," Chem replied, dodging a spear. "They don't want to mix in human business. They don't care who rules Xanth."

"Well, go anyway. I don't want you getting hurt here."

Chem nodded. She was sensible enough to grasp the reality of the situation. It was best to keep all expendable personnel well clear of the moving Gorgon so that no accidents could happen.

The Mundanes, meanwhile, were shaking their heads, reorienting. Some tried to attack the running ogre, thinking he was fleeing them. That foolishness was rewarded immediately; Smash swung his free fist in a surprisingly wide arc, knocking them away. It was an almost idle gesture for him, akin to the swatting of flies, but the Mundanes flew through the air and did not move again after they plowed into the earth.

Other Mundanes returned to their original mission, advancing on the castle. Their numbers had been depleted; there were fewer than a hundred remaining. Some contin- nto the glade, trying to ascertain what was happen- and these the Gorgon quickly dispatched.

soldiers stopped to pick up the items the ogre wn. Imbri had forgotten about those; Smash had called them spells, so he must have believed they were magic that would help in the war effort. She galloped over, but was too late; the Mundanes were already opening one box. Whatever the magic was, the enemy had it. As King, she was not handling such details very well.

There was a scream, followed by frantic activity. The Mundanes started desperately swatting at something, stomping their feet, and fleeing the region. They ignored Imbri.

In a moment she realized what it was. Smash had picked up the box of quarterpedes left by Good Magician Humfrey. It must have washed into the jungle undamaged. The terrible little monsters naturally attacked anything they could reach. They were all over the Mundanes, gouging out two bits of flesh with every pinch, a scourge not even brute soldiers could ignore. In a moment the area was clear— clear of quarterpedes, too, for they were all on the Mundanes. Screams and curses in the distance bespoke the location of the affected individuals. What lucky mischief for the Castle Roogna defenders!

The second box remained. Imbri remembered this one; it was lettered PANDORA. She wondered what was inside, but knew better than to open it herself. She picked it up with her teeth and carried it with her; maybe the Gorgon could identify its contents, since she had packed it for the Good Magician.

Soon Imbri judged the ogre to be far enough away; the sounds of boulders cracking and trees being knocked over had faded in the distance. She wondered idly whether the quarterpedes would have dared to gouge at the ogre, had he opened their box. She trotted back toward the Gorgon's glade circuitously, avoiding Mundanes. "Start again, Siren!" she sent.

There was no response. "Hey, Siren!" Imbri sent again, in a stronger dream.

Still there was nothing. "Gorgon, tell your sister to resume singing," Imbri sent.

After a moment the Gorgon responded in the dream. "My sister has been taken by the Horseman!"

Imbri's confidence collapsed like a wall struck by the ogre. Too late, she realized what had happened. The

Horseman, confined to Castle Roogna, had heard the Siren's song, faintly, and felt its compulsion. Since he could not reach her, he had remained partially transfixed, perhaps walking in place against the wall, perhaps in imminent danger of stepping out to be gobbled by a carnivorous plant. The moment the song stopped, he had been freed— so he had acted to eliminate the danger. He must have been able to see the Siren from an embrasure, and could work his magic on whomever he could see. Or perhaps her song had enabled him to focus sufficiently on her. He had connected her to the gourd. She now had joined the Kings.

"We'll have to fight without her," Imbri sent. "Do not be alarmed, Gorgon; she is well enough off in the gourd. Just protect her body from the Mundanes, and we shall rescue her when we rescue the Kings."

"I'll do more than protect her body," the Gorgon said grimly. "I'll petrify every last ilk of a Mundane!" She walked purposefully around the statues, holding her veil away from her face, looking for enemy men. Imbri was glad she had cleared the area of friends; this was certainly dangerous territory now!

But it wasn't the same without the Siren's summoning. The Mundanes were becoming aware of the danger. Some formed a phalanx, not looking out; others located the Gorgon by looking at her in the reflections of their shields. They blindfolded some of their archers and gave them instructions on aiming their bows by using the shield-reflection technique. The first arrows missed, but the Mundanes' aim was improving. They might not be in the centaurs' class as archers, but they were good enough. The Gorgon had to keep moving to avoid getting struck.

"We need to reorganize," Imbri sent. "You must back up against Goldy's tree, Gorgon. Then Goldy can protect you. Blythe can help a lot, too; I don't believe your power affects her, since she is already made of metal."

"My sister mentioned that Blythe was immune to the glare of a basilisk," the Gorgon said. "Mine is no worse than that."

"Get on my back; we must hurry."

Carefully the Gorgon mounted. Then Imbri galloped on, while the Gorgon glared about, leaving a trail of statues in their wake. Many Mundanes had not yet gotten the word; they soon got the look, and that finished them.

A centaur galloped back. It was Chem. "Why isn't the Siren singing?" she called. "Is something wrong?"

Imbri quickly sent her a dream of explanation. "Get away from the Mundanes," she concluded. "They remain dangerous."

"So I see," Chem agreed. "One thing I can do. I can circle around and carry my friend the Siren away to safety."

"An excellent notion," Imbri said, and the centaur galloped away.

They set up by the yptus tree, with Blythe Brassie protecting the Gorgon from hurled spears and close arrows, while Goldy Goblin used her wand to remove any archers whose blindfolded aim became too good.

They settled into a war of attrition, with the numbers of the enemy steadily decreasing, but their alertness increasing. The Punics tried to swamp the Gorgon with another phalanx; Goldy and Blythe disrupted it, loosening it so that some Mundanes inadvertently looked out—and turned to stone. That messed things up for the others, who found themselves in a pileup of mixed living and stone bodies. They tried to charge with a huge tree trunk as a battering ram, but Imbri sent a dream picture of a tree to one side of the real one, and they oriented on that and charged harmlessly by. When they ground to a halt, realizing that something was wrong, and looked back, the Gorgon got them all stoned with a single glance. Others tried to use the stoned bodies of their companions as weapons, picking them up and shoving them toward the tree, but the statues were too clumsy and too easy for Goldy's wand to move away.

It seemed the girls were doing all right, despite their reverses. The Mundanes were down to about fifty and were fazed by the number of their companions who were statues. Soon they would not have enough of a force left to storm the plant-defended castle and rescue their leader. The day was passing; when night fell, Imbri's power would be magnified, for she would be invulnerable to strikes against herself. As it was, only constant vigilance, the proximity of the Gorgon, and the fact that many Mundanes did not know what office Imbri held prevented her from getting wounded. Had the Punics been able to face her and attack, they would soon have prevailed.

Then Imbri realized that she hadn't seen any Mundanes lofted out of the battle for a while. "Are you all right, Goldy?" she sent in a dreamlet to the high branches of the tree.

She encountered only blankness. With a tired and familiar wash of horror, she knew that the goblin girl had been taken. The Horseman had evidently spotted her, concentrated long-distance, and finally managed to reach her. It surely wasn't easy for him to score at this range, but he had nothing to do except try; perhaps he had missed a hundred chances, then eventually scored when conditions were just right. Maybe Imbri had erred again by not going in to deal with him at the outset; he certainly was causing mischief now! Whom would he reach next?

"I think you should get out of the line of sight of the castle," Imbri said to the Gorgon. "Blythe and I are from the World of Night, so can't be enchanted that way; looking into a gourd's peephole does not hypnotize us. But you—"

Hastily the Gorgon edged around the tree until she could no longer see Castle Roogna. But without Goldy's help, their situation was critical. Now the Mundanes could organize a phalanx without having individual members fly out from it. They had shields angled like mirrors in several places so that they could orient specifically on the tree. There would be no stopping this one!

"We have to move," Imbri sent. "They are too much for us."

They moved, Imbri carrying both Blythe and the Gorgon. The double load was awkward, especially since the brassie girl was heavier than flesh, but the phalanx was not able to pursue efficiently, so Imbri did a lumbering gallop and made it to the protection of the main jungle.

Then she felt the Gorgon sliding off. Blythe grabbed the woman to prevent her from falling, but that was only a minor problem.

They had appeared in sight of the Horseman, and he had been ready and had taken the Gorgon. Maybe it had been a lucky score for him, but the damage was critical. Now they had no really good weapon against the Mundanes. All they could do was hide until nightfall, hoping the plants around Castle Roogna would confine the Horseman until then. Imbri was not especially proud of the way she had managed things; she should have realized that the Horseman would strike again the moment he got the chance.

The Mundanes did not pursue them far, perhaps fearing some new trap. They might be satisfied to have routed the defenders, not knowing that the Gorgon could not turn and strike again. Imbri soon was clear of the enemy, moving through the quiet jungle. She and Blythe set the Gorgon in a pillow bush, covered her over with a blanket from a blanket tree, and left her there; she should be safe for a few hours. Most of the predatory creatures of this region had departed when the Mundanes came, as the reputation of the invaders as hunters of monsters had preceded them. Imbri and Blythe went to the edge of the jungle to watch the Mundanes.

Irene's plants remained formidable. The first Mundanes who ventured close to the front gate got snatched and consumed by the vines and tangle trees guarding it. Pieces of Mundane fell to the grass, and it gobbled these just as avidly. Some plopped into the moat, where the moat monsters fought with the kraken weeds to snap them up. That taught the men caution.

The Punics tried another battering ram, charging up to the moat and hurling it across at the wall, but the tentacles snatched it out of the air and dumped it back on the men's heads. A real battering ram, which was a horned and hoofed animal who liked to charge things headfirst, would never have made the mistake of charging a tangler.

The Mundanes consulted, then scattered. "What are they doing?" Blythe asked.

It soon became apparent. They were gathering dry wood. "They're going to use fire," Imbri sent.

"Oh, the plants won't like that!" the brassie girl said worriedly. She had learned about plants during her prior visit to the real world, when she had traveled with the ogre. "But doesn't water stop fire?"

"It does," Imbri agreed. "But the Mundanes have proved to be resourceful before; they must have some way in mind to get around that."

Imbri looked at the sky. The sun was now descending, as it did every day about this time when it got too tired to maintain its elevation. Soon night would come. She doubted the Mundanes could free their leader before the friendly darkness closed. "When night arrives, I will enter Castle Roogna and confront the Horseman," Imbri sent. "You must go then to rescue Goldy Goblin from the yptus tree and bring her to where we have hidden the Gorgon."

"Yes. I will keep them safe," the brassie girl promised.

The Mundanes rolled small boulders into the moat, slowly filling it in at one place and forming a crude causeway. They shoveled dirt and sand into the interstices. The plants and moat monsters were not smart enough to realize what the men were doing, so did not oppose it directly. They tried to grab the men as morsels, but left the boulders alone. In due course the causeway reached the castle wall, so that the Mundanes were able to march up to it, while fighting off attacking tentacles.

Now the Punics brought their collected wood and piled it against the wall where the causeway touched. But the vines grabbed the sticks and hurled them back, perceiving them as useful missiles.

"I could get to like such plants," Imbri sent appreciatively.

This did not balk the Nextwavers for long. They started their fire away from the wall, then drew burning brands from it and threw them at the plants. The plants threw them back, but received a number of scorches in the process. It was evident that before long the Mundanes would be able to clear a section of the wall. They weren't approaching the front gate, for that was guarded by two ornery tangle trees; but here at the ramp, the wall was less heavily defended.

Of course, the wall itself remained behind the plants, and that was excellently solid. They would have to batter a hole in it, which would take time. Imbri judged she would have about an hour to deal with the Horseman after night fell. But she wasn't sure, for the Punics had surprised her before with their savage cunning. Still, these ones must have been active for a day and a night and another day without rest; they were bound to give out eventually.

Darkness closed. "Go about your business, Blythe," Imbri sent, and phased out.

"Good luck!" the brassie called after her.

Imbri started to neigh a response—and discovered that she still held the Pandora box in her mouth. She had been so caught up in events that she had never noticed the way it propped her mouth open. Well, she would simply have to hold on to it a little longer, since she didn't know what it contained. It was bound to be important, though; hadn't Humfrey said his secret weapon, more potent than any other, was locked up in this box? He had been afraid the girl Pandora would take it out prematurely, so had kept the box.

If she opened it herself, something horrible might emerge to destroy her, as the quarterpedes had done to the Mundanes who opened the other box. If she let this item fall into the hands of the Mundanes, some fearsome thing might come forth to aid them. What should she do? It was a problem.

Imbri suspected she would need the luck Blythe wished her. Everything depended on her. If she found herself in real trouble, she would open the box and hope it helped her. But she wouldn't touch it before then, only when she had nothing to lose.

The castle loomed closer. She had not been able to concentrate on this aspect of her challenge. Now, as she galloped invisibly toward the final encounter, seeing the grim wall illuminated on one side by the smoldering blaze of the Mundanes' fire, she realized why: it was because of the day horse.

She had thought the day horse was her friend. Now she knew he was not. He had deceived her from the outset, running from her because he feared she could read his mind, then meeting her in the form of the Horseman and learning more about her, then returning in horse form to ingratiate himself with her by freeing her. What a cynical mechanism to make her feel positive toward him! Thereafter he had used her to find his way conveniently all around Xanth, learning about the enchanted paths, the invisible bridge, and the nature of the Xanth defenses. Thus *she* had been responsible for the ultimate betrayal of Xanth, setting up a series of Kings for confinement in the gourd. All that the day horse had told her about the selfish motives of the Horseman, such as why he had allowed her to escape Hasbinbad's camp, were true; he had been in a position to know. Of course that creature, in either form, had enabled her to remain free; she was far more useful to the enemy than were any of the Mundane spies! Beware the Horseman indeed! If she had known . . .

Now she did know. Now she was the tenth King of Xanth, and she had to atone for her colossal error in judgment. She had to destroy the monster she had so innocently facilitated.

But that wasn't all of the point now. There was something else. Something more fundamental. What was it?

She couldn't kill the Horseman because of his magic, which would probably continue after him, leaving the Kings in dire circumstances. She had to make him tell his secret, which meant she would have to converse with him, and she couldn't do that because—

Because why? Somehow her mind sheered away as if at the brink of the Gap Chasm. But she had to face the truth, for this was the critical encounter. What was that truth?

She snorted hot little snorts and swished her tail violently from side to side, venting her private rage at the cynical way the day horse had maneuvered her, reviewing it once more in order to evoke the elusive thought she knew was so important. The day horse had played the innocent, pretending to be almost stupid, almost cowardly, when he was in fact none of these things. He had given rides or aid to future Kings of Xanth, facilitating their advance, not from any good will to them, but because he judged them to be potentially ineffective rulers against whom the Mundanes could make easy progress. When each new King disappointed him by demonstrating surprising determination and capability, he took out that King to make way for another, weaker one. Ironically, even the less promising of these, the women, became towers of strength for Xanth, until at last the least impressive of all, Chameleon, fathomed his secret and trapped him.

Least impressive? No, that doubtful honor belonged to Imbri herself—not human, not male, and no Magician. Xanth had at last been brought to the indignity of being governed by a night mare. A creature whose life cycles were equine—

Suddenly, as she encountered the dark moat, she suffered her final, horrible realization—the one that had eluded her before; she was coming into season.

It had been developing all along, of course, in the normal equine cycle. As a full night mare, she had never been tied to it, for she had been mostly immaterial. But once she became a day mare, the things of solid existence had loomed larger, and nature had proceeded inexorably. Now nature said it was time for her to mate. Her mind had been distracted by the crisis of the Kings, but her body had never changed its course.

The enemy she faced was, in his fashion, a stallion.

She veered away from the castle. She could not face him now! She could not even go near him! Her equine nature would betray her! It would not permit her to attack him; it would require her to mate with him.

Yet she could not stay away, either, for soon the Mundanes would break open an aperture in the wall and free their leader. Then Xanth would be finished. The Horseman would kill the hostage bodies of the Kings and proclaim himself King, and there would be none but a discredited mare to deny him. If she were going to stop him at all, she had to do it now.

Imbri wavered indecisively. If she went inside Castle Roogna, she would surely betray Xanth to the enemy; if she avoided confrontation, she would let Xanth fall by default. Which way was she to go?

She turned again. Better, at least, to try! She charged toward the castle, determined to do what she had to do. She might be in season, but she had a mind equivalent to that of a human being, and a human woman could pretty well control her mating urges, such as they were. Imbri had to determine, once and forever, whether she was a civilized King—or a simple animal.

She phased across the moat, through the vegetation and the stone of the wall, and into the deep gray matter of the castle. A ghost spied her, waved, and vanished; then all was still. She made her way to the throne room—and there was the Horseman. her foe, sitting slumped on the throne, a golden crown on his head, a scepter in his hand, sleeping. Such ambition!

She materialized and stood looking at him. He was a fairly handsome figure of a man, with curly light hair, good musculature, and that thin brass band on his left wrist, the only jewelry he wore. Yet even though he was in repose, there was a cruel hook to his upper lip. He was not a nice person.

It would be easy to kill him now! This was the enemy who had plagued Xanth generally, and her personally, for he had ridden her and dug his cruel spurs into her flanks. She could dispatch him with perfect joy and justice.

But first she had to force from him his secret so she could free the nine other Kings of Xanth. If she failed, they would all perish as their physical bodies starved, even if the Horseman died first. If the Horseman won, Xanth would be ruled by the tyrant imposter and his Mundane henchmen. She *had* to succeed—but still did not know how to proceed.

As she stood there in unkingly uncertainty, the Horseman woke. His eyes opened, and he spied her.

"Well," he said. seemingly unperturbed. "So you have arrived at last, King Mare."

He seemed so confident! Imbri knew that there was no way this horrible man could get on her back, since she was fully on guard. Even if by some trick he managed to get on her, he could not remain, since she would simply dematerialize. He would have to get off in a hurry, or she would carry him into the gourd and turn him over to the Kings. He would never get to rule Xanth then! She could attack him, while he could not attack her, not even with his special magic talent. She was one of the few creatures naturally immune to his power. That was why she was here now. He had to know that. Why, then, should he appear unconcerned?

"What, no dreams, Imbri?" he asked brightly. "All this trouble to come see me, and no dialogue?"

"I'm here to break the chain," she sent, trying to rid

herself of the unreasonable awe of him she felt. "How do I free the Kings from your spell?"

"You don't, Imbri! Those Kings are past; I am the next and final King of Xanth, as you can plainly see."

"Not so. I am the present King of Xanth," she sent, her equine ire rising. "I will kick you to death before I let you usurp the throne!" She took a step forward.

The Horseman waved a hand in a gesture of negligence. "So the issue is which of us is the true tenth King of Xanth. You are bluffing, mare. I know you are immune to my power, and I know I can not ride you or strike you while it is dark. I have seen the night world from which you hail! Nevertheless, you are not about to attack me— because all your prior Kings will die if I do. There will be no one to unriddle the enchantment I made."

"Then you *can* free them, if you choose!" Imbri sent.

"I did not say that," the Horseman replied, as if playing a game.

"Either you can free them or you can't. If you can't, then they are doomed anyway and you have nothing to bargain with. If you can free them, you had better do so, or you will lose your life. I shall not permit you to gain the throne of Xanth by your mischief. Either King Trent returns to power or I shall remain King; in neither case will you assume the office. The question is whether you will free the Kings and live, or fail to free them and die."

The Horseman clapped his hands together in mock applause. "Oh, pretty speech, nocturnal mare! But what if I live, and you die, and I am accepted as the final King of the chain?"

She saw that he had no intention of yielding. He was stalling until his Mundane allies rescued him. She would have to kick him. Perhaps when he was suitably battered, and knew she was serious, his nerve would crack. She braced herself for a charge.

Suddenly the Horseman hurled a spell enclosed in an opaque globe. It bounced against the wall behind Imbri and burst. From it a bright light emerged, illuminating the whole chamber as if it were day. It was a sunspot, one of the spells in the royal arsenal. The Horseman had spent part of his confinement exploring the castle and had, of course, raided its store of artifacts. He was, after all, far from helpless—and she should have anticipated this.

Imbri wrenched her eyes away from the blinding sunspot—but too late to prevent damage. Her vision, adapted to night, was temporarily stunned. Fool! She had allowed herself to be completely vulnerable to surprise!

"What—did that sudden blaze hurt your sensitive evening eyes, mare?" the Horseman inquired with false concern. "Do you have difficulty seeing me, King Equine? Perhaps I can alleviate your indisposition."

Imbri whirled to the side, avoiding his approach—but soon crashed into a wall. The forgotten object in her mouth flung out and clattered across the floor. She could not see—and not only that, she could not phase out, because of the daylight the sunspot generated. The scheming Horseman had hit her with a double penalty. How cunningly he had laid his countertrap, knowing she was coming!

"I dislike this, Imbri," the Horseman said, stalking her. "You're such a beautiful animal, and I really do appreciate fine horseflesh. I am, I think, uniquely qualified to judge the best. But you have placed yourself between me and the throne of Xanth and have cost my *ad hoc* allies an extraordinary amount. So I must congratulate you on the way you organized those females, and dispatch you—"

Imbri lurched away again, caroming off a wall. Her vision was beginning to return, but slowly. Things were still mostly blurry.

"Mare—he's got a magic sword!" a voice warned in her ear.

"Who are you?" Imbri sent to the unknown person. How could there be anyone else in the castle?

"I am Jordan the Ghost," the person whispered, again in her ear. "We ghosts have been watching for the rescue attempt, and I was notified the moment you phased in. I know what you are doing, and the great effort you must make. I have friends within the gourd. I will help you, if you trust me."

"I bear a message of greeting to you from them!" she sent as she continued to move. "I forgot to seek you out before, when I had the opportunity. Of course I trust you!" Now she deeply regretted her neglect. There were half a dozen ghosts in Castle Roogna, and Millie, the Zombie Master's wife, had been one of their number for eight hundred years. Naturally the ghosts supported the legitimate Kings of Xanth! "Help me. Get on my back and guide me till my sight returns."

"I'm on," Jordan said. Imbri felt nothing, but that was normal for a ghost. "One body length ahead, turn right. There's a door. Hurry; he's about to strike at your flank!"

Imbri leaped forward and veered right. She misjudged slightly and banged her shoulder, but got through the doorway.

"Two body lengths," the ghost said. "Turn left."

She obeyed and found another opening.

"It is dark here," Jordan advised her.

Glory be! Imbri phased into immateriality and walked through a wall. She was safe now, thanks to the ghost. "Thank you, Jordan," she sent. "Are you still with me? I mean, now that I'm—"

"Oh, yes, I'm still riding you," he said. "The state of your materiality makes no difference to me."

Now Imbri's sight was firming. "Did the Horseman follow?"

"He did not. He remains in the light, sword ready. He is eyeing the box you brought, but not touching it."

"He doesn't know what's in it," Imbri sent. "Neither do I. It's a complete gamble, which I plan to open only when there is no hope. That way it will be unable to hurt me if it is bad, and may help me if it is good."

"That makes sense. But he has control of the box right now and doesn't dare open it."

"Then we are at an impasse," Imbri sent. "He can't hurt me in the dark, and I doubt I can hurt him in the light. If that's a typical magic sword, it will skewer me before I can hurt him."

"It is," the ghost confirmed. "Of course, you could borrow some other weapon from the arsenal."

That sounded good. Imbri knew she had little time to dispatch the Horseman, for she could hear the Mundanes pounding at the outer wall. "What is there?"

"Oh, lots of things," Jordan said. "Magic bullets—only we don't know what they are or how they are used, whether they are for biting or for making people feel good. Vanishing cream, which we can't see at all, let alone drink. Healing elixir. Fantasy fans—"

"What's a fantasy fan?" Imbri asked.

"A bamboo fan that has a magic picture on it when spread open," Jordan explained. "It also makes you think you're cooler than you are, especially when the picture is of a snowscape. Periodically these fans gather together from all over Xanth for some big convention where they shoot the breeze and blow a lot of hot air and decide who is the secret master of fandom."

Oh. Imbri didn't need any fantasy fans. In fact, none of the items seemed useful for her present situation. "Is there anything to nullify his sword?"

"Oh, yes. Magic shields, armor, gauntlets—"

"I can't use those things! I have no hands!"

"Oh, yes, I see. Xanth hasn't had a handless King before! Let me consider. It's the sword you must be wary of. You can't avoid it; the moment he gets within range, it will strike for the kill. I presume that if it weren't for that, you could dispatch him in the light."

"Yes." Imbri knew that even if the Horseman got on her back and used his spurs, he could not control her now; she would ignore the pain and launch into darkness, where she would be in control in either phase. No, the Horseman would not dare try to ride her this time!

"I've got it!" Jordan cried, snapping his ghostly fingers without effect. "The melt-spell!"

"Will that melt metal?"

"Indubitably. That is what this one is for. The Mundane scholar, Ichabod, was cataloguing the spells of the armory for King Arnolde, and that was an old one he discovered before the men were sent away from this region. Too bad he didn't have the chance to finish the job; there's a lot of good stuff here that even we ghosts don't understand."

They trotted down to the armory. The spell was in a small globe, as many were; Imbri wondered what Magician had packaged such spells, for they seemed to keep forever. She picked the globe up in her mouth, carefully, for the ghost could not carry anything physical. She phased back, phasing the spell with her, and trotted off to the main floor.

She heard the crashing of the Mundanes attacking the wall. By the sound of it, they were making progress. Their ramp and fire had nullified the moat and plants in that vicinity, so they were free to batter the stones as much as they craved. In just a few more minutes they would break in. She had to finish with the Horseman before then, for otherwise the Mundanes could go on the rampage and kill the ensorcelled Kings regardless of the outcome of her conflict. Imbri hurried.

In fact, she thought now, she had better make sure that, if it seemed she would beat the Horseman, she finished him off quickly so that he would have no chance to take the true Kings with him.

She came in to the lighted room, where the Horseman awaited her, sword ready. He looked even more arrogant now, his thin lip curling up from half-bared teeth, his brass bracelet gleaming with seeming malevolence in the light of the sunspot.

She was prepared for the light, and the sunspot was no longer as brilliant, so this time she had no trouble with vision. She turned solid in the room, however; any light stronger than moonlight did that to her.

"Ah, I thought I might see you again, King Mare," the Horseman said with a supercilious sneer. "You must meet me—or forfeit your cause." He strode forward, the sword moving with an expertise that was inherent in it, not in him.

Imbri spit out the spell. It flipped through the air toward the Horseman. The sword alertly intercepted it, slicing it in two—and therein lay the sword's demise. It wasn't intelligent; it didn't know when to desist. Had the spell been allowed to pass unmolested, or had the Horseman simply caught it in his left hand, preventing it from breaking, he would have been all right. But as the globe separated into halves, the vapor of the spell puffed out, clouding about the blade of the sword.

The blade melted. First it sagged, then it drooped, like soft rubber. At last it dripped on the floor. It was useless.

Now Imbri leaped for the Horseman with a squeal of combat, her forehooves striking forward.

The man dodged aside, throwing away the useless weapon. He tried to jump on her back, but Imbri whirled, bringing her head around, teeth bared. Most human beings did not think of equine beings as teeth fighters, but they were. However, all she caught was his sleeve; he was moving too fast for her. He was scrambling onto her, ready to use his awful spurs.

She lunged to the side, slamming into the wall, trying to pin him against it, to crush him and stun him. Again he was too fast; he certainly understood horses! He rolled over her back and off the other side, landing neatly on his feet.

Imbri swung about and lashed out with her hind hooves. The double blow would have knocked his bones from his body, had it scored, but he had thrown himself to the side, anticipating her attack with uncanny accuracy.

But she was a night mare, with a century more experience than he had in life. She knew far more about this sort of thing than had any horse he had dealt with before. She spun on her hind feet as they touched the floor and leaped for him again. She knew she had him now; he could not safely leave the lighted chamber, for in the darkness the advantage would be entirely hers. In moments she would catch him, in this confined space, with hoof or teeth or the mass of her body, and he would be done for.

The Horseman had fallen to the floor, getting out of her way. Sure enough, she had surprised him with her speed and ferocity. He had misjudged her exactly as she had misjudged the day horse, assuming that the personality that showed was the only one inhabiting that body. He was accustomed to tame Mundane horses, who tolerated riders because they knew no better. Now he scrambled on hands and knees as she reoriented for the kill. He was too slow this way; she knew she had him.

Then he transformed into his other form. Suddenly the day horse stood before her, massive, white, beautiful—and male. She had, in a pocket of her mind, doubted that her horse friend and her man enemy could really be the same; now that doubt had been banished.

Imbri hesitated. The masculinity of this magnificent

creature struck her like a physical blow. She was in season, ready to mate, and this was the only stallion she knew. If she destroyed him, she might never again have the chance to breed.

He was the enemy; she knew that. Had she retained any doubt, the presence of the brass band on his left foreleg, just above the foot, would have removed it. She had believed that that band was the token of his slavery to the Horseman; now she was aware that it was much more than that. The form of the creature had changed; the form of the inanimate band had not. How ready she had been to believe whatever he told her! She had gone more than half-way to delude herself, wanting to believe that no horse could be evil.

She knew his nature now—but all her being protested against violence in this case. No mare opposed a stallion—not when she was in season. It was as contrary to her nature as it was for a human man to strike a lovely woman. It simply wasn't done. This was no decision of intellect; it was a physiological, chemical thing. With equines, intellect was not allowed to interfere with the propagation of the species. She had always before considered this an advantage. But advantage or disaster, it was so.

The day horse turned toward her, lifting his handsome head high. He snorted a snort of dominance. He recognized his power over her. It did not matter that they both knew him to be her enemy, her deadly rival for the Kingship, or that he was only stalling for time until the Mundanes completed their break-in. The Horseman had occupied her as long as he could, using up precious time; now the day horse was doing the rest of the job. Nature held her as powerless as she had been when blinded.

"Imbri! Don't let him dazzle you!" Jordan the Ghost cried in her ear. He was still with her; she had forgotten him during the intense action. "No male is worth it! I know, for I am a worthless male who ruined a good girl, and now suffer centuries of futile remorse. Don't let it happen to you! Xanth depends on you!"

Still she stood, virtually rooted, smelling the compelling scent of the stallion. She knew she was being totally foolish, as females had always been in the presence of virile males.

She knew the consequence of her inaction. Yet she could not act. The mating urge was too strong.

The day horse nipped her on the neck. Imbri stood still. There was pain, but it was exquisite equine pain, the kind a mare not only accepted from a stallion but welcomed. He was dominant, as he had to be, to be a worthy stud.

He marched around her, taking his time. This, too, was part of the ritual. He sniffed her here and there and snorted with affected indifference. Oh, he certainly had her under control! The ghost had given up, knowing Imbri was lost. Her glazing eyes were fixed on the box on the floor, the one that had the word PANDORA printed on it. All it would take would be three steps to reach it and strike it with a forehoof, opening it, releasing whatever it contained—but she could not force herself to take those steps.

There was a loud crash from the distant outer wall. The Mundanes had broken in at last. Imbri quivered, trying to break free of her paralysis, but the stallion snorted, quieting her. She simply could not oppose him, though all her reason protested her folly. She had fatally underestimated the compulsion of her own marish nature.

"Hey, General—where are you?" a Mundane called.

The day horse shifted momentarily into his human form. "Here in the throne room!" he called back.

That broke the spell. Imbri jumped, moving like the released mechanism of a catapult, turning on him. But as she faced him, poised for the strike, he converted back to stallion form. He arched his neck, eyeing her with assurance, completely handsome and potent. He tapped the floor with his left forehoof.

Imbri, in the process of freezing again despite her best resolution, saw the brass band on that leg. The band that advertised exactly who and what he was.

She struck out with a forefoot, catching him on that front leg, attacking the band. The blow was not crippling or even very effective; its significance lay in the fact that she was opposing him. His shift of form, and his direct recognition of alliance with the Mundane enemy, had disrupted the equine mood. He was not a horse in the guise of a man, but a man in the guise of a horse. Imbri did not breed with a man in any guise. Now she knew, subjectively as well as objectively, that he was no friend of hers. All she had to do was look at that band, to see him as he was.

The day horse squealed, more in anger than in pain. He stomped his forefoot again. He was as handsome in his ire as in his dominance.

Imbri refused to be captured again. The brass band remained fixed in her mind. Her head swung about, her teeth biting into his neck just behind the furry white ear. She tore out part of his splendid silver mane. Red blood welled up, staining the shining hide.

Now the day horse fought. He squealed and reared, his forehooves striking out—but she reared, too. She was not as large and powerful as he, so was at a disadvantage, but she was driven by pure outrage and the knowledge that she was fighting not only for her pride, her freedom, and her life, but for the welfare of the nine other Kings and for the Land of Xanth itself. She was the King Mare; she *had* to prevail.

She whirled, her lesser mass giving her greater maneuverability, and launched a rear-foot kick. She scored on his shoulder and felt the bone crumbling under the force of her blow. The day horse stumbled, limping, then righted himself and came at her again. He was indeed a fighting creature and quite unafraid; instead of turning about to orient his powerful hind hooves on her, he used his head. This was the contemptuous nipping approach of the dominant animal.

This time Imbri kicked him in the head.

He collapsed, blood pouring from his nostrils.

Imbri looked at him. Now she was sorry for what she had done, though she knew it was necessary. He had made a fatal tactical error, coming at her in the mode of disciplining rather than in the mode of fighting, and had paid the consequence. Yet the blood on his pretty white coat, gushing over the floor, horrified her.

She knew there was healing elixir in the armory. She could fetch some of that, and in an instant this most beautiful creature could be restored. No stallion should suffer so ignominious a demise!

"Where are you, General?" the Mundane called, approaching the throne room.

Imbri charged for the door, whirled, and caught the man with a hard kick in the chest as he entered. He went down with a broken groan, unconscious or worse.

"Jordan!" she sent. "Will you ghosts help? The Mundanes are said to be superstitious; they're actually afraid of the supernatural. If you show yourselves to them and make threatening gestures, it may scare them away. I've got to protect the dormant Kings while I try to reverse the Horseman's enchantment on them."

"We'll do our best," Jordan said, and floated swiftly and purposefully away.

Imbri returned to the day horse, determined to force him to divulge the secret. She hated all of this, but if she had to, she would taunt him with the healing elixir, holding it back until he acquiesced.

But she discovered that he had changed again. He had reverted to his human form, in a pool of blood—and the Horseman wasn't breathing. The terrible force of her kick had smashed the bones of his head. She knew at a glance that he was dead.

There was now no way to make him talk. She had in her desperation hit him too hard. She had murdered him.

She stared at the awful sight, her agony for the death of the day horse merging with her grief for the coming loss of the Kings of Xanth. What could she do now? She had squandered Xanth's last chance!

Bleak despair overwhelmed her. She and the ghosts might fight off the Mundanes, but what use was that now? The King Mare had brought doom, exactly as should have been anticipated.

"The box!" Jordan prompted, returning. "Maybe it has a counterspell—"

Listlessly, Imbri put her hoof on the box and crushed it. Thin, translucently pink vapor puffed out, expanding into a rather pretty cloud. It encompassed her, for she made no effort to avoid it. For good or evil, she accepted it.

It certainly wasn't evil. She felt invigorated and positive. Somehow she generated confidence that things would work out after all.

"Hope!" Jordan exclaimed in her ear. "It was hope

locked in that box! I feel it, too! Now I believe that my own long morbidity will eventually terminate."

Hope. Good Magician Humfrey had mentioned that he had locked up hope. She hadn't realized that it was in the Pandora box. She understood, objectively, that nothing had changed, yet the positive feeling remained. There had to be some way!

Imbri's eye caught the brass circlet on the Horseman's wrist. Something turned over in her mind. Why had he never removed it, though it was an obvious hint of his identity? Surely it had considerable value for him. Could that thing be a magic amulet? Something to enable him to convert from man to horse? No—that conversion was inherent in his nature, just as the Siren's ability to change from legs to tail sprang from her man-mermaid parentage. The Siren needed the dulcimer to do her separate magic.

The band—could it be something like the dulcimer, to amplify or focus his power? If the example of the Siren was valid, these crossbred people did need something extra to bring out their full talents. Part of their magic was their dual nature, so the rest was weaker than it should be. A dulcimer—a thin brass band. The magic of the Horseman could have resided not wholly in him but partly in the amulet.

It was her only remaining chance. She had hope; this could solve the problem of the Kings! She took the brass ring in her teeth and tugged it. It would not pass over his hand, so she used a forehoof to crush the bones of his dead extremity together, pulping the appendage, until there was room for the circlet to pass. Then she took it in her teeth and trotted out of the chamber, to darkness.

"We'll protect the Kings!" Jordan called after her. "As long as we can scare the Mundanes . . ."

She sent a neigh of thanks and phased through the walls and out of the castle. She saw in passing that the ghosts were indeed doing a good job of holding the remaining Mundanes back; with the Horseman and one of their own number dead, and with the ghosts menacing the rest, these troops would be quite wary of penetrating deeper into the castle by night. They would not realize for some time that the ghosts had no physical power. She hoped the Mundanes would be balked long enough; the Horseman had lost, but Xanth would not win until the Kings had been saved.

She shot out into the night, the brass band still firmly in her teeth. She knew one person who was knowledgeable about brass. "Blythe!" she broadcast as powerfully as she could. "Blythe Brassie!"

As she neared the place where she had left the Gorgon, she heard the brassie girl's dream response. "Here, King Imbri!"

In a moment they were together. "Blythe, I have a ring of brass I took from the Horseman. I think it connects to his power, but I don't know how it works. Can you tell?"

Blythe took the band and examined it closely. "Yes, I believe I have encountered something like this before. Note how short it is; very little depth compared with its mass. It is what we call a short circuit."

"A short circuit? What does it do?"

"It's supposed to make a wrong connection, to divert power from its proper avenue—or something. I'm really not clear about the details."

"Could it divert light?" Imbri asked, her new hope flaring again.

"Yes, I think so. It might make a lightbeam go the wrong way."

"Like from a person's eye to the peephole of a gourd?"

Blythe brightened. "The missing Kings!"

Imbri looked through the loop. All she saw was Blythe, on the other side. But of course it required magic to implement the effect—and that was the Horseman's talent. He had somehow used the short circuit to connect the gaze of each King to a gourd's peephole, causing the King to be confined to the gourd. The ring could be a short circuit to the gourd on one side and to the King's eye on the other. "But how could the connection be broken?" Imbri asked.

"You have to shield the circlet," Blythe said. "Ordinary matter won't do it, though. It has to be magic."

"I don't have any such magic—and very little time," Imbri sent desperately. "How can I abate its power quickly? Should I just break it? I'm sure I could crush it under my hoof with just a stomp or two, or have the ogre chew it to pieces."

"Oh, no, don't do that!" Blythe said, alarmed. "That could seriously hurt the Kings, sending them back to the wrong bodies or permanently marooning them in the night world." She paused, smiling fleetingly. "Isn't it funny, to speak of anyone being marooned in our world! But, of course, since they don't have their bodies with them—" She shrugged her metal shoulders. "You must interrupt its power without damaging the brass. That's the way such things work. That will have the effect of cutting off the Kings' view through the peephole, harmlessly."

She ought to know, Imbri realized, since she was of the magic brass region. Desperately Imbri cudgeled her mind. What would do it?

Then she had a notion. "The Void!" she sent. "That nullifies anything!"

"Yes, that's where we send hazardous wastes to be disposed of," Blythe agreed. "Things like used brass spittoons. That should work. Nothing ever returns from there."

Imbri took back the band and launched herself north, toward the Void. Then she remembered to veer to the nearest gourd patch. Obviously it did not affect the band to be within the gourd, since the day horse had been there while wearing it and no prisoned King had been released. But the Void was different. Even the creatures of the gourd world had to be careful of it.

She plunged madly through the night world, heedless of all its familiar scenes, and out of the gourd within the dread Void. She suppressed her growing nervousness. After all, Xanth depended on her performance.

Now she ran straight into the most feared region of Xanth—the center of the Void. The land curved down here, like the surface of a huge funnel, descending to its dread central point. For the Void was a black hole from which nothing escaped, not even light. Only Imbri's kind could safely pass the outer fringe of it—and she had to dematerialize for the inner fringe, lest her physical body be sucked in, never to emerge. She was terrified of this depth, for it was beyond where she had ever gone before—but she had to make sure the brass ring was properly placed, that its effect was absolutely shielded. If she set it rolling or sliding down toward the hole, and if it snagged on the way, the Kings could remain captive for an indefinite future time until the ring completed its journey.

She wasn't even sure a direct placement in the hole would break the spell, but it did seem likely, and it was all she had left to try. It was her only hope. If this did not break the chain, then Xanth was doomed to anarchy, for there would be no way to rescue the Kings, and the Mundanes would ravage Xanth unchallenged. The Horseman was gone, but his mischief would remain after him, causing Xanth to suffer grievously.

She came to the bottom of the funnel. She saw the deepest blackness of the black hole. She was immaterial, yet it seemed to suck her in. It had a somber, awesome latent power. She was extremely afraid of it.

She opened her mouth and dropped the brass band. It plummeted as if gaining weight. In an instant it disappeared into nothingness. There was not even a splash, just a silent engulfment. The deed was done.

Imbri tried to turn and depart the funnel. Her feet moved, but her body made no progress. She had approached too close to the dread maw of the Void! Even dematerialized, she could not escape it.

She scrambled desperately up the side of the funnel, but slowly, inevitably, she slid back. Her hooves had no purchase; *nothing* had purchase here! She had penetrated the region of no return. Her fall accelerated.

With a neigh of purest terror and despair, Mare Imbri fell into the black hole of the Void.

Chameleon seemed to float up, her face and body amazingly ugly, but her spirit beautiful. "Chem! Chem!" she called out over the jungle of Xanth. "Chem Centaur—where are you?"

"Here I am!" Chem cried. "Here with the Gorgon. Don't worry, she's thoroughly veiled!"

"We need your soul," Chameleon said, drifting down to join them.

"I have only half my soul," the centaur said. "Imbri the night mare has the other half."

"No, you have all of it now. Don't you feel it?"

Chem was surprised. "Why, yes, I do! I feel buoyant!

But how is this possible? I never begrudged Imbri her half, and my half was regenerating. Now I have more than a full soul; it's too much!"

"Imbri fell into the black hole of the Void," Chameleon explained. "She killed the Horseman and carried his magic talisman to the Void, to free the rest of us from the enchantment, but she couldn't escape it herself."

"The Void! Oh, this is terrible! You mean she's dead, after all she did for Xanth?"

"No. We believe one essential part of her survived. She lost her body in the sacrifice she made to break the chain, fulfilling the prophecy, but her soul remained. No soul is subject to the Void. It's the only thing in Xanth that is not vulnerable to the black hole."

"But it reverted to me! It wasn't her own soul, because the creatures of the gourd don't grow their own souls! They have to borrow from those of us who do. I don't want her half soul! I want Imbri to live! After what she did for Xanth, and the kind of person she was—" The centaur filly was crying human tears of frustration and grief.

"So do we all," Chameleon agreed. "That's why Good Magician Humfrey and I, anticipating this, made plans for such a contingency. We could not act while we were confined within the gourd. But the moment Imbri freed us, Humfrey uttered a spell he knew. A Word of Power. An enchantment to keep a special soul discrete, despite its origin."

"Discreet?"

"Discrete. Separate. So Imbri could live on after her body was lost."

"But how, then—if her soul came back to me—?"

"She came, too. Free her, Chem; the Good Magician's spell enables you to do that, because you have the first claim on that soul."

The centaur concentrated immediately. "Imbri, I love you! I free you! Take your half soul; be yourself!"

Something intangible snapped. Imbri floated free. "Is it true?" she sent. "Am I really alive?"

"Yes, lovely night mare!" Chameleon said. "You are alive in the purest sense. But you have lost your body. You can never again materialize. You are now of the spirit world, like the ghosts."

"But what can I do without my body?" Imbri asked, dismayed. She remembered her awful fall into the Void—and the arrival of Chameleon. Nothing in between.

"That's part of what we arranged," Chameleon said. "Humfrey's spell took care of the paper work, or whatever, so it's all right. We all love you, Imbri, and we all thank you, and we owe our lives and our hopes to you, and we want to be with you often. So you will be a true day mare, carrying daydreams and pleasant evening dreams, much as you have been doing. Only now it is official, and forever. Whenever we daydream, you will be there with your new associates, making sure each dream is properly delivered and enjoyed."

Imbri liked the concept. She no longer liked bad dreams. Still, she was perplexed. "My associates?"

Now several other mares appeared, trotting prettily through the air. They were of pleasant colors—red, blue, green, and orange. "Welcome, black mare," one sent, perking her ears forward in a friendly fashion. "Oh, the Day Stallion will like you! You have such an individual color!"

"The Day Stallion?" Imbri sent, an unpleasant association forming.

A male horse appeared, flying winglessly through the air, bright golden as the sun. "I assign the daydreams," he sent. He swished his tail negligently. He was the handsomest stallion Imbri had ever seen. "But you may choose any you like to deliver. We are very informal here and seldom take things very seriously. This present daydream is an example; we're all linked together in it, and we're all helping with it, so as to introduce you to the nature of your new work gently. All the recent Kings of Xanth and their friends are sharing it. Soon they must revert to normal consciousness, to transform the Mundane Wavers back into men, one at a time—King Trent transformed them all to stinkweeds, and the castle smells awful—to see if they're ready to swear allegiance to the present order, and to see about King Trent's retirement so he can spend more time with his wife, and about King Dor's permanent assumption of the throne of Xanth—these things must, after all, be accomplished with the appropriate ceremony—but first they wanted to see you properly established in your own new employment. We have never had a King among our number before."

"But I'm not King any more!" Imbri protested. "Now that the real Kings have been freed—"

"You will retain the honorary title, King Mare Imbrium," King Trent said with a smile. "You are the one who saved Xanth. We shall fashion a statue in your likeness and never forget you."

There was a murmur of agreement from all the others in the collective daydream—her friends.

Suddenly Imbri knew she was going to like this duty. With that realization, she looked up and saw that it was day. Time had passed between her descent into the Void, the final breaking of the chain of Kings, and her reanimation as a soul-horse. Now the sun was up, but there was a light shower, as if the clouds were shedding tears of joy at the salvation of Xanth. Perhaps it was some weather overlapping from her region of the moon, the Sea of Rains.

There, in the bright misty sky, was the many-colored rainbow she had always longed to see, spanning her horizon.